COVID-57
Book Two

Glen "Rocky" Meyers

Dedicated to my mother,

Barbara Jean Hayes-
thank you, Mom!

By Glen "Rocky" Meyers

Feral Eyes: Book One

Feral Eyes: Book Two

Sara

Kam: Book: One

Kam: Book: Two

Covid 57 Book: One

Covid 57 Book: Two

<u>The 'NIA' Series.</u>

<u>'COVID-57' is the Seventh of 13 books in the NIA series.</u>

<u>The First Amendment.</u>

Freedom of expression is a fundamental human right and a central tenet of an author's work, livelihood, and American Society. The First Amendment protects freedom of speech, the press, and citizens' assembly to protest or march in groups. Freedom of expression is the freedom for us all to express ourselves. It is the right to speak, to be heard, and to participate in artistic, political, and social life. I am a firm and staunch believer in our First Amendment! Using someone's name, image, or life story as part of a novel, book, movie, or other 'expressive' work is protected by the First Amendment.

Addendum > In many of my manuscripts, I use real-life locations, businesses, and names that I'm familiar with, examples… Shasta Lake, Silverthorn Resort, Jones Valley Resort, Bridge Bay Resort, Lakehead Resort, Iron Mountain, C.R. Gibbs Restaurant, Shasta County Jail, Mercy Hospital, Winn River Casino, and my leading protagonist group from the Bethel Church, and the list goes on… Mary Lake, Whiskeytown Lake, and other towns and places in Northern California. I use personal experiences in writing my stories and try to morph into different characters. I explore my inner personalities, feeling firmly attached to my female side. Therefore you will read about my female protagonists. I write in the first person at a whim; this can be a little disconcerting to the reader or listener. I'm sorry about that. I endeavor to have my characters come Alive and be viable and touchable. Just like you, I have many inner nuances of my personality, and I explore aspects of each character by turning inward and examining their thoughts and feelings; writers can learn more about themselves and use that knowledge to create their character base fully or partially. I fall in love with some of my fictional characters all the time. I can't help it because they're like me in many ways, Lol. Many continue living in my other manuscripts in black and white for eternity. Having the same characters from book one until the end of a series brings a natural form of continuity and familiarity for me and my audience. Developing characters is the most rewarding and exciting part of my writing experience. Thank you for your time.

Let me adamantly make this clear from the gate > Nearly every word I write when penning fiction is just that Fake-fun. There isn't any relevancy to any establishment even though there may be a likeness, my words are fictitious in fictional settings, and I write stories of fantasy and make-believe. No disrespect is meant if I coincidentally broach on sacred ground or accidentally insult an entity or establishment... it's all in fun. Please have fun and smile!

Glen 'Rocky' Meyers.

<u>The NIA Series… Book Seven… 'Covid-57.'</u>

<u>'A Preface.'</u>

<u>An introduction of how's and whys… with explanations.</u>

<u>'I'm a Felon… and enjoy using Disfluencies in my
manuscripts.'</u>

Within most of my manuscripts, I incorporate the use of disfluencies. There are many reasons why I do so. Many purists will find this form of writing unprofessional and of a lower standard… which is fine by me. Some authors have distinctive writing styles, '<u>prose.</u>' In writing, prose refers to any written work that follows a basic grammatical structure. Prose simply means language that follows the Natural Patterns found in everyday speech. It isn't well known that disfluencies pop up in everyday speech or conversations in most languages on our planet. In conversations, it has been approximated that about every 4.6 seconds, a disfluency is used. I try and combine disfluencies to emphasize points or for the reader to slow down and reflect on what was just read. I have fun using disfluencies, and I use them to directly communicate concepts, ideas, and stories to my readers. If you were to really concentrate on a person's speech or a friend's conversation… uhm, or listen to an interview, you might find yourself amazed at how many of these 'placeholder words, filler words you hear. Even some highly esteemed professionals use an abundance of disfluencies.

<u>Please</u> reference this great piece of work regarding disfluencies ("Well, um, you know, you're saying more than you

think.") You can find this article in the November/December 2022 'Psychology Today,' magazine.

To paraphrase, some of the substance in this awesome article is that most of us use disfluencies; for example, have you ever been conversing with someone and lost track of where you were going? You pause momentarily and think of your next words... using Ah, Uh, Umh, then pick up where you left off. Disfluencies can be used to emphasize your topic of choice, aligned with appropriate expressions, and you see this at comedy clubs and in everyday conversations. We roll our eyes and pause and use 'Um'. Disfluencies are common in humorous or even serious discussions. Stop for a minute and truly listen to someone's interview, either on TV or the Internet, Social media sites; you will hear an abundance of Disfluencies. We as a society have become immune to the dozens of common disfluencies many speakers use them for repeating a phrase or revising the sentence structure in midstream. I use disfluencies in my writing for emphasis, and because they're fun for me, I hope they aren't annoying to readers, umh, especially the purists. If so, I apologize, ugh, right up-front. Um, I don't want any of you not to enjoy my books. I do believe that over usage of disfluencies can become a nuisance, Uh.

Okay, umh, so here's the rest of the info that I'll share with you regarding disfluencies. Now I'm not defending my overuse of these words, or maybe I am? In many of my 13-plus written manuscripts, you'll read and see or hear words such as... 'um, uh, ugh, ah, umh, huh, so, uhm, ughhhh, ahhhh, and other variations like... oh, yep, yup, yay, yum, ahoh, lol, lmao, huh, and the list goes on...

The argument can be made; according to some Professors of Psychological Science, disfluencies help listeners and readers concentrate better on the narrative, and the use of a disfluency sometimes tells the audience there is likely new information about to be disseminated. Disfluencies seem to occur at discourse points or are used to indicate a Major plot change of direction. These educated professionals have said that disfluencies 'focus listener's attention' and sometimes allow the listener to analyze what has been said, sort of like a pause for reflection. In testing theories regarding using Disfluencies… when appropriately placed in a narrative, they actually increase a person's attention and memory of what they have heard or read.

Disfluencies have been used to help emphasize the topic being discussed. They are proven to help the listener or reader to remember storylines or points of contention better than most other deliveries of verbiage.

To sum up, disfluencies are used by highly esteemed intellectuals, from our Presidents right down to street urchins. They have been proven to increase listeners' attention. Please try and catch disfluencies either by yourself or others. You might be surprised at how many of them are used in a single day. Like… Well, heck, that said a lot, lol… Umh, okay. Yup!

How I became an author after my arrest for growing and dispensing Marijuana.

I'm sure you've heard the term 'to make a long story short,' which indicates that the story will likely not be short and concise. Lol. I've penciled over a thousand pages in a book named Sacramento County Jail, a harrowing non-fiction venture. Below is a short passage into what caused my life changes and thus led to my creative writing hobby.

In the year 2012, suddenly, health issues befell… my body and mind. I was beyond listless, with no energy or motivation to do anything felt like a Slug. I was a regular at the gym and in the past was active… this all stopped. I sought out professional help. First things first, I had to donate blood for a wide variety of tests. A sex hormone panel, 'SHBG' amongst other tests, was ordered since I was approaching the age of male menopause.

The endocrinologist called me in and informed me that I had several anomalies. One was that I had extremely low… deficient testosterone levels, but what bothered her more was that I'd had the highest Estrogen levels she'd ever seen in a man. In fact, her words were with a smirk, 'Mr. Meyers, welcome to female menopause. Your levels are off the charts.' Thirty-five years of being an endocrinologist, she had never seen these numbers before. After checking with her colleagues, it was decided that I needed another hormone test because there must have been a mistake! My test numbers were impossible to comprehend. Well,… what would you know? Two weeks later, I was called back into her office. This time I didn't witness a smirk from her countenance, nope. She beckoned me to have a seat across from her magnificent mahogany desk. She folded her arms up elbows on the desk, clasped her fingers in a temple, and bent her head down. With her not saying a word, I'd automatically jumped to the conclusion, 'I WAS DEAD,' something terminal. I must be on my way out 🌐.   >>>>>Please visit '<u>Gembooksrock.com</u>' and finish reading… Yep.

<u>Former Federal Inmate.</u>

I am a former prisoner and felon sequestered by the IRS… Federal Government on Marijuana charges… was imprisoned and locked up in Terminal Island Prison for about Seven years. A short synopsis of the events that led to my writing career can be found on my website 'Gembooksrock.com,' please check out my homepage. You will find some interesting tidbits… along with links to my arrest 🌐.

The Military Occupiers.

General Bill Hollinger.
Colonel Ruiz > Lieutenant Noah Songs, Sergeant Briggs,
Corporal Trisha Mendez, Captain Pat Rory, Corporal Chris
Hanson,
Sergeant Rigor, Private Noels, Private Shann Smith, Private
Klaus, Private Drake, Lieutenant Sloan, Sergeant Thomas
Barton, Corporal Tina Bracewell.
Soldiers > Eric, Tom, Ray, Avery, Roger, Becky, Castle,
Bruce.
Deputy Salazar, Deputy Kim, Deputy Franklin, Deputy
Travis, and Deputy Lopez.
Major Richie Bryan > Private Jimmy Neal, Private Remy,
Lieutenant Sloan, Sergeant Barton, Private Freeze, Privates
Savannah, Jordan Hughes, Corporal Ashly Humming, Private
Snyder.
Doctor Cindy Walsh, Doctor MacGyver, Doctor Ivy, Doctor
Lumens, Nurse Spacey, Doctor Luna.

Younger Generation.

Ben Burgess, Catrina Cline, Maddi Taylor, Cody Hoffman,
Ali Schaff, Karen Fleming, Kayla Green, Joshua Strong,
Heather Otter, Lori Chan, Wayne, Vickey, Sally, Homer
Sampson, Bart
Sampson, Lisa Sampson, Maggie Sampson, little Charlie, and
Kaluai.

Bethel Church.

Father Rite, Elder Jeremy, Wanda, Goliath, Venus, Tim,
Kelly, Trudy, Patti, Dan Gable, Jen, Rick, Sister Lizzy,
Brother Thomas, Nurse Becky Hill.

Anarchists.

Brock Dame, Rocky Blake, Latoya White Gore, Bartender Jeff Wilson, Linda Wilson, Doctor Shanon Roble, Jason Roble, Tayshon White, Devon Gore, Shon Peterson, Terrance Hallium, Wendi Feral, Sandi, Lacie Link, Mondo.

-56-

Ben and Cat, and Bethel.

Elder Jeremy led Ben, and Wanda had a hold of Cat's shoulder. Ben thought he'd stepped over a rail and then was slowly lowered down onto what seemed to be a bench seat, and then he felt a seatbelt snap around his waist, and the ride began; the wind started swirling, and yet he couldn't hear any sounds, but there wasn't a question they were moving. Cat had held her breath at first but now was nervously grinding her teeth. The hood over her head blew up a few times. The earth smells hit her nostrils, ughhhh thinking, why the heck did they allow these religious zealots to bind them down? Cat declared to herself, what kind of church has hidden tunnels…. medieval ones!

The temperature was in the cool range, but Ben and Cat were perspiring. Despite no inverted upside-down loops, rocking from side to side, or the scary sounds of the slowing of the rails grinding squeaky brakes, the roller coaster they were seated in…. didn't point straight down with gravity winning nor rocket up pointing into a severe incline. Nor did it hit 95mph with the inertia pinning the rider in their seat. Although, with that being said, it was the most frightening of all rides, no noise, electric with hands bound, blindfolded, moving, and shaking upward only companion was the unknown… try it.

A smooth landing as they stopped, hands upon them 'watch your steps' We walked up a slight incline, then it felt like we were in a box, ah, another elevator the sensation that we were going up, they were leveraged against the back wall, safely held by Wanda and Elder Jeremy. "All right, hold your hands up." In a flash, a snip, their zips were cut…. other hands were pulling off the hoods. The door opens to Gospel music down low.

Ben and Cat react similarly by rubbing their wrists, showing perplexed expressions like now what? New smells strike their senses, incense burning. Wanda leads the way. They walked on marble tile… pictures adorn the walls with religious themes, yeh think?_ thought Cat. The crucifixion grasps her to a halt, and Ben saw drawings of the 11th, 12th, and 13th expeditions of the bloody Christian Crusades, which was a series of religious wars initiated and supported by the Latin Church back in Medieval times battles intended to extract Jerusalem and its surrounding areas from Islamic rule. Ben remembered reading about the sieges being especially brutal, many lives lost fighting over The Holy Lands.

Strange paintings stretched across the wide hallway they walked, graphic beheadings, horses dressed in armor, blood, and guts flying swords ripping skin. He didn't have time to stop and read the captions engraved in wooden frames. They entered a wide corridor with large 11-foot doors closed on both sides. Next, they turned towards a narrow foyer; they stopped before a door with a Goldcrest 'Headmaster,' Wanda knocked on the door, and it clicked open three steps later. They were in an enormous room. Cat first notices the varnished aromas of glossed furniture, a Mahogany theme with giant plush Oriental rugs and tapestries of unique intricacies and complexities pictorial depictions interwoven in the thick fabric hanging from the walls and bizarrely from the ceiling in rows. Bay windows allowed the natural light to flood into the room.

The cathedral ceiling went up in stages… steps. The architecture seemed to be replicated from Europe, and in the early 1500s, the room was about 35ft X 20ft. No one spoke while Ben and I took in this unique space. I walked over to one of the bay windows and looked down upon a lush green grass field and running… walking paths. Father Rite was standing beside a giant high-back chair behind a ginormous desk, and we were asked to sit on a floral-designed sectional sofa... Wanda and Jeremy stood by him in greetings.

Elder Jeremy reached his hand out. Father Rite grasps it covering it with both his in a warm embrace. The same for Wanda... Ben forgoes this with his fist held up for fist bumps. Father Rite went with it, for Cat followed likewise protocol. She knew the three wore other masks, not just the ones on their faces.

Father Rite reached out to the accordion-like coffee table next to the sofa, took out a plastic bottle with a nozzle on the end and a handle with a trigger... gun-like gave it to Wanda "will you do us the honors, dear, please." She pressed the nozzle onto his head, and the end of it flashed Green. This same process was done to each of us. All Greens "were all negative for Covid, so if you want to remove your masks, that will be fine," said Wanda.

Relieved now, bald-faced, we watch Jeremy and Wanda sit down on each side of Father Rites' desk. Ben nor I said nary a word... resigned to observe and listen, the mood was gloomy. The church had lost four young members, and this would be a somber gathering. We understood the intent of this meeting was to recruit some more members, specifically us. Cat wondered how little Charlie was doing. She reminded herself to inquire about the tiny boy. If nothing else, they owed the church and this Pastor dude some of their time. The hood's zip-ties underground tunnels only verified their original assumptions of Bethel being Cult-like, not unlike the majority of citizens in Shasta County.

Father Rite gazed at each of them, bowed his head, and closed his eyes "will you pray with me..." "Yes, Father," was heard from Wanda and Jeremy; we went along with the semantical image, hands together, fingers steepled churched... Amen. We'd watched the Rite Father press a key on his working phone earlier. We now assumed why he did so... subsequently we hear knocks on the outer skin of the room, and he once again traps a monitor. The door clicked open entering were three Disciples pushing carts with Sterling Silver trays. Before us was a flavorsome spread of pastries, mixtures of diced fruit, juices, and tea with a hot pitcher of coffee, all the fixings and condiments in bowls… what I zoomed into was the little sandwich wedges of various meats and cheeses.

We start to indulge with thanks given to the servers when the door clicks open again… of its volition. Ben caught the glowing figure first, all in White, a maxi silk dress with beaded braids in her hair. Even her feet had White flats on them, not a lick of makeup, no fingernail polish adornments other than the beads couldn't see her earlobes, but the woman didn't need to be painted up. She was plain-ass gorgeous. I instantly saw Ben's arousal, tempted state of being. At least, this was my feeling… no question, the girl was alluring. She was mesmerizing. She stood perhaps 5' 11" tall before us in her slim, form-fitting floor-draping dress. Her eyes were assets of Copper color… features of Cleopatra's eloquence, unh, exquisitely beautiful indeed. I had to admit it… she was captivating. ✿

The stunning woman offered up a curtsy. Father Rite broke our trance "please meet my Adjutant Sister Venus. She's, like you've probably heard said, describing others that are highly organized and proficient. Venus is my right-hand lady who keeps track of all my important correspondences and coordinates my agendas. Simply an amazing woman." Venus's eyebrows moved in unison with her facial features, an inviting virginal, twinkled smile of innocence feint fleeting then gone. The introductions were made. Venus offered, "it's a pleasure to make your acquaintance." I guess I was so enthralled or captivated by the girl's charismatic glow that I missed the haversack she carried and lifted it with her left hand taking out a mini-Stenographic machine, a laptop, and a recorder… "Can I refer to you as Benjamin and Catrina?" I'm sure I blushed, not having heard my full name said so officially before with such emphasis like I was about to engage in a Deposition, lol.

My mother only called me by my full-on moniker when she was angry at me or wanted to wish me tenderly... sweet-dreams; I could still hear her low-pitched tone, 'sweet dreams, Catrina, I love you!' dammit, where's my family now? I nodded at Venus, then added, "I go by Cat."

Venus was now staring at my BF, who intently gawked back at her awkwardly, not so subtly... I elbowed him out of the admiring daze, thinking men were so easily confused and disarmed by beauty led by their sexual fantasies of conquest. He muttered, "oh yes, sorry, uh sure Benjamin works, that's fine, but I normally go by Ben, Venus!" Wow, talk about a time-lapse whew, dude, tuck it back in! Then the BF switches gears "why so official..." periscoping at the others and stopping at Father Rite, glancing at the security cameras bobbing from alcoves "a video with audio is sufficient, right I mean no disrespect here to Venus, but I guess...."

"Ben, this is our standard M.O. Sister Venus keeps the minutes of our meetings a shorthand stenographer just like the American Judicial process depositions are taken, all legal proceedings are completed likewise. Of course..." Waving his right arm, "there are three cameras on us recording all... this is mere formalities. Does this bother either of you?"

"No," I answered while chewing on a bear claw Danish "but can we also be provided with a transcript of this like a legit informal interview? Oh, can we expedite this some, please we do have to get back to the Clear Creek area to see our friends this evening to plan our next conference at the Mary Lake Clubhouse..." Cat caught Ben... to her full-on disdain with his mouth open looking at Venus God she hoped the fool wouldn't start drooling "ugh right Ben?..." "oh uh yes for sure Cat!"

For the record, I'm not the jealous type of girl, but... Father Rite then stands up and walks to another desk and takes up a large binder bringing it back, then methodically verbalizes, "you will come to understand we're not in a rush here at Bethel. We like to think we've stepped away from the Rat race, but I will speed up the process. Please refrain from interrupting my dialogue. There are pens and a couple of notepads in front of you if you'd like to take notes or comments.... or have questions to ask after my soliloquy."

I looked at Ben. He shrugged, then I glanced at his crotch, wondering if Ben junior, ah BJ was in his normal state of flaccidness. He followed my eyes, frowning and squinting his eyelids with a negative shake. I put his ass in Check he bluffed; annoyance at least... that's my contention. No, I'm not the jealous type.

Father Rite bowed his head, then crane-like raised it, staring warmly at us, "first, a quick overview is in order. Bethel Church has a Worldwide spiritual congregation. We're not cultish or demonically sinful, nor are we devil worshippers. Here at Bethel, we believe in spiritual paths to enlightenment. In that vein, we do participate in the belief of a devout higher being... and in the Holy Ghost's interventions.... that is, if we are tuned in with our inner spirit. Guardian Angel's seances, paranormal communications with the deceased, raising of the dead, laying on of hands, faith healing speaking in tongues if you want, call us Holy Rollers as some non-believers do. We are Christians first and foremost and have our best goodwill on display always for our fellow men and women. You have nothing to fear from us. Quite contrarily, it's you that can cause us far more harm than added benefits."

Elder Jeremy grimaced, piggybacking Father Rite "yes were Evangelical fanatics, Snake charmers. Actually, you are both here to be sacrificed at the Alter." Wanda grinned at these words. None of the others reacted. Wanda took the **bull by the horns** and continued heedlessly, "categorize us as a Supernatural Ministry... God fearing Disciples we have faith in the 'destiny of enlightenment' which persists to be forthcoming. I ask you, is this the time of cataclysmic preaching and Prophesying of the Apocalypse? Where God comes forth and destroys, eviscerates evil forces which will scatter like Rats running for survival, the Devils Apostates ugh, henchmen will hide in every nook and cranny on this planet."

Whoa, Ben and I were straight erect on the edges of the uncomfortable sofa, speaking for the only person I could... me. I wanted out of this place Now! Ben must have felt likewise blindly grabbed my hand, holding and squeezing tightly.

Father Rite bows "who am I or our living Prophets to say or prognosticate the future... we're mere humans on this earth... flesh and bones, just like Jesus Christ himself. If Covid-57 is the embodiment, unh, the epitome of the beginning of the end of the human race, the finality, well, who truly knows? We do want to be here alive and free, untethered to the manmade Governments of this world. Tyrants, despots, dictators, the power-crazed self-centered masses who will eliminate all others that expose them. These Devil incarnates will impose their wills unless we stand united against..." he sighs, takes up his Orange Juice, and lets the last words said to linger. The room was eerily silent.

Venus was tapping away, her head held high, not missing a phrase, I'm sure. It was as if Father Rite had just plumb worn himself out. Sitting delicately simultaneously, Venus stopped tapping away while Elder Jeremy took up the Gauntlet "we will fight the establishment, not adhere to improprieties against our indelible rights. We are not the Sheep, nor are we the Wolves unhhh, not the hunters nor the prey, not the weak but the Strong of Heart, Soul, and Spirit. I'm here to inform you... reveal and disclose to both of you that we will survive this Purge. This treacherous epidemic/pandemic rages within every Government and hierarchy across the globe. Bethels congregations, brothers, and sisters will not be led to the gas chambers or cremation mausoleums... if the evil entities had their ways. We'd be led to pits.... mass murders the docile

Lambs eliminated." He kneeled for emphasis, waving his left palm before our faces.

"We Bethelites will stand up and fight, were not whom we portray falsely to the Governments of this world we know many of them wear masks underneath, akin to malignant spirits of Satan we have been training and..." jumping up Father Rite his stop sign hands facing Jeremy "hold up Jeremy there is no reasons to continue this rant rah, rah cheerleader montage of hype let's move on with substantiated facts and to why Benjamin and Catrina have been invited here today!"

"I got this, Father...." "Oh, all right, Wanda, but let's stay on point. We've already pushed our schedules to the limit in hopes to facilitate the enlightenment of these two young minds and to persuade them to bring their large group of advocates together to combine and coalesce with Bethel...."

Wanda nodded while Venus fidgeted. "We're the largest institution in Northern California, and that's saying a lot. Our church is a non-denominational neo-charismatic megachurch, and we have over 11,000 active members. We have satellite and affiliated Churches across the globe. We are not stagnant in our progressions. We believe in a Triune God–Father, Son, and Holy Spirit... most importantly, we believe that God is sovereign over all his creation... God is Great!" Amens were verbalized, while Ben and Cat watched the religious threesome nervously.

Wanda rolls her hands onto her lap, "Benjamin, and Catrina, it is true that we had asked our disciples to try and recruit you, and to bring you to us, yes, we'd like your group of youngsters to join us here at Bethel. We are on the avant-garde, vanguard of enlightenment and will not be deterred from accomplishing God's work. In fact, quite the opposite.... we are in continuous flux, with exponential growth on all continents and, I'd like to say, on the cutting edge of religion and life. The Coronavirus saturated the USA and the world starting at the end of 2019, and subsequently, the viral strains morphed with more deadly variants that brings us to 2025 today. Tomorrow Covid will grow even more resilient and virulent; we are proactive and aligned with many professionals in positions of power throughout our Government and now the New World Order. The W/O has mandates of evil intent uahhh things are not what they seem. Benjamin and Catrina, what you don't know is that a form of Genocide and Senicide also referred to as Geronticide, the killing of the elderly and the infirm/weak, has been going on since the inception of Covid-19. Fast-forward… to this very second Democide, a concept proposed by Rudolph Rummel, a political Scientist who wrote the book 'Death by Government,' in 1994. Much of his writing has found its way into the mantras of the W/O. What we can't see can definitely hurt us and is happening across our planet. Government forces are enacting… combat 'the killing of unarmed people by Government Agents acting in their authoritative capacity and pursuant to Government policy of the High Command' which is now renamed the W/O."

Ben had finally had enough… patience diminished, hand and palm up "listen," he smirked with his clever pun, "it's like your preaching to the choir. Tell us something we don't know. We've witnessed the arrests of our families, but I don't believe for a second that our United States military is killing innocent people. They seem to be weeding out people they deem necessary… ugh, I don't know crap…." I somberly see Ben melt before me. His mouth closed. He dropped his head, sad like me. I jumped in and added, "we are suffering our family arrested we just want everything to go back to normal we collectively had agreed to see what help Bethel had to offer Tim, Kelly, and Trudy made it sound like…." then I went quiet realizing I just saw them comatose in the back of the hearses.

This was when the saying <u>you could hear a pin drop</u> was valid. Father Rite gently held up his palms "we have yet to broach the subject of our four Bethelites. Please continue, Catrina." "Ugh, where was I? Oh yeah, we wanted to know what your Church had to offer in these times of strife... look, we're desperate for assistance to find our parents and friends and to understand what's happening here in Shasta."

Everything stood still for a moment then Father Rite said to Ben and me, "please give us a few minutes to discuss this matter. Step out the door. I'll buzz you back in when we're finished... thanks."

We followed his orders, the door closed, and I said, "this is so way weird, and what's up with you staring hypnotized at that girl, huh?" "Oh please, like I'd be interested in a Churchy prissy girl like that. Wow, I feel insulted. Yeah, she's pretty and all but way strange... what are you fricken jealous of? When..." "Shut up. I'm sure they have listening devices in this hallway. This church is like dealing with the Secret Service or something!" then the door clicked open, and we were told to return to our seats.

Not sitting standing before the 4-some, it was my turn to vent "why are we all sitting here? Then you brought Venus in to record what? We don't need a running press conference hyping the advantages of joining Bethal. We..." Father Rite stood up faster than I thought he could move. At the same time, he raised his left forefinger to his lips, miming sshhh, be quiet. A seriously empathetic pain-riddled expression came across the three Bethelites. I pinched Ben's palm.

"Please take your seats. We've decided to divulge some heart-wrenching news; we're very sorry... Ben, Cat, your parents have been murdered by the military!" We jumped off the sofa into the air. Wanda reaches for me "what the fk are you saying" screamed Ben holding his head. I'm instantaneously in shock shaking my mouth, covered by my hands in sudden spurts, tears bursting out, choking, gasping for air falling back on the couch. Ben shouts, trying to catch and hold me. "I'm out of here. This is insanity; how ugh, why would you say that?"

In a relaxed voice, Elder Jeremy stands over Ben and me... "Would you like to visit with our counselors? I think that would be a good thing…" "No," yelps Ben, angrily glaring into Wanda's face. He's up, pacing across the floor while my head is in my hands. "Where's your proof? That's a sadistic awful thing to say to us….." Jeremy interjects, "we're sorry, these are the reports we received days ago. Truly, our hearts go out to you. Some of the details are horrific!…" Father Rite added, "we have been able to infiltrate both factions that have control of our county. They're vying for notoriety and are divisive in separate struggles to make names for themselves, Colonel Ruiz and Major Brynn. Their platoons are extremely dangerous and loyal. We continue our advancement against their objectives, Ben… Cat, you can choose to disbelieve us…unfortunately, that's not going to change what has already been done. You can leave here now out the front door of Bethel. A driver will take you wherever you want to go, or you can hear us out, and please refrain from expletives. It's your choice. We will leave you alone and return in 10 minutes."

Ben takes a box of tissues from Venus and gently clutches my clenched hands as we watch the Bethelites walk out the door. "I don't believe our families have been killed. If so, wouldn't Ruiz announce that on his daily TV broadcasts, I'm sure, for like he said yesterday about raising the rewards to $75,000 for each of us? He went on threatening anyone who was caught assisting us, helping, or harboring, uh, hiding us. The punishment would be extreme, not death! Don't you remember babe, his plea woah statement that if we wanted our families set free to turn ourselves in… so like please our families are held for Ransome, their alive girl!" "Ben, I'm with you. I'd need proof to believe what they're saying, but hey, Rite said we could go, no strings attached, but I'm sick to my stomach. This came out of Right field, and no, I don't disagree with you…." "Babydoll, listen, don't you think that Ruiz wouldn't have emphasized that our parents would be released, let out of prison or lockup if we just gave up….." "Ah yeah, your correct

I'm not thinking logically, boy, just stressed-out, um, spun out Ben," he slouches back with me on the sofa.

I blow my nose, hugging him... muttering, "you know we should probably get out of here and check in with Cody, Ali, and Maddi. We're supposed to meet back up with them at Karen's later tonight. Gosh, we have so much to do. Let's put this out of our minds. It's got to be hype. Why would the military kill innocent people? Uh doesn't make sense... they're not barbarians. This is the United States of America. We have Constitutional rights. No one is just executed. Heck, criminals sit on Death Row for decades before being anesthetized."

Ben and I embraced then he declared, "why would the Bethelites lie to us? What, ugh, trying to use scare tactics, umh, to manipulate us into joining their church? Nope, I don't think so. What ulterior motives would they have? Cat..." I wiped my eyes and took a deep breath... regaining composure, and declared, "I don't think they're lying purposely to us. Possibly they received misleading information from some of their congregation like our parents being shot point blank thinking the machine... like dart guns fired real lead bullets watched them shot and fall, surely they'd appear dead!... sleeping though," "damn, I didn't think of that yep that's it, Catrina!..." "Catrina, huh..." A matching smile broke our cheeks and dimpled epidermis.

The door swings back open at the entrance of the room. Rite calmly walks in and states, "you two haven't a clue as to what masterplan our Government has stamped, begrudgingly I'll get straight to the gist of this meeting... your leaders of a youth movement against the authoritarian Police state of Martial Law that exists in our County and in your group you have Savants umh experts in the technology fields. I've been lucky enough to be privy to the lists of your attendees that joined you at your conferences, and there's a new age new wave of thinking. Gurus in the making.... your people think out-of-the-box.... geniuses in many spheres. With our precocious young adults and yours empowering one another, there are no limits, no obstacles we can't overcome."

He paused, letting what he'd said sink in. Ben and I weren't looking at him, gazing at one another "although there has been a slow sieve, um, a bleeding reduction from your original 1,700 plus crowd, we at Bethel would like your entire group to join us we're congruently harmoniously on the same side!" Father Rite figured he had built some momentum and stepped over the line "the next meeting for your people should be at Turtle Bay Exploratorium... Bethel controls that establishment. We also can provide assistance with limited transportation for the leaders of your 'Think Tanks.' Did you know..." "Wait a second, how do you have all this information about our...." "There are over 35 Bethelites in your meetings. You met Tim, Kelly, and Trudy, who was sent by me to bring you here."

Father Rite nodded at Elder Jeremy, who opened his mouth "did you know that today the military has already tattooed thousands of citizens, and many of them are in your age group of 18 to 29 years old? Tattoos are mandatory. If you are caught and have passed the W/O's gauntlet of qualifications, you're permanently Branded. Besides a Covid-57 vaccine injection that slowly dissipates... its time released into the tattooed person's bloodstream, we are currently dissecting some of our people who have been branded with these Pyramid tattoos and have found thus far a microscopic GPS chip inside of the Yellow dot..." he witnessed shock pounce across our face's "what are you kidding me... just like Veterinarians do for animals to be tracked by their owners... what why?" "Ben, don't get angry with the messengers. We're only informing you of what we've discovered."

I had finally recovered from hearing that our parents were deceased, discounting the ridiculousness of that with basic no-nonsense logic that they, Uhm, the American military, wouldn't execute innocent people. Even if they'd caught and arrested Ben and me for breaking curfews or organizing a subversive group of people to fight for our rights. The worst-case scenario would we'd face possible fines and maybe have to perform some community services, no jail, for we didn't do anything wrong! While I was ruminating on that, Ben spoke up, "we had heard about the colored stamps of Blue, Yellow, and Red. What you are saying is that they're permanently tattooing people. Now that's kind of like livestock labeling, man, and they're moving fast. This can't be legal. What about the ACLU and the preservation of our individual rights and civil liberties? What... huh?"

"No one knows about the tracking chips.... we do, obviously because of the informants that we have placed within Colonel Ruiz and Major Bryan's ranks. Our scientists and physicians are examining the invasive mandated tattoos at this very second. I'm told we're on the brink of developing a portable device the size of a small cell phone that we will be able to place over the Pyramid tattoo and, at the very least, negate the GPS chips function, just one of the many ways we're covertly trying to counter the forces of evil and more reasons for your team of young people to join us. We have a new acronym for you to put in your brain.... its these three letters, 'F.O.E.' This is how we will refer to the military from now on. <u>*Forces Of Evil.*</u>*"*

Wanda seemed anxious for Father Rite to finish when he did.... She retook the floor "you both seem up on your history, so here's food for thought, a phrase that can be traced some 2,600 years ago to the 6th century BC. Then centuries later, this phrase was replicated by one of our Founding Fathers, John Dickinson, who wrote the song 'The Liberty Bell.' This profound statement... still inspires humans to this day <u>'United we stand, Divided we fall.'</u> Will you not join us?" Father Rite grinned, with Venus smirking and Jeremy nodding affirmatively glowingly at Wanda.

Father Rite wasn't finished yet, holding up a clipboard and flipping through a few pages.... "ahh, here it is. The FOE has terminated over 15,000 Shasta residents. This information is from our accountants that are in the field, and this is known to be on the low side of estimates. Bethel hackers intercepted a Red Alert from Major Bryan's network goals to be achieved by the 23rd of July 2025. One of the insidious bullet points read; <u>the egregious reduction of the population in Shasta County to 25,000 or 75% of citizens eliminated, needing 15,000 workers (Yellows), 3,000 Law Enforcement Officers (Blue), and 7,000 upper echelon individuals, the 1% wealthy and the Who's Who (Red)."</u>

With Ben's mouth wide open in disbelief, Rite iced him with, "what colors are you and Cat going to be, do you think?" Raging, I stood up "here we are again, with the military killing our citizens, including our parents. You just said that over 15,000 people have been terminated. That's impossible to comprehend. Where's the Beef, huh proof… besides that, if these tattoos are all that you say they are, then at our next gathering, we will divulge all of what you are disseminating. We will democratically vote on if we as a total group will join Bethel." I paused then, "it would be better to enhance the chances of a 'Yes' vote to supply us with non-subjective proof but validated objective proof, Father Rite. I'll admit your scaring me to death; petrified, it's terrifying. What you're stating is almost unfathomable, but Ben and I are living in a microcosm. We feel the pressure, umh, net tightening. Call it a noose around our necks, an eerie foreboding like invisible weight portending to weaken our resolve. Call it whatever you want, like you say, the FOE, or just plain evil. Something is wrong here in Redding. We shall discuss this opportunity with our nucleus, the reigning leaders of our small group Cody, Ali, and Maddi!"

"Well said, I must say, young lady, you are articulate and worthy of being in the position that you are, and the same for you… Ben, time is ticking. We need to combine our minds to overcome….." Jeremy stopped like he'd been zapped, yanked his cell phone out of his front pocket, vibrating, "we must attend to your advocates who argued the importance of you being here, Tim, Trudy, Kelly, and Patti, who were delivered by the Hearsts earlier… they're in one of our basements, so we must end this…." "Wait," Ben says, "not so fast, please! We see you all using cell phones. Cat and I, along with our tech wizards, were working on alternative means…" Jeremy smirks wide-eyed "our Scientists have utilized miles of fiber-optic wire lines laid underground bypassing stringent regulations and developing another form of internet infrastructure. Personally, it's all foreign to me, umh; perhaps I'm not explaining the process correctly. Suffice it to say our phones work without a glitch as long as we're in this zone and can't communicate much further than a 7-mile circumference."

Wanda listens and says, "if you were to join Bethel's team, I'm sure we can allow you to learn how our technicians circumvented the Government blocking devices, although I might add Major Bryan has his triangular dishes searching us out 'probably as we speak pun intended'…" Venus says, "with a smile good luck with that!"

Since we had them answering our curious minds, Ben asked, "how could you have tunneled from Turtle Bay without them…" "My turn to answer," exclaimed Wanda, "there are tunnels all over the North State. Did you know Shasta Lake has several towns at the bottom of the man-made reservoir? There's been mining operations over most of these lands, like the toxic Iron Mountain!" She lowered her voice.

"We broke ground 19 years ago. Our engineers located three super-large veins… tunnels from the 19th century and early 20th century. We went to work digging and reinforcing, strengthening the ground, and sealing the walls with new-age solutions. We hadn't a clue at how useful the tunnels would be…. and God knows all. We found ourselves preparing for the apocalypse and now have several escape routes not only under and around our Bethel Church but elsewhere…." Father Rite waves his arms, "thanks' Wanda, but I'm sorry all other questions will have to wait. We have serious business to attend to. It's time for you two to decide what your future will be?"

-57-

Karen, Cody, and Ali were restrained in a military van.

Karen excitedly worked at trying to shimmy her body towards her feet's end of the stretcher… the safety belt was snugly encasing her arms above her elbows, but the latch wasn't on her chest or anywhere she could feel it, so it had to be hanging on the side of the stretcher. What she was able to get a hold of was the loose end of the belt, the part that was pulled to tighten the harness like a seat belt.

She tried to pull her shoulders in and wiggle her way… worm her way so that the smaller part of her body… Ughhhh, Karen did it, took the strap over her neck and head with hands freed, sheet off her face finally could see clearly. Karen slowly popped up. She was in the middle. On each side of her were Cody and Ali's bodies covered, seemingly sound asleep.

Karen peered between the seats, dammit… the cops took the keys. She scanned the van's cab and saw the cache of weapons, her mind wheeling like a smidgen of the darts potion had entered her bloodstream, but adrenalin overpowered any side effects. As Karen saw it, there were two choices neither were appetizing other than getting away. She could bolt from the van into downtown Redding without a Yellow stamp or a reason to be outside during curfew, and Martial Law, if seen, would be shot. Peering out the passenger window at the street that generally would be busy only soldiers were out and about. Another option was to steal from the cab a gun and wait for the soldiers to re-emerge from the store at this gas station and force them to drive Ali, Cody, and herself back towards her house.

If she ran, she'd be abandoning her new friends, but hey, they'd just met, again nervously looked out the windows of the cab, crawling forward, snatched a 45 Caliber pistol clicking off the safety, tucking it in the waist of her pants, and jumped to the passenger side and bailed grabbing a camo hat that one of the soldiers had left on the dashboard. Karen looked both ways at the back of the van crossing Pine Street 'from the corner of her eye' the soldiers exited the store. There weren't any civilians on the sidewalks and only a few vehicles. Karen needed to find an alley back street right away before the wild pursuit of an escapee was rung over the alarms. Then there would be drones, choppers, and foot patrols 'what a screwed-up world she lived in,' mumbled sorry, Ali, Cody, unh Cody, yeah, admitting to herself she'd felt some feelings for him, not sure what, however.

Karen was still dressed in Black. The last thing she did after putting on the soldier's hat was to steal his military edition camo jacket rather than sneaking from bush to bush, house to house. An obvious visual bust changed her act. Karen decided she'd act nonchalantly as if she belonged on the streets. Essentially, she'd own it. Karen brazenly and purposely walked down the sidewalk's center with only one destination in mind... and she wasn't too many blocks away from Kayla Green's office.

Dan was the first to recognize a problem... his door was ajar. He watched Jon hit the lock button on the fob, yanked it open, yelled to Jon, "hurry, we ugh, how in the world?" slung open the cargo van's side door, and pulled back the sheets. Jon stood beside him "this is a first, not good, bro!" Speechless, Jon scanned the street's closed storefronts. Karen wasn't anywhere, "hop in, Dan, let's find her!" they jumped in the seats. Dan sees his pistol gone with his jacket and hat missing thinking, "oh, for sure, this will appear on my resume and records, he shouts, "drive, Jon, go now!..."

Jon squeals the tires onto Pine Street, swerving around a left-over grocery cart, three lanes going North "she couldn't have gotten far, Dan!" they scoured the vacant streets and sidewalks, but Karen was nowhere to be found. Dan slaps the dashboard… "How'd she do it? She was plumb out cold, flopping like a dead fish when we strapped her down. Could she be immune to the sleep agent sedative? It didn't last long on her." Jon blurts out, "2 out of 3 ain't bad the real demand wasn't the girl, Dan," ahh, Karen… He then remembers and opens his satchel. "Karen forgot all her identification heck, and we have her home address right here… we will get her again. She's got a reprieve, for now, she'll be free for a short time longer, better enjoy herself cuz…." "I agree, Danny; we still have big money, the big fish strapped down. Let's head in and not say anything about her unless asked," Dan replies "heck, we best just face it and tell the truth. It's not our fault that the darts didn't do their job… and failed to work on her. Besides, you called in three captured…." "That's right, Dan, <u>honesty is always the best policy.</u> The boss will not be angry heck, look who we have in the back!" laughing.

<u>Forensic Doctor, Shanon Roble.</u>

"Lieutenant Sloan, don't delegate this nor outsource it. I want a report sent to my desk ASAP. Whoever she is, she's yanking chains… ughhhh, chains of commands I just hung up after a sweltering barrage, including not-so-veiled threats from one of the Wash. D.C. Directors of the FBI. She wants us to kindly take great care and locate one 'Kayla Green' and immediately remove her from the quarantined area."

"Yes, Sir, I wonder who's pulling the strings and why we hadn't heard of this Kayla Green before?…" "It's a Pathologist, Doctor Shanon Roble. I wanna know all there is to know about her. Who is she? Whom does this Shanon know? First and foremost, Sloan… find her daughter this, Kayla… make this a dang priority. Kayla is

a paralegal who works off of Court Street across from the County Jail. I sent you her address. Get on it, Sloan." "Yes, Sir Major Bryan, this will be my priority. I'll get Private Freeze to pick her up and safeguard her...." "LT, we should debrief her. She's been inside our perimeter for days. We need to find out what she will be telling her mom. At this stage of our plans, we can't allow anything to upset the Apple cart, okay!" "Yes, sir! Major, while we were speaking, I tapped her in on our decisive lists of Yellows. She's not on it, so she is expendable, you no!..." "Don't flm say that Sloan cross-references her on the IMP lists if she's already been delivered to Iron Mountain ... oh man, that wouldn't be good!" "I'm on it, Sir. I'll get right back to you on our new encrypted line the minute I can confirm Kayla wasn't taken already to IMP to the freakin pit, Major!"

Bryan's worse fear could manifest itself. The Shasta County Operation had been a dream thus far, not a flaw unless you count Colonel Ruiz. That is, no credible reports of escapees from the cordoned-off areas. He was still amazed at how pliable and obsequious the public could be to authority figures and the new laws and rules he'd posted for the civilians to abide by. Combine that with 24/7 nonstop radio and TV broadcasts of the dead bodies piling up all over town fear had set in and was as thick as Tuli Fog, and Bryan smirked and snickered.... lol.

Major Bryan shook his head ole history repetitively doing what it does, same ole same mulling over one of his favorite characters, old Harry Anslinger! The propaganda machine's film crew's Covid-57 paranoia was playing to the masses. The first USA drug Tzar Harry J. Anslinger, was called a Prophet back in the 1930s,' and 40's he used the film 'Reefer Madness' to scare the populace to death and to poison naïve civilian's brains for his own agenda ole Harry had ulterior motives. Selfishly he succeeded.... at bringing his agenda to roost! Passing archaic laws regarding Marijuana, and now in every city in America, you can shop at a Cannabis shop. Just like the Nazis or centuries before Genghis Khan, even Caesar used propaganda to inculcate fear in the citizens to obey the rules and not fight against his objectives. 🏵 Making a mental note... Major Bryan snarled into a smile, yeah, when he had time, he'd try and pull up a short excerpt on YouTube of the ridiculous film 'Reefer Madness.' Ahh, he could use a laugh!

Major Bryan nods with a grin in a mirror, thinking nowadays he'd orchestrated an academy award-worthy film of Covid-57 Madness paralleling 'Reefer Madness' he was able to turn regular community members into policing their friends and neighbors. It was a thing of beauty with his brilliant idea of having the neighborhood watchers patrol and report directly to his command. He again laughed hard out loud. We have snitches in every region of Redding and Shasta County. Uh, what a good joke!

Bryan only had to reference back five years to 2020, when society sat up and fought the establishment with protests and marches. The Alpha males and females who had the wherewithal became outspoken and started ruling the airwaves with podcasts and blogs, and violence gained momentum... organizing mobs, riots, and looting... the number of people dying was akin to a gambling wheel, a 'wheel of death' even Bryan's relatives argued against the lockdowns, and having to wear masks everywhere they'd go. It was crazy back at the beginning then the sheep fell in line despite famous actors... pro athletes standing up against the lockdowns. Notwithstanding, the dead were multiplying... Coronavirus victims filling the morgues in freezer trucks and trailers, they argued against Martial law. Now only the younger generations fought still. The older citizens had acclimated and accepted the rules and regulations imposed.

Bryan knew if the W/O tried this lockdown martial law gimmick back in 2019, it would have been a Mini-War the citizens would be bearing arms and joining militias. They'd be breaking down the barricades and blockades, sure some escaped the cordoned-off areas with stories of mayhem sensationalism personified, saying animatedly 'what the military was really doing in Shasta' but who believed them? LoL. Our propaganda machines detailed what we wanted the narrative to be, what the world would believe was our propaganda!

Some of the escapees told the truth with little exaggeration. It was all over the web and social media. Luckily, the cordoned-off area hadn't access to the internet or cell phones, or this scenario would have been far more challenging to maintain. In a few cases, an escapee from our lockdowns would jump on YouTube, telling his or her fascinating story about us killing or arresting people... and what we were really doing in Shasta County. We were ready to attack back and had five others countering the squealing YouTuber calling our intrusion into Shasta a lifesaving miracle and lauding our achievements and perseverance to save the lives of the dying residents in Redding. With culpable deniability, we proved that we used the RFD sleeping weapons on people who fought against the rules and our Martial Law to help them from perishing and succumbing to the latest killer airborne variant, Covid-57! We didn't want to. LOL, uhm didn't want to shoot the rule breakers, but oh well, some of 'em' wouldn't obey our mandates! What the outside world believed, for the most part, was the bullshit propaganda we sold them!

Sure, we are lucky that the populace had been previously conditioned and had easily written off the few that told the truth about our invasion... they were labeled conspiracy theorists and exposed as lunatics. Funny, Bryan mused how easy it was... and how believable the filming of the fake mannequins were... all stacked like deceased bodies of Covid-57 victims! Air Borne killer virus, easy-peasy! We didn't have to do much brainwashing or influencing the citizens to fall into line and obey us. We used the Sheriff and Mayor to verbalize warnings on our television channel for enlightenment... parents, elders, Clergymen, women, and preachers, then passed down to the naive innocent children they were able to swing every single priest, minister, pastor, preacher, and monk except freakin one who refused to play ball, Bethels Father Rite. That bastard wouldn't work with us, but he will! With spiteful anger, he tossed his coffee cup against the fireplace bricks. I will encourage Mr. Rite to see it my way today! Bryan chewed on a raw Carrot chomping away with a dubious scowl.

Bryan felt his cell phone vibrate. It was a text, 'please call me sir,' he thought; what could Sergeant Barton want? He crunched the last of his Carrot, then leaned over the sink washing a tasty Honeycrisp Apple; Bryan was always conscious of his intake, snorted… a 'fruit diet was for fruits!' giggling. Uh, he had to maintain his trim whip-like body. He tapped the speed dial. "Major, I have a bit of distressing news, but I have to commend you for not having to broadcast this over the radio, hell I missed using phones. This new frequency is great. How many are online, Sir?" "Sergeant Barton, never mind that… you stated you had some distressing news. What?" "Oh yeah, uah, the mobile units triangulation satellites have zeroed in on another communication leak. Actually, there are two sources now. One is over where the Colonel is located at Lake Shasta, and the other seems to be transmitting from Turtle Bay and the Sundial Bridge area, and I'm afraid, as you suspected, Bethel Church is in the mix. Unfortunately, we cannot isolate the origination. It's not continuous, Sir… we're within 750 yards square at best from the transmissions, Sir."

Bryan choked on a Grape and stopped filling his blender for his morning fruit smoothie… "That's like 6750 square feet WTHeck, we need to pin it down to a much smaller area. Barton, send over the coordinates and outline or highlight the areas that we need to search. It's time to pay another visit to good ole Father Rite at Bethel!" "Yes, Sir Major, I just sent that to your main page. I'll check in with you a little later have a disturbance at the Redding Airport to handle some of the high and mighty entitled Reds who are fighting the new Tattoos, Sir; it's a fisticuffs out there, uhm., a Federal Judge slapped one of our soldiers, Sir." Bryan chomped on an Apricot "all right Sergeant the elitist 1% entitled are the most difficult to manage they're used to calling all the shots, spoiled rotten pretentious assholes but it is what it is good luck keep me posted" click.

With some scissors, Bryan cut some growing Wheatgrass and started the blender up, adding ice cubes. Five minutes later, while studying the areas that had illegal communications and downing his smoothie, he was clenching his sphincter like Kegel's… fruit equals regular bowel movements. Bryan moved delicately from his desk to the bathroom and just made it to the commode at the same time he released a sustained Kegel. Cusses realized his baby wipes container was empty then his phone rang. Darn, he left the cell on the desk, ft. Then he rebukes himself. What's happening to you, Bryan? You're really becoming a rotten potty mouth with all these cuss words, not like me. What's up as the last feces dropped.

Seven minutes later, he reads a text, 'check in with me please, Sir' from Doctor Walsh… Bryan sucks a bottle of water down. Have to stay hydrated now. What the Fudge is going on? Sighs, takes a shallow breath, holds it releases, counting in a slow mantra, 'Ohmmmmm!'. Taps the phone, now a touch more relaxed. 'Hello Doctor, what's up?' chortles at his cleverness like 'what's up doc.' Oh well, time to be serious. He's going to have to check his anti-depressants must be a side effect or effects… feeling goofy and giddy snorts a snarky cackle "you all right, Sir. Did you just choke? You're not sounding like yourself, Sir" pausing he pinches his nose staring into a mirror silently mumbles yeah I'm back from the dead. "Unh, we, uh, have a problem Sir somehow, Doctor Roble has been chasing me down on our radio channel!"

"Sir, that's exactly why I called you and left you a text. She's causing a stir down at one of our blockades on Hwy 273. I'm staring at her from a distance now…. she's searching for her daughter Kayh Green…." "I know. I was just on the phone with DC and delegated Lieutenant Sloan to find her. I'm left in a quandary, Doctor… what would you have me do? We cannot allow her entrance, uh, need to stall until we have Kayla in our grasp. hopefully, she wasn't transported to the acid pit." "She's not going away, Sir… she's standing with her hands on her hips arguing with a Private right now… do you want me to talk with her?" "No… I mean, yes, crap, this could be our first real glitch, unh, problem. This woman has connections; put her off till later this afternoon, Cindy… okay?"

"All right, Major, shall I give her this new contact number, Sir?" "By all means, yes, Cindy, the last thing we can afford is outside interference will be out of this county in little more than a week, heck, only nine days off. Let's not blow it now!" "Alright, I'll handle it, sir, although I thought we were going to start pulling out of the county on the 23rd." "Nah, that's what we broadcasted to the residents… that was never our intention. We only leave once our objectives are accomplished. Then and only then are we done here, Doctor! Keep me posted" Click.

Like Grand Central Station, his phone buzzes again, peering down at the LCD screen, puzzled, confused. This cell phone was a cesspool of trauma wished he'd never had his tech crew put together this new frequency, no peace, constant bothering… but who could he admonish but himself, uh! "Yes, Lieutenant Sloan…" "Well, Sir, Kayla is not on the pages of deceased up on the Iron unh IMP. I mean, Sir, I can't find her on any of our internal reports. I located her address, name, and social security number that aligned with her being expendable and sanctioned to expire by the 19th, Sir!"

The Major guzzled a 6-ounce container of Orange Juice pulp… residue on his lower lip napkin wiped. "LT, turn this Cowtown upside down, find the bitch" click. He swivels in his chair at his desk at the radio, then squawks, "breaker Major you got a copy… over?" he grabs the microphone. "I'm here, Colonel Ruiz, Sir!… over." "Listen here, Bryan, someone is putting up a stink from Quantico to Langley and the Pentagon next… I'll be getting barked at from the fkn White House. You need to locate a Kayla Green now, right the fk now… over!" Bryan's eyes fluttered, his nose twitched, and his bladder pings…. looks at his glossy manicured fingernails and bites…. yanking his middle fingernail down to the quick. "Yes, Sir Colonel, I'm already working on the Kayla debacle… over." He swipes a tissue out, finger bleeding, throbbing shit that hurts uhhh.

"Bryan, please don't tell me she's visited IMP. Have you checked her home?… over." Colonel Ruiz thinks angrily that Bryan is a fricken retarded buffoon? "No, I mean yes, Sir Colonel, I'm all over this her unh un, I'm tracking her down as we speak. I will find her. I'm personally handling it, Sir. You have too much already on your plate Colonel Sir… over." Ruiz yelped back, "Bryan, wtf is wrong with you? Huh, you sound all messed up, man you okay? Can I count on you?… over." "Uhm, of course, you can, sir. I will get back to you the second I have something to report… over." Ruiz yelled out loud. "Eat Shit!"

Bryan hadn't noticed his office door open, his petite secretary covering his mouth. The radio blasted again as he tossed up a wayward arm and shouted, "get the fk outta here, boy" his secretary eased the door closed. Colonel Ruiz barked back, "Major, this is a priority. Her mother is some big wig Forensic Goddess or something, Doctor Shanen Roble. Now you gotta put this fire out, or it is your burning ass" he chuckled at his play on words "snorting uhh… over!"

Bryan wants to put a bullet through the prick's head and keys the radio again. "Colonel, you have such a unique and clever way with words…. no fear, I'm taking care of it, Sir… over" "See that you do, Lieutenant uh, I mean Major for now over and out!" Ruiz laughed hard, then sneered. Bryan almost runs to the toilet to pee, sits…. lets his bladder go. A phone in the foreground rings, shakes off, foregoes a rinse, screw hygiene, prances over, snatching up the phone barks, "what?" "Major, this is Private Freeze, Sir. The person in question,

Kayla Green, is not at her residence. I've put out a BOLO and APB for her. I'm going to her law office on Court Street next, Sir…." "You listen to me, Freeze, if you don't find her. You'll be lucky to be serving tacos from a fricken lunch truck. Find her fkn ass!" click.

Major Bryan had a massive migraine and walked slowly, holding his head… staggers to his mini fridge, popping the top of some Tomato Juice, and pouring it into a clean glass. Taking a swallow of vitamins might help. A knock on his office door. The trembling secretary cowers his head in and has a large white envelope in his hand, "Major, this arrived a while ago. It's urgent from the White House and has a Presidential Seal on it. Sir, I think you should open it at once, Sir!" "Oh, do you hum? Is that what you think, you piddly squeak Einstein? Wow, your brilliant bring it here and get out!" "Yes, Sir, did I do something to displease you last night? Sir, I thought you were blissfully moaning. It was great…" "Get the hell out of here now, or you'll be a fkn Janitor at Iron Mountain."

He sheds his suit coat, peels the Fed-X packet, opens it, and sees the Official Seal… Presidential orders… scans the first few pages OunLord Kayla Green. No way, Radio blurts out, "Breaker Major Bryan… over." His phone rings. Bryan screams aloud, and the door opens again. "Sir, did you call me?" Bryan waved the secretary off, yanked his bottom drawer open, pulled a flask of Stolichnaya Vodka out, swigged it all down, chased it with the rest of his Tomato Juice, a fkn adlib Bloody Mary yep fk them all

Taps enter on his cell "yes, this is Major Bryan….." "Major, this is the Director of the FBI for the State of California, Agent Rice Captor. I have a few concerns to run by you. First, I'm trying to locate a… Ms. Kayla Green, a Paralegal by profession, with all cell phones down and the internet shut down, her mother has been unable to find her. Why is Shasta County on lockdown? No… let me recant that uhm, I have read the reports of another Viral strain that has evolved, and the epicenter was in the Redding area, uh, Covid-57. I understand the reasons to cordon off the area, but why have all of Social Media and communications been squashed? Believe me, parents and family members are blowing up the phones wondering what's happening in the county...." "Agent Captor, unfortunately, the orders for lockdown and blocking communication here are beyond my rank. I only follow orders.... regarding Ms. Green. I have a search party out there right now and expect to be able to deliver her to her mother shortly!"

Bryan's throat is on fire, and his chest is heating up.... body is now warming into a sweat. During the pause, he hears the Agent clear his throat "well, if you can't explain to me why the outside world cannot communicate with people inside the lockdown zones, perhaps Colonel Ruiz can? Unfortunately, he hasn't returned my calls...." "The Colonel is dealing with his own issues Agent Captor, and yes, I'm well aware of the importance of locating her. The only insight I can offer you about the cell towers and the internet being down is that it's just procedural. We don't want to cause a hyperactive reaction from the citizens that are being quarantined. We want to contain any sensationalism and exaggeration, uah, hyperbole that would escalate the fear of this new contagion being labeled like many of the churches have in the county as.... Armageddon. Can you imagine the riots and chaos that this would cause in every Urban area on the planet?"

Rico, even before this conversation, had decided to make a trip North from his San Diego home "Major, I look forward to a face-to-face with you. I plan on visiting the Shasta area in the next few days. I will be flying to The Redding Airport if you haven't found Kayla by then. I guarantee you I will! Contact her mother once you do. Here's her phone number. Luckily, she's on the outside of your blocking devices, 530-209-5746. Ok, it's been illuminating speaking with you on this cell phone. Can't you understand, Major, why the citizens are up in arms and why the double standard here we speak on the phone..." "Like I told you, Agent Captor, I only follow orders...." "Oh, I got that, and I'm going to the top tell your Colonel to call me."

"I'll find this, Kayla. As far as you visiting this area, I'd reconsider doing that... this new Variant is killing people at an alarming rate. It is now Airborne, one of the main reasons communication has been cut. We can't afford to have the world's peoples in a frenzy when, must contain Covid-57...." "I get that I'm upset that some of my closest friends are unable to answer my calls. I'll text you their names. Can you check to see if there is any information on them? I want them to be at the Redding Airport once I land... they have homes in the Shasta area. Major Brynn, I want you to put out feelers for Rocky Blake, Brock Dune, and Shon Peterson." Brynn nearly chokes on hearing the same names he'd earlier sent to Ruiz, the suspected terrorists out at the lake, "sure, I will run their names. You have a fine day, Agent. I must go!" click.

The first wave of a buzz shutters inside him, and Brynn sways back, reclining in his ergonomic leather chair, thinking, no more alcohol... dammit I have to stay on point. Remember, he said aloud, 'Pressure makes Diamonds' or is it 'Stress can cause Neurosis?' picks up the radio 'breaker Colonel Ruiz... over.'

—58—

Karen acted like she belonged on the streets of Redding.

Karen could have sworn that she'd seen the white van a few times roaming the streets looking for her, but it hadn't turned down the streets she walked, cutting through a park past the Placer Executive Airport to her good friend Kayla's house. But no one was home, not even her couch Potato husband, A.J. She didn't need to break in; just jumped the backyard fence, and Kayla's sliding glass door was unlocked. No sign of either of them…. kind of odd because, checking the garage, neither car was there. Curfews and Martial Law were enacted. Where could they be? Then she saw the newspapers piled by the front door, and wedged in the door frame were cards from Lieutenant Sloan and Private Franze to call number 411 or 911 and to report at once to the Redding Police Department.

Karen left the house, yanking up her mask from around her neck, covering her face, and stopped at a 7/11 store on Placer Street. Happy to see it open, Karen needed an energy drink and some snacks but only had a twenty-dollar bill tucked away in her jeans pocket. Her wallet was taken by the soldiers. A masked turban Middle Eastern lookin older man with kind Brown eyes said, "my 3rd customer of the day, welcome." Karen said nothing; moments later, she stood at the counter before him.

He seemed to stall, egling her, "I need to inspect your left wrist, ma'am uh, Ms. Gable." Startled, Karen looked down, realizing the camo jacket had a name tag. Ugh, the guy called Dan's last name was Gable… I glanced back up at the thin tallish guy "what did you say?" "Sorry, soldier, but there are new rules that are being delegated by the authorities and must be adopted by all shop owners if customers don't have a Yellow, Blue, or Red Pyramid Tattoo, were supposed to push this gadgets button, he holds up a triangled plastic fob then points to the door, do you see that cylinder like post the authorities told me that soon all customers would have to scan their wrists when they visit my store when entering and then when leaving."

"Look," he shows her his underarm from his wrist back. His Brown skin was Reddish with a new tattoo protruding up from his skin, a Large Yellow dot in the middle by the base of the triangle. She'd never seen anything like it before. Damn, they're branding us like cattle and said nothing gazing back up at his inquiring face. Reacts fast, he holds the fob up, "yes, I'm scheduled to be imprinted later this afternoon, umh did it hurt?… I'm really a chicken." Not thinking, whoa, that was

stupid, he stands there, mouth ajar... "But soldier, your skin is covered by tattoos climbing up your face and piercings, in fact, I've never met or seen a soldier with so many piercings or tattoos. How do you mean, uhm, chicken?" Karen blushed and had to think quickly... "Oh, it was the last Ink job. I got a super bad infection, was hospitalized, almost died told myself no more tattoos. Hey, I'm in a hurry... we can talk next time I visit your store!"

Happy to feel the sidewalk under her feet swinging a 7/11 plastic bag, swigging a sugar-free Red Bull that was way weird can't be buying food or groceries without one of those tattoos wrong something is... coming right at her was a Redding cop no time to duck out of the way.

She nods at him subtly when he slows down, then swings the White plastic bag at him like I'm cool. I passed the test at the 7/11 store he kept on driving. So far, so good now.... can I make it to Court Street? Maybe Kayla is holding up in her office.

Now walking with my sonar blinking, trying to stay out of the limelight, aware that the locked-down citizens had eyes on me, so I couldn't act paranoid better to behave like I belonged outside, but I was fearful and truly afraid and wanted to duck between bushes and hide around parked cars, but that would be a bust so I soldiered on. I was partially dressed like a soldier except for my pants. I still suffered from abandonment issues leaving the guys, Ali, and Cody, in the back of the van. It bothered her and continually ate at her inner self like she'd let them down, but hell, there were no keys, and she couldn't carry them on her back, hopefully... they would be fine.

Karen crossed the street, not at a crosswalk, and remembered she needed to return to her house for later tonight. Maddi, Cat, and Ben were supposed to show up by nightfall. Finally, at Placer and Court Street, she turned left North in the direction of the Courthouse County Jail and Kayla's office, which was across the street. 'Please be there, girl,' she muttered over her breath.

Joshua and Heather, under water in Shasta Lake... hiding!

Josh found himself constantly thinking about his relationship with his wise, wisdom-laced Grandfather. Ole Grandad could break a subject down to a gnat's ass. He could take on a phrase and give you seven different perspectives. Grandfather would sit on his porch, philosophize, and mull over critical fundamental beliefs, thinking and continuously analyzing words. History was his favorite subject, but also he enjoyed Science and often discussed human beings, mentioning... saying humans were indeed just animals and easily trained mammals. People were merely more complicated and misplaced in fiction narratives aligned with mental illusions, sometimes lost in prevarications, lost in their distorted vantage points. Grandpa could lose himself and often me and Grandma in one of his circuitous dialogues. He was relentlessly debating specific topics and conversations till we either conceded, uh, or could see or feel his perspective or relate to his way of thinking. I thought, ultimately, Grandad's meanderings were meant to convert us into believing in his ways of thinking and coming to the same conclusion as him. But now, years later, I came to realize he wanted me to dissect and analyze any perplexing issue that could restrain my advancement. As a young boy, I'd conversely tell him I was lost within the sums of his ideas and convictions. One such subject boomeranged back to me now and did Matter!

Grandpa's words... not verbatim, "Was it luck or fate? What is luck? What was fate? Like many, did you make your own luck? Did your luck manifest into perceived fate? Can we decide our fate? Of course, we can, being the only living creature that can envision a future dream or goal. Unlike a foraging, Wildebeest... its goals aligned with all animals whose instincts rule their motivations which are to eat, mate, and survive. Our sophisticated brains enable us to transcend and morph into our destinies with eyes Wide Open.'

Josh had countless verbal battles with 'Papa,' his affectionate name for Grandpa, who'd call their sometimes-heated conversations 'verbal sparring,' for years, they'd go at it. All in the learning pool, he'd say the more I understood and could comprehend, the more buoyant I became. He'd say intelligence was ascertained by one's experiences and memories. Imagine having an Eidetic photographic memory, never forgetting a sentence that matters to you, being able to recall lessons taught physically and mentally, having total recall, uh, memorization. He emphasized patience, unlike Dad, who relentlessly pressed onward over obstacles. 'Go Time!'

Josh silently prayed below the water's surface. Papa would be proud of him tonight. He did learn the lesson regarding patience, uuh, patience, Papa. Yes, now it was my turn to follow Dad's lesson. His rambunctious way was 'all in, go for it.' Heather and I would find out if we had good fortune, good luck… lousy luck, or any luck at all?. They would soon know if fate would smile or strike us down. It was time to test fate… luck… destiny. Josh frowned, took a huge breath, and gulped… just do it. 🦅

Once about an hour ago, they'd waded to the shore and, for the first time, breathed fresh air unencumbered by the bamboo reed… then two drones had zoomed down from the dark sky right at them, so they alligator dived again. Heather seemed despondent back… Josh couldn't blame her much… he was having a difficult time remaining optimistic.

He shook her, startled. Heather clenched his arm, and he started kicking his legs. She started to perform the breaststroke with her arms while remaining tied to his hip. Josh still sat on the partially aerated cooler. They worked their way back to where… uhm, whence they'd started from, the beach… darkness prevailed over them, exhaustion of extremes. Heather was deliriously tired. Her neck was cramped, her mouth inside was raw, and Heather's lips were bleeding from biting on the Bamboo reed. He knew that her body had to be cramping up like his… they moved slowly and steadily, knowing that just having a destination would lift her spirits as it already had for his.

It had been a long while since they'd heard an echo of a watercraft's motor. Happy not to listen to the engines revving through the water, his feet kicking, then he touched down like his favorite game. He backed up and felt the rocks behind him. Then Josh unloosened the straps that bound her to his hip and him to the cooler. They slid up out of the water again, hoping not to have drones above them. Together they sucked in untethered air, unrestricted oxygen. He looked around, scanning the night sky, and whispered hoarsely, "do you see those flashing lights?" she answered croakily. "Yes," "Heather, these are drones seeking us out, thermal scans with night vision cameras." "Oh, fk no, do we need to duck back under the water, Josh? I don't think I can do this…" "Honey, there's two of them heading our way, but they're a ways off. We're going to test our luck, as my grandpa would say. What would be our fate? Come on…. the cave is only 70 yards from here. Let's navigate closer in the water.…." "Josh, it's going to take a few minutes to get my legs working…." "Come on," they dropped underwater again while the drones came closer. Josh had taken into account that there were still two or three boats in sight at the entrance of the expansive arm of the lake heading out into the mainstream.

The search parties had vanished and moved on; no doubt there was another emergency elsewhere that took precedence on the lake. Tapping her forearm, both raised their heads, watching the drones that had 360-degree cameras rotating and focusing on the shores and the water's surface. They were already flying in the opposite direction on their way out of the cove. One notable advantage they had was that the drone operators flew the drones way too close to the water's surface. If he were the joystick controller, instead of flying ten feet above the water line, he'd set the gages at 35 feet and wound out the focus. That way, the cameras could scan a much larger area, including both the shores, and water's surface, and the horizon.

There was just one drone left that was committed to their part of the lake they'd hidden each time the flashing light of the drone got close. By the 3rd flyover, Josh had timed the drone operator. Josh thought of a trick play he'd called when he practiced with the Florida Gators hut-hut-hut 3.5. It almost always got a first down, although this wasn't a trick play in a football game. This was life or death, good luck fated, and that was when he quickly raised his body and said, "easy, we have 30 seconds… try not to splash. We're going to our cave." Their skin was shriveled, and bones ached, finally standing with their bodies hitting the night's air. They fell to the ground, their legs cramped, and their muscles refused to function… no on-call movement. Josh and Heather's willpower to move was mentally supported but not physically possible yet….. they couldn't run up the ravine toward the bear cave. Quickly they stopped almost at once and had to retreat back into the water…. flexing their legs and trying to regain their motor skills. Again Josh and Heather watched the drone fly back toward the entrance to the cave they were hiding in.

"I think I can do it, Josh. How about you?" Josh didn't speak his actions did, though faster than he'd thought he could move, Josh pulled her up. Since they had failed on the first attempt and practiced stretching out their legs…. that test run was over. It was now or never in Josh's mind… their legs back under them, they made it on the next attempt, the last 55 feet with bursting endorphins and adrenalin pumping with just enough light from a flickering moon. They made the final turn dropped down, and started crawling on their knees, tumbling the cooler over, holding each other, sputtering inhalations. Soon enough, they'd learn if the cave was a safe zone. They almost didn't care… but they did. Exhaustion weakened their resolve, and they collapsed onto the dry sand. Were they lucky, uh, maybe?

<u>**Five Soldiers are asleep at Shangri Lala.**</u>

"All clear, I repeat, all clear…" bellowed the Communications Officer. The soldiers lay side by side on the uneven grass. Three wore only underwear. The other two had their uniforms intact, and all the soldier's weapons were taken. Private Drake met with Corporal Trisha Mendez, who waited for Colonel Ruiz, who was stepping onto the dock at Campground Shangri Lala. He was in a vile mood. Drake was glad that Mendez was in charge. Perhaps he'd be easier on her being a female, but not likely, though. Private Drake was doubly enthralled with Corporal Mendez… she was a Psychology major who decided to give up her practice and join the military. Drake had thought when he'd flirted with her that she was full-on into women, but he was surprised Trisha swung both ways zealously! ... Yum.

Colonel Ruiz felt like chewing fricken nails, pissed off was calling it benign he approached the shore staring at Mendez and Drake, shouting vehement assertions dressed with disdain. Mendez elbowed Drake with a frown knowing the screaming words from Ruiz was a precursor of what they'd expect to tolerate. He spewed vile contempt, easily inferred by all within hearing distance that his attitude and beliefs were that Mendez's squad were a bunch of inferior inbreeds. He openly yelled, asking no one. 'Why the hell was I stuck with these idiots, and the fool Major Bryan had the cream of the crop? I'm left with a bunch of fckn delinquents,' he stomped up to the five soldiers…. *Who… Brock, Rocko, and Latova had disabled.*

Corporal Trisha Mendez's medics had the soldiers on stretchers attending to them, and all the Colonel could do was shake his head in disgust.

The floodlights were set up at the scene, along with the lighting from the campground. He raised his hands to the side, palms upward, staring up at the dark moonless night "why oh, why me dammit can't I catch a fricken break? We have all the numbers, computers, drones, helicopters, watercraft, all the technology with night vision heat sensors, the whole kitten-kaboodle, and yet we can't arrest a single perpetrator. Hell, a meth whore and a broken, damaged fkn Eunuch has escaped after killing two Officers and putting my Captain in the hospital, strapping him to a tree. Now he's a raving lunatic, and they're responsible for the beheading of a civilian up on Iron Mountain. The fricken rebels have attacked a Sheriff's Substation that was destroyed by a rocket-propelled missile... a freakin floating toilet blown up by plastic explosives; they've sunk five of our boats, shot down drones, killed our soldiers and deputies and a Navy Frogman. Next, you know their further disrespecting the United States of America by stripping our soldiers indignantly, and the fkn beat goes on...!"

Everyone was fearfully quiet, pretending not to hear Ruiz mutter a single syllable no one burped nor made unnecessary noises. His loud, boisterous voice echoed on, "how pathetic all of you are you call yourselves soldiers?" pointing at Mendez and Drake, who stood side by side, "what do you have to say report at once like now!" Mendez, somewhat tense, took several steps forward "yes, Sir, it appears my soldiers were attacked, most likely ambushed. The perps took their uniforms to move about covertly dressed as our soldiers, sir. Obviously, there are three perps, two males and one female, Sir." She took a deep breath as Ruiz chewed on the end of his cigar. "We know they left here by stealing a Sheriff boat, the same one, my soldiers, arrived here on, unh. All five were shot with our issued RFDs uhh, that's all I have for now. The Medics are injecting them with antidotes to wake them. We will be able to interview them soon, Sir!"

Ruiz seemed only to stare blankly at her, slowly moving his head from side to side... "My compliments Corporal you said all of that without Laughing or Crying with a pathetically straight face!..." "Yes Sir, Colonel Sir saluting," she replied, inhabit. Without gazing at Private Drake, Ruiz ordered. "Get in the Apache's search the Eastern sector of the lake. I'm certain the perps didn't go West from here. That's the direction we've arrived from.... and look for that Sheriff boat which surely is sunk by now. Report back if there's any movement out there. We have pinned down the direction they had to go, either Jones Valley or Silverthorn Resorts, unless they grew fkn wings and have flown off the lake!" "Yes, Sir Colonel Ruiz"

"Mendez, when your Ace team of five wake up, I want you to interrogate each separately, debrief them and report at once to me points to his commandeered houseboat. I will be waiting with <u>Bated breath</u>." "Yes, Sir Colonel, I sure will, if I may say one thing, Sir!" he spins around snake... quickly, staring backward. "No, unuh, no, you may not!" "Ugh yes, Sir," she salutes him, thinking, what a fkn asshole probably better she didn't say what she was thinking, almost smirking at her chosen words which were 'Sir, I didn't know you read Shakespeare's Merchant of Venice in 1605. That's where the words <u>Bated breath</u> originated from!" She absolutely admired <u>Shakespeare's writings and plays</u>. Trisha was a sharp cookie, and serving her country took precedence over her enormously successful psychiatry practice. She dreamed of writing a book and now, with this contemptuous Colonel, had more Raw material... for her pen!

On board his commandeered houseboat, Ruiz grabbed the radio's microphone, 'breaker; LT Snwgs come in... over.' Snwgs almost immediately came in, "yes, Colonel Sir.... over." "Remember the homicides of our two Deputies and the two male black Americans? Wasn't a female missing? Did you ever find her body?... over" "no sir... over." Ruiz started shuffling through a stack of folders. Ah, yes, here are the pictures. "Smugs, check with Major Bryan for any information about gymnast Latoya Gore. Also, check the records for anything to do with this Gore woman…. over." "Uhm, yes, Sir, I'll get that information over to you at once. We'll run the deceased names and find their associates and families. I believe we've had an inordinate amount of calls regarding the three Blacks from family members get right back to you, sir!... over." "See that you do anything from IMP? Where are we at on your investigation up on the mountain, and how is Captain Rory? Has he regained consciousness? What the hell happened up there, Smugs?... over." "Can we meet later off the radio, Sir? I'll fill you in on what's up… over." "Yes, Smugs later, hey, on a side note, have you heard if that Kayla Green has been located?... over." "No, Sir, but I will also check on that for you!... over."

Smugs scowled. It was only going to be a matter of time before the 'Cat's out of the bag' and Ruiz was informed about the Shasta Games and Captain Rory's preposterous stupidity, and he was in charge of the fool. Actually, Smugs had recommended him for the post on Iron Mountain. Already dealing with Ruiz's wrath, man, he just wanted to be on a different project, uh, planet…. relocate elsewhere and get away from the toxic Colonel.

Ruiz pours himself a shot of Dewar's: "hey, Private Noeh, are there any new developments over by the beach where those two escapees went in the water?" "No, Colonel, the drones are still flying. Nothing to report as of yet. My best guess is the perps backtracked into the forest and give us false leads down by the water, Sir!" "Well, then send a few drones back up in the hills. No one can hide from thermal scans, Private…." "Yes, Sir, that's what I'll do. The only other options are they drowned or were picked up by another watercraft, but the satellite images didn't show any other boats in the area before we arrived and cordoned off the cove."

Ruiz's mind reverts hauntingly back to Major Bryan's words at their uncomfortable luncheon at Bridge Bay, the Tail's Whale Restaurant. The names he brought to the table were legends. Could it be?... Ruiz ordered Private Noels to pilot the houseboat towards the Jones Valley Resort while he sat at a desk looking once again at their dossiers. The three were known to live up in the North State, within an hour of where his commandeered houseboat plowed over the lake's wake. Perhaps his tormentors were none other than one, two, or all three of them. Certainly, they knew each other…. the records showed that they attended NIA's 2-year physical education course years back and were instructors. Although, as per their norm, they most often worked as Lone Wolves… squad leaders, then he flipped over one of the stacks of extensive files and saw that Brock Dome and Rocky Blake had teamed up several times in Mosel and in the Middle East during the Desert Storm War and later in Afghanistan. They actually enlisted in the FBI together. Yeah, no doubt it's them whom I'm dealing with.

Rocky was a detonation expert and taught classes on all different explosive materials, C-4, and plastics, and his specialty was underwater demolition work. He was a trainer at 'The Center' as it was known or NSWC, The Naval Special Warfare Center, a leader within the Naval Amphibious Base at Coronado, California. He flipped another page, and an 8 X10 glossy of a handsome Black man grinning with a Sombrero hat, a sign showed in the background Rosarito Beach Mexico. Shea Peterson stood proudly in shorts without a shirt. On his left and right were Rocky Blake and Brock Dome. The muscled three looked like serious Mofos.

Flipped the three Dossiers over and pulled out the financial ledgers. Government checks traced to Cybercurrency brokers, Bitcoin and Ethereum, no taxes out of Shasta County, no land under their names, but what of Charities or business partners, Corporations / LLCs, silent partnerships? How about properties under fictitious corporations, huh? How did they fund their lifestyle? Shangri Lala was rumored to be owned by Rocky, but the paperwork led to an offshore conglomerate. It was a labyrinth of dead ends.

Ruiz mused over his hippy-type girlfriend, that used to work as an investigative reporter for the New York Times and now heads up her own tech company out of Sacramento. She was a Bulldog, uhm, her favorite was doggy… yum, the ex-fling, ugh, they had broken up about seven months back. Their acrimonious break-up was a horrific time in his life. Ruiz thought it might be time to touch base with Ann and try to rekindle, uh, kiss up to Ann McClintock and get her Bloodhounds on these three individuals.

Then like a flash, it struck him. "Wait," he yelped, "Noeh, that doesn't work. The couple didn't backtrack. The Bloodhounds would have tracked them back up the ravine. Also, the thermal footprints were one-way Private. How do you explain that there are too many holes in your theory? The Dogs followed them right into the water, and you said you discounted the variable that someone picked them up for no watercraft were tracked to the cove hours before, correct?"

"Yes, Sir Colonel, that's correct…." Noeh drops down to the second deck with 11 X14 pictures "these are time-lapsed stills. We also have the video from the satellites. If you take a magnifying glass, you can see the entire area around the Dam. No lake crafts out there except for Sheriff boats, look!" He slides another zoomed-in picture of the Northern part of the lake going towards Lakehead "again, see the five boats on the other side of the I-5 bridge trolling for fish, and the two other Sheriff boats, searching the banks for rebels. Remember, Sir, we're the only ones on the lake. Our soldiers are on Leave or break, fishing and hanging out on the lake. The Shasta citizens are Locked down with curfews. With these still photographs, we cover the entire lake; the only watercraft are ours. I also counted seven Sea Doo's all manned by soldiers, who were either on the prowl or in pursuit of outdoor fun and recreation Sir."

The Private unreels another picture of Bridge Bay and the I-5 railroad crossing. Ruiz rolls his massive shoulders. "Sir, these are the latest satellite images just downloaded nine minutes ago..." "Okay, no one picked the youngsters up. Whoa, wait a fkn second, let me see that photo again!" Noels jumps "here, Sir, it's the same. There are only Sheriff boats and deputies." "Get me a map of the lake. Superimpose it right here. Hold on; this is the McCloud Arm of the lake where we're sitting right the fk now give me that magnifying glass, blow this up on the computer, Noels."

A few minutes later, they stand shoulder to shoulder "well... I'll be damned. Heaven forbid, Sir, I see it too. It's them.... even with it being blurry, the night vision shots are clear enough to determine that the perps are dressed as soldiers in that darn boat, sir, the stolen boat. I'll blow it up as far as the dot-pixels will allow and still be in focus!" Ruiz grins, pointing "that girl there is Black as the Ace of Spades. We got them. I knew she was still out on the lake. Yeah, she didn't kill our deputies. Those guys did. I want follow-up pictures with video, if possible. From this timestamp forward, I will trace them to where they went. I'm beginning to feel better, Noels...." Noels joined in with Ruiz's contagious enthusiasm but felt hollow nh vacant, for the Colonel tasked him to change directions in midstream to drop the searches for Josh Strong and Heather Otter, the fugitives he'd diligently sought and felt he was close to capturing empty stomach like left unaccomplished now he was ordered to hunt with fervor the three perpetrators in the stolen Sheriff boat.

"Hey, I have the 8 x10 pictures of the 3-war heroes and that missing Olympic hero gymnast on the coffee table. She's the Black girl on the boat.... her family is putting up quite a squawk along with the mother of that missing Kayla Green girl. I bet you dinner

it's them, somehow....." He pulls up the folder again, glaring at the pictures of Brock, Rocky, and Latoya. Staring at Noels, "I was right. That bastard Brock Dame escaped our net alive! There he is next to Rocky Blake and Latoya Gore. Have you got confirmation on the voice recognition software of the scrambled communications from that Ultralight yet? That would explain how he reappeared nine miles from where we had him trapped!" "No, Sir, I'm still waiting for that."

Meanwhile, Private Noels went up to the upper deck, delegated the pilot to veer East at the mouth of the main inlet, and sat back down in his designated alcove. Computer screens were lit up, feeling inspiration wiring him out. He wanted at least one major success to add to his resume! Replaying Ruiz's demands, 'Noels, I want a blow-up of that photo, all satellite images from before taken on the Sacramento Arm, then Southeast towards Jones Valley get me all videos on the double uh Triple like yesterday.' He'd replied I'm going to work on that, sir. I'm also concentrating on the escapees... Ruiz's orders were, 'stop that bullshit. They are on the back burner. All focus is now on this boat. I want these three perps. I'll hang them from their genitals, get on it, or you'll face the same punishment, Noels!'

Noels hadn't felt the Colonel's wrath before and naively defended him to other Officers; now he understood how fickle and meanspirited the man was not loyal to anyone except himself with the man's final words echoing in his head. Noels didn't debate or rebuke his ridiculous statement of hanging the three by their genitals that would be difficult, one being female... ugh, get a handle on yourself. Stop taking everything literally with no one looking. He swiftly slapped his face and felt better now!

A moment later, the pilot barks from above, "Private Noels, Sir, someone is approaching us on another watercraft." Noels swiveled around the table and passed his three computers up the stairs. He bolted to the Eagles Nest, pulling up alongside the houseboat was a Sheriff boat. He ordered some soldiers to

tie it off after recognizing Corporal Mendez. "Excuse me, Noel's..." "Yes, ma'am..." *"Ask the Colonel if I have permission to board Private!" He nodded, thinking what an odd request mattered, "yes, ma'am," and pivoted inside. "Colonel...." "I heard her send her in!"*

"I did as you said, Sir. The Medics gave the five soldiers shots to counteract the darts. I interviewed them. Here's a consensus of what they said...." "Mendez, relax at ease. I was a bit testy earlier were on the same team. Drop the formalities you're an Officer because of my recommendations. Cut the prevarication and pretense of giving me respect. You don't give a Rat's ass about what I think, but I'll let you know you're dead wrong. I care about our soldiers and my Officers!" "Uh no, Sir, I mean that's not the way...." "Sshhh, what did our soldiers convey to you? Try not to get me wrong, all I want to know is what you perceived happened... uh, tell me what you're thinking, Mendez!" She was now disheveled; Mendez had never heard Ruiz speak to anyone like this. "Sir, in a nutshell, the five implied they were ambushed from the trees East of the water back in the forest on the other side of the campground over by the obstacle courses. They didn't see a single person. The darts knocked them plumb out... before you ask, they will be sanctioned for not following my orders of spreading out and patrolling and searching the grounds. Asinine as it was, they stopped on the pier chitchatting and were picked off easily, Sir...."

Ruiz knew the soldiers were drinking and being irresponsible. "Corporal begin their names and place an asterisk next to them for failure to obey a direct order. Tell them they have three months to make amends, or it will be a permanent smudge on their records. Place them on extra duty. I suspect they were drinking pilfered beer from the campgrounds store Mendez." "Yes, Sir, it would appear so, uh, we found partially empty cans at the site of the attack...." "That will be all,

Mendez, wait. Can you do me a favor, take your helicopter, fly over Silverthorn Resort, and take a complete thermal footprint of the area for me." "Umh, certainly, Colonel, and Thank you, Sir. I will send you the scans as soon as I finish."

Ruiz watched her step back off the deck, thinking, got to hand it to her… Mendez had a hard time achieving her rank, being discriminated against not only being a female but Hispanic like him. "Breaker Colonel… over." "Go ahead, Snugs… over." "The woman that was on the Wakeboard boat was married to one of the deceased… a Devon Gore. Also, her brother Tayshon was killed. Latoya's a famous Olympian, a consecutive Gold Medal winner, and overall Gymnastics Champion. Her name is Latoya White Gore. Sir, her family owns a chain of gymnastics studios in the Bay Area. Her parents are well respected and have several Degrees. Her father has a Ph.D. Latoya's mother has a Doctorate. The family isn't to be taken lightly. They are Scholars with influence uhh, their connections run deep and have caused a major stir… over." Snugs breathed, surprised that the egomaniac hadn't interrupted him yet, and then smirked. How could he? He was pressing in the radio button on the microphone, and then Snugs… let it go.

Ruiz shook his head with the additional facts already figured out who the Black girl was but listened to his LT feeling kind of mellow from the Dewar's shots. He asked, "How influential are her parents? What do you mean caused a stir?… over." "Ex-Presidents Biden and Trump and even Obama have placed several calls wanting to locate Latoya. Sitting on Major Bryan's desk is an order to locate her and her brother and husband and fly them out of the cordoned area, uhm, apparently… Latoya's like a National Treasure. An obscure threat was conveyed to 5 Star General Bill Hullinger that no harm better come to them. Sir, ugh, she is to call home at once Immediately… over." "Snugs, it would appear from her stripping and stealing a female soldier of her clothes that she's fine as far as her deceased brother uh and husband. I'll have to deal with that later. We will save Latoya and get her back to her family. That will be one of my priorities. I'm sure she's been kidnapped by Rocky Blake and Brock Dune. Thanks, Lieutenant Smugz. Switch to our private channel now!... over."

Smugz and Ruiz had a prearranged channel so they could speak privately. The channel they'd been speaking on was a public forum used by the military in Shasta County and was being monitored and recorded for prosperity. Ruiz would definitely be deleting some of the conversations between his Officers and himself before releasing them to be scrutinized by any court of law or military tribunal.

Ruiz slid shut the glass door, turned up some Jazz music, took up a Walkie-Talkie, and disappeared into a restroom in the houseboats master suite "you there, Smugz... over." "Yes, Sir Colonel, uh sorry for putting all that info out on front street on the open radio channel lines... over." "Yeh got to think things through, Smugz now listen, we've got pictures of this Latoya not only wearing the stolen uniform but standing alongside criminals ughhhh fugitives that have attacked and killed our people, maimed our soldiers... murdered is a better description she's a damn terrorist like her associates 'Birds of a feather hang together' LT we will shoot first no questions need to be asked you get that!... over." Anger boiled over the radio while Smugz sat in a Humvee sipping some hot coffee, knowing he better not incense the Colonel anymore but saying to himself. 'Why the fk not... hate for Ruiz overpowered his rationality.'

"Colonel Sir, <u>don't shoot the messenger,</u>" LT grins at Ruiz's temper and egocentric self-importance. "Sir, it's my opinion after reading a transcript from 72 hours ago from Wash. DC that was signed by General Hullinger for the safe return of Latoya Gore to her family. The General issued warnings that if she is being held against her will, there'll be dire repercussions to pay... it would be an error of egregious consequences if we terminate her from the field, Sir… over!" Smugs lets go of the microphone … starts howling hysterically and laughing, thoroughly enjoying himself, wishing he could visualize the ole piece of shit Ruiz. 🔆

"Smugs when we capture her… mark my fkn words, I will personally string her Black ass up from the nearest tree limb. Let's see this… Latoya perform her gymnastics from a fricken rope! Smugs, let me remind you that you're in a world of shit up there on IMP. You got two Officer's dead, uh, homicides, and your ass is on the line LT. Smugs, you can't fricken even handle one project. Chaos and havoc surround and follows your every step. You better straighten this bullshit up. I better receive a detailed report by the night's end, or you'll face my wrath, get that!… over." Smugs was no longer smirking "yes, Colonel… over." "Smugs, lastly, I want you, since you're in Redding at Mercy Hospital, to check in with Major Bryan. I need the entire dossier of Rocky Blake, Brock Dame, and Shon Peterson also run a thorough check on contacts for Latoya Gore, her husband, and her brother. I want to know what the three of them were doing in the North State. Where were they staying,… any friends? Where did the Wakeboard boat come from? Did it come from the Shangri Lala campground owned by Rocky Blake? They disabled our soldiers and stole their boat. They are enemies of the USA and will be shot on sight. There will be no White Flags," he snorts into the microphone. "Shoot to kill… over!"

Lieutenant Smugs had been squelched. He merely acquiesced, "yes, Sir, I will be in touch… over." Ruiz clapped his hands with an uproarious frenzied cackle, cruised out of the bathroom and bolted up the stairs to the top deck, and glared at Corporal Mendez and Private Noels, who stood behind a desk, papers in hand. Ruiz bounced around rambunctiously. They watch their commanding Officer work himself into a joyous frenzy clapping his hands and twirling into a Jig.… WTHeck, they pretended not to notice or look, never seeing the

Colonel act this way. Corporal Mendez tells Noels, "well, I'll leave you with it, okay, Private." His face blanched "yes, ma'am," they heard Ruiz mumble, "I'm fka crazy like a Fox them all I'm the King!"

-60-

<u>Rocky, Latoya, and Brock.</u>

Drinks in hand glasses chimed. The liquid for her was a favorite, a Baybreeze with Absolute Vodka. The guys drank Tahoe Blue Vodka and Club Soda without any fruit, reasoning no sugars, therefore no hangovers. At least that was their premise, umh, excuse. Nonetheless, a celebration was in order and on full display at Brock's compound on top of a mountain.

Brock and Rocky watched Latoya animatedly hop around the Livingroom. Neither could stop smiling as Latoya gave her play-by-play rendition of what had happened thus far. Latoya was entertaining... what a fun gregarious astute announcer she was, sexy-toned and brilliant with exuberance, a joy they'd lost somehow years before. All on the lead lap, umh pace holding their 3rd drinks and last because in the morning a full set of chores waited... But now, the time was for remembrances an anesthesiologist couldn't have concocted, uhm, mixed... a finer brew of friends, accomplices, warriors, the three of them were beyond many superlatives. What was solely important was that they were survivors thus far... in the war on America by Americans... Civil War number 2. They had won the earlier skirmishes!

Latoya, with pain and delight flashing across her Deer Brown pupils, "OmGod, it happened so fast, like a 'B' movie set like orchestrated the police pull us over nonchalantly on the lake and calmly tether our boats together. When we argued with them, they murdered my brother and husband. Then the cop said he was going to have some delicious fun with me before he killed me. Said I'm going to rape you, and you're going to enjoy it bitch! From nowhere in the dark," tears formed but never fell… like her body systemically quenched the excess body fluid sequestered her wet eyes sucked back up in her tear ducts which suddenly lit up, not dwelling on dreadful, horrendous realities staying in the positive vein of the evening she'd vaulted over another hazard, magnificent landing… taking a swig blinking away the negatives.

Latoya wasn't finished. "I was down on my knees first a splash, and then there was only one Deputy left. My hero saved my skin." Rocky was chewing some chips and salsa… he tapped glasses with her, "shoot, I can still remember when you touched my shoulder in the water. I almost screamed like an Alligator got me. OmLord, the calm, cool look on your face set me into another dimension. There we were, holding onto the Wake boat. You then somehow wasted the prick who wanted to abuse me, making less noise than a freakin Frog." Rock grinned. "Oh yeah, that's when you came out of the water, girl, like nothing I've ever seen before from like seven feet in the lake, you catapulted over the railing perfect 10-landing on the boat deck." Rocky ran his hand across his forehead "yep you should have seen it Brock! It was an amazing move, bro!"

'L' didn't miss a beat "yeah, then Rock takes me on a night ride on his missile of a Sea Doo like whoosh, holding on blindly to his underground Bat cave lair, uh bunker," she quipped smiling. They were slightly lit up with a fun buzz. She points at Brock, "then super Brock enters the fray surrounded at the dock that bastard Colonel Oh, shit, Rocky was giving him some shit on the radio. It got way intense!"

"We umh, I mean Rocky devised a diversion," she giggled. Brock and Rocky were entranced by reliving her characterizations. "I was like the navigator online… Rock blew up the…" They all knew where she was going, and instantaneous laughter resulted "damnit, Rocky blew the floating toilet up to Kingdom Kum, then was like surrounded underwater on his amazing water scooter contraption. Then Brock came back into the scene. This is movie material that we should sell to Netflix or Paramount. You fly.... a damn Ultralight flex balls to the walls landing right next to a Sheriff's substation on the water, no less from the sky onto the lake. Shoot a rocket, and wham bam, thank you, ma'am, the substation is in tatters... lol, lmao!" They clank glasses again, grinning hugely.

"Then, of course, James Bond-like you fly off the lake, the military with the Ruiz asshole takes off in quick pursuit, leaving me and Rock free to move. I'm going bonkers like crazy in the bomb shelter, um, bunker, then Brock lands at the campground. That's where I met you, and then it's the 3 Amigo's shoot, wild shit really...." another cheers, accompanied by three sets of dimples displayed.

"We disable those soldiers.... change into their clothes, bam, and escape to your mountain paradise sucking down cocktails alive and living to live happily ever after the end.... yep!" Brock looks over at his lifelong pal with a knowing wink. It was far from over. The saga was only at the starting gate.

After extending her left fist to them, Latoya hops up, "I'm making one last drink. Who's down with me?__" "Latoya, we have a big day ahead of us," says Brock. She puts her hands on her hips and shakes her ass swaying her body. "I ain't trippin,' are you?" Blasting from the past, the speakers of the radio harshly.... imploded all exigency for another totty eviscerated the uplifting, positive vibes. The joyous ambiance took a severe hit while the voice on the satellite channel barked loudly.

Latoya dropped her glass onto the tiled floor. It shattered into pieces. Brock shouts, "Latoya leave it there. Come over here, sit down. I want your perspective on what this asshole says," Ruiz spoke abrasively cocky and confident when they heard him blurt out, "Latoya White-Gore shoot to kill on sight, no questions asked. All of them are enemies of the United States of America...." They had heard their names mentioned before she sank further in her chair, seeking out the men she hero-worshipped. Their expressions taunt firm resolve, nonshocked with no fear placing their glasses down. Rocky steps away; moments later, he hands out bottles of chilled water, still listening to the dialogue between Lieutenant Sungy and Colonel Ruiz.

There was a silence that perversely traveled within their compartmentalized minds, lost in examining their current situations. Three Spirits permeating a forbearance a refrain.... strange laughter amplified ghoulishly like out of corridors of an Asylum for the insane Ruiz's words were viciously spiteful, maliciously exposed he was a depraved lunatic vibrating the speakers with vile contempt/ hatred. "I know you have your ears on... the three of you believe you've escaped and made a fool of me and your Government. I am allowing you immunity. Yes, I'm speaking to you, Brock Dame, Rocky Blake, and Latoya Gore. This reprieve expires at noon on the 17th tomorrow, or we will hunt you down and purge you and flush you from existence. The clock is ticking," he howls derisively... 'over!'

Latoya looked blankly at the guys "well, aren't we going to reply and defend ourselves?...." she stiffly stood "we can't let him have his say. How many others heard all of that on the radio, not only military ears! Shouldn't we rebut him, have him redact or rebuke that bullshit ughhhh" declares Latoya! "No, Latoya, Ruiz epitomizes the definition of a psychopath. He's a sinister bully, a cocksure and abrasive evil dude who has maneuvered slithered snake-like up the rungs all the way to Colonel. He's a cunning adversary, an Alpha male not guileless uh, with a purpose to his madness. He wants us, Latoya, to respond. His plan is to anger us enough to rebuke his slanderous statements of falsity and for us to defend our actions over the radio and then have his technicians try and triangulate our position. There's no telling what nonsense he will spew from his vile lips.... Colonel Ruiz doesn't speak the truth unless it favors his mindset. Latoya, all you have to do is look at the bogeys on the lite Green screen behind your head!" Latoya rotates around. There were seven icons... markers moving on the monitor near their location "see them all within 15 miles of us: right now! That's one of my radar systems displaying Ruiz's airplanes and helicopters waiting with sophisticated tracking systems wanting to triangulate our transmissions. Ruiz is maybe the Devil incarnate, but he's no idiot fool!"

"That's right, Brock, I'm concerned that we probably will need to move off your mountain, brother. Consolidate. It's time to meet with Terrance Hallman and our home team at NIA." Rock sucked down the plastic bottle of water and continued, "it's apparent they have the direction that we went when leaving my campground. It's only a matter of time, don't you think?" "Yeah, surely... they have satellite images of us on the boat and most likely will be investigating the Silverthorn area soon enough. You may be right, bro, but let's not panic. We have escape routes...."

Latoya raises her head and looks up at the wooden beams and, peering into the open ceiling rafters, "can't they just fly over us, see us, and attack? I mean, like in the movies, jump out of helicopters Rambo style propelling or repelling... which ever, like drive Army tanks up the road and smash us were not invisible yah got all kinds of buildings up here!"

"Go ahead, brother, do the honors" Brock nods "well, Latoya, you would normally be dead on correct, but for a National secret innovation.... coined or named <u>'Simulated Camouflage,'</u> very few are privy or had ever seen, or read about this innovative supersecret technology. With that being said, not many people have even felt the fabric that covers my entire complex. The simulated netting is above my entire encampment, a special net designed in labs in Silicon Valley. Its indigenously fabricated with the foliage and terrain, including the trees corresponding with the saplings and plants living naturally up here in Northern California. An ingenious camouflage netting has been woven through the existing Redwood, Oaks, Pines, Maple trees, and so on. I've personally flown over my mountain top umpteenth times. It appears vacant of life other than Deer and

Brock sips his water and crushes the plastic bottle. The room had morphed from exaltations to eerie contemplations of their reality "in the daytime tomorrow, you will notice all my buildings are underneath the canopy of trees sewn through…" radio again comes to life. "Latoya, sweetheart, I realize you're being manipulated, perhaps maybe even held against your will, a prisoner of the traitors I previously mentioned. I'm on your side… your parent's mother and father are heart-stricken. I spoke with your mom. She's having a nervous breakdown because you and your brother and husband are missing. She's been prescribed psychotropic medications. Please talk to me so I can connect you to your mom. You're not like the scum that holds you. Help me help yourself and, for God's sake, your poor mother, please, Latoya. I implore you… please have the compassion to get a hold of me. You have the numbers to call. Latoya, you're a National Olympic hero and Gold Medalist many times over. Now it's your time to become a military hero too!" Ruiz pauses, grinning with a howl allowing for his words to sink into the pathetic girl whom he wanted to chain to a wall he was pacing before his desk. The houseboat lurches to the right. He swayed with the movement and re-clicked the microphone.

"Pick up the radio, save yourself… escape Latoya. I've directly spoken to our President explaining your situation ugh, Latoya, we know that you're an innocent bystander, not part of the Rocky and Brock conspiracy against the USA. Our President told me personally to extend a full pardon, total Amnesty. Reach out to me and escape your captors. I'm here for you and will fly your parents to Shasta for you to have a family reunion!" Ruiz clicked off the microphone on his radio and cackled, shaking his head. 'I'm good; should have been an Academy Award-winning narrator!'

Latoya grimaces and mumbles out loud, "my poor mama and papa OmGod, I wonder if my family knows that Tayshun and Devon are dead? I guess there's no way for them to know, and what the hell has happened to their bodies?" Latoya dissolves in front of them. Rocky looks to his bro, who holds his open hands up, gesturing to him to nurture her and hold her.... this was the body language telepathically conveyed. Rocky stood feeling the residual effects of the Vodka. A fun time passed.... pivots left two strides, arms pulling her into his brawny tight pectorals. Latoya willingly grasps him, leaning into him and sighing with sudden spurts of tears.

Latoya shivers not of temperature but of body, spirit release vibrates now, clutching him tight, tears willingly spilled, Brock stands and walks outside. His Dogs surround him, the hovering sound of the whirling rotors of a chopper above... it was a moonless evening. The camo nets brilliant manufacturing technology allowed him to see clearly into the night while he was invisible to the eyes above. He leans over and kneels, taking his animals in. Stands reaches up on a wooden beam and pulls down a Tupperware container with doggy bones wagging tails. He disperses some, then Brock shifts directions and walks to the automatic feeders ensuring his family of animals was going to be fed. He prepped his Stallion 'Sunshine' saddle, stirrups up, and glided for a midnight ride run. They cantered away into a gallop led by his Horse. This was Brock's kind of peace and Heavenly bliss. Swinging in his porched hammock, stirring awake as his dream of horseback riding evanesces over a hill, which was long ago.... would this ever be again?

Lieutenant Smugs depressingly stood over Captain Rory's gurney.

Captain Rory was totally enthused to be the lead actor in the latest Shasta Games movie and video game. Rory was grinning, gallivanting about on his 500 cc Quadzilla 4-wheeler motorcycle. He oversaw his Kingdom, taking up his iPad to see what was happening. Captain Rory was his name, this he was relatively sure of…. he was living inside a colorful, action-packed true-life video game, being the main character of a spinoff of his favorite novels and movies, the Hunger Games. The latest filming of his Shasta Games was ongoing…. Captain Rory was the Star…. where were the Director and Production manager, his filming team, and the crew? Oops, suddenly Rory snatched back his arm Ughhhh something had a hold of his arm ohhh uuhhh, the excruciating pain!

Doctor Lumen, head of Neurology at Mercy Hospital, held Rory's right hand up. "The good news is Captain Rory will recover from all his physical injuries," the Orthopedic Surgeon stated. "The surgeries in his shoulder went without problems, and he has a few Titanium screws and a wire mesh plate from his Labrum to his rotator cuff. A full recovery is expected with total movement. His ears were chewed off, but that is only cosmetic. Fortunately, our staff was able to kill the insects that burrowed into his inner ears. He shouldn't lose much hearing, but we won't know until he regains consciousness. Apparently, the animals were snacking on his flesh…. where possible; we stitched him up. Rory will need further operations and skin graphs and transplants over open wounds, they chewed off three of his toes, but he should walk again without a significant limp but…." "Doc, tell me something; I don't know, like is he going to have any brain damage? Is he going to…?"

"No, Lieutenant Snings, I cannot see the future. Yes, he should regain consciousness, but that's not what concerns me. It's his EEGs and brain scans that are revealing major deterioration. I've never studied a human brain that looks like your Captain… Lieutenant, after his second MRI, I'm going to advocate that you fly the Captain down to Napa to one of the finest technically advanced Neurological Hospitals in the World. It's part of the 'NIA Complex' amazing results have been exalted from their new Sciences… and Stem cell therapies! Captain Rory is far from any form of recovery physically or specifically mentally; he is… well?" Snings shook his head with a scowl starting to walk for the door.

Then Snings turned around "excuse me, Doctor Lumen, maybe sometime later, not now… we might transfer him to Napa, but right now, we're in the infancy of an investigation in which Captain Rory is an eyewitness. He needs to stay here till he regains consciousness my team and I need to speak with him. This is where he will remain… thanks for your diagnosis. I need for you to….." Suddenly, Rory bucks up, trying to break his restraints from the hospital gurney. Rory lunges his head at them like a Serpent growling Wolf, howling like a Coyote. Startled, the Doctor jumps back behind Snings. "This man needs specialized help, don't you see this? I can't believe you think Captain Rory will regain his conscious state of being, come on, Lieutenant, please look at the devastated person before you! How can this shell of a man be able to assist you in whatever investigation…." "Doctor Lumen, the Captain, stays here if you have a problem with that. Consult with Colonel Ruiz." Doctor Lumen utters to himself, looking at Snings arrogance and stupidity personified, finally proclaims, "listen, this man isn't a man any longer. He is an animal lost in a convoluted Zoo." Snings waves him off and walks away. Doctor Lumen said nothing else, took up his clipboard, and went in the opposite direction… 'Why waste a breath on uselessness?' One thing was for damn sure he wouldn't be conversing with that piece of crap Colonel Ruiz. He watches Smogs enter the elevator, thinking they're two birds of the same feather. They must breed stupidity around here.

<u>Doctors Shanon Roble and Cindy Walsh at the Barricade.</u>

Doctor Walsh wasn't a happy camper, not her forte dealing with her peers, albeit one who may have a higher influenced perch. Enjoyment was always found with the regular folks she'd digested and metabolized them with her daily cannibalistic approach being superior intellectually… above the lower class. The less educated or informed clones of society. Cindy detested the ignorant commoners. She was highly esteemed and, in her estimations, the most intelligent person in any room. Some thought the same of this Doctor Roble person…. but they were wrong; she couldn't hold a candle to her. Doctor Roble was weak, and she'd put her in her stationary place!

I had to admit that Doctor Roble did have an impressive pedigree. She laughed at that thought pedigree like a purebred dog. No, her resume glittered like Gold. She had a list of notable followers and accomplishments and, on top of that, an additional number of utmost sacred advocates. Many believed this woman walked on water; she was what the old saying was, <u>'it's not what you know, it's who you know.'</u> Of course, she knew many people in high places; how couldn't she with her position? Cindy didn't like Doctor Shanon Roble way before she'd met her. It wasn't professional indifference nor any form of jealousy, of course, she knew she was a much better leader. Why else was she in charge of being the Medical Examiner and Pathologist for the Sharta project when this so-called expert lived on the County line?

Sadly, Cindy thought it was wrong of her to have a predisposed dislike for the woman but couldn't put her finger on it… was it because of her haughtiness? Cindy had read online some of the news articles about Shanon's innovative procedures and being awarded honors. Her pictures showed matching eyebrows and Eagle Brown eyes. Shanon was not sexy on the feminine spectrum gauge or meter, but definitely handsome with gritty overtones. Shanon looked like no one to fk with. She was in search of her daughter Kayla. Cindy had no children and was always married to her profession, but this 'Shanon squawked like a mother's Hen nah, she acted like she was every Hen's Mother!"

Shanon watches the Doctor maneuver around a few Humvees and Jeeps and past a line of soldiers. The Sergeant held up the caution tape, and Cindy walked past the barricade's Orange and White barrels. "Hello, I'm Doctor Walsh..." "Yes, greetings, Doctor Walsh; call me Shanon, and I'll refer to you as Cindy." Cindy is taken aback by the woman's brazen self-importance and entitlement but maintains civility... unh barricade side manners.

"Cindy, my daughter, has not been heard from since the 5th of July. Today is the 17th.... where is she, and what the Hell is going on behind these barriers? Why are all communications blocked? What's really going on here besides that? Why are you here, Cindy? This is my territory, like my backyard. Why am I, not the one in charge here? I don't ...." "Shanon, surely you've followed the news reports and watched the headlines and the documentaries filmed within Shasta County. There is a new contagion, Covid-57, a new killer variant. The bodies are piling up it's now airborne...." Shanon yanks down her Black mask. "Cindy, you can fk with others... don't try to triple-talk me. There's something sinister going on, it smells, and for the military to fly in 15 medical specialists such as yourself the day before this new outbreak stinks and infers more than words, yes conspiracy tell me what the fk is happening...?"

Shanon studies her peer, although it would be better if she didn't hide behind the overly large mask. Cindy pauses "as I said, the pathogen is airborne loss of life is in the thousands. I've not slept in three days. I'm in charge here, not of my own volition. We have searched Kayla's home and workplace, but we have yet to find her. She's not in the hospital, no police reports. I'm doing all that's humanly possible. L..." "How about turning back on the phones, huh? Cindy, that's not getting it for me, airborne... ahh, why is the epicenter here, and nowhere else does this new Variant exist? You tell whomever you report to, whoever is in charge of this puppet show, that if my daughter is not located by tonight, I will." "You will do what, Shanon?" Shanon pauses for a moment and requalifies her approach, swiftly takes her phone out of her purse... looks at the blank screen, then calms down, staring around at the nosey soldiers and the frowning Sergeant. This isn't the time, thought Shanon. Her phone was not connected, and the blocking device used by the military was working against her. Shanon nixed her next threat... that she would break down the barriers with force, that was fricken silly. She needed time to think this out. Heck, she was on her own alone and surrounded by this woman's military team of guards.

Cindy went lightning quick from a dislike for this woman to detesting this entitled, hateful pompous, uh, Doctor bitch. She was in control, slipped down her mask, spewing some of her own vile contempt, "Shanon Wtf? You stand there all high and mighty you think you're the only mother that has a lost child wanting to know...." "No, I'm not the only mother, but I'm the mother who will take a scalpel to your carotid artery. I like you less than you hate me. Now get my daughter here pronto or face the consequences!"

Shanon spun around, emotionally charged marched back towards her minivan and out of the cordoned zone, not pleased that her eyelids were moist. Three soldiers stood in her way. "I'm sorry, ma'am, once you enter the zone, we must keep you quarantined!" "Oh, Hell no! you don't... Don't touch me, or I will have...." Cindy shouts, "Let her go. I'll take responsibility for her for now?" Shanon bent down and under the caution tape and strolled gingerly, wondering if they'd shoot her in the back. Something was 'Way Wrong.' It was like an enemy force had landed in Northern California checked her phone still no service started the minivan up and squealed the tires as best she could away.

Finally, after a few miles, she entered the small town of Cottonwood; the screen on her phone showed three bars. He answered on the 1st ring, "Hi Rico, it's me. I'm at a stalemate here at the gates of hell Redding, no cooperation heck Rico you...." "Stop, sweetie, breathe, relax. I'm waiting for an emissary to arrive when he or she arrives. I'm flying up there pronto. I'm sorry I didn't leave sooner but I couldn't. I will explain it when I see you. I have to go. General Bill Hullinger is waving me in. I'll talk to him about knocking down the blockade and get to the bottom of what's going on up there will get Kayla out, sweetie gotta go," click.

<u>Doctor Cindy Walsh was beyond her limits.... Irate!</u>

"Calm down, Cindy, I've never seen you this worked up...." "No, you calm down that bitch threatened me." Cindy went into a temper tantrum. "Sharon is going to become a serious problem for us. Major, listen to me. The scary thing is her ferocity.... Lioness like.... the woman's vibrating jowls, aghhhh. Umh, I don't think she's fln around shit. Damnit, I've said more cusswords in the last 30 minutes than I've used in the last three years. I'm pissed!" Bryan clutches the phone tightly. This wasn't something he needed at this time "all right, I will disburse another 15 soldiers to search for this girl but tell me again about this Sharon Doctor she's putting up what demanding a time limit I mean..." "yeah she's going to bust our blockade she thinks she's General Sherman...." the door bursts open without a knock slim-Jim secretary belches out "5 Star General Hullinger wants you to contact him at once Sir he sounds angry and is fuming I told him you were unavailable like you ordered. I have his number, ah he also gave me an encrypted radio channel, gosh I hope you're not in trouble, Major..." ..."Get out of here!" he yelled.

Cindy exhales, "whoa, I heard that… why would 5 Star General Hullinger be in a tizzy to speak with you? I heard he had a large spread East of here in Shingletown…." "Cindy, I wonder why he didn't contact Colonel Ruiz after all. This is his puppy, his mission. I'm second in command. This has got to do with something regarding your Doctor Roble." "We just have to find her daughter, Major…." "I know, Doctor, if the General involves himself, we could lose containment. He's not part of our special counsel, and he is not in the loop nor part of the New World Order. The integrity-based guy wouldn't play ball." Bryan stated, "I have to contact him; I'm allocating another 25 troops to find Kayla!" click.

Less than an hour had passed, and Shanon arrived back at the barricades. Cindy watched as the minivan returned and parked. Shanon only gawked at her from the other side of the barriers. Then she got out and started stomping back and forth, strange thought Cindy, the maternal bonds and all. Sadly she'd never had that chance…. infertile had a hysterectomy, not a choice cancer, ahh, mandatory.

Cindy had a scheduled autopsy at Mercy Hospital for Corporal Hansen, who got killed during that sick game up on the mountain… it would have to wait, thinking you get more with Sugar than Salt she'd put on the fake front uh façade in a chance for new beginnings told the Sergeant to call Shanon back over. Cindy doing her best to smile, waved at her Shanon saw her and started running, then Cindy put the stop hand up slowly and deliberately. Shanon made her way over and uncompromisingly glowered at her… the expression left nothing to analyze, ughhhh, pure disdain.

"I spoke to the Major in charge of this operation. As I speak with you, he is releasing an additional 25 soldiers to find your daughter. We will find her. I'm sorry if I seem so apathetic, and we got off on the wrong step. That's not my intent just been crazy busy and stressed out. I know that's no excuse." Shanon only frowned tersely, glacially saying, "you better find my daughter, and I hope she's safe." "Doctor Roble, I was only trying to commiserate with you...." "Cindy, okay, I'll play along; why does this new form of Martial Law impose sanctions on communications? Besides being inherently wrong, it's unconstitutional. There are thousands of relatives and hundreds of thousands of loved ones across the planet who have tried to get in touch with their families, mothers, fathers Grandparents, Aunts, Uncles, husbands, wives, and children, all locked up behind your cordoned-off area if all is above board then why not allow freedom of speech Cindy?"

"It's way above my pay grade... I'm not an Infectious Disease Specialist nor a Virologist, and I cannot argue with the methodological geniuses that our military has employed to test this new Variant Covid-57. Shanon, one thing for certain it has mutated yet again and is airborne-like. I've told you there is a fear that Wi-Fi waves, frequencies, cell towers, and satellite feeds can spread it. Bizarre as it sounds, the virus is possibly spread through the airwaves. I don't know, don't shoot the messenger...." "Come on, Cindy, what is this? A Sci-Fi movie, we know better than that subterfuge bullshit. We don't believe that it's, geez, what bullshit uh nonsense a virus spread by satellite feeds and phone towers. Wow, how straight-up ridiculous." "Yes, true, but on the 23rd, they're supposed to lift the ban on communications and cell phones, and the internet will be up again, and by the 27th, Redding will be back to normal that's how I understand it?"

"Cindy, sadly, I've heard several dates, always changing. I hope you are right about the 23rd. Who is truly in charge? Is it Major Bryan or Colonel Ruiz? One of my closest friends has been in touch with 5-Star General Bill Hullinger. He has a place up here, and rumor is he is furious and will get to the bottom of this ballcrap." Cindy now knew how the General had got involved and couldn't wait to call Bryan. This Witch is causing all kinds of trouble. "I want inside and to be able to look for

Kayla myself… who do I need to speak to? I am far from the only parent wanting to see and talk to their children." Shinon holds up a notebook with names covering the pages.

"The CHP and the National Guard have moved over a thousand vehicles out of the Redding area. There are camps of displaced people all the way down to Red Bluff. This is absurd, yes, at least the daily broadcasts keep hope sustained, but enough is enough. I will be back. I have to make dinner for my other children and husband. Let me know if I can enter this forbidden zone, or just please find my daughter Cindy!"

Cindy was relieved that she was leaving and pivoted. "Oh, one other thing, ugh, comment or call it an observation, you have a cell phone, obviously speaking to the Major. That's apparently how you knew about the additional 25 soldiers he was allowing to search for Kayla if the virus can be spread with a cell phone…" she frowls at Cindy. "You understand this… something is rotten here. Horribly wicked stuff is going on, pernicious shit and your horns are exposed, missy!"

Cindy huffs, twirls around, silently screams, 'I hate that fkn bitch,' walks back to her M.E. Hearst slams the door throws it in reverse… and stops cold why the heck is she so bent out of whack? The woman spoke the truth. She knew when she signed on that it was going to be for the long haul; she would travel and be an intrinsic part of Major Bryan's team. The goal was in place and was already in stage 3. They would, as a team, undermine Colonel Ruiz, or like she enjoyed referring to him as the 'Blockhead Fool.' Private Remy was in the process of subtly reducing, uh, killing Ruiz's loyal Officers, and we were replacing them with user-friendly hand-picked cogs. Yeah, I suppose I am an evil bitch so fkn what… It is, what it is, Yep!

It has been said that <u>Money can't buy you happiness.</u> I wonder who made that pathetically wrong saying up sure, money isn't everything, but the Oceanfront property and the signed contract for 5 million dollars and the 'net' ah paycheck of $100,000 a month till death do us part works fk yeah! She smiles and says aloud, 'we have to find that lil brat before her mother rips this scenario to shreds. This is our first mission… we knew we'd face obstacles but had contingency plans across the board; uhhh, nothing to deal with a Doctor Shanon Roble!

<u>Maddi at Bart Sampson's house.</u>

Maddi unhinges her anchored eyelids… a red glow pulse finds her eyes reflecting… imbuing a luminescence; the numbers flash, changing to 3:37 am. Maddi was damp, no better to call it wet… soaking drenched, and burning up with fever, she pulled the covers and sheets off her body. The cold air was hitting her body, and she shivered. It felt weird, as if something had changed wrongly. Felt discombobulated and dizzy, stiffly laid on her backside… Wthell?

In a daze for sure, waking inside an alien cubicle, disillusioned, disoriented head on the tracks of a Freight Train, no saliva, unfocused where? What was going on? It was pitch-dark inside the room except for the Red LCD display memory recall not working. My neck, arms, and body aches, my nasal passages are clogged, I can't breathe, and I am claustrophobic. I curled my lower lip up and quivered. This reality had smashed my optimism, and hope… was squelched. It was day three, or was it seven, lost in space. Covid-57 had taken control of my body and mind… I was dying. All symptoms were united, with known deterioration dead soon.

The bed-shifted weights gravity rolled me closer to him, an estranged foreign dizziness that seldom had I dealt with in the past. I was sick, very ill… ugh, Sick. "Here, Maddi, take these pills. They will make it easier now for you to sleep and feel less pain, Bart handed me a bottle of open water. Drink it all, babe, you're dehydrated….." Wait, did he just call me baby babe? I drank, hurting to swallow, found a damp cuddily pillow, and turned it over to a dryer side still moist, but I didn't care. I was sort of comfy, closing my eyes. Would I wake up again?

Thinking, questioning… the drapes of my eyes closed, had I ever in my short life come to life woke up and not had a clue as to where I was, have you? Oh yeah, a few times when I was drinking like a fish, but I'd much rather be hungover than minced Covid meat. I couldn't focus. Am I mentally stable?… Heat flashed over my skin. I trembled… I was always daddy's girl and mommy's good girl, not the party slut loose, easy to screw, nope, nor did I play the conquest games hard to get, and then get got! I never considered myself sexually frustrated and was able to self-manipulate myself. Mom had that talk after blood started to drain, and the bush was getting thicker… now growing into a woman, you know, the talk.

'Here's mother's little helper' bought me my very own Pink Rabbit vibrator. Nope, not sexually frustrated. Our family wasn't prude like we had open understandings, and most everything was on the table for discussion. The only time I woke up unaware of where I was, uhm, I was wasted in a state of inebriation, totally intoxicated. My mind was elsewhere and had vacated my cranium. I was a senior high schooler… playing a game called Beer Pong ugh, with Yeagermiester and indulging in smoking on a seven-person Hooka pipe. I was ripped. Nope, there had to be another word other than inebriation. My forcefield was reduced gone disappeared. It was survival at one point relaxed to a slobbering slug. I tried uh preempted my boyfriend Alec with a slurring preamble; now, please, you better watch me. Don't let me go tonight. I'm intoxicated and buzzed to the max. He acted like he understood my slurring intentions, he held me and laughed loudly. It was strange indeed because we weren't party animals. I guess I let go of my inhibitions that night forced by willingly ingesting aphrodisiacs.

The bed jousted, shaking me awake uh, was I awake? Not cognizant forced a blurred eyeball outward tomb-like darkness. A heavy arm slaps across my back whoa, shock, it pummeled me. Bart's skin, smell against me.... out went the lights once more.

Hours ugh, days later didn't know feeling like Death on a preheat diel complaints were too numerous to detail list body aches, cramps, not menstrual.... migraine trains, can't breathe coinciding with an all-consuming fever concluding Barts Q-Tip proofed tests certain Covid-57! A slither of light shined on the wall thirsty and had to pee, hangover on meds, needed an Energy drink or coffee, maybe both.... umk, wishing for a bowel movement later. But now I was constipated, maybe just gas non-filtered from that crevice. I kicked my right leg up, pushing the sheets off of me, lying flat on my back, flicking blinking crusty eyes.

From hot sweats to cold flashes of frigid ice OmGod, I hadn't a stitch of clothes on. I'm nude, naked, huh uuhhh, and I'm fricken naked! Goosebumps and pronounced tenseness reverberated in my sick and tired mind, yet I was in overdrive, analyzing couldn't focus as to when I disrobed and why I would. Heck, even my ankle socks were off. I leveraged into a sitting position, re-corralling a sheet, and my elbow propped me up.

No, nope, Screamed silently.... no way, please say it's not, so please, Lord, no, yep, my inner thighs were sticky as were my Labia's my vagina had been penetrated having sex enough times to feel the aftereffects Bart had raped me! I couldn't come to believe this, no memory whatsoever; suddenly, the virus took a back seat to being violated, and emotions reared up, anger, humiliation, and hate belched up from Bart's betrayal. The bastard pervert, I reached my forefinger and middle finger down below my slit. Slimy lubrication... was rimmed around my hole.

I rotated on the bed, pulling both my legs up to my breasts Indian style, my back against a wall feeling an odd distinct burning pain. I shifted again to my back and spread Eagle. Oh no, omg... reaching my hand further down past my Taint, more lubrication. My Anal cavity was on fire. He sodomized me.

When I spread my legs apart instantly, I felt a stinging fiery pain, and the air burned my anal opening. I spun my head back and saw a tube of KY gel with the cap off. Black spots bounced across my eyelids, and I felt like passing out, hyperventilating without full breaths, sick, physically abused, and mentally wrought in confusion. Shaking with fury, my adrenal gland shot a load. I abruptly stood up, leaning on his bed.

I couldn't grip it, saying to my inner-self, repeating it over and over, Bart raped me. Bart Sodomized me. He Raped my body. I needed to call the police and report the dangerous freak. Beads of perspiration comingled and dripped down my upper torso. Why couldn't I remember his assault on me, man I had to be totally unconscious when dead to the world to not feel my body being penetrated? I'd never allowed my butt to be entered violated, not even a baby finger. Nope, that was an exit hole, not an entry. The burning like hot coals up inside my torn anus, mortified, treated like an animal, the relentless excruciating pulsations only increased while I dwelled on the process. I needed a shower, ugh, bath, and an ice cube up my butt… help!

No need to preserve his semen… DNA was all over my skin. Obviously, Bart didn't wear a condom… because if he had, there wouldn't be the pasty Peter tracks on my trimmed pubic bone area, all the way up into my belly button. My thighs were already turning a bruised color of Purple, Black, and Red with distinct fingertip marks where he held me tightly in place. The demented perverted bastard, I'll kill him.

I searched the room with my eyes still leaning against his bed for a weapon. The dude was into necrophilism, screwing the dead. How could someone, ugh, a guy… Stop! I need to assess and figure out what to do. I can't call the police, have no phone, and I'm wanted with $75,000 on my head immediately, I'd be in handcuffs. I would be arrested, need to go to a clinic or hospital for DNA retrieval, a rape kit… file, and press charges. Oh yeah, the light blinked on, sure. Bart knew I couldn't report him or go to a clinic hell, go anywhere he believes his sexual assault rape was a foolproof crime… what recourse did I have?

I hobbled over to the window, opened the curtains, and blinked backward. The time was already 11:15 am. I'd slept for another nine hours since he gave me a load of medications and stuck my head out the window… no window screen long ago. I mused I could climb out, or I could go to Homer and Marge and tell them what their son had done to me. How would that go? Probably not well, daddy dearest had gleamed at my breast like a hungry Wolf smiling at his son when he found me in the closet … uuuh Mr. Sampson, your son raped me! His retort, "Sorry Maddi, you can't rape the willing!"

I grabbed a Brass lamp, yanking it from the receptacle. He still snored lightly. I crept up over his prone body, his head laying sideways on a Simpson's pillowcase. I swung the lamp's base downward, busting his skull wide open. A crackling sound, blood spurted up and out… stopped held up why? Stepping away from the tittering ledge, my conscious state saw no one in his bed. It was a wishful daydream…. the perpetrator was already gone!

Thinking about it, I was locked in Bart's bedroom, but I could merely jump from the window and leave. His parents were aware of the reward for my apprehension yet kept their mouths shut. That was the only positive of my being given refuge here. No, the best move for me is to leave here. I must risk it and retrace my steps back to Karen's.

If I killed the degenerate with one slam of the lamp, it might have been worth the risk, but if I only dazed the freak, he was much stronger and would overpower me in seconds, then where would I be? The best thing for me was self-preservation. I need to get a clean Q-Tip and apply it to Bart's DNA, take the evidence with me to prove the vile acts then a quick shower. The rapist wasn't due back from his job at the hospital till about

5 pm. I am disheveled, obviously hallucinating, stalled within a delusional fevered mirage, but for certain, he did rape me. What was left of my mind was in tatters, my body in disarray. What recourse do I have? Help, I plead with my inner self. Please help me! A car door slammed shut outside of the window.

I sneaked back to the window, placed the lamp down, and raked my squinted eyelids open. Yep, it was the freakin Neighborhood Rats patrol making rounds. Dammit, I bit my upper lip decisions confirmed, take a DNA sample, shower, get his filth off of me, out the door, and risk getting captured. What the Hell? I will deal with Bart later with Ben, Cat, Ali, and Cody. They'd help me dole out revenge. Bart would get what he deserved, which is castration!

I sputter awkwardly, sore, and feverishly to the bedroom door. What's this, I ask? A pushpin of Blue in color buried in the hollow wooden door, a Lime Green note inside a dark green envelope.

Cautiously I pulled it out and opened the triple-folded paper, and on page one, in odd print, not cursive, I read, "Maddi, you were Terrific with a Capital T, the best loving I've ever experienced. You're a fka Tigeress in bed, kind of kinky never did the backdoor before felt weird at first, but awesome can't wait till I get home and try it again. Your so damn sexy and beautiful I want you forever. I love you, Maddi. I think I always have. I'll bring Pizza home, all right, and medicine for you to take to feel better, okay? Hey, take… a shower, seeya soon, don't let Covid get you down- Love Bart ....."

P.S. > 'I hope your bite mark doesn't leave a scar. I had to wear a Turtleneck undershirt. Maddi, the hickey is Sick!_ Bitch!'

P.S.S… One complaint, girl, I'm not Alec. You called me your ex-boyfriend's name a few times, but it's okay, I understand. I'll make you love me more…. not jealous kisses and hugs, cutey pie!

When, I lost my equilibrium and slid down back against the closed door grasping his love letter. Ok, fk no, not possible. Fell into a fugue lost in a quagmire, imagination warped; (Suddenly, on a movie set script flowing film crew grinning insatiably, a Law-and-Order drama unfolds before my veiled eyes… 'it dawned on me like CSI America What a scintillating uh, maybe 3-part series.') > <u>News bulletin…</u> 'The violent voracious greedy, forced copulation rape sodomy of a cute virgin ass Maddi the homespun victim, a sweet prosecution team warms up the jury!' 'Bart Sampson, that man sitting next to his public defender, she points angrily vehemently. Take a long look at him. He is a predator of the worst kind of breed an RN, a Nurse by occupation, an imposter, a deceiving pretending monster who uses the tools of his trade to drug and disable his vulnerable victims. Bart drugged Maddi, raped, and sodomized the poor innocent girl! I stared at the jury, letting a few tears cascade down from my blushed cheeks, and cautiously and timidly bowed my head onto my folded arms. No one spoke, waiting for me to regain my composure. Slowly crane like I raised my head back upward, allowing a fading hurtful pout to pass across my sad countenance, carefully shyly avoiding the eyes of the 12 jurors who try to zoom into mine, conveying pure innocence personified… yep Me!'

My Prosecutor vixen pranced to and fro in front of the intensified jury cage, 'Bart drugged Maddi before we detail his aggressive behavior and violation of unnatural acts on the poor girl here before you… penetrating her sacred flesh, look at the vile creature, this diabolical cretin. The man is sinfully sinister!' She did a pirouette. 'Better beware said my lead big-haired fake boobed savior peering at the seven females of the jury…. look at him and memorize that smug face; he could be coming for you! Bart's Public Defender, Mr. Manning, jumped to his feet. 'OBJECTION,' your Honor, please, isn't this a bit over the top

unh … personal, my sister is on the jury, oops …
'SUSTAINED!'

Maddi's lead advocate… the prosecutor's fierce expressions were orchestrated with hours of practice in front of mirrors. 'Let me paraphrase that, ugh, no rephrase uh Bart's mental approach, his fiendishness sadistic disorders lurking evil, misogynistic disdain for you and us the double Xer's clever he is you ask how clever?' *The Judge seemed perplexed he didn't hear anyone ask how clever.*

Bart is as clever as a razor-sharp cleaver, cunningly knowing that Maddi would wake much later from her assault and assume properly that she'd been raped and violated because he forced debilitating drugs into her … that induced a stupor a fugue what's he do huh? Think what you would do if your mind were as twisted as his… 'She unfurls a pretty Lime Green note, sure he leaves her a witty love letter… 'Exhibit F' if it would please the court, she whirls it around in the air above her perm. Bart's Public defender pounds the laminated table jumping to his scrawny feet and rubbing his hurt fist 'I OBJECT,' the Judge leans over, burping his bifocal's slide down his greasy angular beak, saying, object to what? The Public Defender gloatingly swaggered up well. Why Exhibit F shouldn't we start with Exhibit A, sir? Sustained Strike that pointing at the erect studious librarian-type/court reporter, who does a giant wiggle, trying to warp her head to see him. 'Make that Exhibit A,' the Judge nods approvingly at the Public Defender. 'Nice Catch!'

CSI America attentively watches with bated breath, wide-eyed, chewing popcorn. It was an intense trial with running monologues taking interviews. Bart is guilty as a 3-dollar bill. The gambling bookies are laying odds and over-under's on the time he's going to receive in prison… announcements by the prosecutor on the Courthouse steps. The media stacked up on the stairs. "Yep, we nailed him. His DNA was all over Maddi, the poor victim. The CSI Captain steps up and squints into the floodlights, annoyed, shifting to his dimpled side. I should remind my audience I was the one to scrape Bart's fingernails that had scratched Maddi's thighs and glutes!

Back in the Courtroom, silence permeated the rows of benches, the audience's nail-biting tension cutting the air. The Judge looked squeamish, with a putrid clenched muzzle and a loud flatulence. He quickly stands to inspect and yells, somewhat embarrassed with his mallet crushing a drink coaster. Recess rings the bells Recess a bell rings in the distance uh in the far distance.

Evil noses curled up turned into sneers when Bart catches Maddi's jaded spears (eyes). She asks, big hair, "well, how you think we're doing?" "don't you worry, precious Maddi… Bart will be strapped to Old Sparky this afternoon. You can flip the switch and watch his long Blonde hair and testicles turn frizzy. The guy doesn't know it, nor his pathetic pretender defender Bart will be electrified toast burnt within hours!"

The trial resumed the players in position.... what would Bart's attorney come up with. It seemed to be one of those stereotypical open-and-shut cases guilty off with his head seeya. The rail-thin advocate for Bart stands periscoping the interior of the standing-room-only crowd of spectators. He shook his head ('I have nothing to say in Bart's defense, Ladies and Gentleman of the jury. I've heard all the testimony and heard it said a picture is worth 1001 words.) He yanks from his shorts an 11 X 14-inch photo and waves it around. 'Now let us all in this courtroom and across the globe… Look at Exhibit F,' he clicks on his laptop, and the enormous screens light up around the courtroom. 'Yes, this is Indeed… <u>Exhibit F</u>!'

Bart's Public Pretender bounces up before the Jury, waving and gesturing his hands in Maddi's direction, and declares to Maddi… 'You're so fked. Please, all of you, look at the bloodsucking Hickey with her DNA and proof of her incisors fangs, not a hickey uah, Maddi was a busy insatiable Vampiress.' The crowd goes berserk crazy. The Judge pounds his gavel, screams, and shouts obscenities. 'Order In My Court

Now!' he stares, drooling at the screens. Bart's public defender yelps, ("We're pressing charges for assault… arrest, Maddi put her in chains!")

Maddi is gasping, her face against his bedroom door, waking from this Nightmare… Dreaming of this warped scenario. A smell hits her from the other side of the door; she squeezes her head downward into the carpet close as she can to the 2-inch opening at the bottom of the door. Saw black holes, um, a nose sniffing and snorting the family Guard Dog. Uh, tired, Maddi crawled back to the bed, plopped down, rolled to the dry side of the bed, looked at the nightstand, and saw the pills… yep Bart was looking out for her, Gulp nighty nite now!

–62–

<u>Father Rite… Ben and Cat at Bethel.</u>

With Elder Jeremy beside him, Father Rite walked with a purpose; Wanda was trying to keep pace Ben and Cat were on her heels. They were shellshocked with the horrifying news… far too much to assimilate oh absorb the matter-of-fact statement that their families had been eliminated and killed by the military. This stuck like tar to their hearts. This caustic information was way too bizarre for them to comprehend… they asked for proof, but none was forthcoming. The Bethelites only changed the subject each time Cat or he tried to gain some leverage and evidence that the military had gone Rogue and was assassinating innocent civilians. Behind them, uhm, pulling up the rear… the Caboose was the girl in all White Satin… Venus. Who seemed to float with ease, impassively, and unenthusiastically without a care, then she disappeared into an alcove.

Ben noticed, along with his GF, that they were yet taking another detour up a circular staircase down another hall. Now the maze continued. Heck, he thought he'd need a map or schematics to maneuver around this Church. The walls were dull White with a bubbled texture, no pictures. He felt they were somehow on the outside of the main entrance of Bethel; Father Rite stopped at a steel door and entered a code. The door zips open in a brief instant. They could see inside a vast room; computers and cubicles were everywhere, with at least 35 people working if there were one. The inside of the spacious room resembled a computer laboratory at a University with screens, monitors… keyboards clacking away. He glances at Cat, who nods, matching his thought; impressive indeed.

A hulking man, Ginormous in all extremities, approached us. We stood eerily transfixed. The giant could have been on Ripley's Believe It or Not… near 7 feet or taller and a muscled 375 pounds, indeed a fearsome individual cartoonish, ahhhh, unreal-like, whoa, the dude could be scary. Father Rite says, "this is Goliath. He's in charge of security here at Bethel." The Giant bends his head with acknowledgment releasing a weary suspicious stare at us, then finds Rite's gaze. "Yes, you cleared them. They're okay, we can speak…Goliath, moments ago, I got your warning beep… what's the matter?" Goliath's baritone vibrates. "Father, I buzzed you because we've experienced unusual traffic flow and flyovers by Apache and Blackhawk helicopters, and an AWAC surveillance plane has been wrapping a circular nothing pattern above our properties in search of signals, I'm guessing, and sir, add to the fact that they've got a mobile unit with satellite dishes down on Hilltop Blvd and Lake Blvd running an inept triangulation of our property…." "What? This is against our agreements with Major Bryan. I will address this at once!"

Goliath bowed his enormous skull 'Father, for the first time since the invasion, we're exclusively on their radar. No question they are trying to zero into our mode of communications"

"What's your advice? Shall we go dark and scramble our frequencies again?" "Yes, for a few hours more, Major Brynn's so-called tech wizards are totally confused. They haven't figured on below-the-ground fiber optics being utilized by us; we need to go dark at a minimum of three hours, Father!" "Goliath, thanks for the heads up...." He raises his massive hand. "Father, the posers keep coming in. The last day we've got 17 soldiers that want to join our church... infiltrators, sir, and you know that's not happening!"

The giant seemed to stop over us taking us in with a hazing glare. "Father, I'm not questioning you, but do we need more recruits?..." "Yes, you are and don't... thanks for the information. I need to get to the 1st-floor basement and use our radios till you get the phones back up. Thank you, Goliath!..." "Oh, almost forgot the 3rd-floor basement awaits your new friends... you're welcome, Father Rite." Venus reappeared with a worried expression.

Rite said, "well, that changes plans; Ben, you, and Cat follow Wanda... Venus, record all, please. Jeremy and I will start in the Cathedral with our church officers planning the upcoming meeting with Major Brynn." "Yes, Father," Wanda waves her arm off. We go in slow pursuit stopping at a bank of elevators. She sticks her forefinger on a keypad, and the door opens... hits the button labeled B-3. We fell so fast, like a Magic Mountain ride Cat, and I grabbed the walls. The Bethelites were veterans and only bent their knees like shock absorbers. Venus subtly grinned "it takes some time to get used to it. I'm sorry; I should have warned you." The elevator racks open to a humongous loading dock, forklifts jockeying about with hard hats on. Stacked pallets upon pallets, all packaged in a light green shrink wrap Wanda noticed our curiosity... "All necessary supplies from canned foods to toilet paper, for our congregation to subsist when things get worse, and that's the direction it seems the FOE or World Order is heading." We resumed walking. Wanda pointed to a temperature-regulated glass enclosure "that's filled with insulin and other perishable Pharmaceuticals.... that we will need to sustain life... the lives of our worshippers."

We continued walking down a ramp stopping at a garage-type door on a chain. Wanda pushed a round Green button; up the door went. The first thing Ben and Cat saw were Army boots, then the camo fatigues of two soldiers, a long-extended Van beside it, were two stretchers with Cody and Ali's faces either dead or soundly sleeping sheets covering the rest of their bodies. Cat nearly tripped, running. I was frantically on her side, sliding to a stop. She places her hands on Ali's face. I put my fingers on Cody's carotid artery. Cat nods happily... "He's alive..." "so is Cody...." I relayed, relieved; we smiled wide, weary-ass grins, pulling back the sheets and looking them over. Yes, they had all their body parts attached. Cat went about hugging each of them... it dawned on me angrily. I stood "why are they here? What did you do, kidnap them? Where are Maddi and Karen? Explain yourselves now!"

Wanda rolled up her eyelids like annoyed, then peacefully beckoned us over to some chairs while Venus took her radio out.... "We need injection antidotes inside Unit A+ of Unit B-3 garage # 1 on the double Venus out!" moments later, "10-4 Venus on our way out"... Wanda showed us her patented reassuring smirk while we sat down. "You're familiar with the military's machinegun-styled RFD, which fires darts. Your friends were shot by two of our Bethel brothers. She waves them over and introduces Jon and Dan to them. No shaking of hands nods only. "Could either of you explain to our new friends here why you shot Cody and Ali?" "Ahh, sure, Wanda, but perhaps it's better if you listen to the military's emergency phone line that all citizens are encouraged to report all lawbreakers for possible rewards. This is the report that led us to intercede and save these young men ahh... with the help of our Dogs," Dan explains, standing in front of them.

He taps the recording machine, "hey, this is Jimmy Mastery. I want to report three people breaking curfew. It appears there are armed bulges under their jackets, all dressed in Black, and they just crossed Hwy 273 from Clear Creek Road. I want the reward. My phone number is 530-222-2242." "Jimmy, are they on foot, bike, or vehicle, and you failed to say which direction they... "They're on foot going North ducking and hiding like criminals. I want the rewards on these...." "We're on it, Jimmy thanks for doing your Civic duty will be in touch with the reward details." click.

Dan walked in front of us, stopped raising his head, and continued to explain why our friends were unconscious on the gurney's before Cat and me... "then the radios came online. The MP's uh military police, along with a batch of soldiers, were sent out. The police went to Red Alert. Two Humvees and a helicopter with two drones were immediately sent in your friend's direction to capture them or kill them. What you didn't know is that a neighbor of Karen's family is a member of our Church who works with our security detail. She reported two young people, along with Karen leaving, so we were already aware that there was a problem. This neighbor, who will remain anonymous, loaned us her trained Canines agreeing to let them join us in trying to make sure we got to your friends and

intervened before the military could capture them." Jen nervously raised his arms. "Dan, you're forgetting what the neighbor also said, that is... that during the late evening, her night vision sensors picked up a female leaving Karen's house at around 3:45 am...." "Oh yeah, that's right! Anyways we made it to where your friends were hiding in a 2-story office building complex and captured them; rather lucky to have not been shot dead or injured... your friends are trigger happy!" Dan whipped up his eyebrows, wiping his forehead with the back of his hand.

"Elder Jeremy had heard the earlier reports and had ordered us to take action. Mind you, if we were five minutes later, the three of them would have been captured by the MPs and likely would have been restrained in the brig being interrogated. We joked several times about the monies. They have a cool $50,000 on their heads, the same as both of you. I heard it was dead or alive!" Jon added, "Dan and I did as Goliath had ordered and spoke like we were part of the invading troops just in case any of the Officers were using those listening probes that could enable them to hear our words. Therefore we bragged about the monies we were going to collect. We never mentioned Bethel, ma'am!" "That's good; you two deserve praise. I will be informing Father Rite about your good deeds..." stated Wanda.

Cat and I were befuddled and annoyed at how fast our lives had been altered. "That's great, Dan and all of you." I vented exasperated, staring at Cat's perplexed face. "We're being hunted for forming a so-called insurgent group of young people to fight for our Constitutional Rights, such as Freedom of Speech because the Government has blocked all communications illegally. How about our rights to decide what we want to ingest or, ugh, forced vaccinations leaving a permanent Tattoo on our skin...." Cat jumps in. "Yeah, and didn't you tell us that these new brands, uhm, tattoos have hidden tracking chips inside the ink umh, what irritates me is you people here at Bethel were spying on us joining our conferences. I wonder how many Bethelites are in our separate think tanks?..." I took the ball "besides that, Karen's neighbor was spying on us like surveillance and following us. Are you people not the same..." "Ben, wait till you jump to conclusions, don't cast stones at the only liberal thinkers and doers you have left to aid your movement and agendas," said Wanda.

Wanda continued the debate, "Remember when Tim, Trudy, and Kelly talked you into going to our Bakery at the Sundial Bridge to meet with our Church leaders your plan at that time was for all of you to meet back up at Karen's home the next night. At your Mary Lake conference, little did you know there were a few spies that had allied themselves with Major Bryan, and they'd reported your friends left the building with Karen. Therefore they had an idea… of where to find Ali, Cody, and Maddi. They'd already sent a team of soldiers to her ranch home only minutes after they had left that same morning that girl was seen leaving Karen's house. Father Rite and the officers of our Church had wanted to spare your group from a form of Genocide!"

"Genocide like the Nazis… please define exactly what you and Bethel think is going on here in Redding Wanda?" demanded Cat. I added, "by the way, the girl seen leaving Karen's was one of our best friends and my brother's ex-girlfriend Maddi. Where is she at?…" "Yeah, that's right, Ben. Where is she at since you guys have these plans to enlist and recruit the members of our group and to follow us and spy on us? Tell me!" yammered Cat.

Suddenly it dawned on me… laying on stretchers disabled by darts were Cody and Ali, but where the heck was Karen? Didn't Dan say they captured all three of them? I stood back up and raised my arms up "where's Karen at Dan? You said…" Jon twitched, saying, "I had to use the bathroom. We stopped at a store, and while we were in the store, she escaped. Before you ask how she wasn't like your friends knocked out from the darts, we can't answer that possibly she was immune anyways she bailed out of the Van…." "Did the military arrest her? Where is she at?" asked Cat. Dan nodded. "We monitored all the radio transmissions and did search the downtown area for her. We have to play it close to the cuff, even while inside the Van. Well, we don't discuss anything but what the military would expect us to talk about. They have specialized trucks that use newly modified listening spheres like phalluses with dishes. All they have to do is point it at a house or vehicle and eavesdrop on all conversations within; therefore, we couldn't contact other Bethelites in the area."

Wanda rolled her head on her meaty shoulders "we don't know where Maddi nor Karen is, but my best guess is their probably looking for their families!" Quickly entering the space were two people in White overalls with Medic insignias on their backs carrying old, like Western days rucksacks. They didn't even look at us, just beelined directly to where Cody and Ali lay dormant.

"Your friends fired their weapons at us meant to kill us, and they were not shooting darts. Dan and I were lucky that we had some combat experience, or Cody, Ali, and Karen could have killed us btw if we were real soldiers of the incumbent forces, uh FOE forces of evil... and were fired upon, they'd been executed on site without jurisprudence that is the unspoken law on the streets now you fire at a soldier you die" blurted out Jon!... Jon flips a switch on his pocket cam points to a small monitor on a wall, "watch our pocket cam... video of when your friends tried to kill us... before we disabled them!"

After the short pathetic action shit was over, neither Cat nor I replied. We had no defense; we just went in a different direction "how long till the boys are going to be able to speak or to come to life? Will there be any side effects from the darts? Any residual effects that any of you are aware of from being shot?" asks Cat. Wanda took the question, "the concocted sedative solution in the darts usually lasts between 7 and 11 hours, depending on the individual's constitution. People's internal systems are all dissimilar and have various resistances. For instance, we've witnessed Heroin addicted people having to be shot with additional darts. Some are completely immune and wake up within minutes. It depends on tolerance levels the darts contain super strong tranquilizer mixtures. As far as residual effects, we've noticed none but drowsiness and some sleep even after waking naturally."

"Karen," shouts Jon like a light went on, "was she a Heroin addict? I mean, I know I shot her several times, yet it had no effects...." Dan adds, "speaking of her, she's a slippery gal spunky was the last to go down fighting gun blazing were not sure maybe she had a built-in resistance to the darts formula. One thing for sure Karen's resourceful stole my hat, jacket, and gun, was able to unstrap herself from the stretcher, and disappeared out on the streets!" I said, "Karen might look like a rebel and drug user with her piercings and the tattoos covering her skin, but I'm told she's not a drug abuser, just a tough girl, a survivor we had only met her the night of our Mary Lake conference...." Moans and groans are heard. Cat was moving her feet in a split second, racing over to the stretchers. I was on her tail, followed by the slower-moving Bethelites Cody was gesticulating, arms and legs waving, moving in unnatural motions like he was spasming, yelling indecipherable words, gibberish then Ali's eyelids flickered open Whites lit up full-on fright.

The guys were coming to life, and something chewed up flipped from Cody's mouth. Dan points it out, "look just like Karen. They chewed up some notes they didn't want us to be able to read...." Cat nodded "we have drop-off areas for our group to be able to communicate and to be able on the fly to change meeting spots since this is the only way left to us...." Venus shuffled forward, "just like during Hitler's reign. The Jews had a whole network intact for communications!"

Ali rolled up on the stretcher's edge and looked around, seeming to try to take it all in. Cody was still in flux, not focusing then, a radio blasted words out on Dan's belt 'we've spotted a violator on Court Street by the Jail!'

—63—

Karen Fleming searched for Kayla Green.

Karen cruises down the street like her name was on the street sign, but it wasn't... Court Street was pretty much vacant. She was walking behind a Law Office across from the County jail, checking for Kayla's car, not in her usual parking spot, dammit. Karen hopped up the steps peering around, then knocked on the back window of Kayla's office.... all was dark inside. The lights were off on the ground floor where Kayla had worked as a Paralegal.

She stepped back, stretching her neck up to see better uh, and caught a light aglow on the 3rd and top floor, thinking each floor denoted a different law firm, yet no vehicles in the parking lot. From out of nowhere, skidding tires, loud screams of voices shouting... "Get down, or we will shoot you dead!" With the stolen military jacket, could she bluff? The only advantage she had was the Rhino skin armor wear her father had gifted her and the weapon she'd taken from the van. "Get down now..." bullets ricocheting off the pavement, a barrage of shells, real bullets, not darts, were fired from multiple directions. A long echo existed then a soldier squealed in joy. "We got her!"

Karen ducked behind a shrub as they swarmed in. The apparent homeless woman lay splayed out in pieces. They had murdered her; Karen froze, knowing they had thermal seekers. Her tough persona cracked, tears flowed, and she crawled deeper under the shrubbery, trying to hide in the dirt. Watching as best she could, a covered truck pulled up, and two medics grabbed the Ragdoll woman, one from her legs and the other from her arms, and they slung the emaciated victim into the back of a truck. Then instantly, everyone dispersed like no big deal... done!

After what seemed to be an eternity of time, Karen crawled out, going through her mind thinking, what next? Kayla wasn't at her home.... nor at her job. Maybe her husband AJ and she had escaped the Redding area. She was about to take off and try to make it back to her family home, instantly a feeling she couldn't describe to anyone who hadn't felt it before, a sensation as if someone were staring at her, a 6th sense she'd read if a human were in tune within the ethereal space they inhabitant, vibes aligned with intuition could be assimilated. Karen was on high alert, awareness like a live wire.... a tingling foreboding premonition was lighting up her conscious state. Karen believed in her mother's mystic beliefs and knew she had unworldly powers. It wasn't make-believe or fiction. Not only was it inertially possible via her psychic intuitions, but it was also reality. A ringing sound resonated from her inner ears uhm, an alarm telling her to freeze. Someone watched her every move. Slow as Molasses, she subtly starts to shrink down her knees, bending into a squat, a stinging chill retreating from her skull to the nape of her neck, dropping downward and tingling down her spine. Was it, Foe or Friend?

She didn't run periscoping around… saw nothing, no one, decided to explore this feeling, stumbled apprehensively down the back sidewalk of the building, and trended farther next to an Emergency exit sign and stairs. Karen started climbing them and knocking on each door, first hesitantly, then rather aggressively, no answers, ugh, still on edge. She banged on every door on floors #2 and #3, but not a peep in return, nothing. Back on the ground floor, Karen searched and found the Redding Electric company's meters for the law offices on the first floor; the electric meter indicator barely moved. No one appeared to be using any electricity. On the second floor, the needle indicator moved but… at a turtle's speed, but then Karen swayed back and gawked… The third-floor numbers and indicator were running at a Rabbit's pace, huh?

Karen again strode out to the curb, glaring at all the windows. Sure, a few lights could be seen, but the building was dark inside. That much was obvious, all being the same…. this was congruent. The problem was that Kayla worked on the ground floor. The feeling that someone was watching her came and went. Karen asked herself… why was there so much power being consumed on the 3rd floor? Karen decided to play out a hunch just like she'd done dozens of times since she was a small girl; her inner guide had never failed her unh. She paid heed to the non-regulated, harkened voice speaking from within a voice that resembled her own. Reached down under a bush and snatched up a medium-sized rock.

Racing up the stairs to the 3rd floor, pounding on the doors with the meaty part of her fist holding the rock, yelling, throwing caution into the breeze, "I know someone is in there… open up…." A shadow floats snake quickly across the peephole, and Karen cries out. "I need help. I just saw you open up; please help me!" Those last three magic words did the trick. The metal latches were clanged the door swung out over the threshold. Standing before her was a China doll Asian with unsmiling eyes. Behind her was her best friend Kayla, all 5'11ish, towering above the 5-foot Asian girl. What a contrast to the small-boned tiny girl was Kayla's tall, big-boned beautiful figure…. she threw her arms out wide. Kayla was grinning wide, her expansive eyes unblinking, showing dimples popping on her cheeks. Karen leaped inside, rudely brushed by the slim figure…. then ensconced in a long minute, embracing one of her bestest friends. They were shaking and quivering her GF and her together. Yes! 🦎

Before Kayla could introduce us, no joke, the diminutive female screamed a blood-curdling howl. We glanced… Reptile quickly at what brought this fearful reaction. Omg, the parking lot was entrenched in military vehicles. Kayla turns to Karen "how could you lead them right to me? They've been searching for me on loudspeakers shouting my name. Why Karen, what's wrong with…" "sshhh, I didn't, I promise." We fell collectively to the floor listening, laying on our stomachs huddled together against a wall in an office with a placard on the top of the desk the name… Lori Chan. Pictures adorned the walls, desk, and lamps table her family!

The computers were running, and it looked like they were working on something. Instantly they heard a loud bang-battering ram like a crushing shredding explosion. Sounds burst in the air from at least two different bullhorns, a discordance of verbiage with the only consistent words…. Kayla *Green. The loudspeakers came at them from different angles from the front of the office building and the back, the only exits were canvassed. "Ms. Kayla Green, please come out. Uh, your mother* wants you.... You're not in trouble; you are safe. Please come out now!" Karen stares at her friend's expression. Lori states, "what are they saying? Are you kidding me? Your mother, uhm, mommy wants you. Wtf? The entire platoon is hunting you, Kayla, for your mother. Who the fk is your mother anyways?"

Kayla blanched bleach white, her wide eyes in shock. "Ugh, uh, I um, I don't get it uh, you know my mom, girl, she's just a doctor, a Forensic Pathologist who does subcontract work for the FBI and CIA, you know these secretive acronyms used by our Government...." "I don't like it," says Karen. Lori waves her head and nods down up, not good. "If you don't go out there, we'll all be caught up, Kayla!" "Oh no, I don't want to get either of you in trouble because of me; they're only after me...." "Oh shit, they're on the second landing there goin to search all the offices were busted oh damn as they hear the doors below them busting open "There's got to be 35 troops out there...."

Kayla pushes herself up, standing with a determined expression portrayed, "both of you go hide in the janitorial room. I noticed an attic opening. Try and get up there, there only after me...." Ironically at that very second, flashing on a large TV screen attached to the wall... was Colonel Ruiz holding up a picture of Kayla. Then he barked that Kayla Green is wanted with a $50,000 reward for her capture. She wiggled her head, whispering, "go now, please hide!" Lori and Karen ran and disappeared, afraid for themselves and their friend Kayla.

Kayla unlatches the door. At the same time, it gave way with a launching battering ram pummeling the hinges. Kayla was greeted by three sweating, hyped, and angry men who held weapons at her throat and head. She'd watched the patrolling posse of soldiers outright kill people on the streets below and also witnessed the covered trucks pull up to the back of the County jail and counted the gurney's leaving with sheets covering inmates. "Get on your knees, hands behind your back now!" The hyped, overzealous types, she thought, not shaking nor acting like her inside, which tumultuously somersaulted like a rollercoaster. There had to be nine soldiers staring her down, then they spread out. A distinguished man with a Gold nameplate with Yellow stripes steps up… Private Freeze.

"Help her up; what are you doing? She's not a prisoner or fugitive…." Kayla regains her feet. "Come on with me, Kayla. I'm relieved to…." "Where am I going, Mr.?" "I'm Private Freeze. You're not in trouble. Your mother is waiting for you." Down the stairs, Kayla followed closely in his footsteps. A woman standing against a Black extended Hearst flashing a peace-sign mask, Kayla heard the words. "Well, well… well, I'm sure glad to see you, missy. I'm Doctor Cindy Walsh. Come on, get in. I have a cooler with cold drinks inside and snacks. Your mother is waiting."

Cindy had broadcasted the fortunate luck to Major Bryan, who sent out bulletins across the military radio bands… relief, uhm, post-coital bliss like nearly… while General Bill Hollinger cheered. Many of the power players exhaled all the way to the hierarchy of the World Order and members of the Presidential cabinet that were privy as to what really was happening in Shasta and the overall plans worldwide. Calls went out to FBI Director for the State of California, Agent Rico Captur, who delayed his trip North from San Diego, happily speaking with his good friend Doctor Shanna Roble.

On the other side of the coin, Colonel Ruiz was engaging in a heated one-way conversation with Bryan. "It's like I've said many times, 'One bad Apple spoils the whole bunch,' and that Apple could just be this Kayla Green. We need to debrief her. Do you realize what an amazing feat my command has accomplished, Bryan? Not a single resident that was in the epicenter of our invasion has escaped our military zone. Kayla will be the first. Sure other fools have gone to extreme measures after getting past our blockades, causing social media stirs across the planet, which our positive propaganda experts shot down as another insane conspiracy freak. Still, this young woman has a built-up audience that lurks waiting. I've gone over her resume, and there's no fricken dirt. She's an outgoing woman with tons of powerful acquaintances and friends. Look what her whore of a mother has caused with her connections. Let me tell you, Major, the 'Fruit didn't fall far from the Tree' Kayla, by trade, is a renowned Paralegal working for the largest Law Firm in Shasta County and going to school with a goal to pass the Bar Exam and open her own business. People will listen to what she has to say… what we must know is precisely that… before letting her leave our control."

Major Bryan was still simmering over his middling statement about what he had solely accomplished, giving him zero credit. Sick and tired of the abrasive Colonel, and decided what the heck, "Colonel, you're not the 'Lone Ranger.' Yes, this is your operation, but we're in separate sectors, and I believe I deserve some of the credit here. This is a team effort. I mean, don't you realize I'm…" "Bryan shut the fk up. It's just like you to hog in on my achievements and triumphs. You just follow my orders. I could have picked anyone to be in your position. You are fortunate that I chose you. We need to be clever and try and debrief her before Doctor Walsh drops her on the outside of our forbidden zone to her pestering mother."

Kayla puts her shoulder bag on the floorboard along with her purse she grabbed after being accosted. "I'm so happy to see and meet you," said Cindy for the second time, for Kayla hadn't muttered a syllable. "Tell me, what were you doing in Lori Chan's law office? Kayla, why were you not in your own office? Why haven't you been to your house in the last week? Where have you been? We have been broadcasting your name on the emergency channel nonstop and on all Television sets. Geesh, we even had our patrols ringing out your name from mega-horns on the streets. Kayla, it wouldn't be an exaggeration to say that your name has been mentioned hundreds of times. We've been searching for you, young lady, for days. What's going on with you?" Cindy watches her bend down and pull out a half drunk plastic bottle of water and gulp the rest down. "Is there anything bothering you, Kayla? Are you hungry? You haven't said a word. Should I take you to the hospital? Are you traumatized? What's up, girl?"

"Please just drive me to where my mother is; thanks...." Cindy, beyond perplexed, at this girl's attitude, she should be grateful. Cindy had read the texts on her proprietary military edition cell phone. *"Don't let her out of your site. Try to debrief her. Find out what she will say to the world once we free her. If she doesn't cooperate, take her to Mercy Hospital to the basement!"* Cindy pulled the death wagon; Hearst to the curb stopped, leaned over stared at the girl. *"Listen, I know this has been hard on you in these chaotic times. I can try and provide you with answers to any questions you may have. The dynamics have been altered with the Covid-57 Variant, which is airborne now. This restrictive Marshal Law is a bitch for all of us you have any stories to add uuh uh, I'm kind of keeping a running journal as an amateur author writer and hope to write a book. Please humor me with some anecdotes of your experiences, some tidbits, something juicy, Kayla, won't you please?"* Cindy made a mental note to have the entire office building that Kayla was caught hiding in searched and also to have the computers in Kayla's paralegal office and Lori Chan's law office confiscated and analyzed by a team of CSI types, due diligence was indeed necessary.

Momma hadn't raised any fool. This hippy woman with flowers beaded in her lengthy hair, her peace sign medallions and necklaces, and her matching face mask.... she was one of Them! The enemy, she had to be thoughtful and diligent. "Doctor, I see you have use of a cell phone. Can I perhaps use it to call my mom?" Cindy looked down at her phone, pausing. "No, it's not that I wouldn't let you, but it has a limited range here in the city limits. Your mother is out of range; sorry, hun." "Well, I have nothing to report. I kind of just went into a cocoon hermit like I saw nothing out of the ordinary and just wanted this to all be over. Tell me, Doctor, when will that be? How much longer will the citizens of Shasta be enslaved!" Whoops, she thought… the wrong word but tightened her lips.

The doctor pounced, "Enslaved? How do you mean?" Cindy ensured the speaker on her phone wasn't blocked thinking… and questioned Kayla. "What a strange word to use, enslaved like incarcerated or imprisoned…." Then Cindy wizened up and remembered what the Major had mentioned at their last meeting about the missing girl's law office that was adjacent to the County Jail, where they'd scuttled the inmates off and up to the IMP pits. "Can we get going? Why are we parked? It was a wrong choice of words. I meant the citizens being locked down under curfew orders is all." "Did you, by chance, see the trucks across the street from your office pick up the inmates that were taken to a cleaner facility? Many are in hospitals, and others are given pardons. Well, at least the nonviolent offenders that must have appeared gruesome, their bodies covered in sheets carried out, ugh?" Kayla didn't bite nor add what she was meandering over while this huntress detailed exactly what she'd witnessed. What about the homeless downtown who were shot where they laid the encampments and tents of the destitute bagged up and thrown into the back of waiting truck beds. Anyone not dressed in a uniform was captured and taken away if they fought… which she saw many that had, they were once again fired upon.

Cindy was losing her patience and getting nowhere ughhhh started the vehicle up. Kayla relaxed more. "Thanks for picking me up. I'd much rather be in here with you with the air conditioner blowing than one of those Jeeps baking in the afternoon Sun." The car veered sharply to the right onto Placer Road, "whew, where are we going? This isn't the way…." "I'm sorry we can't allow you out of the Redding area before you are checked out at Mercy Hospital. Kayla you could be infected with the new strain, got to have some tests, unfortunately… I will contact your mother and let her know you are safe, and soon I will deliver you to her!" "What, no way....." "It shouldn't take long, I promise. Also, I think it would be prudent for you to visit with one of our on-site Psychologists. Just procedure hon, relax ok." *Kayla glanced at the handle on the door, wondering if she should try and escape looked in the side mirror and realized they were being escorted by a Green Humvee a few yards back from their bumper.*

Kayla stressed to the max and wanted out of the hippy Hearst!

I drifted off and wondered where all the people were taken to.... the news from several hospital employees that had come to visit her friend Lori told us that the medical facilities were overflowing with family members searching for brothers, sisters, daughters, and so on. No one had a clue as to where the citizens captured were taken; Kayla had never heard a word from any of them! She tried another tact. The last place she needed to go was to that hospital.

Kayla pulls her mask down to clearly speak, "Doctor Walsh, I'm not sick. I don't want to go anywhere, but out of this curfew lockdown, I guess I'm a little paranoid hate to admit it, but I've been hiding out, afraid. My home was a large walk-in closet. Uhm, I haven't had the inkling nor bravery even to look out the closed drapes of the office windows, just hunkering down. I know, pretty pathetic I'm afraid of catching the virus and barely have eaten a thing, my mom would say. That's good, Kayla. You needed to lose some weight anyhow!" Kayla laughed, and so did Cindy, who thought that sounded like the controlling bitch, Shanon!

"Can I get something out of your cooler, please, Doctor?" "Yes, call me Cindy dear, and of course, have anything your heart desires." "Thanks.... I'll grab these peanut butter crackers and some Cranberry juice." Cindy's cheeks raised "yes, that's what they're here for; enjoy, Kayla; please take whatever you want." She yanked the Hearst again to the side of the road. Excuse me for a moment; I'll be right back. There are some sandwiches also premade; please eat. I'll have you to your mothers soon enough!"

Kayla subtly watches the Humvee park a few yards back by the same curb, the dark-tinted windows blocking her view of the occupants. Cindy strode around to the passenger side. Kayla watched, not obviously staring at the door latch, taking the handle in her right hand and pulling it up. It was not restricted, free, and not locked. She wondered if this was a one-way trip. Weird vibes, whom was she conferring within the Humvee twisted her head to the left, shifting her butt around. It would take perhaps three seconds to get out the door, but that was only the first step... scanning the road and bright sunshine blasting off the asphalt, she'd be a running casualty easily shot down; escaping would be hopeless. Kayla had to use her brains... be savvy, for it was apparent she was in danger. The question was how, um, to escape this toxic situation. One thing was for certain she wanted nothing to do with going to that hospital.

Cindy stands beside the door and doesn't try to get in the Humvee. The passenger side window drops. "Have you been listening to our conversation Major?" "Yes, I'm listening. Do you believe her, Doctor? We need to get the pressure off of us. It's amazing what one person with connections can do. Her mother is a pain in the ass, no?..." "I'm not sure, Major. She seems genuine. I'm not prepared to make the call if we take her to the hospital, which might be prudent but could cause more strife from Mommy dearest!" "Do you have one of the tester lollypops for Covid?..." "Yes, in my briefcase...." "Test her and if she's clean, take her to the Hwy 273 barrier and drop her off. Let's get rid of her...." "Okay, Major, it'll be done!" She was glad that she wouldn't have to detour from taking the girl to her mom. If she had said she'd eye-witnessed a tragic scenario, Kayla might not have made it to her mom. Then Cindy frowned and bowed her head. Nope, if Kayla had seen anything toxic, ugh, that she could detail... about what was happening here in Redding, the girl wouldn't be breathing long.

Kayla watches the doctor and her head and takes a sip of the Cranberry juice, wondering what to do next? Cindy returns to the Hearst and opens the driver's passenger side door. "Hey, is everything all right?" Spies her opening a briefcase "yeah, just getting one of the latest testers out. All you have to do is put it in your mouth and suck on it for about seven seconds. If the lollypop turns Red, then we're off to the hospital. If it remains Yellow, then off to meet your mother!" Kayla sighs inwardly. Oh yes, coolly says, "well, heck, I can't wait, uhm, give me that lollypop!" Moments later, the lollypop showed the color Yellow. Cindy flipped a U-turn; the Humvee fell off their tail, and Cindy pushed in a music CD old school. Since there were no radio signals in the area, 'the best hits of the 60s and 70s played,' and the atmosphere in the Hearst no longer felt terminal. Not so strangely, the first song that played was 'American Pie' by 'Don McLean.'

<u>FBI Agent Rico Captor had already informed Kayla's mother of Kayla being located.</u>

FBI Agent Rico Captor just pressed end on his cell phone… relief was exhibited. He'd known Kayla since she was born and loved the little girl. He checked that Big Girl now. Like Volleyball big. His next call was to Shanna "Rico, what is it? What's happening? I…" "Calm down, woman, calm your ass down. No hello or hi, just what is it?" Pauses a vacant line…. his phone rings back. "I lost you, Rico. What's up? I'm sitting in my minivan with the whole family back at the restrictive barricades….." Rico declares, "Seconds ago, General Hullinger called me and told me that… all's well. Kayla was located sound and safe at her Paralegal office, no wear for worse….." "Oh, thank you, umh, thank goodness you mean no worse for wear. I knew I could count on you, Rico." He could hear Jason, her husband, in the background whooping it up and then heard her two other children screaming with delight, shrilling pitched joy. "Yep, all is good, or was it thought he?"

"OMGod, I appreciate all you do for me, Rico…." "Hey, that's always a two-way street. Thank you for being there for me as well think I'll call Wendi and take her on a Harley ride down the beach!" "Hey, say hi to Ms. Feral for me…. when are you going to pop the question? Ms. Captor sounds better, right?" matching laughter. Rico said, by the way, Wendi and I will be going to the San Francisco Zoo to visit her favorite Gorilla exhibit and will be making a trip up there to Shasta later this week. Seeya, hey, say hi to your family…." "You just did, uhm, you're on speaker! Be safe, Luv ya bye" click!

—64—

<u>Major Bryan tries to assert himself.</u>

Finally, the worm had turned, and his stress was reduced…. With a triple expresso in his left hand, Colonel Ruiz and General Hollinger off his back, he checked his look in the floor-to-ceiling mirrors, stepping into his shower, the hot warmth soothing his bare skin. Glad that LT Sloan and Private Freeze came through, and don't forget Doctor Walsh. He mused that she's been invaluable. The heat had been alleviated. Kayla Green delivered to the pesky Pit-bull Doctor Shanon Roble less than an hour ago. Yep, whew!

Major Bryan had free sailing from here on out, toweling off, realizing the Shasta mission had been flawless. His team joined the elite <u>'cream of the crop'</u> status. He'd chosen the perfect crew ak squad, which performed with utmost proficiency and competence, with not a single complaint. Even the useless Rodent Ruiz had evolved into less of a scoundrel or scourge. He's been completely taken out of his hair, and what hair! Not a follicle out of place.... thick as a Porcupine!

Bryan took the time to gloat, checking out his timeframes and bullet points on his interactive spreadsheets and maps of the inoculated areas, grinning at his schedule all _major positives.... Major his fine ass._ Major Bryan was 21 hours ahead of the original timetable. Even though the W/O had extended the date for the conclusion and the military occupation departing Shasta from the 23rd to now the 27th of July.... Bryan was in charge of the winning team and would separate himself from Ruiz soon enough!

He and Ruiz had been invited to the third World Order convention, with all the world's leaders attending this mandatory conference. It would be held this time, not in Geneva but in his hometown of San Diego, actually, on Catalina Island. Ruiz, he thought, was about ready to pass the gauntlet to him. He'd be the main presenter, ah speaker at the conference detailing their success story with intellectual articulation verbalizing how his intricate plan.... umh, he cracked a smile glancing at himself grinning touching his dimples Me, handsome debonair ahh I would have a standing ovation once finished detailing how easily Shasta County had been reduced to just 25% of its population.... Smiling at how his team of experts had organized the branding of the leftover chosen populace, the colored Pyramid tattoos were ingenious; he would be King, uh, no Emperor, lol.

Bryan flexed his glutes and muscled thighs in a mirror mulling over the truth. If he didn't prefer a man's touch, he'd be the envy of every adult woman's dream squeeze. He knew this and used it to his advantage. No didn't bounce around like a Fairy, not a flagrant gay person, nope, nor a closet dweller. He was omnipresent and omnipotent!

Dressed again, he would shower three times a day if he could.... it always was refreshing to be cleansed... yep, another delicious change out of his clothes, um, fresh again. Bryan and his upper echelon of officers had taken and overanalyzed with open minds everyone's opinion counted all hypotheses and assumptions in theory applied and calculated then refined each priority. Their conclusion or call it an educated estimation they could take California from a population of around 40 million. Well, wait, that was an old census back in 2023. Since the latest Covid variants, the population was now about 36 million. Bryan could adjust the population to where the W/O demanded…. leave nine million people alive in the state, ugh, take his crew about, ah, maybe three months. Too bad he couldn't just poison the water sources, but no, the process was going to be replicated like here in Shasta, a selection committee of who would survive the Government's purge. He laughed out loud.

The Board of Directors of the W/O would be bowing, kissing his Brown suede shoes, and they would vote him the overall President when they saw his algorithms that made up his plan uh concept had been in motion for 45 months part of his innovative brand-new agenda was parked on the outskirts of this county! He would be more affluent and have more notoriety than any human on earth, counting one of his idles, Donald Trump or even Elon Musk! Bryan was still pissed off about how Trump got screwed in the last Presidential election… illegal collusion galore! But hey, which politician made it as far as he did and wasn't a Crook or someone who didn't take advantage of all the loopholes provided by the paper pushers?

Bryan, again for the hundredth time like an addict, pulled up the three-dimensional design that the structural, technical engineers had experimented on trial-and-error countless times. Finally, his dreams and ambitions combined with fortitude had brought fruition to his entrepreneurial concept, from modest thoughts of simple scribbled sheets of designed plans that were somehow molded into a unique innovation. Grinning so wide, afraid he'd tear his cheeks, Yes me… Major Bryan's signature is all over it… forget about it! All the non-believers and skeptical, cynical folks who laughed him out of their offices he'd proven them all wrong had successfully taken what he'd learned by studying history and brought a modified new mindset to the forefront. Better than the archaic concentration camps, gas chambers, passe antiquated oh yeah, there must be better descriptive words than brilliant his portrait and name would go down in infamy, statues erected, movies of his life autobiographies he'd be treasured... history was his slave!

Gloatingly gazing at the packet of 8 X 11 color aerial pictures of his dream machines parked side by side front to back on I-5 North and South, nose to rear bumpers on Hwy 44 West and East the same could be said for Hwy 299, his solution to the dilemma the world now faces were parked with generators humming. His invention was precisely what the W/O had needed. He'd read long ago in an Entrepreneur Magazine 'think out of the box' pun intended. Bryan smirked... fill a need, and the consumers would be knocking your door down.

Wait until ole Ruiz gets ahold of his ingenious idea movies would flow like Niagara Falls. Forget the billionaire's.... paltry sums. The richest Kings would grovel over him. Hell, he could buy an island and countries. Once they bought into his concept, all power players would want to hobnob with him. Bryan would be Royalty; everyone would want a piece of the action! Best yet, this wasn't one of those grandiose pompous grandiloquence schemes or ideas ala pipe dreams nope.... lol he liked those words.

Hail to the Chief played his cell phone ringer on loud "Major Bryan, this is Sergeant Barton Sir, here we have just confirmed Bethel Church has broken the no communications ban. We could easily surround the Church, Sir, and make our way inside and search every square foot of the buildings. Many of the congregation have been caught breaking mandated curfews. Our switchboards have had hundreds of calls complaining that we were hypocritically allowing Bethel to break the rules. Many are asking why the double standards; Sir, we must quell the rebellion. <u>Nip it in the bud you</u>…." "Barton, stop enough. I wanna try the diplomatic avenue at the onset were to close Sarg don't want to rock the boat." He lets the line go silent, sipping his fruit smoothie.

Then he laughs "do you know what Ruiz and I plan for the 27th not too long from now, hmm?" "no, Sir…." "Well, neither do any of the Goodie 2 Shoes that reside at the White House and Congress… Senate and House of Representatives no Barton, only the chosen such as yourself are privy as to what actually is occurring here… and worldwide soon enough what we're accomplishing here will be replicated. Remember, I chose you and the rest of my squad personally. Just follow orders…." "Sir, I was told that we have to get those Pyramid tattoos. Everyone is calling them the Blue Dots… I, for one, don't like tattoos. It's like being branded my family, and I don't believe in vaccinations, Sir and…." "Barton, don't buck the system. Your either part of us or you're not… contact that Father Rite; we'll see him this evening. Tell him it's a mandatory meeting!" "Uh, yes, Sir, and thank you for believing in me, Major. I will not let you or my family down, Sir!" "See that you don't!" click.

The intercom squeaks. It's his boy toy who's invaluable in more ways than Bryan would want to concede. "Are you busy?" then he snickers. "Uh, that's right, Sir, sill me your always busy unh, can I cum in and help you relieve any of your pent-up frustrations, Sir? I will be quick and succulent as always. I promise that Sir, um, it won't take you long,… um-yum for you to succumb, Major Sir…" a smart "ah relent yah no unh capitulation" lol

Bryan grins, saying to himself, 'see, I love that dude' "sorry, can't cum right now. Check the day's calendar. Ruiz is already on his way…." "I did, Sir, that's why I said quick. He's still 15 minutes out!" "all right, you've convinced me… lock up the office entrance and cum and get some…." "It already is… Bry-baby." "Don't call me Bry during work." "Stop it, babe. I will be in Bry. Let me try out my new comfy knee pads!"

Major Bryan sat back, relaxing, putting silence in mode on all his communications primed and pumped up uhhh, stress relief drained soon… "Wow, Bry, hey look at you, babe, you're raring to go, unuh yum ready and willing my handsome, manly hunk"… deep kisses with downward momentum!

Colonel Ruiz meets with Major Bryan.

Precisely 13 minutes later, Colonel Ruiz stomps into Bryan's office, "what the hell is that smell in here? Get your freakin Queen to get me some coffee, don't play fricken games with me, Major. I have contacts in high places. All through our Government and the ditat hierarchies, word is you are undermining me here, stabbing me in my back, trying to make, um, build a name for yourself at my expense. I will not stand for that. You're disrespecting me. That's a dangerous thing to do, Bryan!"

Bryan swivels his rolling chair and stands up from behind his glorious desk… "So you don't enjoy the smell of my integrity-based persona… and besides, I never shirk my duties or didn't carry out your orders, Sir. I'm sorry that you're not a fan of my Sage and Lavender incense. I haven't a clue as to what you are insinuating, Sir." Bryan pushes the intercom, "I need a fresh pot of coffee and condiments…." "Yes, Sir, right away!" Bryan mused, usually I'd be full-on testy and argumentative…. stress relief brought welcome composure with confidence. He stated, "Colonel Sir, you would be hard-pressed to find another person under your command as loyal as I am to you. Never would I betray you, never have. I'm not a slanderous backstabbing snake in the grass person like many of your people. I'm confused by your allegations… what's the problem, Colonel?"

Ruiz was busy looking at his Tablet, reading something, it seemed. "Please, Colonel, do me the justice to allow me to be judged fairly and face my tormentor's… uhm, enemies, the scandalous scumbags that you listen to that talk behind my back and yours too! <u>Where's the beef?</u> The proof I want my accusers to look at me in my eyes, sir. Remember if they're talking about me, whatcha think they do behind your back?" Bryan… cackles.

On cue, timing being everything, a knock on the door, and a tray pushed in. Private Jimmy Neal, his personal secretary, strolls in. Ruiz slides out of the high-backed chair staring at the display of pastries on the cart. Jimmy said, "Major, here is a copy of your last memo…." Jimmy winks at Bryan, not seen by Ruiz. Jimmy then said, "I just received confirmation that it was securely received by all parties…." Bryan gawks at him inquiringly, not giving away his utter bewilderment "ugh, well, Private, go ahead and read it aloud…." "All right, quote verbatim. I'll start at the first paragraph." Ruiz was busy making his coffee and loading a paper plate with goodies. "I'm extremely proud of what our combined forces… uhm, our teams have accomplished thus far. Colonel Ruiz has been a breath of fresh air, a supreme leader, and a troubleshooter. His ability to adlib is second to none. Always has contingency plans and alternative reactions to any negative happenings…." "Let me see that," yells Ruiz.

He grasps the 8 X 11 paper scanning it, nearly blanking after a long minute; he reads the last sentences 'General Hullinger, besides all those updates, the true measure of success is we're well ahead of schedule here and will shine at the next W/O Convention at Catalina Island… thanks and contact Colonel Ruiz if you have any further questions.' Ruiz is stunned and bewildered for the first time in a while. He seemed to be backpedaling. Bryan stares at Neal and then pounces while the momentum is in vogue. "Yep, I'm undermining you disloyal all of that." Then he sits down, realizing he never saluted the Colonel when he came into the office wanting to be on even ground, saying... "Does that sound like a traitor, a man betraying you, Sir? Well, does it?"

Ruiz's mind in turmoil puckers his lips, no mask on perplexed stare; he'd come here to his underling's office angry and raging, ready to rip the queer apart with his bare hands had heard from a supposedly reliable source that Bryan was complicit and working with accomplices behind his back. Some pictures and paperwork were shuffled to his superiors that showed up on the desks across Washington D.C. Ruiz had a heated one-way conversation with the US Attorney General about the IMP acid pits and Captain Rory hunting inmates above Iron Mountain in a so-called game. He defended himself as best as he could. Mysteriously the missive sent to the White House distanced Major Bryan from that operation, explaining that it wasn't Major Bryan's sector. In his eyes, it only made sense that Bryan was the culprit. Why divulge this information unless it was advantageous or for ulterior motives? Thus it was Bryan! Ruiz was highly agitated that this information was leaked to Wash. DC, and of course, he was being held responsible because he was the man in charge of the entire Shasta operation.

Puzzled and not mentioning the real reason for his impromptu meeting, he sat here chewing an Apple Fritter... leaned down, picked up the communiqué peers at Bryan, and rereads, stopped fidgets about "I'll check my sources Major and get back to you in my way of thinking it would be perspicuous to me that you'd want more of the credit for this operation... It's way ahead of schedule, far exceeding anyone's projections. Honestly, I couldn't have done it without you, Major. You've been a proficient protagonist and a steadfast unrelenting force to be reckoned with and an asset. Although I definitely disagree with your lifestyle choices but were appearing Golden to the W/O and our political regime, and that's what it's all about!

There was a pause, then "Brynn, who do you think could be sending reports out to DC about one of our covert tasks? The Iron Mountain Project has imploded… someone sent pictures and top-secret internal reports about our Captain Rory; this is on you, Major. In fact, I was kept in the dark for days. We have to locate the source of the snitch, uuhhh, Rat. I want him or her in the Brig for insubordination. This reflects our joint operation diminishing my leadership. Who else could be responsible? Let's be proactive, all right?" Brynn nodded. "Colonel, I respectively disagree your Lieutenant Snngs is in charge of the IMP elimination sector, and Captain Rory is under his command; thus, he's directly associated with you, Sir." Before Ruiz's rebuttal, "yes, Sir, I'm on it! I'll see what I can ascertain for us. Is there a chance that your lead LT Snngs could have accidentally leaked some of what Rory had said?" Ruiz scowled with a lingering grimace… "not a chance he is loyal, and besides, Captain Rory hasn't been able to communicate he is lost in a fugue, insane! I truly don't have all the information about what went on up on that mountain still kind of in the dark, but I will get to the bottom of it once I control the other issues out on Shasta Lake. Snngs has described what these demented Officers were up to. They'd set up a game for hunting some of the terminal prisoners. Surely it's his command, and I will hold him responsible why the hell would he leak anything to anyone? That's absurd, Major."

They sip some coffee "let's switch gears, Major. I'm actually thinking of taking the microphone at the W/O big-wig ordeal down in Catalina Island and then passing it to you to conclude the details, rejoicing over our concerted success in this mission. I have to confess I'm a bit concerned about this plan that you've concocted to start on the 25th; shit, it could implode. It has catastrophic calamities written all over it; surely we haven't weighed the repercussions. If the world's populace or just the U.S. citizens get a whiff of what is planned, there would be an uprising unlike any seen ever before! There would be a major exodus of regular citizens joining militias, uh, people that are law-abiding citizens that listen to us and follow the rules of our laws. They'd be joining insurgent groups and mercenary encampments. I'm telling you they would come out of the woodwork. <u>Every Tom, Dick, and Harry</u> will be up in firearms. You and I would become the world's most hated, reviled men hunted and skinned alive, and that is if we're lucky!"

"Jesus, that's a lot to chew on, Sir," Bryan smirked, leaving a lingering smirk upon his smiling face. "Very true, Sir. All you expounded upon could come to fruition, although there is a flip side <u>other side of the coin.</u> We will be the two individuals who will be exalted and worshipped as innovative Savants, the <u>'Cat's Meow'</u> honored by the only people who matter to us, the power brokers of the globe! It's like you, Colonel, instantly becoming a 7 Star General everyone will be in Awe of us, Sir." They drank some more coffee in silence, Ruiz mulling over the discussed topic, Bryan contemplating, gosh, how amazing was Private Neal? So shrewd I owe him big… the fake news memo was beyond wise what a move. The guy has so many redeemable attributes… he is a keeper as he readjusts his flaccid package.

Out of the hush, "we need to discuss the Shasta Lake issues. I have Private Noels researching Rocky Blake and Brock Dame. I don't believe Shon Peterson is involved, but we've scrutinized all landholding associations in Shasta. I also want to borrow your Lieutenant Sloan to investigate these three ex-military men. Frankly could order her to do so, but Major, I respect the fact that LT Sloan has been part of your team for years. Sure, she'd be obedient and adhere to the chain of command, but the order coming from you might have better results; IMO, what do you think?"

Before Bryan could reply, he continued, "furthermore, I want you to task her to research and investigate all there is to know about Josh Strong and Heather Otter, the escapees who we believe are guilty of several murders and with the assault and near death of Captain Rory, we've lost them somehow.

They have escaped by the lake. Of course, much of what LT Sloan will recover will be redundant, for Private Noels has already given me a partial report. We have family addresses and some surface material like schools, arrest records, and their associates, but the more heads and minds engaged, the better. I'd also like you to add the black woman Latoya White Gore to Sloan's plate. I've come to respect her diligent analysis and would appreciate your assistance in these matters!"

"Colonel, I will do as you request, but if you would allow me or indulge me, Sir. In my opinion, using your verbiage, it's… true that two heads are better than one. In fact, the more analysis, the better to envision a more detailed picture. A spontaneous thought I'd like for you to give serious consideration to is to do absolutely nothing cease and desist, Sir!" "WTHell Major, are you fkn sniffing glue or downing Bath Salts ugh, Meth, our Officers have been attacked, murdered bombs detonating all over the Shasta Lake area. Our soldiers have been beaten and robbed. We've lost seven boats in total. Two Deputies were shot and killed in just one incident. Do you want the total of the crimes against us? Ahhhh, it would make for a mini novella. Just forget it. Why don't you tell that to their mothers and fathers… wives, husbands, and their families? There's no way I'm just going to turn my tail and run or hide these facts."

Ruiz wasn't finished glaring at Bryan… "It's an <u>eye for an Eye.</u> I will not bring any of the felons to court. Nope, their justice will be doled out by me, <u>lock, stock, and barrel</u> full of lead after a bloody bout of torture, vengeance, and retribution with retaliation for their crimes against America, a payback for you and me! We're the USA Military, the most powerful entity on this planet, not going to let a bunch of old former has-beens make fools of us, Period, or some juvenile delinquents. You get that, Bryan!"

Sighs filled the room silently. Jimmy listened via intercom and shook his head. Bryan thinks, first of all, Heather and Josh aren't juveniles... Ruiz must be referring to the young people who are revolting against... "What's up with you, uh, the <u>Cat got your tongue,</u> Bryan?" "No, Sir, just mulling over what you've said certainly, if you don't mind me saying you misunderstood my discourse, um, dissertation. I meant no disrespect for the loss of lives or physical pains and suffering nor mental transgressions uh injuries caused by our mutual enemies, I fully am empathetic and commiserate with your position, and without a doubt, you have to make examples of these lawbreakers, perhaps like in Roman days hang there bloody Skulls from tree limbs you must respond. Yes, Sir... unemotionally and strike unhesitatingly, you are our leader... and I would expect nothing less than your undying resolve and proactiveness to prosecute and bring the offenders to their knees. All guilty parties, Sir, should pay!"

Ruiz sat there utterly open-mouthed, blankly catatonically, nearly stupefied, wobbling his huge noggin. "Wtf did you just try and say, Bryan? Plain English, no mumbo-jumbo articulations or whatever you call it, no false kissing ass you don't like me, I don't like you not two fkn Peas in a pod okay were opposites that don't attract." He mumbles aloud 'thank God or whatever' "we work extremely well together cohesively I'm the motor fuel uh gas you're the wheels. Tell me what your thoughts are?"

Private Jimmy Neal snorted, morphing nearly into a howl covering his mouth, his speaker phone on mute on his desk in the outer office. 'What a pompous asshole the Colonel was saying he was the motor and my BF the wheels really, what a backward analogy he was the true chump, ah moron.' He turns down the volume and hears, "Colonel, sorry that you felt I was not straightforward enough; let me boldly say what I'm thinking I___"
"Bryan, why is it that you can't stop running at the mouth? No bullshit, short and concise. I don't get it. It's like you constantly try to triple-speak me acting as if you are this sophisticated academic professor and I'm a lowly student taking notes subjected to your

verbal lashing. I'm no fool." He pulls a mini recorder out of his vest, "all of which we've discussed is recorded."

The Major showed zero concerns and barely acknowledged the device coolly said, "when you go back and listen to our banter, you may conclude that I have been judiciously attempting to do as you have asked… to give my opinion verbally now. Can I continue, Sir?" His cheeks puff out, an exhale… inhale Amber in color "go ahead, Bryza." "Thank you, Sir, to complete my thought process before the interruption." Bryza points to a large calendar on the wall behind him and asserts… "It's July 18th, soon we're scheduled to turn Shasta County back on… allowing the internet, phone services, and social media to be once again active. I believe the chatter and noise from Shasta will explode. I think we should put that off, Sir. As you are aware of… our master plan for annihilation begins the same day, the 25th, and continues until we exit the county on the 27th. Isn't that correct, Sir?" "I'm listening; go ahead…" "Well, I know we're planning to leave a skeleton platoon of enforcers to monitor the aftermath. All of our assailants, uhm, the rebellious few along with Heather and Josh, Rocky Blake, Brock Dame, and Latoya, will they not be dead as doornails, sir, by the 27th? I'm only stating the inevitable truths that you know to be true, so why waste man hours?"

"Colonel, here, look at the map," the Major stood with a pointer stick. "77 soldiers have lost their lives since our occupation. Seven Officers have been killed, with 171 injuries sustained. Pardon me for my bluntness, but you've taken the lake catastrophes personally because the perpetrators are ex-military and former FBI Agents who have chastised you, egging you on, playing on your ego, and…." "That is enough; your point needs no further elaboration, but in the same vein, the uprisings have, for the most part, been quelled… still I will not rest till we arrest the perpetrators at the lake and the guilty parties who have assaulted our troops."

Ruiz stands "hold that thought; I need to use the restroom. Yes, we have uprisings in almost every sector in Redding, from Whiskeytown to the Trinity County line to Palo Cedro. They have been reduced to the smallest of percentages, one of the reasons I made this trip was to cover several topics. I heard you have a meeting at the Bethel Church with Father Rite. Is he not cooperating, and could some of the rumors be true that he is leading the resistance? We both know we have to reign in the Bethelites!" Ruiz put his coffee cup down and exited the room.

While Ruiz was out of the room, Bryan studied the latest information on the ongoing investigation of the Bethel Church. There was a horde of data, so he scanned over as much as he could before Ruiz reentered the room. "Colonel, you are correct. I have a meeting with the Preacher. It's arranged for later this evening. I will keep you posted, sir. It's essential, and I believe in keeping Bethel in our cross-hairs. It's hard to comprehend the enormity of the organization. Uh, the institution they are by themselves rebellious, even dating back to the infancy of Covid. I think I read files about March or April of 2020. Bethel disregarded all emergency mandates and wore no masks at a religious revival or something at the Sundial Bridge. They had concerts by the Sacramento River, like Evangelical seances right out in the open in spite of the lockdowns and rules that everyone was to wear masks. I went through the local paper, The Record Searchlight, online. The freakin Bethel Church had pictures of young people dancing and cavorting about praying as they do right out in the open wearing no masks." Bryan inhaled largely, wide-eyed, and resumed, "Bethel Church is proactively doing what they feel is needed for their congregation and Christians worldwide, sir."

Ruiz snarled perturbed and wiped his face, "Yeah, I heard they have a presence in many other countries and a huge following up here in the North State. We must tread lightly... Bryan, we can't have anything leak out about what we're going to accomplish here! There also connected politically and have tens of thousands in their worldwide ministry!" Bryan reaches into his desk, "Here, Colonel is an extra packet of our surveillance of the church and where were at thus far." Ruiz takes the thick packet. "Major, you know they're nothing more than a cult-like Jimmy Jones and the Peoples Temple drinking the Cool-aid. Besides, if everything remains the same, they should all perish, Parish, get that one!" Lol… They collectively laugh.

Bryan thinks what a dumb-ass Ruiz was, but true, by the 27th, any of them that pass his scrutinization will be tattooed. Only about 25 % will be saved if they're worthy and meet the necessary criteria. "For now, I concur with you that we should minimize collateral damage and mitigate exposure, Major… thanks for the tasty coffee and the invigorating banter. Keep me in the loop… see you soon, Major."

The Colonel stood. Major Bryan matched him and then gave a genuine salute "thanks, Sir, we're on the same page and team. We shall overcome all obstacles and persevere. Have a dandy afternoon…." Ruiz pivots… "Dandy wasn't a word I'd use, Major, but I get your gist. Good day!"

Bryan and Jimmy listened to the outer door slamming shut; he shouted, "okay, Jimmy lock the office door and get your butt in here." "Oh, Bry, I enjoy the way you say that, although feeling it would be much more fulfilling!" . Seeing the Major's face, he "I was only kidding.…" "Sit, Jim…" "Yes, Sir." "You heard our every word what's your take?" "I believe Ruiz doesn't have proof that your actively undermining him, although he is certain that you have a hidden agenda to raise your value and diminish his, yet he gave you props, Sir. Was openly honest about his feelings for you and yours for him like no worries."

Jimmy Neal showed an odd expression. Bryan shrugged as if, what? "Ruiz is a psychopath who is coy feigning ignorance or bland stupidity like that character, you know, the dumb acting old Detective movie Columbo who was always pretending he was a bit slow in the thinking department. All you have to do is replay the last statements he made. His verbiage and articulations were dead on with proper terminology. The fellow is no fool, no siree!"

"No, Jimbo, I go along with that. I'd like to know who he's connected with up the food chain. I don't know. I just can't figure out how he landed this mission above me. Someone in a high place within our Government is a cheerleader with Pom-Poms shaking and waving a fan of Ruiz. We need to uncover who it is, dammit. It's not what he knows but whom... there's no doubt there."

-65-

<u>Josh and Heather.</u>

Cool darkness engulfed them uncomfortably.... they tried to snuggle each other Heather Jigsaw puzzled into Josh's chest, his knees bent, locking her into a fetal position. His warm breath on her neck and his arm pulled her back against his upper torso. The musty smell of the cave was oddly reassuring.

Heather listened contently to Josh's regulated release of Carbon Dioxide eyelids flickered open and close she couldn't sleep wired out, waking abruptly in a shaking tizzy, constantly reminding herself she was safe and no longer underwater in the lake. They were inside their sanctuary in the cave by Shasta Lake. Safe and snug inside the cave... it was much cooler than the outside air of this July evening. Rather than replay her past life... like was her standard program when she fought to sleep. A "Ground Hog Night" constantly dredging up memories, ugh, all the negatives she was either responsible for or felt resentment toward. Heather was finished making excuses. It was what it had been, and there was no hiding the truth. Like Joshua Strong had taught her in such a short time,....

Integrity is how she wanted to live the rest of her existence, but because of the circumstances she was engulfed in… umh, she was unsure and sadly insecure. Heather was too weak to revise and power up her new mindset tonight. But yet, on the fringes… she imagined a future, uhm, a fantasy of what could be. Could it be possible for a venue change, uh, a new beginning, no more drugs waking up hungover, not knowing where she was? Could that really happen? From slut chasing the drug guys addicted… Slash to a respectable person… a real-life 'Pretty Woman' movie book, lol. Thinking not skeptical per her norm, she closed her eyes, tugging on Josh's arm… hand placing it across her heart, holding on tight.

Her mind still whirling when she should be full-on exhausted; why not flee into my subconscious dream of what will be, could be? I experienced it 3rd hand in my life of inner hope, an inner voice that predominantly spoke to me and was on my side a positive outlook, oh that was until Meth. Drugs had manifested within selfishly manipulated excuses… a plenty. I did this-that because I was high on drugs or stole this… that because I was withdrawing

thawing suffering Jonesing with spasms of pain disconnected, always chasing the buzz, the euphoric ecstasy, the high that was never as good as the first-time temporary bliss into forever trauma agony and misery.

This equation was leveraged yep by my sick, tainted mind concentrate Heather, 'leave me alone,' she whispered, 'let me go.' Concentrating on breathing, and finally located peace and tranquility, sleep… rest. Her dream side took her on a Fairy Tale ride her horse-drawn carriage galloped like the wind, her Prince Charming by her side Joshua Strong umh was it love, adoration, hero worship, a combination of yes and no he was my friend heck isn't that the best way to start a relationship sleep well, Heather!

Josh blinked awake instantly frozen in place, pinging pulsating bladder, frontal side comfy warm, backside cold, smelling her hair in the cave… a musty dampness felt in his bones they'd stripped off their wet clothes after digging out the tarp and stuff they had buried before escaping into the lake wrapped themselves in jackets and the sweatshirts that Captain Rory had issued them at the start of his Shasta Games hunting party.

Slowly not wanting to disturb Heather, he pulled the tarp back and couldn't see a thing, not even the walls of the cave. She tossed and turned with a moan. Josh crawls backward in the direction of the exit, and the fresh air of a moonless night that was breaking up not long till the nuclear reactor in our sky-lit back up. He shook himself off and crept over to a boulder looking out on the surface of the dark water of the lake. Surprised by no green or white or Red lights of watercraft, he could spot just one flashing drone which was flying low a far distance from where he kneeled.

He rolled his shoulders…. oddly he thought, why would they call off the man-woman hunt? They were trapped, and still, he couldn't figure any way back to the civilization he'd left when he was captured. They'd either have to climb back up the mountain or drop back to the beach and water, whatever. He was tired and a bit uneasy being nearly naked… he knew he should wake her up. They should move out, but where? Some ideas flashed within but exhausted mentally and physically, he kneeled and alleviated the spiritual side with a short prayer. He squeezed back beside her… she shivered "oh, your freezing." Pulling him tight seven minutes later, rest found them sleeping soundly.

July days in the North state of California are hot and dry for the most part. This was the time for outdoor fun on the large bodies of water. They saw the light beaming in from the cave entrance, teeth grinding as they slowly untangled their limbs. Josh was the first to dress in the still-damp sweats and venture out. The heat from the sun was already blasting… Josh checked the watch he'd stolen from Captain Rory… crap; it was almost noon. Heather and he had slept like 13 hours unreal. He emptied his bladder again while scanning the sky and water, but nothing nada. It appeared that the search for them was over way weird, or possibly the military thought they'd escaped the area and were far gone. Either way, it was time to move out.

Bending his head down said into the cave's opening, "hey, Heather, it's 15 times warmer out here. Come on out here." Josh had glassed the hills, mountains, and the surrounding area. All was safe, it seemed. She said, "ok, then you can help me…. come here." Adjusting his eyes, he stepped in with a grin "aah, brunch, wow, thanks, Heather, I'm starving." The cooler had remained somewhat cool inside. "Josh, we will have sandwiches with some soggy lettuce heck, we even have some potato chips," he winced as his head bounced off a jutted-out rock near the cave's entrance. "Ouch," she laughed, "this cave is better for short people!" he smirked, "you mean shorter Bears!"

After replenishing their empty stomachs with nutritiousness and packing up, she leaned over and kissed him plumb on his lips. He shyly pulled back and then went in for another inviting peck. "I know what could start us out with smiles…." "No, there's time for that later. We're running late, girl" he embraced her and once again went over the plan.

After some much-needed sustenance, they'd packed up…. and left the cave. He points to the Southeast. We will backtrack towards the Shasta Dam, staying in the forest overlooking the water. Our goal is to get to the other side of the Dam that's where the ATV offroad area is. I used to mountain bike when I was a kid, and then later raced motorcycles there. It's a paradise for dirt bikes and quads. Then we will cross the Sacramento River and connect with the famous River Trails that will lead us past the Sundial Bridge. Friends of mine work there in a bakery owned by my Church, Bethel.

Heather's expression quirked up, looking at his face "your one of these Bethelites, Josh. Whoa, what? a freakin Cult member, I would never take you for a crazed…." "Shush, yes, and proud of it; in reality, without the Church, I may not be standing here next to you, Heather. I got a full-ride scholarship to the University of Florida. I was going to compete for the starting quarterback position for the Florida Gators." He stopped pulling her over a stump and some brush. They packed just the bare essentials for a lighter load, hiking and hiding in the tree line with the goal of trying to stay close to the mountain ridge.

Heather saw that this was a sensitive subject, so she subtly changed her tact "ok, go ahead, you were trying out for quarterback for the Florida Gators...." "Umh, I started football practice, not feeling like myself?..." "How so? What do you mean...?" "It's hard to explain, like something unknown was attacking my energy levels. I felt way tired and sapped of my motivation, ughhhh, like depressed and downed out all the time. I was feeling no pain nor any symptoms heck. I was a stud who worked out five days a week along with running obstacle courses. I pulled a groin at practice and went through a typical physical the doctor didn't catch it, but while I was dressing, I felt this small bump in my scrotum sack that I'd never noticed or felt before stopped and showed the doctor, who frowned and referred me out immediately to specialists. Anyways I was diagnosed with testicular cancer... my life stopped... vaporized that very afternoon. Believe you me, I was devastated and fearful, with so many emotional waves of despair that I couldn't even think straight. I was a plumb mess." She clutched him, leading him to a boulder to sit next to her.

"I went straight into Chemotherapy, refusing surgery, becoming less than a man castrated. A Eunuch.... that wasn't going to happen, I'd decided man Heather, I was filled with anger and was full-on hostile, always asking, 'why me?' I went from the Macho-muscled Alpha Male hero on campus stud to a wimp in no time. I don't want to talk about it anymore. Suddenly my virility was in question. Sports boyhood dreams, career aspirations, life's fantasies out the window, girl's marriage… babies, life went topsy-turvy uh upside down. I did have the opportunity to save some sperm in one of the banks. Still, why would I want to take a chance of passing on this curse?" He dragged her up "come on, we have to go…." "No, finish; you never mentioned how Bethel came into the picture?" "Uhm, all right, a quick synopsis I lived within the doldrums, left the University of Florida tail between my legs back to Redding, and a goofy friend kept prodding me to come to Church with him, mind you. It was hard for me even to hold my head up. I became a hermit."

He stalled… she shoved him, pushing his shoulder gently "unhhh, okay, I downed a bottle of sleeping pills, yeah, the easy way out. The church guy stumbled on me at my apartment, drowsy adding one thing into the other with my propensity of constantly whining, wanting my life to end. Ahh, my mantra of suicide… for cancer to kill me fast ughhhh anyways. Bethel circumvented the situation by surrounding me with their followers…. Bethel Church maybe castigated by non-believers but I'm living proof of the congregation performing miracles, without the church I'd be dead Heather… come on, before I get emotional, let's go!" She reached out and hugged him swiftly tightly, didn't say what she was thinking 'what a precious man!'

Josh yanked her hands away, glassy-eyed with restraint in his achy voice. "Please, enough of this; come on, now we have to…." They walked, making their own trail… trailblazers. Heather was lost in thought, following in his footprints… awhile passed by, then he spun around, pointing look! A sign was posted. Yes, they'd discovered a motorcycle Black Diamond trail or part of a track. Heather, still elsewhere in her mind, mused back at his painful disclosure, almost wanting to slap herself. Ugh, how embarrassing for him, oh, so wrong wondered if the poor guy could even get it up, would Viagra or something like that work? Ahh, sex. I wanna have him inside of me, feel him feel me OmLord is that even possible? Sick that it mattered, but Heather admitted it did! How shallow she thought he had intimated previously, his penis still functioned with hormone shots. It's not that important, and Heather kept repeating, uh, telling herself, although an aching fact lingered, yes, it's very important to me! Heather realized that Josh was sidetracked, unh, preoccupied with religious overtones, and with his allegiance to Bethel… Which in her mind, ugh, Bethel was for witches and warlocks, a totally strange brew of people indeed! Heather had known some of the Bethel crowd and was invited once to a home that was fricken decorated to the hilt with sorcerer stuff. The entire contingent of Bethelites was playing a game called 'Dungeons & Dragons….'

66

Colonel Ruiz visits his favorite Bartender, Jeff Wilson.

On Hilltop Blvd at a fine establishment named CR Gibbs, in a booth in the back of the restaurant on the other side of the lounge, Colonel Ruiz sat impatiently waiting on his Officers. The bartender was busy but amazingly proficient. Strange how Jeff didn't waste a step; Ruiz watched him, wishing some of his underlings could be so calm under fire. The guy didn't sweat his middle name should be 'Multi-task.' Jeff always catered to him, was as cool as the other side of the sheet… Ruiz scrunched up his nose, whew, not like that. Jeff was cool as a cucumber, and it seemed that when he was under fire with a dozen drink orders, he relaxed even more. A solid character under pressure. Ruiz had noticed a few plaques on the walls from the Redding Chamber of Commerce 'Jeff Wilson was voted the number one bartender in the city multiple times…

Five cocktail servers stood in a line. Jeff was memorizing food orders. Three blenders were whirling, shaking two stainless steel cups... Martini's. Jeff was tapping the cash register, and the assistant manager was running drinks. There was a line at the door, a hostess was seating the arriving soldiers, and busgirls and boys were cleaning the tables. The food was Chef Special magnificent. Ruiz was pissed off because LT Smngs was once again late but mused that this Jeff bartender was worth the show and decided to lose himself in analyzing how each sequence or task worked like a fine machine at the restaurant, so he counted nine employees on the floor most didn't cover their Yellow Dot Pyramid Tattoos.

Tired of sitting at the table approached the bar where all his troops would acknowledge him with salutes and get out of his way, moving to a bar stool that was occupied temporarily, the soldier got up after Ruiz beckoned him to do so with a wave of his hand. Ruiz told Jeff he'd take another Scotch and be right back.... walked to the open grille, cooks in total, eight all wore the Yellow Dots. One thing brought giddiness, ahh, happiness. Major Bryan was definitely a keeper. Every worker he saw had fresh Pyramid Tattoos, all vaccinated with GPS trackers and with other additional experimental mind-altering drugs.

Ruiz decided to take a short jaunt to the CR Gibbs hotel, which was attached to the bar and restaurant, and curiously checked the clerks... The concierge and the Valet guys, damn all the employees and managers, all had been tattooed. Inner joy resulted in Ruiz smiling and mumbling 'yes.' Back towards the bar after a quick stop at the bathroom, where another employee passed out a warm cloth rag wearing a bright Yellow Dot. Moseyed out back to the bar stool disregarding all the salutes wearing his patented sunglasses eye covers that left his vantage points anonymously registered. Colonel Ruiz looked at his bar stool, where an MP stood guard as he had requested. It was his.... then Ruiz periscoped around and noticed his large table booth was filled with Officers and soldiers. It wasn't his booth anymore. Two brash young soldiers sat with females, and a Private had a gal on his lap. Jeff saw the annoyance on Ruiz's countenance and could be heard from a distance telling them…. 'That table is taken. You need to get up.' Ruiz was five steps away when the loudmouth soldier belligerently scolded Jeff. "Who the fk are you, bartender boy, to tell me that this table is taken? Dude, yup, it's taken and is ours!"

Jeff had shouted again…. at the table's occupants after spying on the Colonel using his innate bartender's skilled peripheral vision. The soldier yelled back again, "I don't give a flying shit whose table this used to be. It's ours now!" The three of them hilariously laughed. The big Red-headed guy took the Colonel's Scotch that had been delivered and downed it. Jeff bellowed, "you shouldn't have done that, soldier, if I were you…." The soldier slammed a shot glass onto the table. "Hey, dude, where's our pitcher of beer?"

Jeff pivoted and leaned over towards Ruiz. "I'll get you another one, sir, oh I'm sure you can handle these thugs," and grinned then ducked back under the bar top in control, knowing the other soldiers that had saluted Ruiz before the rowdy ones showed up were waiting for the Colonel's well-known reputation uh temper to flare up. The others didn't care, or like the brass Officers and soldiers who'd stolen Ruiz's table or else they'd warned them… lol, all waited for the show that no doubt was going to play out!

Everyone once again saluted and gave respect to the Colonel. The three at his table worked extremely hard at standing at attention to salute him…. two follower-type soldiers moved out quickly the disrespectful three were wedged between the table and rounded booth seat. Ruiz hovered, lowered his hands up and down, palms up like fanning a fire. "At ease," he glared. "This is my booth. Where's my Scotch at? I heard you don't give a flying shit…. huh, whose table this was….." Instantly, five MPs stood to his left. "Lock these fools in the Brig now!" "Colonel Sir, please, we didn't know," cried out the female Private. "Sir, we're sorry we didn't mean any disrespect…." Lieutenant Snugs walks up, standing abreast of

Ruiz. "Well... well, if it's not Seth, Tami, and Rick. Wt'hell is wrong with you three? You've been 86ed from two bars in just under two weeks, Colonel. I have a better idea. Instead of putting them in the Brig, I could use them up at the crater, unh, you know Iron Mountain, we're short on personnel up there, Sir!" Smirking fully with a wink.

All of a sudden, Tami screamed, "no way, not the IMP, that's the pits, the worst job ever. I'd rather go to the Brig!" Seth drunkenly nodded... all of a sudden, hush found the group. Rick, the Scotch thief, pleaded... "Please, Colonel, I'll buy you a bottle of Makers Mark....." Seth hollers, "we'll wax and shine your Hummer, Sir, and Tami will Armor All and spiff up the interior, Sir. Don't send us to the acid uh lava pits!" A low rumble started throughout the bar like a cheer. Ruiz could have sworn it all started with Jeff Wilson, the bartender.... alcohol-enhanced chant IMP... IMP, IMP it got louder, drowning out the jukebox and surround sound, then louder Snuggs Crocodile smiled, teeth bared, saw Ruiz's lopsided swirl brows furrowed, raised his arms, bringing them back down several times to lower the chants, shouts loudly. "All right, ugh, okay!"

Ruiz turns to the MPs "arrest them like catch and release..." he snickered. "Off to the IMP," he ordered the Military Police with a wave of his hand, then added... "They're restricted not to be allowed to leave Iron Mountain till we move out of here on the 27th. At that time, I'll decide if there will be any other punishment for the obstinate threesome. Oh, and yes, I like Richey's idea my Hummer can use a shit and shine....." Jeff rang the bell behind the bar, and soldiers fell about the place all over themselves, laughs and cackling, and the chant boisterously began again IMP... IMP! Until the three of them were cuffed and escorted out of the lounge.

Ruiz says, "sit-down Snuggs, let's chat...." "Yes, Sir, what's on your mind?..." "I've been giving it a lot of thought. You realize we've got less than five days left here. With that being said, I'd like to bring the criminals to justice, the rebel factions that have attacked and killed some of our regiment!" "Sir, it's of my opinion that it isn't an organized rebel group, more random retaliation as you and the Major are well aware of… there have been literal tens of thousands of frantic calls by Shasta Citizens in search of loved ones. They've witnessed us 'Darting' family members with our RFDs, and they demand to know where we've taken their loved ones. If we placed ourselves, Sir, into their shoes, seeing our kinfolks taken and never seen Sir again…" he paused as Jeff approached.

"Excuse me, gentlemen, Lieutenant, what are you having this fine afternoon?" "A Long Island Iced Tea sounds refreshing, please." Jeff puts down Ruiz's Scotch… "Here you go, Colonel, this one's on the house!" "Thanks, Jeff…" "You are most welcome, sir. One question, if I may, I've heard over the days about the IMP, how the soldiers don't want anything to do with that posting!" he chuckles. "Kinda like in history class during World War 2, none of the Nazis wanted to be sent to the Russian Front!" Snuggs waves his arms and hands up frivolously. "The IMP is the Iron Mountain Project. I'm sure you are aware that it's one of the worst polluted lands on the continent or planet for that matter. We're trying to accomplish a feat. Uh, my goal is to leave this beautiful Shasta area better off than when we were forced to cordon off the area. Call it a clean-up exercise. The soldiers are in charge of cleaning the area up, Jeff. They have to wear space suits." Colonel Ruiz throws in his 10 cents "uhhh, there's no restaurants, entertainment nor bars, or drinking establishments up on the mountain… it's not allowed once you're assigned there; it's all work, no play!"

Jeff nods, "thanks for the explanation doesn't sound like a place I'd like to go either. I'll be right back with your drink and then take your food orders. The food specials are on that Blackboard over there," pointing. He walks away stifling pent-up hatred towards the Officers and the entire lounge full of soldiers because his lifelong love, Linda, his wife, had been missing for over a week. A friend of theirs had witnessed Linda get shot by one of those RFD Machine guns, then bagged up and loaded into the back of a covered truck with the acronym IMP on its sides!

Jeff had attempted to visit the Iron Mountain encampment but couldn't get close… to many military personnel, so he took up his concerns with his beloved friends. Jeff belonged to a group called the Redding DogPound, a Harley motorcycle group. Well, not only Hogs, ugh, but any type of motorcycle was welcomed. It was a fun group of diverse people… not one of those biker gangs. Made up of mostly middle-aged successful citizens who also loved to ride the open country roads in the County and elsewhere as a whole, they alone were responsible for seven kills of Ruiz's soldiers. It was unavoidable… they were riding on Drycreek Road in the country, minding their own business, and were ambushed by troops shooting darts at them, hitting five of them who subsequently crashed their bikes. The group of 17 riders stopped sliding all over the graveled soft shoulders to help their compadres who were shot. Jeff heard a soldier shouting, who he later found out was Private Remy… "Let's put these dart guns away and bring out the AK-47s. We hunt them now, shoot to kill, do you understand!" The DogPound came together, lifting their unconscious brothers and sisters, and yanked out the protruding darts and then their own weapons… typically a docile group. Still, since the Martial law and insane restrictions, they no longer were meek Lambs. Each one of them was armed to their teeth.

Jeff recalls the deadly story; we had ducked into a grove of trees, our bikes were left scattered all over the road, then we heard echoing from the hills over a radio Breaker LT Sloan this is Private Remy… over. "This is Lieutenant Sloan… Private… over." "LT, I have an issue out here on Drycreek Road. A motorcycle gang is once again breaking curfew. There are about 20 of them. We darted some of them. I saw them pull out some weapons… over." "Listen, Remy; we just had another uprising over at Wnn River Casino. The Natives started using weapons against us. The Indians were restless, not going quietly nor obeying our curfew. It was a hellacious battle, not going to put up with that crap again. Kill them. Anyone that carries a weapon is open territory….over."

Jeff shook his head, making a pitcher of Margaritas that was days ago. We shot and wounded 13 of them, of which seven died. Jeff scowled and snarled, remembering wounding a soldier with his 30/30 rifle that had shot one of his friends. Ironically later that same afternoon Major Bryan and a group of his Officers had met in my lounge. That's when he listened to Private Remy detail her slanted version of what really had happened in the shootout, lying outright, then the topic had changed like no big deal! LT Sloan and her new husband, Sergeant Barton, were celebrating with the group. Excitedly, boisterously bragging at how their objectives were progressing, the more alcohol I delivered, the louder their voices became.

Bartender Jeff Wilson was a main protagonist in the Rebel movement, he was invaluable.

Colonel Ruiz was still meeting LT Smugs. I'd just delivered a second Long Island Ice Tea and brought Ruiz some more Scotch. He heard now via his left earbud from the tiny listening device inside the flower arrangement on their table. "May I ask what the status is at Shasta Lake?" "No, you may not. Smugs were pulling off the lake and securing the perimeter. There have been way too many Shasta residents escaping into Siskiyou and other adjacent Counties…." "Well, Colonel, aren't you concerned that once we power up the internet and cell phone towers, social media will go Viral with our attacks and killings? You know how people sensationalize everything! It'll drive a sort of hysteria, I'm afraid!"

Ruiz guzzles his Scotch... waving the empty cocktail glass up "actually, it's expected our public media machine has already been pumping out propaganda 24/7 since before we captured Redding on the 5th of July, we will weather the storm and move on to the next region... Umh, city, this will become redundant to you and us, Smugs. Remember, we're only setting the example of how to control the populace, along with reducing the number of residents to 25%. The sensationalism you speak of will be coming from every country on the planet. Imagine that we have nothing to worry about. Remember, I'm like you... I am just following orders!"

Jeff accidentally knocks over the blender after hearing Ruiz's last statement, flustered and highly agitated, having to stay composed, finding it hard to listen to the earbud and concentrate for the love of his life was still missing.... Ruiz says at the table, "Like the song by 'Linkin Park,' 'In the End,' well the title of that tune relates because <u>in the end</u> there will be at a minimum 75,000 deceased people in this area by the time we pull out LT on the 27th. The loss of life is part of the Covid-57 façade." They tap glasses, and Ruiz lowers his voice slightly....

"We've been broadcasting the horrific details all along to the outside world's populations. We have a few Hollywood producers and filming crews exploiting the mayhem of what this killer variant is doing up here in the North State. It's being aired while we sit here we have professionals, politicians with military leaders stacked upon Governors, Congressmen, and women doing interviews about the mass casualties in Shasta County warning everyone to stay away and to feel lucky the new deadlier Variant that's now airborne has been contained here in Redding. This is a preemptive attack on civilization and will

cause fear across the globe. Then we continue on, soon, societies will become acclimatized to death all around them. The hyped advent of Covid-57 will change people's mindsets. Rather than fighting and organizing insurrections, they will be fighting to survive and just exist."

Smugs clacked glasses... "Yes, Colonel, I've watched a few of the infomercials with the actors wearing Hazmat uniforms like space suits, the stacks of corpses, the outrage across the globe. Fear is palpable. I get that, Sir. Just look at the stock market last week. It dropped over 7 %. We are in corrections mode across the world markets. It's nice that most of us got a heads-up and shorted the indexes. Yep, we're in a Bear market. Many traders and stock funds are in the Red, and they are getting margin calls. You know, Colonel, I don't believe many of us... our troops nah speaking for myself, if it weren't for my family being given a pass guaranteed safe harbor, I wouldn't be part of your killing machine!"

Ruiz Frowled angrily, clenching his teeth.... his furrowed brows vibrated growled, tapping his empty glass on the table. "Lieutenant, you are a main cog. You're the man that runs the Killing machine, as you refer to it as, Iron Mountain. It's your baby," cackling... "Finish your drink and move it.... I'm holding you culpable for Captain Rory and his clowns. I got more relevant people to speak with. Private Noels will be here in less than five minutes, and unlike you, he's punctual!" Smugs refrains from a verbal sparring match that he'd lose, bites his tongue, and salutes.... "Yes, Sir!" Lieutenant Smugs snarled while bending his head down after hearing the name Private Noels. Ahh, Smugs still needed to address Noel's attempt at blackmailing him for what he'd found in Sargent Rigor's motorhome, yeah got to deal with that snake in the grass. Smugs wondered what Noels had done with the 'Headboxes,' the decapitated victims of the Shasta Games. Smugs arose after tightening his boot buckles, displaying a scowl... "Hey, Smugs, if yah don't like it too bad, somebody's head had to be tied to the Iron Mountain debacle. It's yours, Smugs.... it's too late to turn back. You've signed the contracts, uhhhh as I heard it, many in your family would meet their demise if not for you signing on! They wouldn't even qualify for Yellow Tats.... now get out of here!"

Right on time, Private Noels is pointed to the table by Jeff… LT Snuggs leaves without acknowledging him. They didn't care for each other. No love lost their thought. Snuggs, who sees an oversized briefcase in the Private's hand, overhears Ruiz. "Have a seat, Private! good to see you…." "Yes, Sir" "I called you here along with Corporal Mendez. Oh, there she is…. wave her down now we're only missing Private Drake." "Nope, Colonel Sir coming through the other door now is Private Drake," Ruiz smiles. His Shasta Lake team of Noel, Mendez, and Drake was on time and ready to receive new orders.

They properly show due respect with salutations, scooting around the table and booth as Jeff sends a cocktail server over to get drink orders and to offer appetizers. Ruiz waits till the server leaves, making note of 'Mormon' Noels ordering Cranberry juice Virgin. The guy never has any fun, huh…. "You're here because we're entering the closing phase here in Shasta as expected; we're experiencing resistance. The longer family members are missing, the more frantic and aggressive the local folk will become. This is per norm." He unrolls a map on the table…. "Each of you will take your platoons into these sectors."

Ruiz pounds the table with his knuckles, then went silent as the drink orders are delivered "put away the RFD's no more darts. Shoot not to maim but to kill. That's an order. Anyone who carries arms against the US military is our enemy. Do any of you have any questions or comments regarding this binding order?" "Yes, excuse me, Sir, but I followed up on your last demand." Noels opened his briefcase and quickly shuffled through a packet of 11 x 14 pictures printed on glossy paper taking out the first sequence 1,2,3,4,5, and placed them on the table. "Colonel, your suspicions have been warranted and proven out. These are zoomed-in close-ups of the perps." He passes the first two photos over the table. Sir, here's the proof…. "Driving the stolen Sheriff boat is Special Operations Agent Brock Dune to his left is also a decorated military hero Rocky

Blake in the middle is Olympic Gold medalist Gymnast Latoya Gore." Ruiz didn't interrupt, but this information was old news. Sure, he didn't have glossy pictures, just fuzzy satellite shots.

Noels continued, "as you can see, pictures three and four are from Silverthorn Resort number three is a picture of Brock picking up Rocky on a Sea Doo he was sinking the Sheriff boat number five is of Brock loading a Jeep up without a license plate." Ruiz abruptly said, "let me see those..." he snapped them up "well, well where's proof of where they escaped to!" "The last photo in the sequence is the three of them leaving as you all can see, they extended their middle fingers up, flipping the Bird up at the sky an 'fk-you.' It's plainly obvious they're well aware that they were on blast, Sir!" "Noels, I think we get the picture, pun intended," said Ruiz. Corporal Mendez speaks up. "So, Sir, this proves what you've always said that Brock Dane escaped Silverthorn when we had him cornered... but why would they bother to sink the boat if they knew that we were taking pictures?" Noels answers, "I think we can safely say they assumed is all, and just in case the satellites didn't have their images, they sank the boat covering their bases, a calculated move."

Ruiz shakes his head negatively "why couldn't we have followed that Jeep with its heat signature?" Private Noels took the horn, "We did just that. It disappeared from our satellite, Colonel; per your orders, we have hired the best sniffers on the planet, a Canine unit of Bloodhounds that just landed at The Redding Airport. They're from the Vancouver-Portland area, the famous Feral Feedback Kennels. Sandi, the trainer, is being flown out by helicopter to the Silverthorn Resort area and will be walking the areas shown in the pictures. Oh, on another side note, Sir, I haven't been able to find a single landholding in either Rocky's nor Brock's names. As far as the girl Latoya, she was on vacation with her deceased brother and husband. They were from the Bay Area; her parents are making a stink applying major pressure....." "That's enough, Noels....." Ruiz waves to Jeff for a repeat performance, saying, "Look, if the Dogs locate them, we will annihilate them, but they account for a total of three individuals. We now must concentrate on the numerous gangs organizing covert militias to squelch the resistance and stop the exodus of escaping residents from the cordoned-off zone. This county remains shut down until we complete our mission. Many of the escapees are deceiving the public with statements and interviews on YouTube, TikTok, Instagram, Reels, and that kid's channel, Snapchat, ughhhh, and even Twitch. Those social media sites are nothing but trouble. Ugh, Facebook is the fricken worse by far!"

They nodded, then Private Drake perked up "back to the Jeep and threesome, I've taken my Apache over the tree lines scouring all below from Jones Valley to Silverthorn. All the hunting, fishing cabins, and hidden retreats have been vetted and searched, nothing no sign of the assailants. They have to have a concealed place such as a bunker, Sir, uh, they just didn't disappear!..." Corporal Mendez threw in her 2 cents "I think they have to be off of Bear Mountain Road or Dry Creek Road. There are literally hundreds of ranch homes up there!" Drake adds "strangely, we see them in the Jeep driving up the boat ramp Southbound..." Taking another manilla envelope and scattering half a dozen pictures out. Private Drake further expounds, "there is no sign of the Jeep on any of the roads exiting the Silverthorn vicinity. My team of surveillance experts who scanned all the satellite images in the time period that the Jeep had disappeared not only didn't spot or see any sign of the Jeep, there weren't any other vehicles spotted on any other roads leaving that mountain!"

Colonel Ruiz waits till the server vanishes again, "all right, we have multiple fronts to deal with. I've ordered and tasked Major Bryan to deal with Bethel Church's hierarchy and their unruly congregation. They seem hellbent on fighting against our military occupation at every turn. That Father Rite needs to be reined in. Ruiz grasps his drink and downs it with a leftover sigh…. then on top of that, we have to deal with another group of young rebels who have formed an insurgent militia to fight us not physically but technically, trying to overthrow our controls of blocking the communications in Shasta County. Also, I've left that to Major Bryan." Ruiz stares at Jeff, who seems to be tuned in, at the bar. He waves his empty drink glass and nods aggressively.

Ruiz then continued barking, "our duties are to tighten our control over our borders here and kill the rebels that are leveling arms against the United States Military. We can now ascertain that the numbers against us are growing exponentially. But again, the numeral Uno… mission is to capture Brock, Rocky, and Latoya's heads on a platter. Which one of you is looking for advancement, huh?" They nod with perky grins. "We meet back here on the 25th same time, same Bat channel…." Grinning to himself at how clever he was, they sucked down their drinks… "Get out there; you have your orders now…. shoot to kill!"

The Officers walked away; at the same time, a server with a large tray showed up with baked Halibut Crab cakes and a crock of French Onion soup, Asparagus with a yummy Rice Pilaf, and some Garlic toast. Ruiz licked his lips, expounding, "Oh Yeah!"

Jeff ducks into the office, checking to ensure that all said at Ruiz's table was being recorded with a grimace and a sideways smirk, wishing he could have poisoned the bastard, but his hands were tied not a happy camper had to maintain his allegiance to the resistance movement. Jeff walks to a private storage area where the most expensive liqueurs are locked up. He takes out a delivered note given to him only minutes before… bam his heart cracked, and Jeff yelped out internally. No!… the love of his life, Linda, was taken to Iron Mountain. This was just confirmed that her name was found on a ledger…. that a double-spy had been delivered to Bethel Church… 'Oh please let my honey and lover….' Jeff stopped moving…

leaning against a wall in the C.R. Gibbs storage room. Jeff wasn't a religious man, not a praying type of individual, but he gritted his teeth and said aloud, 'Linda, I love you. Please be okay. I'm coming to get you, babe!'

A few minutes later, Jeff knew he had to keep it together and stepped out with a firm countenance on his face, seeing his second-in-command Judy who was an on-call troubleshooter for the restaurant, bar & grille. Judy gave him her typical inquisitive stare, and Jeff had a thought flash by his blinking eyes… Judy played like she was subservient and almost kiss-assing at times, constantly questioning him about Linda and what he was doing with The DogPound, uhm, his motorcycle club. She had asked him pointed questions about several of the members. Something clicked suddenly, and Jeff remembered Judy asking him where Mondo was at. Judy had proved to be loyal on several occasions, and Jeff trusted her and told Judy where one of his closest DogPound friends was located, 'Mondo'… who was wanted for revolting against the military blockade. Mondo was stowed away in his bunker on his property with other members… oh no, she wouldn't. Judy reacted nonchalantly as if no big deal, then not 24 hours later, Mondo's bunker was raided. *"Hey, there, Jeff, is everything okay? I saw you duck into the liquor room but brought nothing back out. Is there anything I can do to help?"* "Ughhhh no, Judy, I was *checking our inventory of Hennessy Cognac. We're getting a lot of orders for shots of it___" "You know Jeff, Hennessey is actually Brandy, uuh___" "Yes, Judy, now please bus the tables in the back room; we are going to have a large gathering of Officers here in less than 15 minutes."*

Jeff checked on the bar area and quickly disappeared back into his C. R. Gibbs office, tapped on the in-house computer, and searched the archives. There it was, Judy Smith…. Jeff had watched her cavort around Corporal Tina Bracewell and even hugged her. Jeff had inquired about the Corporal, asking Judy how she'd known her; Judy's reply was oh, they'd gone to elementary school together... they called themselves blood sisters but were just old friends. But the files showed, in fact... Judy and Tina were distant, albeit consanguineous cousins. Someone was leaking information about Jeff's connections to the underground movement he was involved in. Better keep an eye on Judy. She portrayed a nincompoop, ditsy and unobservant, could she be the person who was responsible for Linda's capture? Judy was one of the few that knew where Linda was hiding out by the lake... after my lovely wife delivered the cache of weapons to other members of my Dogpound group of dissenters. It wasn't an hour and Linda was splayed out on the asphalt in front of their cabin by the Lakehead Resort. Instantly anger boiled over, and Jeff went ballistic, realizing that there wasn't a question... Nope, Judy was a snitch and was responsible for his wife Linda's capture. Jeff emptied his Visine container into Judy's flavored mineral water... 'There yuh go, Judy, have a good night!'

Colonel Ruiz chomped down on a piece of Garlic toast after dipping it into the crock of cheesy French Onion soup, mulling over what he'd find out after dessert... having slipped a listening device underneath Major Bryan's fat desk couldn't wait to access the faggots conversations after he had left Bryans office. Something smelled wrong... rotten Bryan was a mortal enemy! Then switched gears, thinking about his antagonists... Happy that ole Feral Feedback was hired to locate Brock and Rocky. They have some great sniffing Bloodhounds on the ground rubbing his significant snout. Ruiz's intuitive nose was never wrong.

Brocks Mountain Ranchette.

Brock finished brushing down his Horse and worked his way over to the rest of his animals, checking to ensure they were A-Okay. He felt safe standing on the grounds of his ranchette. Brock reentered his main cabin to find both Latoya and Rocky snoozing

A few hours later, Brock flashes awake, Glock in his right hand and a combat dagger in his left sprung up on the go, a high-pitched tone moving triple time, passing Rocky down the hall.... his cameras were motion enabled, the alarms rang out; monitors were buzzing with troops and Dogs heading up his mountain, not three and one-half miles from where they collectively stood breathless. He enlarged the live video feed; Rocky, behind his back, said, "Lookie there, it's one of our NIA partner's Canine teams!" Noticing the Dogs vests of Red, White, and Blue with a Gorilla mug in the middle, an insignia of the infamous 'Rocco the Gorilla'... Wendi Feral's dream business and there was her partner and friend Sandi leading the search for them.

Brock had to shake his head at the Irony that the military had subcontracted out Feral Feedback, who was famously hired out by the FBI and Rico Captor. Their animals were second to none. What the military failed to understand was that the owners of Feral Feedback belonged to their secret organization NIA.... we are forever tied to the hip. And yet oddly, the Dogs were on a beeline trajectory right toward his property. Rocky was perplexed, "hey, there's twenty-five soldiers if there's one." Brock snorts. "I know, my friend, it's disrespectful that they didn't send at least a hundred after us! A pitiful 25 or so, huh? You want some coffee or expresso shots while we enjoy the show!"

"Thanks, bro. When will the Dogs come across the sensors?" "oh, about another 300 yards or so. They still have a steep climb. Wendi's Canines are impressive; there on a direct route...." "Yep, as we'd guessed, the satellite cameras caught our images at the dock, but they surely couldn't differentiate where we went. Surely they pulled pictures of Bear Mountain and Dry Creek roads, knowing we vanished into the forest." A few moments later, they sipped steaming coffee... a noise Brock spun around. "Oh, good morning, sleeping beauty," whispers Rocky smiling... "how ya sleep, girl?" Latoya put her hand in a karate chop over her eyebrows, trying to see past Red stained, droopy eyes. "I'm not done with the sleep thing; boys heard some noise out here and freaked out." Latoya removed herself from the den with a bottle of water. Shaking her head at the hyped-up twosome. 'Ugh, where do they get the fricken energy?'

Back on the monitors, "ok, now watch the Dogs. It's a high-frequency sound that's radiated from high up in the trees. I've installed these transmitters in a circumference around the diameter of my property, 2.3 miles away. It's similar to the annoying sounds that humans can't tolerate, the scratching nails across chalkboards. This is how it was explained to me by Wendi Feral. Dogs invariably feel pain in their inner ears... it's like a blaring wailing siren. A special team of Scientists developed this technology to eliminate man's most basic and reliable hunters.... Bloodhounds. There nearing the forcefield, as I like to refer to it now, Rocky watched their muzzles and subtle head bobs rocking their big floppy ears sideways now there turning in unison, following the frequency parallel to the sound emitting device, Walla foiled again by technology but yuh know, we need to get out of here today brother!" "I agree, Brock, I agree.... let me get sleepy head up your right, pal. We must plan our departure."

<u>Lieutenant Smugs.</u>

A call over the radio unhinged Smugs, Rory's previous doctor at the hospital where Rory was being treated had called and instructed him to go to the Neurology Institute adjacent to Mercy Hospital to meet with a Premier Neurologist who was in charge of the entire Neurology Department. Smugs would try first to see Rory instead of checking with the guards he'd instructed to stay by Captain Rory's side. He'd see for himself if Rory had regained consciousness. Smugs didn't want any more meetings with haughty doctors and to circumvent meeting with this Neurologist and cut to the chase and would speak with Rory himself.... good idea, but it proved to be a feeble wish for Rory was still sedated and delusional. Rory was still growling like a Saber-toothed Tiger. Dammit, Smugs didn't like feeling like he did, felt slightly buzzed still from his visit with Colonel Ruiz at the Restaurant, super dehydrated.

Lightheaded Jonesing for one more drink. That's the problem with booze and him… it was always just one more drink chasing a euphoric high that always ended with the same result a massive hangover of throbbing Hell. That's why some of his civilian buddies would say if you never sobered up, you never got a hangover. Yeah, he wondered if Ruiz was still drinking. He disliked the man intensely and concluded he'd made a deal with the Devil, his family safe and sound. This was his only leverage for signing up for this murderous mission tapped # 3 inside the elevator the door opened to a thin short man of Asian descent. "Lieutenant Smugs, I presume the front desk let me know that you were on your way up…." Smugs thought; what a brain he assumed, like duh, his name was above his heart on his uniform, and I'm the inebriated one?

"I'm afraid I've got continually bad prognostications for you; your Captain Rory is exhibiting hallucinatory convulsions. We've had to place a mouthguard over his teeth. Are you familiar with Grand–mal seizures, usually due to Epilepsy, Lieutenant? Fortunately, he's not still losing his bowels and urine." Smugs said nothing. The Doctor went on as if speaking to himself, "We've exhausted our expertise. Captain Rory needs special attention and treatments beyond our scope of expertise. Each scan EEG shows irregular brain activity, almost animal-like comparisons, and his Neurons and Synapses are firing well... Most patterns of his brain's activities resemble what we've studied in Primates, sir!"

"Wtf Doc, what Rory has turned into a fkn Monkey?..." "No!" quickly stepping away from him, then regaining his stature stoically steadfast. "We are limited here; all my staff and I can do for him has been done. Now what's left for your Captain Rory is us trying our best to comfort him. I have only two recommendations for you. I will have my receptionist give you their business contacts. May I suggest that you transport the Captain to Forensic Psychologist Doctor Milo, a world-renowned Neurologist who has just opened a new clinic in San Mateo. Although I'd choose NIA in Napa, one of the finest institutions on the planet but last, I read there's a 7-month wait to enter their facilities." Smugs declares, "Listen, I only need him conscious for a few questions, isn't there a way to shoot him up with adrenalin or something...." Somewhat annoyed with this subservient fool's attitude along with his stench of alcohol, the doctor whirled around, "Lou-Lou could you help the Lieutenant out with the referrals? I must attend to another brain injury. Have a good evening, LT."

Smugs shrinks down sadly, disgusted that he had two Officers dead and one civilian beheaded in this macabre game invented by Captain Rory. How would he ever know what happened up on the killing mountain? He understood the parallels of the hunting games, but there had to be more to the story. Smugs had to locate the escapees, Josh and Heather. They will know far more about the inner nuances and details of what happened. Gladly Ruiz doesn't have all the facts about the hunting game under his watch, ahhhh, yet... that is! Smugs knew he had to capture the escaped couple before Ruiz's search party did so. In the forefront of the Lieutenant's mind, a question that always lingered... when would Private Noels bring out the missing headboxes that had previously been filled with decapitated skulls.

Snings dropped down the elevator out the door into the warm evening. His driver saw him pulling up the Jeep "where to, Sir...." "TMP soldier," mulling over when the task of dismantling the entire operation would be finished, the orders from above were to leave Iron Mountain like it was when they arrived. He had plenty of soldiers to complete the job, but his main concern was that no human remains nor proof of what the Lava Acid pit was used for... never ever could reach the light of day, or he'd be known or referred to as one of those Concentration Camp Commandants.

Karen and Lori.

The soldiers left faster than they arrived, snatching Kayla up, and were gone, not bothering to search anymore. They got what they came for... Karen leans over the sink in the bathroom and washes her face with cold water. Karen gauges her next move. Should she go back home, or could she make it back home through the mazes of soldiers and civilian snitches? Questions linger without any confirmed answers, mere assumptions would Ben and Cat show up at her home like what was planned? Heck, were they still free or even alive?

Lori Chan was making her way down from the attic where they had hidden while the raid was goin on, "I want to apologize if I was the cause of the cops raiding this building, Lori!.." "No, Karen, we both know it wasn't your fault they had already been here twice before looking for our friend Kayla although, for some reason, this time, they were extremely motivated and decided to bust every door down in this entire building all I can say is her mother has some major pull...." "Yeah, I've met her knowing Kayla way back when we were in the same class in elementary school... she's a powerful, assertive woman for sure."

Instead of risking leaving the office building, Karen had agreed with Lori to stay put, for the military had already searched the building thoroughly, and they were safe for now. Besides, there was a cafeteria downstairs. Jeesh, they could just hunker down here till after the internet and cell phones were turned back on… why not?

<u>Nearly two weeks evaporated into the Covid-57… Abyss.</u> 🙂

After almost two weeks later, they were comfortable with each other's company, lives on hold but at least safe from being arrested, staying indoors a positive for sure.

"Can I ask you a question?" Lori nodded "of course…." "Interrupting was a TV broadcast. Karen reached over, snagged the remote, and turned it up. Flashing at the bottom on scroll mode… were the words all cell towers will be attempted to be activated by the 23rd at 1 pm. Wi-Fi should be up and running also. "That's total bullshit" yelled Karen. "They were supposed to turn everything back on July 21st." Lori put up her finger "sshhh" The announcer continued speaking. "The current time is 5:11 pm. The temperature is 91 degrees; it's still a hot one out there. The manhunt continues for these 57 people. Please, citizens of Shasta, help us. These are… extremely ruthless and dangerous individuals with rewards on their heads. The rewards vary from $125,000 for Rocky Blake and Brock Dame to $100,000 for…" narrator kept naming fugitives wanted with reward apportionments; Lori says, "hey, I made some iced tea do…" "sshhh this is important." Karen locked on the TV checking the pictures of the most wanted then she gasped hearing "please residents of Shasta we have many outlaws and outright criminals out there hurting people. They are amongst us we need your help… Remember, if you assist us in capturing a Rebel by providing a reliable tip, you can collect cash, and don't forget, just like with all the monetary rewards, there's a boatload of other prizes given out with commemorations of recognition!" The continuous scrolling list of rewards and names streamed across the bottom of the screen, $75,000 rewards led us to these individuals Trevor Lawrence, Jill Hale, Jamie Gaumer, and Latoya Gore. Their pictures filled the

screen. Also, others we need in custody, and you have the chance at collecting the 75 thousand dollars for Ben Burgess, Catrina Cline, Maddi Taylor, Cody Hoffman, and Ali Schaff ..."Wait, unh," Karen screams. "Is this current? This can't be current; this has to be a replay!" "yes..." Lori backs away with a perplexed complexion.... "You hear the announcer mention this is up to the date of 7/22/2024. Why, what's up Karen?"

Karen found a chair, sat, and started to explain the history of what happened when Cody and Ali, and she were captured by the military and how she escaped the van... Lori looked at her, stunned "why are you just now telling me this?" Then she heard her name Karen Fleming $35,000 her picture was stolen off of Facebook. "Wow, your money sitting here, girl...." Lori chuckled lightly. Karen rolled her eyes and restarted her story from the point of their capture at the office building and of how she escaped the Van. "The soldiers didn't turn Cody and Ali in for the rewards. Whew, something was not right, weirdly wrong! Who wouldn't collect the money? They were soldiers, right uh?" The announcer continued on the TV with rewards for various crimes all the way down to $5,000.

Lori sat still, analyzing all that she'd heard, while Karen quietly speculated how Cody and Ali could have made it out of the van. They were totally out, knocked unconscious Karen checked on them before making it out the van's door. She'd previously wondered how she missed the scrolling names, then realized they didn't watch the boob tube much and spent their time reading paperback books they'd found next door, the old-school way of entertainment. Karen saw her perplexed expression, "are you good, uhm, ok, Lori?" she nodded... "Well, there's one way of knowing if they got the boys for sure, Karen. We can call the 611-reporting number to check real-time and to pretend to have information on one of the guys. Let's assume they will trace the call so we can make the call down on the first floor where they broke down Kayla's door, use her phone to call in the tip!" "Okay, I'll play devil's advocate. Why would they have Cody and Ali's names on the wanted scroll bar if they'd arrested them?" "Karen, didn't you say that they were strapped on stretchers when you left them?" "Yes, but we've been fine here. Aren't you okay with just waiting it out, Lori?"

"To answer your question, I'm not fine at all. I'm terrified no mortified would be better, like frozen in place, Karen. I've personally locked myself up here since the military attacked our town. Then Kayla joined me a little while afterward. Luckily, there was a deli on the first floor, or we'd have starved by now. I saw the troops shoot more than a dozen innocent people at last count, uhm, 15 uuuh, most of them appeared homeless, and the soldiers just bagged them up like lost stray dogs. Then Kayla and I saw the troops go into the Shasta Jail and take the inmates out on stretchers with sheets covering them, stacking them in covered trucks. Last night you and I witnessed a big 4-wheel drive truck being pulled over with teenagers breaking curfew. They were all shot and dragged out of their vehicles! I don't think I can leave here! Where is my family?....."

Karen hugs her rubbing her head. "We have to do this; come on; your idea is the only way to really know if they have Cody and Ali and just running old information of them being wanted. I want to know what happened to my friends; let's call the tip in!" "Okay, it's my turn. I'll play Devil's Advocate. What if your friends are still out there?..." "Well, if they accept our fake tip, then they had to have escaped the van, and then I must go to my house immediately. That's where they probably went instead of going to Bethel, which was my second choice cuz Cat and Ben went there after the conference at Mary Lake?" Karen grabbed the soldier's hat and his jacket that she'd stolen from the van.

Down the stairs and into Kayla's Paralegal Office, they went punched in 611 on the plugged-in phone. "Redding military services, can I help you?" "Wow, no recording, that's surprising...." "No, ma'am, the Government understands that during this stressful time, when a person calls 611, they should hear a human being's voice, not a machine. So, with that being said, my name is Brandi. Can I help you? I see you are calling from 711 Court Street... is this an emergency? I can patch you through to a 911 operator." "No, nah, is this the tip line? I want the $75,000 rewards for Ali Schaff and Cody Hoffman. I know where they might possibly be hiding out at... are they still fugitives, Brandi?" "Hold on, what's your name, please?" "umh, Ann Rudisel" "Okay, Ann, let me check and see if that reward has already been claimed."

Karen covers the mouthpiece and looks at Lori, who taps her Apple watch and whispers, "we got to move; they could be on the way...." "No, Ann, the rewards for them are still valid...." "I thought I saw them on Hwy 273 by the 'Extreme Burger Joint'...." "At what time was this?" "Uh, less than 35 minutes ago..." "Thanks, Ann. Stay where your at will send an MP to you. Meanwhile, here's your special code that's time-stamped if they do find either Ali or Cody, um, or both of them. You'll need this number to collect the rewards. Do you have a pen or pencil?" Karen realized this call now was a mistake but had to play it out no way she should hang up on this, Brandi. That would cause Red alarms for sure. "Okay, Brandi, go ahead...." "It'll be Z123FK757. Did you get that?" "Yes, thank you," she hangs up, taking up Lori's hand "we got to hide their coming. You were right; that was asinine, uh, stupid!"

They spontaneously run across the street, panicking. Instead of running back upstairs, they hid behind a delivery truck, huffing, "I didn't hang up cuz they'd race over here, so I played along. I bet the Military Police are on the way... but I did find out that somehow Cody and Ali escaped that van. I need to make it to my house. I want you to come with me, Lori.... Yuh can't stay here, now, girl." "I'm with you! Follow me, Karen. There's a car on the third level of the parking garage. It belonged to a secretary who was caught on the streets during curfew. I know where she hides her keys." They make their way to the second landing, that's where Karen realized she'd left the gun she'd stolen from the van in Lori's office. A screeching sound… Karen stops and points at the office building that they'd just left as a Humvee was parking at the curb by the office building…. five MPs got out, not in a rush nor wearing patented masks.

Karen wore the soldier's jacket and hat she'd stolen from the van Cody and Ali were last seen in. Karen could blend in some, although there weren't many troops walking the downtown area of Redding doing rounds like at the beginning of the curfew. But Lori was a standing casualty. She wore a Black and White skirt and blouse with flats on her feet. They kneeled behind the 3-foot block wall in the parking garage, looking down on Kayla's first-floor office. Despite it being warm, Karen shivered, placing her hands in the jacket's pockets. What's this? She says to herself… glancing down at a card that was in the left pocket, phone numbers on one side…. casually flipping it over 'Bethel Church' a triple take. "Hey, look what I found in the soldier's jacket Lori?" she blankly stared, reading the card 'Father Rite of Bethel Church' phone numbers, email addresses, Twitter, Facebook, and Instagram addresses. Then underneath, in deep Blue ink, 'Cody, Ali, and Girl on Hwy 273 by Extreme Burger!'

"Lori, we have to get to Bethel Church right now. I'll explain on the way, but let's wait till it's dark…." "Fine on foot; it's about three miles from here cross-country. We'd be sitting Pigeons in the car anyways. I've noticed the troops pulling over vehicles checking paperwork, and oh, have you seen the latest Tattoos?" Suddenly, the squealing of tires careening up into the parking garage… "Oh fk!"

67

<u>Doctor Walsh versus Doctor Roble.</u>

Doctor Cindy Walsh takes one of the dozens of cell phones the military technicians had calibrated and taps in Doctor Shamon Roble's number. Cindy hits the speaker button and waits for Shamon to answer her call. "Hey there, Cindy, I'll be approaching the barricade in a few miles. Soon I will be disconnected because of your occupations blocking devices.... you do have my daughter Cindy?" "Yes, mom, I'm with Doctor Walsh...." "OMGod Kayla, oh shit, I've been worried sick over you. I love you!" Somberly, Kayla replies, "I love you too, seeya in a minute...." "Are you all right, sweetheart?" "Yes, mother, just tired; I can't wait to hug you."

Shamon tells Cindy on speaker, "thank you for finding her like you said you would. I'm going to park where I was before." Cindy pushes End on her speaker phone, feeling negative vibes, not saying a syllable to the despicable woman... "you didn't sound too enthused, not excited to hear from your mother. Why? Is there something bothering you? Tell me, Kayla!" "I'm deliriously famished and need to sleep for like three days straight. I've not had any rest, is all." "Famished, ahh, didn't you have something to eat? I think famished is the wrong word. I..." "Yes, I meant discombobulated, just burnt out...." Cindy parks and Kayla opens the door; suddenly energized, she grabs her bags and purse and walks past the Military Police wanting to run, but while her heart is beating out of her chest, she has to play it cool. Kayla walked around several barriers and saw her mom... tears strained out; Shamon's gentle smile of adoration beamed out to her. They run now, hugging in mid-stream, a mother and child reunion indeed! Cindy gawks back at the scene, seeing the Roble clan all hunched together group hugging... aww chucks!

Cindy flips a dick and U-turns back towards the hospital, happy to get the pressure off and return Kayla to her mom. Now back to business, she contemplated what it would feel like to have a child missing, what kinds of exhilarations of pumping endorphins would explode when reunited, a different form of elation much different than sexual bliss or spousal love and adoration a child that came internally from your body wow a weird concept sadly, she'd never know!

Kayla.

"Mother, unh, mom, we have to do something. I need to speak with Uncle Rico OmLord, and they're killing innocent people, really murdering harmless naive citizens right in the streets. Wait till I tell you what I've witnessed taps her bag. Mom, I've got over a hundred digital pictures. I love you, Mom; thanks for saving me. They've kidnapped AJ…. you must help me please, mother, find him." Shawon's strong jaw clenched, her brows furrowed, eyes narrowed, squinting her muscles flexed…. tension found her knuckles. White-hot gripping the steering wheel. "Don't worry, honey; momma will figure out what the hell is happening and handle it. I knew something was wrong about this clandestine war on the residents in Shasta County, this bogus new Covid-57 strain being airborne. Well, hell, are you telling me the wind no longer blows? Damn, last I checked, it was flowing 19 miles per hour South, so why hasn't anyone in Tehama or Cottonwood fallen ill and died from this new bullshit Variant?" Kayla, in tears, her siblings held her tight in the mini-van. Jaxon, her step-father said, "AJ made it out honey, I think…. wait, I haven't heard from him in over a week!"

Maddi inside Bart's bedroom.

Knock, knock… Knock, a light's silhouette breaks across the wall from the hallway. Maddi tried to rise up from the bed… like a rusty crane; her drugged-out head moved achingly slowly. "Maddi here is lunch for you," she gauged the voice, a feminine high-pitched shrill. It was Bart's mom Marge Simpson. Marge wore a large mask and had gloves covering her hands, " I hope you feel better today... soon our phones will be turned back on. I'm so excited; ugh, Bart will be home at around 5:30 pm; you okay?" Maddi didn't say anything just wanted to melt away and die.

Maddi wanted to yell loudly, shut up, shut the door, and get out of her sight, but her raw throat felt like the membrane was peeling off in skin flaps down her esophagus. This prevented her from speaking or muttering a single syllable. It was as if Maddi had multiple maladies, and no matter how much water she drank, her mouth still remained Death Valley dry. The worst was the sledgehammer pounding in her cranium, with no power to resist the intrusion of Marge Simpson. Maddi imagined her neck as an industrial crane... dropped her head, and she bulldozed back into Covid-57 Hell. She looked at the additional pile of pills wishing for one of them to end her life. Maddi sucked down another bottle of water, trying to battle her drug-dry mouth, her nose clogged like mud. She was suffering,... rolling to the side of Bart's bed, clutching a damp pillow, and slipping back into her coal-black abyss.

<u>Bart Simpson at his job.</u>

At Mercy Hospital, Bart was having another of his typical days well, since the Coronavirus hit back in early 2020, humanity didn't exist in his warped mind. Bart became nearly robotic, with mundane thoughts that brought feverish contentment. Just bag them up no need for last rites or Hospice... all Bart had to do was fill out the small toe tag done deal name, age, and Social Security number. If possible, the date and time of the person's demise. Attach the death tag to the big toe on the left foot and wait for the orderlies to move the White sheeted gurney away. Hurry because a lineup of waiting gurneys was in the hallways on every floor of the hospital.

Heck, even the lobbies had gurneys lined up in the order they came in. First come, first dead, ▓ *... Bart wonders, 'why do we sterilize needles? Heck, the hospital was running low on supplies. Why not just reuse them, hum?'*

Absorbed in his work alone in his mind, he'd been so proud when passing his medical exams; now Bart was a full-fledged Registered Nurse with aspirations down the road to continue to Doctorhood. That cost serious bucks. One of the main reasons that the five Doctors on floor number seven in charge of his wing had achieved doctorhood was because they were fricken blessed. They were all Silver Spooned born Guppies with the right blood, ugh heritage, ahm pedigree to become Doctors or whatever they aspired to be. Imagine what luck to wake up shot out of the womb, privileged, born into the top 1 %. No worries, huh, your special Why? Bart couldn't stand these privileged pieces of shit. Yet wasted his time dwelling further... oh yeah, because you were hatched wealthy and rich, no worries if you make mistakes along life's journey; daddy and mommy's money will save you and put you back on track. Bart despised them with a passion. Each of the wealthy offspring bore the Red Dot Pyramid Tattoo like they were special or something. Lord knows he hated their perfumed stench.

Staring at one of em sitting at a table, most likely talking about him... drinking her Mocha-Latte sneeringly, 'hope you enjoy the squirt of Vixine bitch I put in your drink' should have you on your knees in front of the commode for hours, he cackled. A scowl-ish snarl displayed covertly under his mask as he passed her by. Doctor Ivy would be in stomach cramp hell within an hour. Bart had to be careful because they could test for Vixine, sparingly using it at times, being cognizant of the cameras.

He recalled yesterday's replay as the witch walked up to him like Hella proud, "I got my first tattoo ever, and it didn't really hurt. I think I'm going to be getting a bunch more. I can certainly afford it. Her nose twitched up ghoulishly 'uh, mine is pretty, Amber, all the Doctors get Red Dots. We're at the top of the food chain. Yah, no, I'm sorry, yours is a putrid Yellow!" she giggled with her crooked grin... nope, they never got along; Doctor Ivy was a raging scumbag!

The morgue in the basement had more traffic than the Emergency rooms no more Freezer compartments available... where to put the dead? Too bad there wasn't a commercial uh industrial chipper to just feed full bodies in and then blast out one-half-inch chunks. I heard they'd be great fertilizer hell; the grass would grow Greener!

Intrigued by this morning's events, never was his family so unified, right down to his teenage sister, prodigy Lisa whom he loathed at times and then loved. It was the sibling rivalry typical 'love hate' heck, both twats Lisa and Maggie were at times intolerable. His lovely mom had called for a meeting, the family meeting scenario, lol. The vote was unanimously distributed, rare indeed, but with a caveat that he would continue to drug Maddi. Then on July 24th or, at the latest, the 25th, he'd drive her down to the Police Station, turn her in, and collect $75,000 and the other perks such as food rations, the Lottery, etc. The reason for waiting until then and not already turning her in for the reward was that many times they'd witnessed the controlling military raising the rewards limits. The police patiently kept increasing the rewards heck. Maddi and her group started out with like a $15,000 reward, he thought. Each increase drove more fervor from the bounty hunters and citizens to utilize all their resources to locate the rebels.

Although... truth be told, he also held out hope that Maddi would break and tell him where her friends were, and they'd be rich in reward monies. What his family had decided was actually brilliant. He knew where his brains came from for sure, umh, the Caveat he liked that word um, wasn't sure if he was using it properly ughhhh... anyways his family had chosen him to pick her brain to try and find out where the rest of the group was, each of them worth an astounding 75 K. He almost drooled, chomping on his upper lip, there was no love lost between Ben, Cody, or Ali and him. Bart did like Cat some, though, but could you imagine an additional whopping $300,000 for the package deal? Yep, he'd first try subtle manipulation, then ole Maddi would need to be gagged and bound. ❄ Oh yeah, I'm going to really have some fun, watching her suffer, uhm, yum, her suffering pain while enduring his insatiable form of torture. Bart re-adjusted his swelling crotch. Soon enough, it would begin. Oh, can't fricken wait!"

Feeling frivolously giddy over the prospects, he stabbed the death concoction into another woman's IV, chuckling to himself. Add to that the military was set to increase rewards any day now, he mused why couldn't he bargain with the police…. they'd listen to him 'say, hey, I know where they're all at, set them up. I got Maddi… give me 75K per head, or was it dead or alive? Could I collect… with their corpses? Even better fun, <u>Fun till daddy takes the T-Bird away</u>? Oh well, enough of the fantasy of what can be. I have to make it happen and need to bring it all to fruition. Thinking he had more 'Death Angel' work on his wing to attend to, it was a different performance every day. Oh, how he enjoyed watching their eyes blink out seeya, "What a Job!" Unfortunately, Bart didn't have a sexy victim left on his floor, but there were always new arrivals. ❄

Lastly, while he wraps another toe, he wonders if mom is playing her part in feeding the bitch? Keeping Maddi sedated…. Mumbles, 'Maddi, you were always too good for me, always teasing me, selfishly chastising and frustrating me, punishing me with your outright cruelties, in high school me the little Freshman you Senior Royalty.' Don't say hi to me in the U-Prep high school halls, no your way too good for lowly Bart, goading your friends to hum the Simpson tune, mocking me with 'where's daddy Homer? Oh, that's right, he's at home with Marge and sisters Lisa and Maggie! Lol'

<u>He or she who laughs last laughs best of all,</u>   ... I gotcha now, Maddi. Yep, your ass is literally mine, bmo, giggling out loud, yanking his mask off, and showing a tooth display with a wicked lopsided Cheshire Cat smile. Muttered. Yep, profoundly the other night, uhm, what a night it was. ...... I did get that ass, he roared again, pinching his cock, a bit sore still, tight little virgin tunnel... Yup!

Back to mom, his orders were only two Ambiens crushed up. Maddi was building up a tolerance to some of the barbiturates. He and his family needed her to be able to call Ben or Cat when the cellphones were turned back on or tell him where they were at. Uh worst case is that I could text them with her phone, but they might want to hear her voice or Facetime her. The goal was to locate her friends and collect the monies, and Bart would be a Hero given the Golden Carrot. Bart and his family would be rich, and then he could continue his medical career.

<u>Maddi still in a daze, sick.</u>

Maddi couldn't swallow sandpaper Sally, parched lips and aching joints like her bones were going to break through her thin skin. She removes herself like a 97-year-old frail twig... hands held out like a walker was needed and drops to her knees at the door. The night light provided enough illumines downs the water and the Orange Juice in a flat-Jack seven seconds. Aah umh; starving, Maddi ate the cold egg, ham, and cheese sandwich. She gobbled up all that Marge had delivered to the room. The clock radio showed 10:51 am. How much longer did she have till she succumbed to the virus? Burning like hot coals, her bum was raw... along with her groin. Bart had violated and raped her; he wasn't going to get away with it. Yeah, despite the sweet note from Bart... Maddi knew Bart had raped her; thinking again of the love letter and supposed hickeys proving otherwise, she was a willing participant, but why couldn't she remember even a second of sex with him? It had been months since she'd engaged in any kind of sex. Crawling back to bed, the fever was less, it seemed, or maybe not. She felt like crud, uh, leftovers. 

Maddi laid her head down, cuddling to pillows, rollin her tongue around her gums. A sharp jabbing stick below her lip line digs her finger in her mouth, pulling out something hard, probably gristle from the ham, and flicks it away… out went the lights.

Bart…back at Mercy Hospital, providing his form of Mercy…

Bart was in the safest place in the hospital, he thought humorously, the men's restroom once again counterfeiting one of the Doctor's signatures for prescriptions of various drugs that he needed. Dad's Morphine, Oxycodone, mom's Xanax, his sister's Prozac, of course, he smirked, signing a scribbled name to the last script for his mother's little helper. He would pull, also, come through as he always did. The alternate would be hell the family would revolt against him being addicted. Their withdrawals could and would be painful for Bart too. Uhm, Bart didn't forget to write some prescriptions of pharmaceuticals for himself, he regularly took a six-pack of feel-good pills.

Dammit, his pager blasted off, beeping… bed two, the fricken idiot pushed the Nurse's call button again. The fool was dying Withell just fricken get it over with. Dammit, Bart angrily glares. Red-faced in the mirror doesn't wash his hands… feces fingered on a messy wipe. Who cares? He had a bout of Colitis which had him making way too many treks to the toilet. He steps out to his left…. "Hey Bart, you have company on 13." He brushes by the vain privileged girl, wanting to slap her. Pound her into oblivion, uh, ram it in her to the hilt, oh she thought her shit didn't stink because she had been 'Well-Born.' Bart sees a group of three people around a patient's bed, all wearing masks with gloves. Bart quickly stops at the Nurse's station and

146

grabs a clipboard… who the fk is in slot number 13? Heck, that space had rotated out two bodies already this morning. Josh checked out the next would-be victim Ms. Becknell 39yrs old, Covid-57 diagnosed.

Bart slides on some blue gloves, bites his lower lip takes the palm of his left hand, and runs it down from the top of his forehead past his pronounced chin morphing into a sad empathetic Nurse. Bart's act was practiced… his other mask evolves into what the family wanted to see; his eyes could be called compassionate the pain for his customers was validly espoused. Glad they hadn't X-Ray vision and could see beyond his masks lol… the husband was shaken, his eyes Red with pain. The two children, both preteens, a perfect mixture of boy-girl, looked over her Bio personal facts that only Bart kept, she was like Scum, thoughtless evil, a scourge of her profession. Uh, well damn, someone had to do it. She was an AUSA, a lying and conniving manipulative bitch, a Federal Prosecutor. The worse of, the worse she'd get her convictions, even if she wronged so many with deceitful coercion destroying families without remorse. Now it was her turn. 🦅   But hey, there was evil that needed to be stopped, vicious, violent criminals, not passive marijuana growers, that she cannibalized. 🌙

The husband, the same filthy profession, what a match! The guy saw his name tag and acknowledged, "Mr. Sampson, how's my wife? Will she recover and pull through? She's a strong woman?" His agonizing expression matched their children,…"It's a good sign she's not on a ventilator, right? Where's the Doctor she was supposed to meet us here?" the children had their paws out, touching Mommy.

Bart felt it was a touching display of emotions, pure human if he cared… that is, the orders from above his chain of command don't ever give false hope empathy based with synonymous words and phrases. 'Should I tell Mr. Becknell that we were out of ventilators. They were all in use on this floor and the other seven floors that were flooded with dying patients.

Sure, they were supposed to get another crate full today, but he better not tell the truth self-preservation meant following proper protocol. "Your wife is stable, fighting the virus stronger than most. I expect her to be one of the few blessed to survive Covid-57. I don't want to provide you with unwarranted hope. Let me check on where the Doctors are at?" "Why does it seem she's having difficulty breathing, wheezing, and struggling for air?..." "Hold on, I'll page the Doctor, but yes, you are correct her not being intubated or on a ventilator is a net positive!"

Bart grinned broadly and pivoted away.... Omigod, the tag... it slips off the clipboard. Omg, I silently react, watching it, oh shit.... fluttering, landing right on the husband's shoe. Lightning quick, the guy picks it up and holds it up before his... "What's this, huh?" Damn, I was stuck shit fit, dammit should I say, duh what's it look like blushing at my stupidity. 'Uh, it's your fricken wife's last piece of jewelry, a Toe Ring' uhhhh, no, that wouldn't be good. <u>Ash, how to recover the dude reaches out his paws aggressively, grabbing my shirt. "Is this what I think it is... is this real are you condemning my wife to death...?"</u> Now the guy had switched gears, still clutching my Nurse's uniform, and started screaming... other Nurses and a Doctor came running, just what I couldn't afford. The irate man was distraught, with anger spewing dribble from his lips. Any second, he'd be swinging fists at my chiseled, handsome jawline.

I went slack, not attempting to defend myself or to grab his clenching tightening grip on my shirt, nearly strangling me "unh, sir, I'm sorry, it's my fault I just filled out Toe tags ahead of time...." "What's going on here?..." shouts Doctor MacGyver. Suddenly I was surrounded by backup. My team had arrived, and the husband, AUSA, unclenched me and released me with a huge sigh.... my switchblade knife slowly tucked back away. Almost!

'Daddy, what's wrong?' asked his daughter. 'Yeah, dad is mom going to be ok?' questioned her brother. 'Yes, said their father'... as Doctor MacGyver reached out to tug on his sleeve.

"Let's talk in private… it is better," the angry, distraught father bellowed. "I'll be right back stay with your mother!"

I am the odd guy out following my advocate doctor and the brutal husband. We find an alcove over by the Nurse's station. The husband held up the toe tag, saying… "What's this about Doctor?" pointing damningly towards me. Doctor MacGyver looks directly at me… with two other nurses joining in, I knew it looked like I was being insensitive, but I had to escape this confrontation. I must save face; I'd already been written up twice in the last three months and couldn't afford a 3rd write-up… which meant a 2-week suspension. Therefore digging deep with true conviction, I'd use the human way… 'Pass the Buck' strategy.

I stepped forward into the middle of the fire and apologized to Mr. Becknell, scanning my colleagues, saying, "when I arrived this morning, bed 13, uhm, slot thirteen was filled like every other one on this floor and at our hospital with Covid-57 patients. The nurse before me didn't do her job. I'm sorry, but I hate to throw Nurse Spacy under the proverbial bus, but her patient Ms. Gil had expired. All of Ms. Gil's attached monitors… uh, her vitals were turned off; therefore, it was a foregone conclusion that she'd expired. Nurse Spacy was well aware of the woman passing. I quickly inputted the information and filled out the toe ring for her to be taken to the morgue. It's been a trauma-filled morning, and no, I'm making zero excuses; orderlies came up and rolled Ms. Gil out. Not 15 minutes passed, and bed #13 was occupied again; meanwhile, I was attending to my other fourteen patients. Another three had succumbed to the new variant. I was frantically trying to bring down some help from the 8th floor, at least another LPN calling for all hands-on deck because the machines started goin bonkers. Ughhhh, I yelled into the intercom again that I needed help from anyone that was available. Please come to floor seven on the East wing. The alarms were wailing, and two of my other patients needed immediate attention. I tried to multi-task when my newest patient in #13 had gone into Cardiac Arrest, dying, so I'm facing four more deaths. frankly, I was losing it, so I started filling out the toe tags, distraught and overwhelmed…. here look!" I reached into my top pocket, pulling out another five toe tags.

One of my gullible colleagues, a cute RN, put her hand on my shoulder. The other bowed her rotating head. The Doctor was blank-faced. I had them backpedaling momentum on my side, so I piled it on…. "Finally, some help arrived. I started in a zombie trance filling out toe tags for the expired not yet getting to our computer banks network software system to input cause of death time. You know all the prerequisites while working on the tags. Our staff had pulled the gurney out of 13 and, unbeknownst to me, had moved and hooked up this gentleman's wife, Ms. Becknell."

I stared into the now gullible four faces guessing the prominent expression per average was confusion gawking at me. I inhaled a large breath; no one spoke, so I did…. "I'd finished with our deceased patients when several call buttons flashed and rang. I went immediately to attend to my patients, not realizing they'd already removed the expired patient that was in slot 13, walking by in a hurry. I grabbed her clipboard and filled out a toe tag, not recognizing there was another patient in the deceased place… my bad, my fault. I'm so sorry!" I heaved up a crying moan and tried to shake despondently, covering my grinning face in my palms and bending down as if I was going to fall.

I held my breath fla—A what a performance even the husband, guiltily ashamed, shook his noggin and bowed his head Doctor MacGyver then reached out, "Nurse Sampson, why don't you take a 15-minute break? We will handle your workload and floor and catch you up!"

Trying but failing to wet my eyes, I blinked excessively, shrinking my tail between my legs, metaphorically wagging ass. I sauntered away sadly… recused. Under my mask, cheeks cramping, dimples flexed… Yep!

Maddi

I was a mess, determined to shower and bathe, but I couldn't very well climb out of the window and take my keys and go inside my home next door for something out of my wardrobe that was neatly displayed in my walk-in closet. I'd be caught for sure by either the boobytraps set up by the military or the Neighborhood watchers. Wobbly, I stood up noticing throw-up ah vomit by Bart's door, not recalling when or if I did so. My mouth had the distinct sour, acidic taste of barfing. It had to be me. I took some worn clothes that were strewn across the floor, trying to wipe the mess up. Tossing the soiled clothes in his hamper, making a mental note to get a wet towel from the bathroom and do a better job. In the time that I'd been here, I'd gone through all the clothes that I had brought in my backpack several times… lucky that Marge washed regularly. I decided, for a change, to put on one of Bart's t-shirts and maybe find a pair of shorts that I could tighten around my waist. I made my way to Bart's drawers looking for something to wear, not much that would fit me. Bart was much larger than I was, although I did find a sweatshirt T-shirt with U-Prep Highschool's logo. I'd have to re-wear my bra. I checked each drawer for any shirts that would fit better. I scavenged for a smaller pair of shorts, happy to find a 34-36 that would work with me pulling the drawstrings tight. Still nauseated, I tittered back, losing my balance grabbed the desk drawers, which couldn't stop my momentum and only slowed the gravitational pull downward, and I hit the carpeted ground. Luckily my head slammed on the side of the bed.

My body spasms like a severe spinal tap… stabbing and crushing my skull. I flopped like a fish on a boiling hot boat deck… to my bruised knees. I tried to push myself up while vomiting some more… angrily; I kicked the useless drawer and puked again. Whoa, stinky smells emitting from way, deep in my bowels. I laid there for who knows how long... but when I came out of the funk, somehow, I felt better. I can't explain it uhm; maybe my body was regurgitating poisons. After downing bottles of leftover water and sitting against Bart's bed, trying to focus, my head seemed to clear the cobwebs somewhat.

My brain seemed to be in gear for the first time in a while, not in reverse or neutral. I could think rationally for the first time since I'd been locked in this room. I took Bart's shirt off... which was a mid-dress on me, and his shorts in one hand and wiped the barf up. In the other hand, I was multi-tasking towards the door. It wasn't locked mommy Bart forgot to lock it and cracked it open none of the pets were there. I listened to a movie or show blasting loudly, which had to be an old rerun of the Simpsons. Bathroom-bound, it was empty. Thankfully, I locked the door and emptied my pent-up bowels, happy that the laxatives were working, flipped the sunlight on the vent fan, and nearly fainted... freakin screamed silently into the sink mirror... who the fk stood in from of me? ME!

Talk about leftovers, like homeless checked to see if all my teeth were intact, thought of a line my ex–Alec would say, then snapped no, it didn't apply, pulled the drapes back, it was the same bathtub we had next door in my family home. I turned the faucet on hot inside the same identical bathroom that I'd grown up with. Trying to get that inappropriate popular saying off my scaly tongue, 'rode hard put away wet,' there, I said it okay.

Was slightly lucky despite possible repercussions. I found under the sink a new toothbrush that I confiscated as my own, wondering to myself, when was the last time I brushed my teeth? I gargled and then took the toothbrush again over my teeth, this time more confidently and appropriately. Despite my gums bleeding, I was no question feeling much better, I showered off. I was pleasantly surprised by seeing a good selection of body wash shampoos and soapy sponges. I plugged the tub after the initial rinse and sat down, oh my, it felt so damn great. Aah closed my eyes must have extricated the pills with vomiting and didn't feel the effects as much. Even the migraine headache had relented, and aches throughout my body were less… lol except for when I'd fallen in Bart's room. I no longer felt I had a fever. Maybe I had beaten Covid-57, or could it have been just a horrible flu? Ugh, no, Bart and I tested positive for Covid. I still had a seriously stuffed nose, and my sinuses and ears hurt, but it did seem I was in healing mode.

I dozed off… awakened to cold water, reheated, and laid back down enjoying the new steam 'knock, Knock' "Maddi, are you okay?" 'Oh, crap.' "Yes, Mrs. Sampson, I'll be out in a few minutes." That was the extent of our conversation. I waited for a few minutes, then struggled up. I must say, as I wiped the residual steam from the mirror, I felt 1,000% better. I definitely was on the road to recovery. At least I could see the onramp sign to survival. After all, Covid-57 wasn't running at a 100% mortality rate with this mutated virus. The last numbers reported were that 79% of people died in less than four days or 91 hours, and hell, I was way past that… in the first 48 hours like that show many went belly-up. It had been many days since Bart had confirmed I had the killer Covid variant.

In the bathroom cabinet, I took two towels, wrapped my hair, another for my body, and a wash rag for cleaning up my mess in Bart's room peeked out the door no one, odd I knew there must be four other people in here somewhere still curfew out there on the streets the only ones in the family that had permission to leave was Yellow tattooed Bart and his mother who worked as a manager at a fast-food joint.

Back in my sanctuary flipped the lights on, opened the shades, and pulled back the curtains stubbing my baby toe on the darn drawer lying on the worn carpet that had fallen out when I reached out to save my fall earlier. I bent over to ugh… Wtf is that on the rug underneath where the drawer slid in? It looked like some books; ahh stretched my arm in ohmy three journals. Whoa, good hiding place if I hadn't fallen and accidentally pulled the dresser drawers almost on top of me? The bottom drawer had come entirely out; otherwise never would have seen what was underneath it, sitting neatly on the carpet in the left corner stacked tightly. I carefully took one out. It was latched closed with a brass lock fitting like a jewelry box on the front cover, it read.

'Bart Sampson, 10 to 15 years old, the next was the same style except the latch was worn out. Bart Sampson, 15 to 20 years old, both were 6 X 9-inch varieties. At the bottom was the last of Bart's journals or diaries. It was a 7.5 X 9.75 composition journal. Bart's Black Book was written in the title line, which was Black with Silver speckles. Bart had a girl's Pink scrunchie wrapping around it. Age 20 to current... times, with a smiley face.

Wow, now it's up to my conscience and integrity and nosey self. The battle was on. Should I read it, would you? Tempted like the cookie in the jar, one more freakin potato chip, one more drink, kiss, or breath of air... this was way wrong. It's Bart's personal thoughts like, could I betray him? Heck, my morality's sense of right and wrong, it's not even good to think about it ... betraying him was wrong. What if it were my Diary? How would I feel? Wasn't it "Do onto others as you'd like done to you?" I started guiltily, begrudgingly inching down the Pink scrunchie feeling like I was pulling underwear off a naked Dead body. I mean, this was none of my business. He would be pissed to the max. Reluctantly the scrunchie sprung off like a rubber band.

My paws are on the cover of his Diary. Do I pass the restricted virgin zone? Is this like being violated? Your mother finds your love journal, uhhhh.... but didn't he violate my body and ravage it while I was unconscious? Trying my best to leverage a reasonable argument.... ugh, I opened it an inch. Wait, stop all these warning signs converged sirens, trains whistles, air raids, horns honking pros/cons. Could you look into his eyes after reading his most profound thoughts, feelings, and insecurities damnit 'Curiosity killed the Cat, uh, but I'm Maddi and not a Cat.

For Christ's sake, my inner self started to dare me. Are you afraid? Goading me into this immoral, corrupt distrustful deceitful form of betrayal… I fought mentally and spiritually to justify this depraved act, almost sweating, then decided I'd suffered enough and mulled over the Pros/Cons once more… I'd weighed it all sufficiently, bit my inner cheek, shook my head, and paused.

I think if I were writing and you were reading, you'd assume that Maddi wouldn't have wasted this much of our time to not open the damn diary wrong knock, Knock. "Hey, Maddi, are you decent?" I dropped the diary, panic-stricken, and yelped out louder than normal, "I'm naked; don't come in"… quickly. I placed the journals back where they were, snatched up the drawer, and couldn't find the grooves finally did and carefully slid them in. I hopped close to the door and opened it a crack. "I'm sorry….." I lean out with Bart's shirt on his boxer shorts hanging so weirdly with a pocket in the front for easy access to my clit. I supposed just joking. Yep, I was in a creepy mood.

"Maddi, it's 1:35 pm. All our cell phones should work with the internet and our computers, but my phone remains busy with Facebook, and not any of my personal sites are coming up on my iPad. Homer's phone isn't working either uh, none of ours are up. Can you check yours? We have Androids; you and Bart have Apple iPhones, right?" "Yes, wow, that's exciting. Let me check." I ducked out of the way, and Marge rudely pushed the door wide open "Oh my, you have no clothes, darling. I can rewash your clothes…" she laughed, covering her mouth "you're in Barts boxers…" I think… don't care about anything except my phone R.U. Kidding me, I shout, "that's right, it's July 23rd. Wow!" I unplug and power up the iPhone jumping up and down its on–it powers up. "OmLord … my lifeline truth phone… yes!" 🌸

Staring unbelievably at the screen, "oh hell yes, I have 1,321 texts. No shit, but it is locked up. Let me reboot, Marge, dammit. I have a ton of Social Media hits and messages from people outside of Shasta County. This is the best surprise oh…..." Then again, my phone locked back up, rebooted/ locked down, and all the while, Marge just stood there doing the same with her Android. She squinted her eyes looking me up and down… "I can't believe you're in Bart's underwear!" "Uah, sure am, Mrs. Sampson tried a pair of his shorts, but the drawstring broke. At least I can pull these up way past my belly button." "I betcha that Lisa's clothes will fit you. Maggie's are going to be too small, let me check for you; meanwhile, undo the bed sheets and covers. I see vomit on them. Maddi, open the windows and let some fresh air in here… it stinks!" "Yes, ma'am, I will, thank you….." wow, I forgot that she was always bossy, but hey, I could use some clothes for sure. Sadly felt a looming loss; my iPhone would power up and load my programs. It was like a prick tease, then phase out!

Despite that fact, at least the icons and apps that were now active on my phone went into my text and tried to input a voice text nope, then typed in a group text to Ben, Cat, Ali, and Cody also added my parents and family members "hey guys I'm held up at Barts house next door to my place sick for days I hope ur safe luv yuh guys Maddi 🌸.

Pressed send tap fizzled out, locked up again, and tried futilely to reboot…. ugh, Nada. 🌫️

I was careful not to come into plain view of the snoopy neighbor's binoculars…. which could be my downfall. I opened wide both of Bart's windows and partially closed the curtains so I could anonymously move about the room. Interestingly enough, I was feeling better way better. All the Covid-57 symptoms were lessened, breathing was definitely impaired, and the pressure in my nasal cavities was still enormous. But I had thought no doubt the worst was over. My body aches and shifting migraine like my head was going to explode had been reduced felt like I was recovering from a massive hangover and needed to rehydrate.

There I stood out of view, breathing in the fresh warm air iPhone stuck in my left palm like the good ole days, an added appendage remembered almost funny in one instant and pathetic in the other… hell I'd only been without a cellphone to use for maybe 19 days since I was twelve years old. That's when my parents grounded me, and hey, that was in my entire life. I was blessed to have a cell phone just before I had started Junior High School, and my cell phone was always near me…like a lifeline. Yep, totally addicted; no excuses, none applied.

A brain fart… uhm, mine circled back cautionary apprehensive feelings of dread as if a major flaw were my undoing, pushed this shadow away, hopefully trying to power up my cell… battery blinked now dead crap needed to charge it been like ten days since, but didn't I just unplug it? Anxiety debilitated my soul, what the hell was up… felt as if an ominous dark cloud of despair hovered over me and was going to annihilate me. Intuition back working internally functioning at three-quarters power instinctually felt danger bad omens, fear hackles raised up inside my mind, had an undaunting compulsion to bust out the window and run away as fast as I could. Uncomprehending this nervous energy like I was being cannibalized within awful terror engulfed me with paranoia, and my intestines cramped from fear like I was going to be attacked and gutted, um, disemboweled. What was it? …what's wrong? My mind was communicating with me… yet I was flummoxed, weary, for I couldn't relate?

Then at the threshold of the door, Marge stood, her hands held out to me… "here's a couple of tops to choose from, some sweatpants, socks, and underwear… Lisa said. No worries about getting them back to her. Covid has us all in fear." Marge placed the clothes on the stripped bed, wearing gloves and an overlarge mask. "It's going to be a hot one out there already 101 degrees. Go ahead and shut the windows. The room smells better, and the Air Conditioner is blowing. No use wasting energy!" I thought, all right, closing the windows down, knowing that people were using precautionary measures when it came to this new variant that was airborne. Even touching something of a person who was infected could transfer the virus. I looked at Bart's warning sign on the outer door, thinking they should disinfect the bathroom.

I bounced past the filters in my mind, Walla running on about five cylinders of eight. It strangled, ahh, stifled me. I sent a failed text, but what if it's held in cyberspace in stall mode and sent once the systems are back running optimally? Then a negative epiphany struck me, lopsided I'd screwed up. The Police, without question, monitored all my friend's phones and my iPhone. I just gave them my location am I being paranoid freaky another look at my iPhone still charging with a power bar signal and no connections. So they couldn't trace my whereabouts.

Ms. Sampson was gathering the bedding "thanks for the clothes; tell Lisa I appreciate it, please." She nodded with a peculiar stare, then walked out, "I'm going to get dressed...." I closed the door on her heels and stripped off Bart's clothes and put on a stereotypical girly outfit looking much better.... let my hair hang dry, put on socks and my running tennis shoes, pulled a brush from my purse along with my makeup bag, time to appear human on Barts stool in from of a dresser a vanity mirror brushing the knots away, time to make decisions I was feeling well enough to get the hell out of this room.

I pulled my shoulder-length hair into a ponytail, took a hair tie colored purple from my purse, and freeze.... brain freeze, Pink scrunchie spun like a top, oh fk the scrunchie that rubber-banded off of Bart's Diary, where was it? I scrambled around the bed on my knees, pulled out the bottom drawer again, and stuck my head inside, not there... Oh, no way! Fright with a tinge of terror struck me, my wet ponytail slapped my back. My mind was in a tizzy. Omg, where could it be disheveled until I wasn't... lol. Sure, the Pink scrunchie is in the washing machine with the sheets and covers and pillowcases... where else could it be? I exited stage right, knowing the house was a replica of mine. Beelined to the laundry room, passing by the open kitchen, frightening Maggie... Woe! shrieked out... "You're sick, Maddi; stay away from me. Get back in Bart's room; you're not supposed to be out...." Her ghost-like stare was unsettling.

No rebuttal, nope I was the Black Plague, purge death walking the paranoia justified still soldiered on lifted the prehistoric washing machines lid whirling around the sudsy hot water-flash of dark Pink... fished out the soaking wet scrunchie squeezing it best I could. Dammit wadded it up in my hand and vacated at once. Now I was in need of a hair dryer I didn't have enough time to put it on the hot window seal. Dang, if this weren't such a serious matter, it would almost be funny.

Passing me near the hallway was Homer, whom I shocked. He backed against the wall "what are you doing out here? The bathroom is the only place you're allowed to go...." I gripped the scrunchie too tight, and water dripped from my right-hand Homer was scary. "Bart is on his way, taking a lunch break from the hospital. He should be here any minute; please, Maddi, get back in his room." "Thanks, Mr. Sampson..." not the words I wanted to expound to him.

Back in my prison cell, my phone was completely charged with full bars signal strength to the max, but strangely my Apps were frozen on the positive I had full bars and a strong signal the cellphone towers were back functioning, right? Again after rebooting, the screen froze up, frustrated plugged in next to the large mirror was a hairdryer took the scrunchie out, flipped the switch to hot, and wedged it against a pillow for I couldn't hold it when it got too hot... A honking sound was heard... arched

my chin up, peering out the window. Bart was in the driveway
'Trouble Cometh!'

-68-

<u>Bethel Church.</u>

<u>Ben sat his elbows on a desk, recalling what had occurred about Two Weeks prior, replaying the excitement at finding their best friends in the basement of Bethel Church, floor B-3. Where Wanda, Venus, Don, and Jen stood watching Cody and Ali coming to life impatiently annoyed were Cat and me. The situation quickly got out of hand. Cody was adamantly against joining Bethel or having anything to do with the Church. He vehemently argued that we must leave Bethel immediately and call for another meeting of their group of protagonists. But things have changed since his awakening literally Two Weeks ago.</u>

In the last meeting only this afternoon, with Wanda and a group of the leaders at Bethel, Ben declared aloud to all, 'we need to get in touch with our leaders and arrange another conference. Instead of losing members of our group, we should be adding to the resistance. I don't care that the military has labeled us rebels, we can only communicate word by mouth unless we get to our designated places where we exchange notes and information. If Father Rite promises security, we'd appreciate using the Turtle Bay Convention Center, he did offer it earlier Cat and I, with Cody and Ali, need to get to our swapping note-hiding places by this evening. We can then make the meeting for tomorrow night....'

How time had passed without a single conference or gathering of our young resistant group stuck at the church, the whole county had turned into a war zone.... Our last meeting was on the 9th of

July. Today the 23rd of July, is the day the authorities promised to reactivate all phone towers and internet hookups. ✳

Cat and Ben's reunion with Cody and Ali.

Ben lays his head down on his palms upon a desk and drifts back some 13 days ago to when Cat and he had been escorted to the basement with the Bethelites. There they discovered Ali and Cody deathlike on stretchers with Dan and Jon dressed as soldiers…. how much had changed? Boom, Ben suddenly morphed back into that time frame… good and intense memories.

Cat and Ben with Wanda in one of the basements at Bethel, 13 days previous.

Cat had confidently said, "we will be prepared to fight to our last drop of blood…." Wanda interrupts, "the dynamics are changing. You or we must evolve within this new paradigm also…." Cat frowns. "Wanda, please spit it out. Get to the point, you people seem always to be less than forthright, always talking in circles," as Cody moans awake.

Flustered watching the Medics work on her friends, "I mean, this is frustrating all this secret agent stuff…." Wanda scowls "to the point, huh, well as you requested, uhm, Bethel is the only true force that opposes the military, and the FOE 'forces of evil' we're the only alternative to subservientness and kowtowing unh, groveling on your knees. We will not allow nor condone your group of youngsters to supplant and undermine us to obliterate all that we have accomplished and all we plan for the future. You will play by our rules and mandates, or you're on your own either way… Bethel will survive!" Automatically even the Medics mimed making the sign of the cross like Hallelujah!

Cat grabs Ben's arm a stare-off standing next to their friend's stretchers "what are the rules we must abide by?" asks Ben. "My friends, the rules are elementary, very basic, common sense oriented," relayed Venus without expressive features. "First, accept the fact and acknowledge that we at Bethel are calling the shots, you cannot jeopardize what our objectives are. No one except your initial leadership needs to know that Bethel is the protagonist. You will need to sign an NDA contract amongst many other restrictive clauses that I'm working on..." Venus pauses for the obvious retorts knowing they were forthcoming, and Ben obliges, "what's an NDA?..." "It's a nondisclosure agreement contract. Before I continue, I will need each of you to agree to this compulsory stipulation?" Cat finds Ben's eyes... a nod of conformity following a firm resounding, "Yes, we will sign; please go on Venus."

Venus stoically moves on deliberately "next, all attending parties to any of our conferences have been disallowed any cellphones or any type of recordings. Here at Bethel, our ceremonies and performances are a private matter, we control all reproductions and promotions of our gifted spiritual gatherings. There will not be any miscellaneous varieties of communications unless there in-house... why? We're already risking our sovereignty if Major Bryan and the Occupiers locate our ways of communicating... which I can assure you they're working and analyzing this as we're speaking. Bethel cannot afford this intrusion... Major Bryan is flummoxed as to why the cameras were stifled by our blocking devices when Father Rite and Brother Jeremy had enabled both of you and Charlie to escape their clutches from our confection shop at the Sundial Bridge. We are afraid that they may be able to trace you to our Turtle Bay Exploratorium!" "We agree with that, Venus certainly, that should go without saying, but yes, we concur," relayed Cat. Venus doesn't miss a beat "thirdly, and most importantly, all the tattooed uhm vaccinated Yellows, Blues, or Red Dots will allow our Bethelites to administer a deactivating device to their tattoos…. Before making the trip to our Turtle Bay conference hall, the tattooed will agree to be scrutinized, or they will not be allowed to join us. Each will need to have the installed tracking GPS chip that is under their skin disabled by one of our hand-held lasers. They cannot be tracked to our properties!"

Ali moves, and Cody coughs. They seem to be re-emerging back to conscious states of being. Ben exclaims, "Venus, how do you propose to do that? we will have to round all the participants up for a pre-gathering to have their GPS disabled!" Cat elbows to the forefront. "Why not use Wayne's parent's places of employment like Simpson College or Shasta College, maybe borrow their auditoriums…." "I guess that could work," adds Ben, "it has to," agrees Wanda "that's not a bad idea."

Venus looks down at Cody, who is blinking awake, Venus says, "great, without any enthusiasm. Oh, lastly and imperatively, a deal breaker is you….." Exploding upward, Jack in the Boxed-up, Cody screamed out, arms gesticulating wide-eyed and blanched skin. "What?" Cat falls instantly towards him, as does Ben. "Relax, bro, your safe," he says… she hugs him "it's all right…." Dan passes her a bottle of water, "here, drink some water, Cody." Cody looked bewildered in a manner of shock, barely holding his head up… he swallowed some water and sank back down on the cot, bewildered. The last thing Cody remembered was that he was shot by the two soldiers standing in front of him.

Venus is undeterred right back where she was before the interruption, her robotic monologue droned on, "at Bethel, using a common analogy, we're the General Contractor, your group of youngsters are sub-contractors, we are in charge, all orders must be obeyed to the letter of our laws no deviations any and all decisions are democratically derived and settled upon in design…. at least. We will convene all together and thoroughly hash out any concerns you might have…. weigh the Pros/Cons so we can move in unison together as a cohesive team against tyranny and the tyrants that want to terminate us all! Do you understand this is mandatory, no ifs ands or butts ughhhh, it's a deal breaker!"

Cody edge's himself up, trying to understand what is happening, "no way, guys, what the hell? We aren't going along with their rules. We can't agree with that. I'm not signing anything!" "I'm sorry, brother but your wrong. I feel compelled to do just that we have no choice but to.... unah, things have changed since you were knocked out in this...." "How long have I been out? L..." he stammers, seeing Ali next to him, covered mostly in a sheet "shit, I was darted, huh, whoa." He rotated his neck and saw Jon and Dan, "you guys fk, I tried to kill you OmGod!"

Wanda bowed. "God is mighty; God is all... God was looking over you. Your safe now give yourself onto the Lord I...." "What's this preaching? Where am L...?" came a raspy, wickedly dry delivery with a follow-up, "Cody, you guys, what's happening?" another water bottle was given out. Ali... sucks it down. Ben lends a comforting hand to his pal's forehead. "Cat and I will try to explain most of what's going on since you've been out of it. Suffice it to say Bethel saved both of you from being captured by the military, so were pun intended 'Blessed' to have them on our side!"

Cody was nearly cognizant... rebooting internal systems in recovery approach and finally was able to sit up, swinging his feet out and down to the concrete floor. Looking at his friends and then swaying his head about "where are we?" "We're in the basement at the Bethel Church...." "You gotta be kidding me, Cat... what why Bethel it's a sham, scam witches and goblins talking in tongues dancing around fire pits, roasting marshmallows like goons laying on hands hell they think they can bring back the dead fk guys they're a bunch of holy rollers they do Sacrifices man oh man ain't nothin legit about these Hocus Pocus practitioners!... Don't you know guys were heathens as far as they're concerned, like infidels? I ain't no believer like the rest of you!"

Dan stepped forward, frowning. "That will be enough expletives, Cody, please no more cuss words. You are intelligent enough not to need filler words...." Cody seemed not to register him and continued pretending that he wasn't interrupted. "Bethel brainwashes the young like us. They use drones to drop pamphlets and brochures all over the County, spreading their scriptures of disease and preaching prophecies of fakeness. It's an ah fricken Cult, Dude!"

Out of nowhere, a stinging slap across his cheek, tenseness/ agitation. No one moved, but all were loaded springs, Dan and Jon were in aggressive poses. The Medic's suddenly looked like predators one wrong blink would cause chaos. Cody rubs his left palm over his stung cheek and slowly pulls his chin up to see who just whacked him, Red blushing anger matching retaliatory eyes, brows furrowed in rage. Venus stood staunch wanting his glare unmoving, waited until he'd focused on her, and calmly mentioned, "Mr. Cody, you're quite alive because Bethel had chosen to risk our sovereignty willingly. You will not continue to disrespect us in our place of worship if you so like we can dispose of you umh set you out on the curb," she wanted to say like Trash but instead said, "pose the four of you on Hilltop Avenue asleep." Instantly noises from all around them in crevices behind pallets RFD's pointed Red Dots fluttered over the four of them "don't move!"

Cat gritted her teeth fk. 'Venus is a serious bitch. I wouldn't want to cross her unemotional demonic persona' thinking, 'how do I defuse this situation?' Slowly like trained performers subtly ever so smoothly, slowly the Bethelites backed away from us... intruders. The Bethelites lowered the Dart machine guns and stood at ease.

Cody's gleaming gaze never recoiled nor wavered. Cody couldn't break the spell of Venus... his heart rate shot up.... fk she was the most beautiful creature he'd ever laid eyes on, even all the models or porn stars that were photoshopped. This girl in the Nath, um, naturally rocked! The spitfire girl was in all White with mesmerizing eyes and plush luscious pouty lips dying to be kissed and explored. Oh my, those ear lobes... suckling sexy sexuality dripped off her pert tasteful nose... penetrating Greenish speckled retinas–pupils stared into his eyes. She was so stunningly gorgeous. Cody could swear she was a living fricken Angel, unh... not mentioning Venus's magnificent Aura hell, Cody had forgotten what was going on... spellbound. Wanda had witnessed the overtly testosterony by other males before almost smirking, 'Boys will be boys,' mused how easy it was to disarm them with a pretty girl. She wondered what it might 'feel like to totally become discombobulated by a visual mirage of physical images and imaginations of seducing desires; she affirmatively nodded. <u>Men disarmed like puppies: that's why we females are the strongest gender and foremost assassins!'</u>

Cody shook his shoulders and grumbled, "a side effect, possibly I don't feel well; tell me again, what's your name?" pointing at Venus. Wanda had had enough takes the lead "now that Venus has reduced your macho impudence, Cody. I'm afraid you haven't been properly introduced if you will permit me to do so." Still, Cody couldn't demagnetize from Venus, fantasies bouncing in and out man, what would she look like naked feel like yum. I'd eat that girl up, I would...." Demonstratively Wanda effusively elucidated once more, "Cody, I'm over here," snapping her fingers! Bam, like Bewitched, he breaks out of his self-imposed stupor. "Yes, uhhhh yum yeah, I'm here! Sorry, this medication, those darts, ahh."

The temperature cooled, and the weapons were no longer in sight. Ali stopped blinking and decided to interrupt with a biological need, "hey, excuse me, everyone, I haven't the foggiest idea about what's goin on but," playing on Cody's words purposely adds, "I'm sort of dizzy and dazed, and definitely confused, but I do have to go pee badly?"

Dan laughs first, then Jon and Wanda display Pumpkin smiles, and Venus pushes her delectable tongue an inch out of her lips, moving slowly from side to side, further entrancing her prey. It seemed the ice had been broken and the semi-standoff waylaid "well, certainly you may use the closest restroom, Dan can you guide our new friend, please." "Of course, Wanda," Ali demonstrates a wobble of uncertainty, his balance still affected by the dart's juice; Dan grasped him, and off they went.

Before they got a few yards away, Wanda said, "Ali, Cody, obviously Dan and Jon are the saviors that got you out of the mess you were in; now your safe. I'm Wanda, and the woman in White is named Venus...." Cody mutters, "perfect." Ben points, rotating his arm and finger in a circle "and who are these folks with all the rifles." "Oh, there Bethelites that are only here to ensure a peaceful resolution. Let us leave you four alone to discuss your options; remember, no pressure from us. You four can leave right now, as I've stated, we'll drop you off, or you can play by our rules...."

<u>**Ben blinks awake and reemerges back in the present time.**</u>

Ben raises his head up from the desk at the touch of his girl, "hey there, why don't you lay down, honey? Your moving, babe...." He rotated his head up.... "Heck, I was just replaying the scene in the basement days ago, wow, that got intense for a second what time is the ceremony in the chapel? A knock at their door, it was Wanda "good afternoon Benjamin, Catrina, please gather your friends and join us in the chapel. It's so nice that you all will attend the Wake."

Dan and Jon were in the hallway, and Venus stepped up from behind Wanda. "Father Rite, Elder Jeremy, and the Officers of our Church, along with some of our Prophets, will ooh, God willing, bring the four members of our congregation who risked their own flesh and blood to save your lives when, we will be...." "ah, excuse me," Ben said, "I uh we will forever be grateful to them they did sacrifice their lives for Cat and me… we wouldn't miss the 'Wake' for Tim, Kelly Trudy, and Patti." Cat shows respect for them bowing her head adding "we were fond of them they were precious we became instant friends they died too young were so sorry <u>it's true only the good die young</u>." Cody, perplexed, sat on the couch alongside Ali inside Ben's and Cat's suite. Cody said, "I must confess I didn't care for those Bethelites when I met them at the Mary Lake Conference, but I'm genuinely sorry. I know they were killed by the military chmy that's so sad!"

Venus walked deliberately into the room and stood in front of the couch, staring at Cody… raising her palms up at breast level. "We must rejoice and express joy and be glad for Tim, Trudy, Kelly, and Patti. They are special spirits who will return to us from Heaven from human death, they will return to complete their missions on Mother Earth this evening. There will be a re-awakening!" She leaned forward, finding Cody's gawking stare explicitly closing within inches of his face staring at him not mockingly but confidently. "We will be raising the dead this evening, God willing… Amen" Amen, then Amen was heard from all directions, echoing even in the nearest hallway. Dan harkened the sacred word with Jen at his side. Amens solemnly espoused.

Cody couldn't hide his shock and shut his mouth. Ali was lost, and Ben and Cat were bewildered watching Wanda close the door, and they were left alone… Venus peeps her head in quickly with the last words… "If you want to attend the ceremony, a pew is reserved for the four of you. The ceremony starts in about 55 minutes seeya there!" Her Angelic White glow disappears, and they're left alone.

<u>Major Bryan and Colonel Ruiz</u>

Sergeant Tom Barton decided he had to play the Wolf in a disguised uniform… He was speaking with Major Bryan. "They are having a real shindig at Bethel this evening for the four freaks that committed suicide rather than face interrogation and give up the Rebel group's leaders uhm, you won't believe it, they're," he snickers lol. "Going to be raising the dead...." Sergeant Barton leans down, looking at his clipboard. "Yes, we have proof that Ben and Cat were with a young boy at 'Sunshine Sweet Goodness,' a Bethel bakery. Instead of being debriefed, ahhhh, before getting interrogated, they dropped some suicide pills...." "Yeah, Sergeant Barton, tell me something I don't know...." "Sorry, Sir, ugh, well, Major, that's what Father Rite said." "Sergeant, I can't believe the gall of Father Rite to invite me to his raising the dead séance. Geez, please.... I'm not going to waste my time going to one of their seances, umh, rituals of raising the dead don't you remember years back in 2019 when the Bethelites were determined to bring that sweet innocent girl back to life... huh? How'd that work out for them? Please!"

"Yes sir, Major, your correct...." What Sergeant Tom Barton could never divulge to the Major was that he was a staunch and steadfast believer in Bethel's Church Ministry and beliefs. He and Lieutenant Sloan had given Father Rite a forewarning of the military occupation in Shasta County. Indeed his new wife, LT Sloan, and he.... would be standing in front of a firing squad if Colonel Ruiz or Major Bryan knew that information... nope, he didn't dare counter or argue with Major Bryan. Several times he had in the past tried to defend Bethel... nah, but that didn't work out well. Barton was chastised to the hilt. Barton had relatives that attended The Bethel Ministries one of his cousins who had been unlucky in love joined Bethel's single group and promptly found her 'Soul Mate' and what's it been 13 years now. Five children later that joined in on Young Saints Summer Camps, yes Bethel was about Jesus Dinners, and when he'd last attended an 'Abounding Hope & Joy Conference, Barton had left a changed man for good. What Major Bryan also was unaware of... was that his new bride, Lieutenant Sloan's parents, were deeply involved with Bethel, not only with participation in many of their noteworthy events but gave Tithing every month. Barton and his wife, Lieutenant Sloan, also donated to the church's causes. They would remarry at Bethel and be Baptized after the military occupation was over, and Father Rite promised them a wonderful ceremony.... Yes, my wife and I would try and run interference and do our best to keep the gentle, kind folks at Bethel breathing unhampered."

Bryan had way too much on his plate already. "Sarg, why don't you attend the ceremony and keep me posted on the show? I've heard it's a real extravaganza; they go all out, but afterward, you make sure and alert ole Father Rite for him to make time for my next visit. We will then pin down their illegal communications and possibly finally surround the Church's grounds and take them all to Iron Mountain or, better yet, my CTS trailers" "Yes, Sir, I will do so and keep you abreast I don't think I can record it but will try hey what are you talking about CTS trailers?" "Never you mind, Sarg, soon enough.... C.O.S. change of subject, Barton, before you go to Bethel, I have pressing issues to deal with. Bring our finest communications experts here to my office, the ones that graduated at the top of their classes at MIT. I hear the couple are technology wizards uhhh, what're their names?..." "Umh, you mean the twins Private Hughes the brother and sister team ah Savanah and Jordan, I believe...." "Yes, get them here on the double!" "Okay, Sir, I'm on it." Barton was still thinking about what the Major meant about Bethel and his CTS trailers, 'what was that about?'

Major Richey Bryan's CTS innovation becomes a reality.

Bryan could barely keep his mind straight, enjoying and reveling at his genius.... giddy with anticipatory tingles throughout his body, the Semi-Trucks the 18 wheelers had entered Shasta County from all thoroughfares he'd positioned some of them at the fairgrounds off of Hwy 273 and the Civic Center with the majority of the truck and trailers parked on the runways at Redding Airport he also took advantage of the Executive Airport off of Placer Street and the vacant mall lots. Bryan's specially designed trailers were parked and waiting for him. In less than three hours, the show would begin. He had seven of them prepped and ready to go his invention and entrepreneur concepts acronym C.T.S. would be operational, and people in high places would grovel at his knees. Bryan would be like an Emperor this afternoon!

Bryan sent Jimmy Neal, his Private secretary, to ensure all was done according to his planned details…although at this time, more pressing troubles that they'd discovered emanating from several mountain ranges uh areas around the County had to be squelched. How to deal with Colonel Ruiz's problems that ultimately would affect his stature with the W/O and might hurt his advancements up the ladder of succession… ascension, he nodded his head back in his ergonomic chair, kicking his feet out, dropping like dead weight into a power nap.

During nappy time his faithful Secretary had repositioned himself back at his desk and had peered in to see his Major resting. Then the twins stepped into the office. Not having a clue as to why they were there, he stood up. "I'm Private Neal please have a seat for a few minutes the Major is busy… what is it that you want with the Major?" "This is Private Savanah Hughes, and I'm Private Jordan. Sergeant Barton ordered us to get over here on the double… we haven't a clue as to why we're here, hoping you could inform us of that?" Jimmy didn't bother with their annoying play on words, 'get over here on the double,' obviously being identical twins. "Pardon me for a moment, please have a seat… there are some snacks and drinks," gesturing over to an alcove. Jimmy knocks slightly on the Major's door and subtly enters; Bryan was oddly grinning, breathing in a resting pattern. He tapped lightly on his desk, not touching him for the last time he'd awakened him that way, he nearly got knocked out. "Sir... uuuh sir." "What is it? Haven't I told you...." "Uh, Private Hughes in the double are here!" "Oh, why didn't you say so? Bring me a triple expresso and have them wait till I buzz you!" "Of course, Major, but can I ask why they're here?...." "No, you may not now move it!"

<u>Private Savannah and Jordan Hughes.</u>

Minutes passed then the intercom buzzed, "send them in, Jimmy." After introductions, "what do you know about these Shortwave transmissions that have increased 1,000 percent since our arrival Privates?" Jordan spoke first, "yes, Sir, we've found literally dozens of channels and thousands of transmissions, all between 24100 to 25000kHz or operated in the 24.1 to 25MHz frequency range. As you might know, Shortwave radios have been used well before the First World War and have a range of 2 to 3 thousand miles...." "No, I didn't, and that's great Intel... but what's important is I want to know where they're being broadcasted from what base or whatever?" Savannah steps forward. "Colonel Ruiz has had us analyzing the transmissions. Unfortunately, their actually highly sophisticated operators. All the broadcasts are encrypted in number sequences. Major, our Government doesn't want to admit that they exist. They're called <u>'Numbers Stations,'</u> and operating illegally, they transmit from unregistered transmitters, which are hard to locate because of the nature of radio signals. Major 'Number Stations' are Shortwave transmissions normally from Foreign Intelligence Agencies to spies in the field... of foreign countries. They carry encrypted messages in arranged groups of numbers and letters using either automated voice or digital mode. Some even use Morse code!"

A long pause "what's the chance of us locating the Rebels who are using this form of communication?....." Jordan's countenance betrayed him "uuuh, Major, we've been working on this for now over a week and are no closer than when we started. The system may be antiquated and archaic in nature, but it is foolproof. Even our most sophisticated computer algorithms can't break the codes a site online to familiarize yourself with the nuances of Shortwave Number Stations is 'PRIYOM.ORG,' much of what you'll learn is classified and you...." "Listen, I don't give a hoot as to researching this matter. This is part of your expertise. That's why you're here; get me answers. Don't give me any details other than answers.... now get out of here until you have something useful." "Yes, sirs," they salute in unison, gone.

62

From the beginning of Major Bryan's concept... to the fruition of his accomplishment.

Shaking his head, glancing at his Jaeger-LeCoultre wristwatch, ah better get spiffed up. His 'Show and Tell' was in less than two hours. Dwelling back to its infancy, his concept was what consumed the Major's every waking thought. His meetings with dignitaries from Langley to Quantico and the Pentagon right through the front doors of the White House. Everywhere he turned high-ranking Officials in the Government had further invigorated him. The powerbrokers had bought into Bryan's creative visions, um... brain thrust. Bryan was jubilated with pent-up excitement that he'd finally triumphed. It had all come to him in a revelation, a daydream while watching excerpts of documentaries of World War 2. Where the Nazis utilized railroad train cars and had retrofitted them into moving gas chambers. Then his astute, brilliant mind had morphed in time... to New York City. Back in time, when so many citizens were dying of Covid that they had refrigerator trucks and trailers freezing… the corpses.

Amazingly one morning… he woke up enlightened, um, fricken elated, buzzed with adrenalin, and started to work on his first draft, drawing upon his engineering degree from MIT. He was now energized that the ultimate rewards of Billions of dollars and prestige were within his grasp! The fruition of a vision… his Legacy had just rounded the bend… Yep!

The city of Redding and the County of Shasta was chosen to be the model by the W/O because the location was easily cordoned off. An added advantage was discovered once we infiltrated the area, and that was Iron Mountain. The goals set forth were to reduce the population by 75%, and the open acid pit filled with boiling chemicals left inside the crater from decades of mining was perfect. Like an open Volcano… Iron Mountain would leave no bones, the conveyor belts moving the humans, dead or alive, to be vaporized no uh none, not a molecule of DNA would remain. Even with five conveyor belts running nonstop at the last count, we'd only reached 25,137 human eliminations… melted away as of noon today.

In other cities worldwide, it was just not feasible… where could the authorities stuff and hide or dispose of all the dead bodies that were eliminated. Indeed the crematoriums would be stacked and inefficient with no Iron Mountains. Logistically it didn't equate even in this county; unfortunately, because of time constraints… for most of the time was spent and wasted on transporting the human cargo miles and miles out of the way. Heck, if you picked up 15 living bodies in downtown Redding, it would take you three and one-half hours to get them on the belts, and beyond those facts, the bubbling chemicals would kill our soldiers if they accidentally had a malfunction on their spacesuits which had happened more times than he'd like to admit. Nope, metropolitan, and urban areas didn't have…. an Iron Mountain at their disposal. Get the pun, lol disposal. Gosh, he was so damn clever! When it became apparent back in 2020 that Coronavirus was devastating to the world's inhabitants, Covid-19 wasn't going away. Sure, it was evolving into different variants. Delta and Omicron too many names to keep track of… numbers worked better.

The killer virus kept on mutating again and again in 2022 and 2023. The pandemic went underground, yet the devious epidemic had grown legs… killing and ravaging masses of people in other countries, powering up once more to attack North America again. It was like the 'perfect storm' for many of the powermongers who were patiently waiting to pounce. Many commoners didn't know the difference between a pandemic and an epidemic. A pandemic affects large masses of people, typically across our planet, and epidemic falls between the two. It is an outbreak that is actively spreading… this was Covid 37-47 hiding and recharging for its final assault.

What we learned from the initial onset of the pandemic was that necessities became scarce, and shelves in our major Box stores were not stocked… and were empty. From toilet paper to food, our resources became stretched and limited. Essentially, we were running out of supplies and the basics of life's wants and desires. The writing was on all the walls…. it didn't take long for the Government leaders in every country in the world to comprehend what the ending result of this voracious virus could be. It became inevitable…. everyone in power knew it would be impossible to find viability and sustainability for the overpopulated planet. This brought stringent measures forth. We could no longer feed the populace. Therefore, we had to reduce the number of breathing humans…. pretty simple, actually, Cut and Dry. Even with Russia invading Ukraine and the horrific killings and death registered, the numbers of allowable living was far from the W/O's mandates as sickening as the annihilation of Ukraine, unprovoked terror… what we were engaged in would re-write the history books and be omnipresent across planet earth.

<u>The 'World Order' had its inaugural… first mandated meeting.</u>

The conspiracy to take control was agreed upon by the powers to be at the first initial secret meeting back in June of 2021, setting forth the wheels of change. It was the first time the World came together, uuhhh, well, at least the leaders. The W/O conference was an eye-opener, and subsequently, it became a quarterly occurrence, and the next one would be in Major Bryan's hometown of San Diego on Catalina Island. What wasn't disseminated to much of the world's populace, ugh, the one's not in the Need To Know, was that Covid was devouring many more humans than had been divulged. The virus was growing more potent and more virulent every single week that passed… with more death and mayhem. The malicious killer wasn't going to be stopped. Unfortunately, each vaccination was temporary. To obviate the ultimate ending results of the pandemic, it would be prudent to eliminate redundancies ughhhh, unwarranted people, and no reason existed to keep feeding the overbreeding of useless pariahs.

Overwhelmingly the W/O voted on Shasta County being the test area being in between mountain ranges, should be easily isolated with only one Interstate Freeway. Right after Bryan flew out of Geneva, Switzerland, his mind whirled, revolved, and evolved. How the hell could he take advantage of what he knew was imminent and forthcoming? There would be no stopping the reduction of breathing mammals had to admit only to his inner being that the idea first surfaced when New York City faced the fiasco during the initial breakout of Covid-19, where bodies were stacked by the hundreds in the back of 40-foot trailers pulled by Peterbilt's, Kenworth and White Freightliners uhm, diesel trucks. The trailers were refrigerated, essentially morgues on wheels parked on New York Streets. There was no room for the dead in traditional morgues or funeral homes. The cremation centers were stacked with rotting skin and organs, bodies decomposing. It would take weeks for the City to catch up un, so like a necessity, the human mind found alternatives… our resourceful talents proved that we were at the Top of the Food chain… yet the food chain was shrinking!

Major Richie Bryan spent days with manufacturing companies, dealing with patents, and copywriters…. covering all facets of his new innovations. He also visited crematoriums and commercial morgues. His visions were attainable, although it was sort of push that came to shove… trial and error. He had many failures, mainly power source problems, breakers, and too much voltage was needed… prototypes were kept as secret as 'Area 51s' visitors, ugh, Nevada's occupants. Bryan had many a sleepless night, always persevering in determination with discipline. Now there were 57 of his truck and trailers parked in the Redding City Limits. *His Corporation C.T.S. Incorporated. The acronym C.T.S. was for Cremation Trailer Systems!*

Major Bryan was nearly giddy with anticipation, his planned show and tell in place!

Bryan Later that morning, placing one foot in front of the other on the tarmac, walked around the 11 CTS trucks at the Executive Airport, tingles lifting off the nape of his neck ahh sweet, then off to the Redding Convention Centers parking lot where other identical truck-trailers were displayed each useable trailer was 48 feet long with customized height and width wide loads down the highway, 397.77 square feet of useable space inside the trailers, rotating shelves had been built on both sides. Bryan smirked when one of his favorite Officers approached. "So these are the puppies the real deal Major?" "Yes, Private Remy can't say we'll not have other revisions, but as of now, we have yet to discover any flaws!" "Well, Sir, if there as proficient as you've told me, why the heck do you have so many of them in this small city?..." "Private, there's power in numbers here in Shasta. I have 57 of them for the Show and Tell. There are going to be 37 leaders from the largest countries on the planet. They're all here to watch them in action. Besides those individuals, there are too many dignitaries to name. I'm glad each will be wearing badges with their names and countries..." Remy hummed, then chortled, "that explains it. I've seen snobbishness, or I'd refer to it as outright snootiness, from many foreigners inside the Convention center and at some of the lounges and restaurants in town...." He nodded, lowering his eyelids. "I hope to obtain massive orders for my CTS Corporation from India, China, Russia, and England. They've sent representatives. We have shot-callers from nearly every country on Earth. Uhm, even the less populated countries such as Australia. Heck, even Germany's Chancellor contacted my Corporations headquarters and ordered 75 CTS trucks unseen. This is capitalism at its finest, Remy!"

"Sir, off-topic, when are you going to allow me to eliminate that pesky Lieutenant Smugs, bah I..." he stuck his arm up. "Stop now is not the time to discuss our other agendas...." "Sorry, Major, that was rather crass; uhhh, so when do I get to watch how one of these trailers works? I must confess that the graphic designs and colors are amazing, like 3-dimensional Black and Silver like the Las Vegas Raiders...nice." "Private, you will have to be patient like the rest of my audience. I'm waiting for a select group to arrive, and I ordered a round-up of non-chosen civilians without the credentials for the Yellow tattoos. Their expendable and will meet their demise sooner than later lol... Why not today!" Remy didn't laugh along, but neither frowned; just a touch passed even keel, knowing she'd got her family protected. "I hope to have at a minimum 55 live ones delivered via covered trucks soon enough!"

"So, who are we waiting for from our team, Sir?" Bryan looks out and scans the parking lot but doesn't answer. "You know I was there at the hospital a total of three times to take out Captain Rory but failed because he was constantly under guard. I had my favorite 'Liston Amputation knife' up my arm sleeve but couldn't get close to the dude's neck!" "Sshhh…." he slaps his palms together swiftly, moving closer to the big woman and placing a hand on her shoulder. "You're still my best Assassin, and as it turns out, Rory is no longer a threat. The guy's brain is fried, uh, dead they are going to take him to NIA, the Napa Insane Asylum. Captain Rory, I believe, left a couple of hours ago, so he will not be informing Colonel Ruiz of our attempted hiring and recruitment of his sick soul… we've already got one of our team ready to replace him, and the idiot Colonel will most likely add him to his team of Officers. Damm, I'm counting on it, Remy, so relax 'all is well that ends well,' hey, on a separate matter, have you had anyone approach Lieutenant Snugs as of yet to offer him a position with our team rather than eliminate the guy?" "No, Sir, and I'm glad you brought that up. I spoke with LT Sloan, who said Snugs is a known womanizer… look at me; I'm not the gal for that job. The dude doesn't like me already, and heck, I'm the stereotypical female military enlisted Lesbian." They show matching grins, and Remy continues, "anyways I think it would be a good idea to encourage someone else to have a talk with Snugs and help recruit him to our way of thinking. Maybe Major have cutie pie Corporal Ashly Humming to start working on him… she's fricken sexy as all hell. I tried hitting on her a couple of times but shit, and she's full-on heterosexual, a spit-fire… umh, and no doubt a Snugs type for sure, Major!"

Bryan let out a howl… "If I were into women, she'd definitely be enticing Private, okay, if sexpot Ashly can't reign in Snugs, you can use your favorite tool that… Liston Knife, on him! But I'll leave it up to you, and yes, true-that LT Sloan could have most likely swayed Snugs into willingly joining us. Snugs would be a much greater advantage to us alive than dead too bad Sloan just got married to our Sergeant Barton. She was our number one recruiter… oh, speak of the little devil. Here she comes!"

In the next seven minutes arriving on time was his trusted nucleus there to support him and to watch the exhibition, the trusted leaders that would follow him traveling from city to city and state to state… Grinning wide, his CTS Cremation system would soon be in all 48 continental states and hopefully every populated country across the globe.

Beaming smiles, Salutations with salutes, and ongoing acknowledgments from his loyal Officers lining up were LT Sloan and Sergeant Barton, Private Freeze, and Private Remy, along with Corporal Ashly Humming and, no doubt, secretary Private Jimmy Neal bringing up the… rear! Driving up in another Golf cart was another group, including Doctor Cindy Walsh. There was definitely excitement in the air, which was at a cool 93 degrees for July in the sun of Redding… Bryan was proud as a strutting Peacock.

Covered box trucks arrived on time, all drivers were MPs, and the military police were out in more significant numbers securing the Convention Center's grounds. They'd received death threats the more prolonged the siege ah Martial Law went on, the more the natives became restless. The whining beep, beep of the backup warning sounds as one of the drivers is backed up to the stopping point by one of the C.T.S trucks. Soldiers with RFDs out awaited the back door to be rolled up. Major Bryan took the clipboard and Tablet to match up the invoice with the names of those who were inside. All identifications had been scanned with all the other necessary important information, along with additional pictures of his first real-time executions. He would start with 33 victims. Bryan was on Cloud 9, totally invigorated and exhilarated to the max.

<u>First demonstration by Major Richey Bryan of his Cremation trailers.</u>

The soundboard was ready, the cameras rolled… his audience was filled with dignitaries that were packed under a giant circus tent covering his finest prototypical CTS trailer. Major Bryan sanctimoniously grasped the microphone. Rockstar like… spins around and says, motioning outward with his hands on the makeshift stage. "Okay, I want you to observe carefully, uh, watch this Presentation. This is the sequence for humane and dignified elimination, uh, purging of the miscreants. First, we walk over here and pull out the control box…." Bryan grins while placing his index finger on a scanner. A slot on the cab of the truck slides open. "It's all wireless!"

Bryan reached into the small compartment and took a device about the size of a video game controller out. He then hands it to Remy, who checks it out and passes it through the crowd. It had green, red, and blue buttons with various switches. The box was lightweight and made of Titanium and aluminum.

The controller box was returned to Bryan, who said, "everything is labeled; the legend is on the back of the box…." He takes it from Private Remy and flips it over, showing the audience, then flips a switch, and the whole side of the 45-foot trailer starts to retract up like a garage door, grinning at their amazed stares. 'Surely I'm a flex genius. Bryan knows all of them should be on their knees bowing hands waving in sycophantic fawning motions towards him for he was no doubt God like, yep it's me!'

"What you see here…." as he walks, holding his hand out, "these are body slots on retractable rollers; there's a total of 14 in each row with five vertical rows," smiling largely for those of you mathematically challenged that's 5 X 14 equaling 70 bodies per loading. Each space is 3 feet wide and 6' 5" long to contain taller folks, every single side of this design is exactly replicated. Meaning, what you see here is spacing for 70 human bodies with the same on the other side of this trailer, which should tell you, at minimum, we can cremate 140 bodies instantly and at the same time!" he paused for effect. "Please, folks, conceptually think of this trailer as a gigantic Vending machine with similar movements and rotations. It will adjust to almost any size of human!" Bryan pauses for a moment to let what he'd explained sink in "with the latest laser technology, each slot uses an actuated adjustment system to squeeze each slot within 5/9 of an inch of the next occupant." He grinned widely and raised his arms wide open.

Sergeant Barton raises his hand. "Major Sir, but....." Bryan's first expression of anger vanishes, "please save the questions for later... no Q&A till we have a run–through!" "Sorry, Sir." "Our cremation trailers, CTS, are designed for easy loading using a unique patented innovative functioning scheme similar to like I just said, vending machines accordion–like we load bodies instead of candies they're strapped to the ceramic heatproof boards then the next slot automatically rotates down into place for the quick and easy load of the next body, fast, speedy, and efficient!"

Bryan nodded with a fiendish scowl morphed into a teeth–gasping grin, "a picture or video is worth thousands of words; we'll watch this live...." Many of his audience start to pull out their phones to videotape. "I'm sorry, there will be no video, for we don't want my CTS to be leaked out to the public as of yet... hysteria might result!" The crowd of onlookers agreed, nodding wide-eyed, no doubt approving of these necessary constraints. Bryan beckons his trained soldiers who had already taken his exclusive courses on how to use the CTS. "Load them up," he shouts. The soldiers, one on each end of the covered trucks, start to pull out the cots and stretchers covered in white sheets. He walked over to one of the sleeping people "as you can see, we have already wrapped and strapped down their arms and legs to their bodies for speed. No need to strap them down in the trailer slots." Bryan points "each one has a Black hood zip tied over their heads… this makes it more clinical that way, our loading soldiers don't have to deal with the living, breathing human faces. Every one of the chosen has been shot with our RFDs they are merely sleeping soundly, unh, sedated." Bryan looked out at the growing crowd and witnessed stunned folks shockingly covering their mouths. "Oh, for those of you queasy about actually watching this elimination of the misery-laden and sickly people… please folks, realize these individuals haven't long to live anyways there in the last stages of the Covid-57 virus… we're humanely ending their sufferings!"

Major Bryan watches the audience of Diplomats and Officers from across the planet, many in Awe and astounded silence, and says… "Just under 2 minutes, you've witnessed 33 slots being filled in my CTS trailers. That's smooth and slick, with no oversized bodies to contend with, all tucked in… the next step." Out of the sky, a whirling rotor sounds then quickly, a helicopter drops down onto the parking lot. Within seconds Bryan looks on, covering his eyes like the others… sand and dirt with debris fly, swirling inside the open sides of the tent; everything stops suddenly.

Bryan shouts to his Officers… "Ah, great, we've got company; who the hell leaked out that we were here conducting this presentation?" Colonel Ruiz holds his hat and jumps down onto the asphalt… behind him are LT Smugz, Corporal Mendez, Private Drake, and Private Noels. The last to hop out of the chopper was 5-Star General Bill Hullinger. Bryan sucked in his breath, instantly unnerved. He mumbled, 'Oh Fk' now what?' All the military personnel stood at attention as the General sauntered up. "At ease…" he said. The Major approached him, ignoring Ruiz "well, General, what a pleasant surprise, Sir! Would you like me to start my presentation over from the beginning, sir?" "No, that will not be necessary,

Major. I saw 4 or 5 of these impressive trucks over in my neck of the woods, near the Palo Cedro area. Colonel Ruiz was kind enough to arrange for a box truck that had another 53 vigilantes from the Belle Vista and Palo Cedro sectors to be cremated. It was quite the show. I'm totally impressed… please carry on, Major!"

This plainly sucked the air from Bryan's lungs. Squinting his eyes up at Ruiz, the bastard gleamed back a shit-eating smirk. "Oh, Major, afterward you and I must have a lil chat; it wasn't appropriate to not invite your Commanding Officer to this exhibition. That was entirely disrespectful…" "Yes, Sir General, but I thought…." "Not now, Major, not now. Let's get with it. How many criminals are in the cremation trailer?" Bryan was major league pissed off at Ruiz. Again, he glimpsed Ruiz's face, which displayed an inspired gloating expression. "All right folks let me continue, so we have 33 criminals that are in the last stages of Covid-57 with not many hours left to live. They are sequestered in their respective slot's, uhm, last resting spots." Bryan again takes his controller box "now we close the panel on this side of the CTS next, we fire up both the turbine generators." The Kenworth Conventional starts up Diesel fuels puff from behind the 3rd axels, and then another diesel generator starts at the back of the CTS… lights on the handheld box went all Green.

His confidence was renewed, his ego back intact. Bryan smiled at the crowd like an actor who'd stumbled adlibbing flawlessly… he displayed the top of the controlling box to the General and said, "Sir, if you would please push the Red button!…" the General obliged. The sides of the trailer shut similarly again to what a garage door would do, a timer lights up… An inset LCD panel flashes on the trailer, and the 3-minute countdown starts… while they wait, he shifts to a contraption under the carriage of the trailer. "This will extend out 19 inches. This is the vacuum chute. A Hemp meshed bag will automatically be attached after the cremation is complete.

Like at a typical funeral home that gives the family the ashes of their loved ones, we, of course, just want to reload the trailers. With my invention…each body slot has an emplaced vacuum system that sucks out the leftover residue uhhh ash and deposits it right here. Look, all 33 bodies that you saw loaded will be deposited in this bag. All ashes end up in these 55-gallon bags. Each bag has been manufactured environmentally friendly to contain 140 cremated bodies per bag! With room to seal them up. Then they can be taken to the local dumps or landfills."

He waves the wireless box that's aligned with the LCD panel's display on the trailer and shows the timer blinking down to 9,8,7, zero, the vacuum chute arches up, and then a bag was automatically attached. Everyone heard a slight industrial grinding noise, sound then the nozzle retracted back underneath the carriage… done! Instantly the side panel reopens on the trailer where the 33 bodies once were. Bryan was so excited that he nearly pissed himself. Walla, all slots were aseptically clinically cleansed, purified, and uncontaminated… Bryan waves his hands like a magician and says nada word. Nothing was needed to be said while his crowd went into an enthusiastic frenzy, disbelieving what they'd witnessed with their own eyes. "Amazingly stupendous," shouts General Bill Hullinger. "A modern miracle Major," not only was the General shaking his hand, but affectionately was patting him on the back!

General Bill Hullinger was Red-faced with monetary delight swirling around in his future bank vaults. He could count his monies by the millions, he thought, 'what an investment.' Bill saw Ruiz frown and was puzzled… "Hey, Ruiz, ah, Colonel, you are invested in the stock market, right? If you work the Options markets, can you imagine how much will be made on just the Calls? The C.T.S. stock is going to the fricken Moon, dude… but forget all that. We'll get in on the IPO. The initial public offering will make us Billions with a capital 'B.' You just watched a fortune with that incineration! Every country in this world… shit, man, a mobile crematorium, a one-stop shop. Yeah!" "Very true, General, you are 100 % correct," but what Ruiz left unsaid was that he didn't invest a copper penny in the venture that Major Bryan had offered him when he was looking for venture capitalists. Ruiz felt nauseous and decided immediately that he would call one of his brokers the second he could get away and chummy up with Bryan… freakin what a mistake, but he knew he could come out on top with coercion.

"Hey, General Hullinger, can I ask you a question?" "sure-fire Ruiz; what's on your mind?" "You went off on Major Bryan and me regarding the missing girl Kayla Green acting as if you had no idea of what we were doing here in Shasta…." Bill holds his palm up "yes, well, the Director of the FBI here in this state, Mr. Rico Captor, had been barking at me about his close friend and counterpart in the medical field Doctor Shanon Roble. She was causing a ruckus and stirring up some chaos in Wash. D.C. Rico isn't privy as to what the W/O has mandated the man wouldn't go along with the new orders for eliminations. Therefore I had to play naïve and two-faced and unfortunately had no other options. Sorry if I was a bit too harsh, but that's the way the cookie crumbles…. Ruiz, yah got to do whatcha got to do!"

Bryan waited glowingly and patiently for the chatter to quell then with a Cheshire Grin… "Okay, ready for the Q & A session to begin," his head and scalp tingling. He really couldn't be more ecstatic. Sergeant Barton stepped toward the Major. "What if the criminals are over 6' 5" tall, say he or she is seven feet, or what if the victim is grossly obese?" "Good question Sergeant… but let me first correct you we don't cremate victims, only the sickly and deserved. If the body is too long, we've developed this procedure." Bryan walks to the open slots inside his CTS trailer and points…. "The lasers measure each body we are inserting watch this." He pops a switch, and a steel bar starts down towards the bottom of the slot. Bryan continues speaking… "This bar will snap the tibia-fibula without a messy compound fracture, then the bottom tray curls up, folding the feet onto the person's thighs… done! If there is a rare tear in the skin, a vapor mist disinfects the slot for the next cadaver. If the person is too wide to fit in a normal slot, then it automatically widens and squeezes the occupant into the compartment. In some rare instances, we may not be able to load the 70 undesirables, criminals, or Covid victims per side and have to reduce the number depending on how they fit into our slots! But let me repeat that it only happens rarely!"

"The General, along with Diplomats from India and China, and Russia, are openly enthused. The U.K. Ambassador hops on his toes. "Bloody brilliant indeed, boy freakin brilliant you've thought of everything it appears. Wow, I'm impressed, Major." Everyone suddenly applauded a standing ovation began and continued for over a minute. Once it slowed down, Lieutenant Snuggs raised a hand. "I have a question, Sir." "Go ahead, Lieutenant…." "I've been in charge of the IMP stationed up on Iron Mountain, and many times, uhhh, let me backtrack. A few times, a body would come awake like… they had some sort of immunity to our serrated darts. Some would jump up off the conveyor belts on the way to their acid graves. It got messy at times, and we'd have to shoot them dead sometimes they'd wiggle off the belt I…." "LT, sorry to cut you off here, the loaders carry the new edition 15-shot dart pistol. One dart shot back in a moving corpse, and their back in position in less than five seconds!"

Snuggs nods his approval, "how many Rebels can be eliminated in one hour with your new System, Sir" asked Corporal Mendez. "Thank you, this is my favorite part of my invention, the numbers. All right, I've had the specs passed out to each one of you, so let me go over these numbers," holding up a plastic master copy. "Okay, take the dimensions of the trailers into a divisional equation. As you all witnessed, when filled, we load 70 perps per side or 140 in total. The process takes three minutes to dust them, and it should take about 2 minutes to load both sides with bodies using 12 soldiers per side and one Officer in charge of each trailer, so 25 soldiers per CTS. We've done some mockups with weighted mannequins, so let's deal with a best-case scenario of a total of five minutes for 140 perps Ashed. So 12 X 5 minutes is an hour or 60 minutes this…. in a perfect simulation, we'd have 12 X 140 perps in an hour vaporized, which equates to 1,680 souls eliminated per… each hour."

With barely taking a breath… gravity-fed, Bryan rolled on, "now there are 24 hours in every day 24 X 1,680 equals 40,320 cremated in a 24-hour period, and that's only 1 of my Trailers, but let's exponentially take the equation out, prolonging it for 30 days of continual use we'd eliminate 1,209,600 or over 1.2 million undesirables, of course, that's optimal!" Way before the shocked and awed open mouths were closed down…. Bryan added, "of course that's an insurmountable ugh, unachievable number for a continuous 24-hour period. Because we'll need to include the time for maintenance and also have to take into account that our human workforce can't sustain nonstop action. Yep, even with lined-up work shifts, the CTS is allocated for at the Max: 16 hours or two shifts of 8 hours. The trailers can run efficiently for an entire month, and then we must maintenance our machines. These numbers are feasible and doable with nose-to-ass semi-trailers. It will be a nonstop operation. We'll devour, ugh, vanquish 1.2 million to 2 million per week… my system is the most efficient and respectable way of accomplishing the reductions that are regulated and mandated by the W/O. Each country in this world must adhere to the 25% population control mandates or be Sanctioned and excluded, uhm, isolated essentially, they would starve to death and be cut off… without unity and harmony, our society will cease to evolve. Remember that our world leaders have agreed upon this, and my innovative concept will make the transition palpable!"

The Mayor of New York City stood in the back row "what about Cities like my own, sir? How would your process....." Bryan holds his palm up "it's all numbers. Like I've been saying, take three of my cremation trailers running at 9 hours for a month with everything working optimally, and they would vanquish the same amount of cadavers. Ahh, let me back up … if you take the cities of Los Angeles or your New York City, say you have 12 million miscreants that needed to be Ashed, we could line up 10 of my Trailers around your city easily without any sweat in under one month you're done met yours and our goals!"

The bewildered audience wasn't prepared for Major Bryan's demonstration of clinical extermination… a killing system or purgation of living, breathing people on Planet Earth. Some in the crowd of Diplomats couldn't believe they'd agreed with the W/O and were going to be a part of the eradication of mankind. What would the history books write about each of them? Mouths once again gaping open with fixed, dull-witted expressions aligned with unblinking stupider stares! Many in the crowd were naive as to how serious the leaders of the W/O… were. The World Order was almighty and would devour any person who was defiant.

<u>Major Bryan stepped back up onto the makeshift stage.</u>

"CTS Incorporated has manufacturing plants logistically uh geographically based in Miami, Atlanta, Boston, and New York City. Also, we're located in Cleveland, Chicago, and New Orleans, and we're in the process of finishing plants in Phoenix and Albuquerque, which will be up and running later this month. In Dallas and Denver, we're breaking ground. Oh, we took over a dilapidated Ford manufacturing center in Detroit nine months ago. Bose Idaho just sent out a fleet that arrived on the North side of I-5 waiting right now at the Redding city limits sign." Bryan sighed and nodded.

"California rejected all our applications because of the Green Movement... tree-huggers ah, the ecology movement. These naturalists are worried about the fricken sustainability of living humans a hundred years from now. I have news for them...." Bryan nearly tore his cheeks, grinning into a smirk. "Uhm, most of them, they won't live till 2027. My team of executives and the Who's Who couldn't break into California... Nope, the environmentalists rule this state. Every time we'd cleared one hurdle, they'd put up another roadblock with unrealistic regulations. Too much Red Tape, then add to that... unnecessary curiosity. I don't know how anyone gets anything done in California. Therefore we haven't a plant in this state, but no worries, we were able to acquire a Portland-Vancouver manufacturing hub and just landed another manufacturing center on the outside of Seattle in Federal Way, Washington. Right here in front of you folks...." Major Bryan, proud as a Parrot, opens his arms waving. "This is our first delivery to Shasta County from the Seattle, Portland, Oregon plants. We have 57 CTSs here as I speak. They are earmarked for...." Then Bryan noticed the General's scowl and stopped... Bill's hand was held high with trepidation in his voice, says, "Major Bryan, that's all fine and dandy and fantastic you have the United States covered. What about the rest of North America, or for that matter, hey, look around. Your facing representatives from all over this planet. Tell them which plants are earmarked for their sales abroad."

Bryan paused, scanning the hundred-plus intrusive glares, tightly grasping the microphone. "General, yes, I was going to get to that. We will be a world conglomerate. Please peruse the lists of military bases throughout the world where we are setting up our manufacturing plants. Please review the packets that all of you should have received." He paused, guzzling some of his bottled water. "I promise to answer all the questions posed to me, and please go to the many Homepages that are associated with my invention. Just type in CTS.com." He waited somewhat perturbed, trying to prompt his team to ask the prearranged questions. Doctor Walsh raises her hand. "Major, there must be downsides. You make it seem so benign, like a scalpel excising a pimple. Tell us what could possibly go wrong?" Brynn enjoyed her word selection, paraphrasing his question for her to ask... paused for effect, then simultaneously smirked. "Uh, okay, I suppose one of the Trailers could run out of fuel, um, diesel, or perhaps have a flat tire, Doctor!" His answer was designed for wanted laughter, yet none of the spectators played along.

Lieutenant Sloan asks, or better states, "so with the populated East Coast, 25 of these Trailers could incinerate all the deemed unnecessary redundancies Vampires of our American way of life... welfare, disability malingerers, the homeless scammers, criminals all perished in under a couple of months really amazingly the East Coast can be really disinfected of most of the malefactors." "Lieutenant Sloan, you said it best I have nothing to add except this the revolutionary innovations have been modified to handle the influx of certain deaths caused by Covid-57 and the likely Variant mutations to follow. With my cremation trailers, we will no longer be hampered by filled morgues. Our system will eliminate the pressures that this virus puts on our medical professionals. While we're speaking, I have two of these trailers being delivered to both Redding Regional Hospital and Mercy Hospital. They have rotting souls down in the basement of their morgues." He paused for effect. "With this new evolution in technology, our best trajectories are within 13 to 25 months we should be able to survive this killer airborne plague and forever live in splendor!"

More applause... it dies down when Sergeant Barton declares, "I can see there's not much of a learning curve for the soldiers assigned to the CTS force. Aren't you worried about a soldier or a group of concerned citizens, ugh, rebels, let's call them conscientious objectors, with our troops bagging and tying hoods off and then cremating people who are still alive and breathing and burning them to death, don't you think if the populace got wind of your machines, this would go beyond Viral a revolution unh I for one am worried and..." "stop there Sarg..." Bryan shrugs, frowning beneath his epidermis 'geez, thinks Barton, you elaborated a bit too much. It was supposed to be a quick un-malicious question nonpersonal.' "Sarg, we are currently training thousands of our troops at several of our plants, institutional sites, and on some military bases in the next five weeks, we will have our first graduates who will man-woman up our CTS operations." He pops his arms up high above his head "let's not forget that Covid-57 will annihilate civilization, and these machines are a necessity what would the world do pile infected contagious bodies on the sidewalks and curbs of their cities? I have no fear that the World Order will succeed. I want to thank you all for allowing me the time to present to you a new age in American ingenuity!"

He stops and orders the other covered truck occupants to be loaded into the cremation trailer, hollering, "now we will witness the CTS filled to the maximum. All 140 bays will have malefactors, uh, violators, that have gone through our vetting system and have been cataloged as qualifying for disposal for various reasons, mostly violent felonies, along with others who are succumbing to the virus. While my soldiers load both sides of my invention, let me also address the last remaining inquiry regarding how my Corporation will handle the overseas endeavors." The large contingent of Diplomats and emissaries gathered around. "We have been given permission by our Commander in Chief, the President, to utilize Military Aircraft Carriers to load my truck and trailers onto the runways. On top of that, we'll have use of U.S. bases in the largest cities on earth.... goals mandated by the W/O will be met that I can promise!"

A Staff Sergeant steps forward. "Major Sir, all the slots have been filled; here's the remote box…." "Thanks, Surg." he spins back on the crowd who were standing around chatting,… "It's time for the 3-minute countdown, folks." No one spoke while he held the killing box up in the air pressing the Red button, nary a word was spoken. The next sound heard was the industrial vacuum cleaner. They watch the Hemp 55-gallon bag blew up with Ashes Bryan pushes the Blue button, and both sides lift up, not a speck of debris, only stainless steel reflected back on the group. Jimmy, his boy toy secretary, leaps in the air clapping, then boisterously, they all joined in blissful heavenly harmony was felt… Bryan could strut across the clouds.

Bill salutes the Major as did all, "well done, Major…. now if you and the Colonel will meet me at CR-Gibbs in 45 minutes, we need to discuss future operations." Colonel Ruiz starts to follow Bill to his chopper. The General pivots and looks back at him. "Ruiz, I'm leaving alone. You and the Major be there in 45 minutes, okay?" "Uh, yes, Sir General, I know the bartender at Gibbs…. he will give us VIP treatment. That's what I was thinking if you wanted me to go with you, Sir?" "Ruiz, I will be communicating with the Presidential counsel's Covid-57 intervention team of Directors along with all 50 Governors and several of the world's leaders across the globe on Zoom. Ahh, any way you're not privy to those conversations, I know Jeff, the bartender as well…. ways there, Ruiz!" "Yes, Sir, I will be there."

Ruiz agitatedly wandered back to where Bryan was hem-hawing his accolades to a group of admirers. "Hey, Bryan, I need to speak with you in private now!…" Bryan peered around after furrowing his brows towards his fans, peeved "please excuse me, I will be back…." Nodding acquiescence at the Colonel thinking how he wanted to garrote the bastard prick. The arrogant Colonel, as per usual, displayed his egotistical power along with his unwavering conceit, the typical higher-ranked Officer who could ride you hard, debase you, and humiliate you, passing the buck down the ladder.... for you could make your own underlings eat shit, even worse just keep shoveling the shit down the grade.... uh hih, Yep!

Bryan walked alongside the Colonel, who was fuming and couldn't figure out what could be up the stout man's ass. He'd just 'knocked it out of the park' fk Ruiz should be wanting to cajole and cater to him with his CTS Incorporated. Ruiz could be rich, a wealthy guy if he played his cards correctly, but he wasn't, ugh, too stupid.... "I have some bones to pick with you!..." Stopping short and now behind one of the trailers had his index finger pointing in Bryan's face, not an inch from his nose.

Bryan backed up, flabbergasted, believing it's got to do with money, or him undermining Ruiz being a usurper, or maybe not inviting him to this presentation, um, demonstration. Damn, he couldn't guess at... how many times he'd done this asshole wrong, almost funny. Bryan stepped away from the angry man, his back now stopped against his trailer. 'One thing for certain, this dude had a short fuse' suddenly, Ruiz puts his finger down. Shaking in anger, musing this wasn't the way to handle this.... there were at least 175 people out here on the asphalt. Just then, a couple of soldiers walked around the truck. Ruiz straightens his suit; he thinks he'll spill his guts soon enough. Don't kill the Goose laying the Golden unh. Golden Eggs takes a deep breath. "I need some answers... no fricken bullshit Bryan. I have information that's been substantiated and is highly disturbing. I could file charges in the future or next week against you and one of your Officers...." "Excuse me, Sir; you have me at a disadvantage here. I'm in the blind, please, Sir, tell me...."

They wait till another group of bystanders gawking at the magnificent cremation truck and trailer walks by. "Major, in the 19 days we've been in Shasta, I have had five Officers murdered." Ruiz waited for this to sink in. Bryan suddenly stiffens up; this was the last subject he expected to be broached. "Sir, it was the Rebels or vigilantes. I thought we'd come to the same conclusions. How the hell could… no, let me rephrase that? Why would anyone, especially from my team, commit such brutal crimes? What purpose this is crazy…." "Bryan, let me lay this out for you all five murders were up close and personal, meaning the killer had to either know the victim or be able to blend in with our military doesn't take Sherlock Holmes to deduce this. Our specialist's ahh, investigators, unh, and internal affairs have spent hours reviewing the satellite images that could have been useful. Our (IID)internal investigations, uhm inspectorate general, and the internal review board have finished their preliminary studies. They logged hours of interviews of our personnel at or near the scenes of each attack, unhhh murder and…." Out of nowhere, a jeep screeched to a halt next to them.

Snungs pulled up in a Jeep… "Hey guys, you need a ride…." Noticing the intensity didn't wait, hit the gas, and said over his shoulder, "Sir, let me know if you need me!" Bryan had noticed earlier that Ruiz had a thick folder in his shoulder bag, pulling it out. "Here are a few telling pictures. Who is this Bryan?… Of course, it's your Private Remy who was at the scene of two of the killing sites. She was seen chatting, ugh, arguing with Captain Rigors, which in itself isn't sufficient evidence to bring her in on murder charges." Ruiz shoulders up against Bryan.

"Nevertheless, look at these photos at the Sundial Bridge. Private Remy is in her uniform, then disappears into a treed area. Look at this following picture… on the River Trail, it shows a person in all Black clothing with a hoodie… the assailant." "Excuse me, Sir, can I see them side by side?" he stands, holding up the 8 X 10 glossy pictures. "Your correct, Sir. I do see the similarities in the body type or size, that is…. but look carefully. You're proposing hypothetically that Remy entered the trees at mile marker 1.7 miles. Now look at the second picture. Ironically, the killer steps out into view. See the

2.5-mile marker, which would mean she would have to have skirted the River about 3/4 of a mile. That's nearly impossible, Sir, for the river abutted the trail in many spots, and along the bank, it's filled with boulders, rocks, and Blackberry bushes and is impossible to navigate by foot, Sir!"

Ruiz not impressed soldiers on "there were three reports written up regarding the incident at the Bethel Confection Shop named "Sunshine Sweet Goodness" where four cult members committed suicide. Remy and Captain Rigors got into a heated confrontation. A shouting match with threats doled out by both. He ordered her to leave the premises; there's your motive by itself." "Well, I wasn't made aware of any of this, Colonel...." Ruiz rolled his shoulders, chewing on gum and spitting it to the ground looking at the report. "When the manhunt began searching for the fugitives Catrina and Ben by the Sundial Bridge area, there were no civilians. All my troops and your Private Remy were the only ones on site. Here's the last picture of the assailant in Black... Remy is like 6'3" tall, this figure meets that description according to our forensics CSI Team. Look at the zoom-in and enhanced enlarged photo." Ruiz then growls aggressively, pointing his forefinger... "See the shoes, their matching military editions with the same scuffs on the left toe. Here's a picture of Remy's left shoe... they're identical, Bryan freakin Identical! Circumstantial evidence as good as my damn DNA."

By now, Bryan was plainly sweating and breathing in duress, trying his best not to show a nervous disposition. "Colonel Sir, why are you discussing this if this is what you believe? Why don't you have Private Remy in the Brig under arrest? Besides, why would she do...." "Major, it's the devious mind behind the opaque pictures whom I'm after.... Yup, the Puppet Master, and who the fk do you think that could be Rickey?   Huh, Bryan, and even more interesting than that is each replacement I chose was less qualified than his or her predecessor, weakening my team, and remarkably most of the replacements on the list of interviews were connected to you." Ruiz paused, gloating with a perplexed scowl, and squinted his eyes, measuring the effects of his words on the pathetic pansy. He noticed Bryan was sweating profusely.

"Bryan here's some food for thought. I bet you didn't know I'm a history buff... Are you familiar with the great tactician Hannibal The Carthaginian General, who almost toppled Rome? Hannibal in the spring of 217 BC. Famously let his army including 38 elephants, over the Alps and came within sniffing distance of conquering Rome. He was known as one of the great tacticians of all time history... Hannibal's strategy way back in history followed the Latin phrase 'Divide et impera.' Yes, the infamous strategies first indoctrination... 'Divide and Conquer.' Hannibal would input loyalists, ahm, spies into his enemy's regiments...." "Wait, excuse me, Sir, the last I looked... we're in the same military, aren't we on the same team Colonel? Correct me if I'm wrong, Sir, but I mean, what the...."

Ruiz fumes scowling and spitting mad, "we both know that's untrue. Surely I'm in charge and was at the outset of this operation. Then we chose our loyal Officers for our teams for two distinctly different objectives. I was to handle security blockades and Law Enforcement; yours was a more technical selection of whom we allow to survive the scrutinization and vetting processes etc." Ruiz bites down on the tip of a cigar staring at him.

"Bryan, take a look at these photos first, Remy, on the 5th floor of Mercy Hospital. Oh, BTW, this was taken 55 feet from Captain Rory's room. I'll humor you. Let's call it happenstance but wait a night later. What do yuh know, there she is again, back on the 5th floor. Do you want to explain this twice as being... a coincidence? Her excuse this time was that Remy was searching for Doctor Walsh. Everyone knows her office is in the basement, uh Morgue, furthermore, what would Doctor Cindy Walsh have to do with the living, huh?" Ruiz inhaled large "now check this picture out a 3rd trip up to see Rory!

Snaugs appropriately asked her again why she was trying to get in to see Captain Rory. She said that she was there to interview Rory for Doctor Walsh… Bullshit! So Bryan, why Captain Rory, why did you send her Black Death to his room… why?"

The Major had been in precarious situations many times before and had learned not to blurt anything out better to digest all information and plead; the Fifth… watches the Colonel spit out the end of the cigar and light it. "Bryan, it's all circumstantial, isn't it, you think? We could arrest her and make a case just for her matching shoes and taint your Sainthood… uh image with the General and the W/O. We both understand that the vilified individual never fully recovers when something is alleged or suspected. Many believe the person guilty despite possibly being innocent. Your clever, a Wolf dressed in a Lamb's clothing. Yuh got the rest of them fooled. They don't see you're a snake in the grass like I do." "Just you wait for a second here, Colonel L…." "Shut up or I'll ruin your big show and have your Remy… faceplanted on the asphalt; now you listen up. It's true that I failed to invest in your CTS, but you're going to let me in now. I want to get in on the preferred shares in your CTS Corporation. I want warrants, ugh, options to purchase company stock at a specific price before the Initial Public Offering, umh, IPO. I don't want anything for free I'll pay you what you paid, and your venture capitalists paid face value, all right… Major?"

Bryan sighed inside, relaxing a little; now he knew what a shakedown felt like. It's generally about money uh, greed or lust, and or power had to be one of them. Shifting a smile beneath, he coughed, his taunt snake skin shaking… lol "Yes, Colonel, I will work out a deal for you to invest in my company's stock before it IPOs and shoots higher than Apple, Tesla and becomes a Trillion dollar enterprise or as many would say shoots to the Moon but we need to do that tomorrow before the explosive news and the IPO is priced out, and I'll do this not because you think you have leverage over me regarding Private

Remy… hope I could use your aggressive nature in promoting my um, our Corporation and with you having a Dog in the fight you will bring in larger and more influenced investors IMO."

Ruiz nods, furrowed brows easing, "ahh, it's fine that I wasn't invited to your presentation. Lucky, I have my own Moles spies from inside your team Major. From here on out, you better keep me in the loop… oh and that's so nice of you, Major, to allow me into your lucrative venture, but I'm not quite finished with your Private Remy. I…" Bryan knows he's pushing it by interrupting this narcissist but holds his palm up. "Yes, Sir, I will keep you in the loop from here on out…." "Major, your Private has a troubled mind. We ran some background research on her heck. Remy signed a plea deal… either entered the military or was going to do an 11-year spread in prison for cutting up her girlfriend, her lover. Oh, and here's a tidbit that we find so culpably interesting her father is an Aichmomaniac, uh, a knife collector, actually Bryan, selling knives is his business. Each of the murders was accomplished with different and rare knives. The last knife used to nearly decapitate Captain Rory was an Obsidian Scalpel, a super rare surgical knife. Circumstantial evidence shows her left shoe, her description at the river, Remy's daddy dearest is a knife collector, uhm, seller… Need I say more, Major?"

Bryan says nothing mulls over a rebuttal, and then thinks better of it as Ruiz grasps his shoulder with a thud and turns into him. "I'm aware you are trying to supplant me to jump over me. We're a full team. We complement each other… stop undermining me. This is your last warning Major, and if anyone else gets the Knife, I will purposefully cut the rope on the guillotine chopping your vile head off. Did you get that, Bryan? I despise your queer ass. Watch yourself!" "Yes, Sir, I understand where I stand…." They walked back to the crowd, which was dispersing. Bryan mused who the hell was betraying him. Whomever it was wouldn't breathe much longer. That's a promise, and Bryan Never Breaks A Promise! ◀

While walking and talking, Ruiz blurts out, "you are aware that we're going to be using real leads from now on out on all fronts fighting firepower with likewise forces. Many of the Rebels in the area have body armor. There are way more of them than we ever thought we would encounter. The RFD Rifles firing darts are useless in penetrating their body armor. We're loading armor-piercing ammo from here on out, and here's some more food for thought. Our Intel has discovered a large contingent of militia members forming up. They have camps in specific advantageous points in the mountains here. Unlike what you and I originally conspired to believe, they have formed a divisive and organized resistance. We thought most of the citizens had been beaten down by years of Covid mutations heck, the Omicron was nothing compared to the last strains. Human resolve in fighting for survival can never be underestimated, Major!" He blew out a long puff from his cigar and laughed hysterically… <u>"But you know what our planned exit party for Shasta County is going to result in… we'll smoke them all out. Puff goes the Dragon!"</u>

Bryan decides it's time to change the subject matter. "Now that my CTSs have arrived, we are in the process of dismantling Iron Mountain. From here on out, Sir, all the bodies will be transported to the nearest trucks. We will leave Iron Mountain as it was… there will be no evidence of us even being there, Sir!" "I'm glad you took my orders seriously, Bryan, and by tomorrow afternoon, when we flip the switch off the blocking devices and allow communications to go back to normal, didn't you say you'd have completed the tattoos and selections of who remains alive and useful anyone with Red blood pumping from that point on will be terminated on site unless their Pyramid Tattoo glows!" "Yes, Sir, I'm on schedule as I've told you, and we received the last shipment of our specially designed scopes that will pick up the tattoo specs." Ruiz didn't bother with replying. He had his own agenda… "what I'm telling you Major is you better finish up your processing before we flip the switches back on, for anyone that doesn't display the colors of Yellow, Blue, or Red will be expendable we will shoot to kill that includes you, Major!"

Bryan was frustrated with this moron's constant threats but soldiered on. "Like you, Colonel, I will receive my Red Dot soon, and my staff and officers have their Blue Dots. We're going to be good…" he stopped and displayed a cool, confident expression. "I've read the latest specs on our scopes technology, and the beauty of it is we can zoom through vehicle's metal ah steel and see inside of the automobile or hell, even in the trunk, to see if there are any humans that are not vaccinated with our tattoos there will be nowhere for anyone to hide. Now with the tracking chip in their skin, we will know how many times a person at work uses the restroom," lol, laughing, they both finally grin in unison.

Ruiz looks down at his Red Dotted tattoo peeling up his sleeve. "It's not so bad, Major better get inked up. We're blessed that our tattoos are just for anti-vaccination protection and, of course, ultimately us… not being misconstrued as a Rebel or a Lowlander. Major, I wouldn't want in my blood… what's in all of the lower-class tattoos or even our soldiers and Officers. Isn't the Blue and Yellow vaccination tattoos all the same, Bryan?" "Of course, Sir, no doubt… we are of the upper echelon. We are not subject to those rules and scrutiny, no GPS chips, no invasion of privacy heck, better yet, the other inked individuals have time releasing drugs systemically melting into their bloodstreams, sort of like castrating the human will and drive for independence all we need from them is to keep us comfortable and for them to do their jobs which coincidently is the same thing!" They howl again now, actually having fun.

Before the subject could grow old, "heck, Colonel, we are the elite gifted top of the heap or as they say, 'Cream of the Crop' 1 %, and if the lower-class had any idea what is planned for their 7-month booster shots they'd run… each 7-month booster will close down any of their resistance to our control

I've been told the human work-force will be Zombies doing our bidding without remorse their satisfaction will be garnered by our patting them on the back 'atta boys' lol like docile puppy dogs!" "Bryan, I personally had discussions with the President and his Cabinet, who willingly received the <u>Pyramid Tattoo Red Dots</u>. We have a much stronger vaccine with additional time-released vitamins and nutrients. In fact, our tattoos monitor our health. If we have a bout of high blood pressure or Hypertension or need insulin, hell, you name it, our phone will be notified, and a Doctor will be on call waiting for us to be treated. Amazingly, it's like wearing a life insurance plan!"

The Colonel snaps his radio off his waist and radios LT Snugs to pick them up. "I will concede I feel sorry for our soldiers and law enforcement agents unless there part of a wealthy Monarchy or have influential connections uh family in high places, they will be emblazoned with Blue Dots, and that's forever." "Yeah, we're blessed, Sir. The only Reds that I know here are General Bill Hullinger, Doctor Cindy Walsh, and you and I, oh besides the Diplomats and Representatives from the other countries that enjoyed the presentation..." Ruiz said, "wait, Bryan, with all your influence and pull you couldn't get your Ass grab boyfriend a Red Dot lol..." "nope Sir, Jimmy is all Blue!" Ruiz howls "yeah not Blue balls I betcha!"

Before Snugs drove his Jeep up, Private Drake screeched the brakes to a stop in his Humvee. "Colonel Sir, you got a radio transmission to contact the General!" Ruiz realized he'd had his radio off while confronting the Major, twisted the switch, and turned the mic back on. "Breaker General, this is Colonel Ruiz... over." "Yes, Colonel, I'm sorry we will have to postpone our 3-some get-together till the 24th at 1530 at CR Gibbs. I have an impromptu high-level conference in San Francisco.... over!" "Yes, Sir General, we'll be their good luck!... over."

Ruiz ponders what can or will happen in the next three or four days. One thing was for certain they were pulling out of Shasta on the 29th of July. Private Remy following through with the Major's last order, watched the Colonel's every move through the binoculars held in her left hand. Her right hand was squeezing the handle of her favorite Black Obsidian blade.

–70–

<u>**Karen and Lori in downtown Redding.**</u>

They stood in the parking garage across from Lori's office building. For the umpteenth time, Karen checked out the card she'd found in the arresting soldier's jacket pocket; maybe Cody and Ali were at the Church. She and Lori had discussed their options and concluded that if Cody or Ali had been arrested, there obviously wouldn't still be a viable reward for them. That goes the same for Maddi, Ben, and his girlfriend, Cat. Karen had listened to Lori's logic, for she was academically brilliant, but in the end, her street smarts won over. Somehow Cody and Ali had escaped the van. After weighing the alternatives, 'stay at Lori's office, go to my house, or head to Bethel, the choice agreed upon was Bethel. Lori's words echoed, 'how could Christians not allow them refuge?

Lori whispered, "there's the car, what do you think?" "It would be too dangerous to drive, Lori. For one thing, we don't have their colored tattoos nor any of the necessary paperwork, shit; look at the streets. Not many vehicles are moving out there…. likely, we'd be yanked over by the military police! Lori, you have been held up in your legal office since the military invaded with Kayla…. you know you probably, unh damn, I bet you uh, why didn't you apply for a work visa or whatever you're an attorney you might have qualified for a Red Dot?" "Unh yuh think so…. well, I stayed undercover for the same reason you haven't applied. There's only a limited amount of Reds, Blues, and Yellows being approved. I'm 29 years old without partners and struggling to survive, spending all my grants and inheritance from my parent's accidental deaths. I'm a first-generation College Graduate. My family is from South Korea no chance for me to be accepted with the strict criteria and guidelines for admittance into the vaulted esteemed Red Society." They watched another Jeep pull up.... "Karen, I guess I could have tried for a Yellow Dot, but then again, I heard that if you are overqualified for the low-end Yellow, you were declined. I rationalized that because, well...." a Drone swiftly flew over them.

"Well, what finish what you were going to say...." "I had a couple of Paralegals try for a Yellow, and they were turned down while others that barely graduated high school were accepted. We assumed that they desired worker bees and non-motivated, proactive individuals. Of course, that's just my speculation, and Karen, I've hidden in my office for another serious reason...." "Ok, I'll bite what reason?" "Some of the highly educated employees at my 3-story building, umh, Attorneys like me, have never been seen again. I heard they'd entered the screening service centers for vetting for whom would receive the colorful tattoos. No one has seen them since, not their family members... and besides that, Kayla and I witnessed atrocities committed by the military police. It was brutal, Karen, like I've told you at least a dozen times, and girl, I left out that I had been dating an attorney next door to my office. My boyfriend Kim went to Lowes to be qualified for a red dot and never was seen again. He is gone, uh, Kim disappeared without any clues!"

They were still hunched over behind an SUV in the adjacent parking garage on the second floor. The sun had set over an hour ago. They were in downtown Redding on Court Street. Directly across the street was the County Jail, and down the block was the Courthouse.

"Not that I want to play the Race card, but I also was informed that mainly Whites, um, Caucasians were getting the Yellow Dot. My Asian friends have been turned away at an alarming rate, and as you can see, I'm 100% Asian, so yes, I hid and don't feel guilty for doing so, Karen!" "Wow, girl, don't get your freakin panties in a bunch… crap. You're an intense one, aren't you?" Karen shook her head, "I couldn't even make Yellow okay I come from a White trash family… felons and drug dealers. Did you see on the TV where if you're a felon, forget about applying unless you have seriously provocative arguments of contention or connections? It's again who you know, girl…." "Yeah, they call it mitigating circumstances…." "What's that mean, Lori?" "Unh kinda like you have good excuses for being a felon, uh criminal. Ugh, like you robbed the pharmacy for insulin before you were going to go into a diabetic coma or shock." They laughed, breaking some of the tension. "Okay, I get it hey, look at me. I have piercings all over my body, and in some places, you wouldn't guess, and at least 75 % of my skin has been inked, uh, tattoos everywhere. My uncle owns a Tattoo shop in town, here, see my left forearm. It's wrapped with Tribal Tats what would they do? They couldn't put the Yellow Pyramid over it. They'd have to remove these tattoos nope… I wasn't a candidate."

"True, I agree with you, Karen; let's crawl out and take another look at the streets. You know they got those night vision scopes and all…." "Yeh, we can't hover in this above-ground parking garage forever either we make a run for it to my house or Bethel!" They lean over the concrete and watch MPs across the way check out the legal office looking for the caller of the tip. It was dark except for the streetlights illuminating the streets along with floodlights and flashlights held in hands once again, searching Lori's building.

Karen whispers while simultaneously rolling an elbow into Lori's shoulder. "A couple of the MPs are heading in our direction; it's time we take to the streets. Bethel is perhaps three miles away…." Karen wished she had cell phone service, but the Government claimed to be turning that back on tomorrow afternoon. Karen and Lori couldn't see that far in the dark night. They moved under fluorescent lighting. Karen glanced at the Bethel card she'd taken out of the soldier's jacket pocket that she'd stolen. Lori crouched down, and they dodged from the car to the next vehicle and made it to the bottom floor. Hearing footsteps, they waited till all was clear and darted quickly across the street behind a large hedge.

Everything was going well; they stopped at intervals. Not many of the troops were out, and fewer Yellows were driving to their workplaces. Luckily they were still in a commercial area, for if not, they would have to watch their backs in residential areas, for all the citizen snitches would turn them into the authorities in a split second. Then, Lori had a second thought… 'A friend that worked on the 1st floor had told her the soldiers had gone house to residence throughout the entire city, ordering everyone out with many of them put in busses…. everyone had to be processed for their tattoos, maybe there wasn't as many people in the homes to snitch anymore?'

They passed the old downtown mall working their way towards Bethel Church ducking behind cars at the vacant dealerships on Pine Avenue nearing Lake Blvd. So far, so good, well, except for being dry-throated and thirsty. Lori snatched her roughly by the jacket, pulled her down, and whispered, "Look across the street…." Karen, with a hushed sound, "I don't see it…" then did. A Red glow of a cigarette or something being smoked it lit up a burnt Orange. They focused and saw three soldiers standing on the side of a bicycle shop under a dull light. One was playing with something in his hands when suddenly a Humvee drove by floodlights lighting their faces up. They were smiling widely, and one of them was staring right at her.

It all happened, as some would say, lightning quick; instantly, one of the guys waved at them and pointed up into the night sky above where they crouched. Following her head movement, Karen looked up with Lori and saw a Drone standing still, silently focused on them in the night's air, a blinking Red light. The drone seemed to point at them. It couldn't be 15 feet above the ground hovering. No…. suddenly, time stalled and stood still. Slow motion existed. They were pinned between a Ford Expedition and a Dodge Charger on their knees. Karen watched the Amber dot fluttering around, then it stopped on Lori's chest…. Lori bends her chin down to see where the red dot had stopped. The drone had them in its site…. locked them down…. Karen shouted, "Let's go!"

They jumped up and ran while hearing the soldiers wildly howling hysterically, letting the both of them run like Rabbits then the guy controlling the Drone pulled back the joystick while tapping a button twice; loud, rapid-fire 45 Caliber bullets rang out of the drone. The girls stumbled and fell on the pavement; the soldiers hooted and hollered. One said, "you saw neither of them had tattoos…." "Yep, it's hunting season now, call them in, and let's bag some more and make sure we get credit for these kills." Another of them stated loudly, pointing at the joystick. "It's my turn next," the leader holding the joystick exclaimed, "okay, pal, no worries, it's your turn, but do you think we should make sure that Rick and Todd don't pick those girls up?"

Why? Asked the eager one "ugh, cuz the rumor is those two dudes are into Necropolis acts…." "What the hell is that…." "It's screwing dead people, uhm, raping their corpses!" "shut the fk up, no way!" "yeah, it's sick, but that hippy Doctor Walsh got some fresh cum, uh, sperm off a dead freshman cheerleader the other day. DNA, the idiot freak pervert didn't wear a condom; he's in the Brig right now…. what a freak!"

Josh and Heather.

Josh caught Heather when she stumbled and let her go after a quicky hug; back on the trail they went wrapping around the West side of the Dam, staying hidden in the tree line. Now walking parallel to the 8th tallest Dam in the USA, following the

Black Diamond trail signs an obstacle path down to where the water spills from the Dam, the Sacramento River Trail was their destination. Josh took her from trail to trail in the off-road area behind the Shasta Dam. Where they were hiking… was designated for 4-wheel drives, quads, and motorcycles. It even had a racetrack for mountain bikes. BLM forest land was on the West side of the Sacramento River. Josh excitedly chewed some beef jerky with Heather sitting abreast on a flattened-out boulder. It had taken a considerably longer time to cover the distance from the beach below the hang-gliding platform. The Sun would retreat into another hot July evening in another hour or two.

They held field glasses and were meticulously searching for soldiers, not leaving the sky out of the mix drones could be killers so far, mostly. What they saw were some troops out on their days off. Some were fly fishing, others were riding dirt bikes, and a few were even flying kites. The soldiers were in leisurely pursuit of outdoor fun and recreation; they counted eleven soldiers that were in the way that they had to traverse. Only 33 minutes prior… two motorcycles almost ran into them on one of the Black Diamond tracks as they continued to work their way laterally instead of down a steep decline.

Josh pointed out several Ultralights and high-flying planes. Heather rolled her hand over, aiming out at drones flying back and forth over the Dam. This wouldn't be easy; neither spoke nor hadn't in over 15 minutes, and this was oddly comfortable. It felt like they were one in tune, chugging some water and staying under the tree cover, mostly Pines. The hard part of the hike was behind them. Bethel and Turtle Bay were within a Bloodhounds olfactory scent. They were close, but close only mattered in the game of Horseshoes or hand grenades. This was a life-or-death mission, and no one had to tell either one of them that!

They were at around 3,300 feet in elevation, peering down on the start of the Sacramento River that flowed from Shasta

Dam, which appeared almost parallel to their position hiding in the forested trees. Many of the soldiers were half-dressed in shorts without shirts. "What the heck do you make of that? They all have matching Blue tattoos on the same spot on the underside of their left forearms. That's weird, huh?…" "Yes, girl, it is rather strange for sure heck, check it out… look, even the guys fishing have the same ink… maybe it's like a gang tattoo." Heather zoomed into three women who laid back on beach towels wearing bathing suits. "Wow, it's exactly like Captain Rory's Pyramid tattoo. Josh, no shit, and he had an oval Blue Dot in the middle, and I can't find anyone out there that doesn't have one of them tattooed on the same spot on their left forearm… that's way weird? Like a cult marking or something."

Josh only shook his head and rolled out a small tarp "let's take a break here; we have a great vantage point and can see for miles," taking off their backpacks, dropping the cooler, cleaning the ground of pinecones, and fallen limbs, and twigs after a few moments they had a resting spot. Collectively they were extremely exhausted, muscles ached and sore they'd rest a few hours, hoping the recreational area would empty out of troops and they would leave once the Sun went down. Then cross the Sacramento River and follow the paved trails to the Sundial Bridge next to Turtle Bay, miles of paths all connected. Gladly, he tugged off his sweatshirt, made a pillow, laid on his side, and tapped his hand down. She kneeled infatuated, noticing he'd had dirt in the creases of his dimples, and watched him smile. "Come here…" holding his head up by a propped elbow.

Heather leaned down, kissed him once, twice, then dived in, engorging his mouth with her insatiable lust. Damn, she wanted him now…. he pulled her tightly toward him, fully engaged. Josh tried and wanted to feel the enraged passion he knew he should have sensed. Lastingly, Josh went for it and forcefully pinned her to him with rabid unrestrained sexual desire, and she attacked him like a

Lioness in heat. Josh yanked her down onto the ground, both breathing in gasps like pups in heat. Heather was wet, grinding her moist, lubricated lips…. labia's rotating her hips aggressively. Heather mounted him, straddling his waist. Tongues danced in unison as if their awareness was formed over years of loving sessions.

Swiftly he rolled her off "wild woman, stop this…. it's not the time and place, girl…" her Feral Eyes glistened, panting in unabashed animalistic behavior in heat, "Wtf Josh, you prick tease…. cmn on babe, you were giving as good as I gave you nghhhh you can't do this Josh you want me…." "That's right and wrong, Heather; the right part is I definitely desire you; the wrong factor is I can't do that right now. I'm so sorry it's ah um uh…."

Heather saw his eyelids puffed out, his embarrassed, demoralized expression instantly twisting her gut. Mortified OmGod no… short of breath feint, she gave him a peck on his pouty lips, knowing it was his lack of testosterone. He'd told her he'd missed dozens of his necessary injections. Heather said nothing and rolled her back toward him. Josh took his left arm and wrapped it over her dirty T-shirt. He folded into her, kissed the sensitive nape of her neck with a warm, sucking kiss, and breathed her skin in. Josh enjoyed her smell, pushing his nose into her hair. They rolled over and cuddled, and both fell asleep in less than seven minutes.

<u>Heather awakes to crunching leaves.</u>

Rustling leaves…. branches, and twigs snapping, it wasn't the sounds of wind blowing through the mountain trees with limbs swaying back and forth. Suddenly, an abnormal crackle, a footstep over dried leaves. It wasn't him that had awakened. Heather quickly took her forefinger and pressed it onto his murmuring, droning exhale. His baby snore ceased at once. His eyes popped up and open they had rolled while sleeping face to face her eyes were ablaze with terror. The moon was on a full beam. No words were expelled nor wasted. He slipped Captain Rory's Glock out, safety off. Heather had the scoped 22 sharpshooting rifle in moments in her arms. He slid the stolen RFD machine gun with a full 55 darts in the cartridge in front of him, alert, listening wired for sounds.

Noises were coming closer on three fronts from directly down the hill to the left or North and to the right or Southern side of their position. The clear escape route was to the West, which was right back up the mountain. Josh searched the night with the night vision scope. Heather looked through the night vision binoculars, super lucky to have confiscated some of Captain Rory and his Officer's weaponry and special gear a couple of days before. They had burrowed up on the inside of a hollowed-out Ginormous Oak Tree. Therefore, their backs were covered. That was the positive note; the negative was that they'd have to work their way around the Oak to head back up the mountain.

-71-

<u>While Josh and Heather slept.</u>

Three hours previously, a soldier who worked at the counterterrorism center, a cyber-geek who designed robots and had over 11 modernized technical designs and patents pending of new fandangled tweaks of his original Drone's revolutionary innovations, his inventions were in the air all over the world. A Scientific Savant who graduated with top honors from the prestigious MIT with a Master's Degree in Computer Science 'Eric' watched his two friends flyfishing, daring each other to jump childishly into the cool Sacramento River. The river was being fed from the bottom of Lake Shasta's Dam just 300 yards upstream. The Sun was on the down-low.

Eric could never find fun in the way others did. Eric loathed other humans, he felt superior to most of them. People didn't understand him, he was special in too many ways to describe all you had to do was ask him! With that being said, Eric was ostracized and isolated, and he was just fine with that. He was born a different breed of human, unsmiling and serious, and was stigmatized as a dweeb, nerd, yup, categorized as an introvert by many who knew him. Sexually pent-up emotions starting as a youngster had tried men and women gave both a whirl... when sexually frustrated in the past as a teen, he watched some porn but only a few times because he'd realized that sex wasn't his thing. There wasn't anything to match the raging hard-ons throbbing when he'd have a breakthrough on one of his inventions. Eric had decided he was asexual. If you wanted to label him, he was a different kind of person who desires celibacy over chaotic relationships.

Eric wonders why he was dogmatically stuck on this subject... what a waste of time! It was because of the night before... he was dragged to an underground strippers party for multiple birthdays. It bored him to death... He stared down at the motherboard on his latest Drone configuring a test sequence; this is what made him tick.

Relationships had to be nurtured and catered to, and he wasn't a kiss-ass nor a small talk specialist. No, Eric was narcissistic with his time and selfish. In his way of thinking... no one was good enough for him; why waste his time? Eric didn't want to get absorbed or get close to human beings ughhhh they were a foolish self-serving waste of his precious time. Eric deemed others as mere... Steppingstones. He'd use them and discard them and advance past each of them; people were buffoons, or better yet primates... um, Baboons.

Eric was still annoyed from being scarred; his skin was sacred to him, for God's sake. He wasn't a robot or owned by the government or anyone, and wasn't he a free man? Nope, apparently not... he didn't even control what permanently scarred his skin. But now he was branded and marked for life, just like all the rest of the morons. Eric had an ugly blemish staining his left arm, itching the newly branded Pyramid Tattoo with a Blue round center dot. Eric felt humiliated, for it was his skin, not the Governments. The orders were to comply or else visit Iron Mountain and be dishonorably discharged from the military. No doubt remained in Eric's head that the military-owned his body, mind, and skin... proof was inked on his left forearm. Geez, he hated the ugly tattoo. It was going to be his first and only tattoo. It was a nightmare being restrained in the tattoo chair, and it hurt like hell. Eric felt the vibes and was certain something sinister would happen to him if he didn't obey and go along with the orders from above... specifically Colonel Ruiz. Some of his fellow soldiers refused the Blue Tattoo and were never seen again. Enough dwelling on that it was done, as he scowled at the forever blemish on his epidermis. 　. Ughhhh.

Eric watched the soldiers... boys and girls, playing by the river. Most didn't wear the mandatory masks, especially now that they'd been tattooed with the new vaccine. Eric was testing a one-of-a-kind tree drone he'd named his new invention 'Chameleon.' The outside layer of his device could be integrated to match the color and contour of what he landed it on, such as the living bark of any tree. It was just a digital tweak; the drone could take a picture of the bark, and its skin would transform to match. He was ecstatic that 'Camo' could appear as leaves or foliage on a tree. He'd incorporated all the colors of the seasons and had only just finished with the Evergreen perennial varieties, which was an amazing feat in itself.

This latest design is super impressive; nothing out in the world compared to what Eric's drone could do it could not only hover for hours, it could fly at over 77 mph, dive, and lithely do 360-degree flips, somersaults, acrobatics across the sky at extreme speeds, Eric had installed sensors for 'Camo' to be able to maneuver through narrow openings. Eric had shortened the name of his latest innovation from Chameleon to 'Camo.' Smirking on the large side, crinkling up his nose, and licking his lips, Eric was having his kind of fun. Everyone else was into trivial flirting and just living in the moment. Eric wasn't like these fools. 🦎

'Camo' could attach itself with a steel grip like claws into limbs or trunks of any tree and didn't need to move to zoom in or out had a radius of almost a 360-degree vantage point only blockage was the trunk of the tree or what 'Camo' was latched onto.

Eric had been testing Camo out... attached to a Redwood Tree about 55 feet off the ground along the Sacramento River behind the Dam while modifying the wide-angle lens and dialing in the Thermal heat sensors taking dozens of digital pictures of his buddies down by the river. As he was repositioning Camo, he was preoccupied with the newly edited schematics and wasn't paying attention to the scrolling pictures that Camo had sent back to his controller box. Because he was testing one of his newest features, Eric had the alarm motion-detecting system off. If the sensors came upon a person, it would sound off. But because that was what he was doing, lol, peeping Tom-like on his so-called friends, the alarm was off. Then abruptly, from his peripheral vision, Eric caught a lit-up shot of two bodies. Eric gasped, froze, and clutched the joystick falling off his perch on top of a rotted log.

He didn't overreact, just stabilized Camo and calmly pulled back on the joystick, trying to maneuver through some thick branches and breathed in slow gasps as he'd practiced during Yoga lessons. Watching the camera's views from Camo, barely raising his cool and collective blood pressure rate, he pressed the button and took a video. At the same time, he snapped some digital pictures downloading them to his wireless mobile printer, which sat by a shrub a few meters away. He grabbed his backpack and bounced out of sight, took up the first 8 X10s, and exhibited a gruesome upturned sneer he'd seen the two faces before the shots appeared to be about five feet away in a mirror. It was the two missing fugitives that Colonel Ruiz and his forces had been searching for… everyone had assumed they'd gotten away. *Joshua Strong and Heather Otter, you are mine bitches… I gotcha!*

Eric squealed in delight, jumped up and paced quickly to a bush, and emptied his bladder with anxious contractions squeezed off with a little shake. *I needed to run a quick facial recognition test. Eric had that software on his iPad…* Eric steadfastly believed that he had located the wanted fugitives, but just for the record, he'd check out the F.R. software. He flipped a switch on his remote box and tried to zoom into their faces; today's facial recognition programs were amazing. Eric should know he pioneered some of the latest technological enhancements. Although in his book, there wasn't a doubt about whom Camo had located! He'd be rich in money and prestige, a notable hero! *How mom would be so proud of him…* Eric lit up in a glow.

With the tethered excitement of a three-time Tiddlywink Champion, he waddled down to his Playboy buddies, who were scanning the girls on the beach and in the water with their binoculars. Eric was cogent that the kissing, groping lovers above on the mountain could see his every gesture and had to play it cool. Eric's voice is in a monotone, "hey, guys, don't react to what I'm going to tell you. Just act normal and slowly follow me up into the trees, two fugitives that Ruiz has placed a $125,000 reward on." He paused for effect, "There up the mountain, not 300 yards away." "It ue, Eric, don't play with us, dude. No way you're a practical joker get out of here…." "Yes, way Tom… and you, Ray, stay here, and act totally normal don't be staring up at the mountain…. from where they're at, they can see us. Tom, please make your way up with me in a few moments. I'll show you the pictures; remember to act normal!" he said with raspy undertones.

A few minutes later, Tom sauntered up with a cocky shuffle. Eric showed him confirmation flashing the pictures and then the video. His pal couldn't restrain his excitement showing his exuberance by leaping in the air. "You're the man Eric. I mean, your awesome, dude…." They watched live Josh and Heather kissing and frolicking about embracing in a Hollywood love scene. Suddenly he rolled Heather off of him. Tom said, "damn, what's wrong with that dude thought we were going to get a POV, uuhhh live porn, real show fk!…." Eric slaps his back "wow, get with the program. That's unimportant what is to me is whom I will include in my $250,000 windfall. We don't want to alert all the soldiers here, for there'd be a 19-way split; therefore, let's include Ray. All we need is us three we will move out at nightfall, so get prepared…." Tom stared at him, thinking, 'WTHeck, this nerd has grown balls and is now assuming he is in control and the fricken boss… uhhh, that ain't going to work.'

Tom, Ray, and Eric waited patiently for the other soldiers to depart, knowing that with nightfall, they'd be packing out finally; they were the only ones remaining at the river. Eric kept Cama monitoring the sleeping fugitives. There were zero discussions by any of them about sharing the quarter of a Million dollars with anyone else. Eric enjoyed being in control and walked in front of them after laying out the attack "ok, this is how the split is going to work," he'd printed out a contract written with legalese. "I need you both to sign this paper, Tom, and you too, Ray. I'm allocating you to receive 80,000 each, and I will receive 90,000 dollars… that adds up to a cool $250,000! Unh, and hey, that's not including all the other prizes that have been promised for the capture of any fugitives. Oh yeah, and besides that, we'll be included in the Lottery!"

Tom glances at Ray, who says, "hey, wait, it should be an even split…." Then Ray catches a wink from Tom and pauses; Eric adds, "no, I disagree. I found them…." He waved his arm as if whatever handed them a pen, they begrudgingly signed the form. Eric self-righteously states, "Ok, we're not going to call this into dispatch. Otherwise, we'd have an Army out here. Lol, we handle this ourselves and will be Heroes, and who knows? Maybe Ruiz raises our ranks next week.... famous and rich with no worries, we'd be the talk of the military!"

"Yeah, my parents will be so proud and will be strutting around like magnificent Peacocks around my neighborhood and Country Club...." "Shut up, Tom, we have to get going. It's dark enough..." yelled Ray. Tom shrugs and then takes charge "okay, let's take them alive there's a 5 % added bonus for capturing at least one of em breathing... remember the Colonel wants to be able to interrogate them.... and I suppose Eric we will be splitting that in thirds also huh? Grab your RFD, and Eric, you go straight at them up the mountain; Ray and I will flank them. Get your night vision goggles. They won't know what hit them. Their blind up there...." Eric doesn't argue despite his arrogant partner's flagrant attitude and knack for playing the Alpha male. It didn't hurt that all the jerk did was repeat what he'd already sketched out. He wanted to climb the open Black Diamond trail to where the fugitives were. He couldn't very well be working his joystick through brush and over boulders.

"Eric dude are they still by that tree?___" they peered over his shoulder as he pulled up the video from Camo, his drone. The light Greenish screen showed no movement, and there they were, sleeping bodies. "Fk, how much easier can this be? We shouldn't even be late for freakin dinner," whispers Tom. "Let's roll! Shit, Eric, that video we watched earlier of them got me Horney; why wouldn't the dude screw her? She was on fire the bitch is a nympho___" "Tom, stop it___" "I'm just fkn around, is all, Eric, relax. I wanna get a close-up of that, Heather. Her mug shots are hot, anyways just because your Auburn-haired lumpy blow-up doll isn't out of the closet doesn't mean we gotta be celibate stroking off to fkn drones in dresses like you___" Even Eric laughs "your such an asshole Tom!"

"Hey, bro, I have a question?..." "hell, glad to hear you are alive, Ray. For a second thought, you sat there like a lump on a log and thought you were a figment of my imagination!" Ray jumps to his feet, smashing his empty beer can. "Time to be serious, don't forget this couple somehow got the best of Captain Rory, tying him to a fricken tree. He's in the hospital. I'm told the dude is like an animal. He can't speak, is chewed up, and doesn't know his own name! Dude, don't fricken forget this Josh and Heather duo also killed Private Smith and Corporal Hanson. Their no joke ughhhh if the rumors are true, they hadn't any weapons and were dropped off and hunted like Sheep up on Iron Mountain. Ugh, other unsubstantiated rumors I've heard are that Josh and Heather not only tied him to a tree but stripped him naked and tortured him, so I wanna know why we don't just send Camo up there and shoot the two of them with darts how simple would that be?" declared Ray.

Tom finished off his beer and declared, "yeah, it was sick, I heard, Rory. Ugh, I was told that there wasn't a spot on his body that wasn't bitten or chewed. They poured some syrupy stuff on his balls, and Ants and bugs ate him alive. Animals bit off his toes, and his fricken ears exclaimed Tom turning to Eric.... "The next thing yah need to invent is a drone that can drop a net on a person and pick them up and fly off... nah," as Tom slams his 5th beer and opens another, only one behind Ray. They both stared, waiting to hear what their nerdy friend would say regarding Ray's comment.

Eric was infuriated with them. Everything was a party with these goofballs; sadly, that was the norm for the ordinary soldiers, all superficial nonsense. The two of them were the same age as him, in their early twenties chasing girls, getting buzzed, barely being responsible enough to stay out of the Brig. Frustrated, he vents, "most of the time, neither you, Tom, nor you, Ray, even pay attention to me. I'm just a tag-along guy. I'm pissed off it's like all you do is use me.... you both owe me money, always borrowing. I'm like a loan store till your next paycheck...." "Hold up, dude. I know where you're going with all your freakin bullshit. How many times do I have to hear this same shit? You trippin' dude like we're using you ukm, like your one of my Hoes from the hood!

Eric throws up his hand. "Ray, it is always the same thing with you all about the hood... you being raised in a housing project uh complex because your Black I'm not trippin it's you that's...." "Shut-up guys," silence took hold while Tom spread his arms out "enough, please stop whining like women." Tom steps in the middle of them, looking at his partners in the hunt. "Let's drop the arguing and bickering and get back on the topic regarding the couple sleeping up the hill; dudes, we have to play this one close to the vest, uh, I mean, we don't, um, like want to share the money with anyone. We gotta stay focused; this fricken fugitive couple is like Bonney and Clyde. They tore through Captain Rory and our other friends Shaun and Chris, ah, man, they killed them savagely, dude we....." Eric kicks a beer can and gesticulates his hands out at his friends. "Stop! This bullshit, please, guys, be quiet. I've got to plan this out." Tom angrily flips a scowl at Ray, who blinks and nods.

Eric rolls his eyes "okay, yes, it's all true about Captain Rory. It was one of my drones that located him. I was the operator of it. I saved Rory, and truly he was a raving lunatic being devoured by so many animals fighting each other for pieces of him they'd already eaten all of Corporal Hansen, but that's not what's important...." Tom stares at Eric, "Wtf, and we're just now hearing about you saving the Captain?" Eric calmly rolled his diminutive shoulders. "It was ordered from above. Don't say a word about what I'd seen up on Iron Mountain, or else I'd end up in the Brig." Tom laughed as Ray popped another Coor's Lite "remember the couple was being hunted in some bizarre sequel to Hunger Games or something off the record, I did some hacking and found all kinds of classified information. Just last night, I broke their codes; they had new rules and called it the Shasta Games and...." "Shit, what are we doing standing here? We can talk about this stuff later. Let's get all our gear and capture them. There's money up there in those hills," laughs Ray... Tom howls "that was a good one, Ray!"

"This is exactly what the problem is.... you two constantly get drunk on your days off. You don't listen to me at all. If you did, you'd know that while you planned on getting drunk and fishing, I was working on a couple of technical conundrums, uh, flaws regarding Camo's loading gear. I didn't arm Camo's weapons. That wasn't the goal. I planned to come out here to the river and work on its night vision and thermal heat sensor controls, so I can't just fly it up as you say and shoot Josh and Heather with sleeping darts for us to go and retrieve! Furthermore, what exacerbates my mood, um, feelings is that since I told you about the news that we could collect $250,000.... we're in a winning situation here, and you guys are acting like damn teenagers. Damnit, we need to be serious, but nope, you two keep popping beers and don't realize the seriousness of this situation. These fugitives could put us all in the ground...."

Under the Coleman lamps glow, Tom winks at Ray, slyly unseen by Eric. He crushes his can of beer and throws it on the pile on the sand, "Eric is 1,000% correct party time is over. It's time to do this thing! Okay, we have radio communication but anything we say can be heard over the open frequency by anyone, so we speak in a sort of code. In fact, better yet, let's have radio silence full time unless we face obstacles or an emergency...." Eric inhales a full breath of oxygen and takes a gulp of his thermos of iced tea, watching Tom wobble and Ray's gleaming wandering eyes thinking, what a team. "You know what.... I'm having 2nd thoughts. Perhaps I should call this in, guys. We should still be able to claim portions of the reward, sharing it with the actual captors...." Tom shoves Eric, who slips and falls over a root dropping his thermos and Camo's control box.

"You ain't doing nothin' of the sort, dude Ray and I will handle this, you flim laser twerp....." Ray grabs Tom... "No, stop it, man, we're like the three Amigos, man, or like the characters in that movie 'Hangover,' we stick together....." Eric was picking himself off the rocky sand accessing the damage to his elbows and the side of his head, then saw Camo's Joystick with a side compartment cracked and the Red warning light error blinking intermittently. He doesn't bother with his small leakage of blood and crawls over to the controller box. Ray beats him there and grabs it while Tom… anxiously yelps. "I'm sorry, dude, dammit, I'm buzzed. Didn't mean it, Eric," helping him to his feet.

Eric looks at the controller shaking his head in anger and agony, musing, 'I'm done with these fools. We're not friends; I have no friends, heck, never have! Don't need friendships. It's truly all about what they can use and what they get out of the relationship, shallow human beings' He'd read in the Science Digest recently that Psychopaths were born and sociopaths were a product of their lives. Looking at Tom feebly trying to show hints of a conscience, knowing it was a learned reaction. Toss in an act about moralities and ethics. He's a self-centered, manipulating person gaining people's trust and then uses them for selfish objectives. Eric had watched Tom, who'd denied it till this day… Eric saw plainly with his sober eyes. Uhm, I observed the Psychopath drop a pill in this female Cadets brew, then help her out to his Jeep and flee the bar with the woozy female right to his apartment. I didn't see him again for a few days. The girl ended up in Mercy Hospital, dehydrated and oblivious as to what had happened… she tried to press charges against Tom for sexual assault. But the cameras showed her willingly leaving the drinking establishment.

Ray, despite his childhood, had a conscience… he knew he shouldn't say it, but Eric was fed up. "Tom, I'm having some difficulty trying to analyze if you're a raving psychopath or a sociopath or possibly a combination. Don't touch me again, or trust me, you will be sorry!"

Aggressively Tom starts moving toward Eric; Ray intervenes, "wait…." "That fricken Weasel called me a freakin nut. I'm not going to take that he's a chump…." Ray squeezes his forearm, raising his brows, then nods… silent communication, not telepathic, nah, maybe an inebriated beer reckoning. Ray pulls him near and whispers in his left ear subtly. "No worries, it's going to be a 2-way split… Us!"

Tom acquiesced, "ughhhh Eric, I screwed up. Sorry, I'm taking the left flank; Ray will take the right side of where the fugitives are, and you are hitting in the middle. We've got the GPS coordinates of their location input on our Walkie-Talkies. Remember radio silence till we get them, uhm, move slow and steady we aim to get them sleeping." Eric quickly speaks, "first things first, we have to head South to the walking bridge to cross the river, then will separate… hope we're not making a mistake, guys." Ray adds, "didn't the rewards state dead or alive, Eric?" "Yes, don't forget the extra 5 % if we keep them alive. It's for Colonel Ruiz's fun. You know the maniac is a freak. I betcha he wants to torture them personally, or you know LT Snings can be sadistic. They'd have a field day with them. Ahh, the couple could be wearing body armor that prevents the darts from entering their skin, so if the RFDs aren't effective will shoot them with our other weapons."

Finally, 19 long minutes later, together they look up in darkness, a Greenish glow provided by the night vision goggles seeing the ground, trees, and rocks with the Green lens daytime at nighttime. Tom flips them around and waves his arms. They disperse in different angles and diverse paths to the fugitive's meeting spot some 235 yards away. Yay. 🔫

<u>Heather and Josh are abruptly vigilant.</u> 😥

Heather felt an overwhelming impulse like a laser-beamed heat flash struck her… she zeroed in on her aligned reckoning and felt a last-ditch compulsion to relieve her pent-up emotions and feelings. She realized the moment wasn't ideal, but it might be the only moment Josh and she had left. <u>Her hand finds his body in the dark, his shoulder. "Josh, I want you to know I've fallen in love with you, boy. I love you!…" "Ssshh no sappy stuff girl cmm on</u>

this ain't over we're fighters stay focused we've been in worse situations…" thinking perhaps not.

Heather's mind implodes… floods with feelings unreciprocated, leaving her actual heartfelt words in the ether… ignored as chopped liver expressive words Guillotined. 'He never told her how he felt for me. Oh my God, I'm so blushingly embarrassed. *However, Heather didn't pull away from him; unexpectedly, he grabbed her head and pulled her tight to his face with a fast peck. "Babe, we gotta stay focused. That's our enemy coming for us. Let's do this!" Another leaf-scrunched… twigs were breaking and snapping. The noise was coming directly at them.*

Reinvigorated, she whispers into his ear, "you betcha, boy!" a brittle stick snaps to their left-their within 50 yards. She pulls down the night vision goggles. He scans the area with the RFD scope seeing nothing living but the trees. The forest was too thick, no one was on the Black Diamond track. They must be approaching cross-country!

Eric stayed parallel to the motorcycle path that he'd chosen from the off-road map of tracks. He pulled the RFD up and sighted the couple. According to the GPS taken by his drone, they were approximately 43 yards Northwest up the Black Diamond trail. He shook his head in disgust. The two drunkards sounded like Buffalos rummaging for foliage, herbivores, uuhhh buffoons, and he thought they'd surely wake up the slumbering murdering couple. Duh, this is stupid! His advantage was that the track he was on would bend to the West, not 15 yards from the giant hollowed-out Oak Tree that the couple slept in like a mini cave.

"We must stand and fight Heather," murmurs Josh. "I want you positioned to the South with your back to this Oak Tree base, we will be back-to-back like in the movies….." "Uh, why don't we run back up the mountain." "I don't know, it's just a gut feeling, but if this were a full-on assault, wouldn't you think there would be choppers and drones in the air above us with a platoon of troops out there?" "I guess so, Josh but…" "sshh, I see one." He leans into her ear "babe, keep looking if we can see them, they can see us. Our advantage is this Oak." They kneeled against the tree. He then spotted another approaching person from the North and muttered softly, "I have another one… there flanking us, girl," she whispered back. "It's strange, but I only see one. Why aren't there more?" he mumbles "be thankful for our blessings," Josh grasps her thigh and mutters a quick prayer.

Eric stiffened, frozen still as rocks tumbled down the mountain side one of which bounced off his shoulder above him where Tom was moving on the couple… thought, what fools the jerk had caused the control box to crash against the ground? Otherwise, his drone would be sending images from above. They'd all be connected with a rectangular LCD screen inside of their goggles. Everything would have been synched. They could have watched the fugitives, but alas, Camo, my drone was without controls, damnit a costly mistake.

Josh left the present, drifting back at an image from his gridiron days in Gainesville, Florida, at the Florida Gators practice field. One of the coaches was ex-military and fondly used analogies of war and battles, comparing them with football strategies. The Coach would say, <u>"It's all right to panic during a broken play but not to the point of being paralyzed if you freeze up… Nothing good will come of it, a turnover, fumble, or tackle for loss, all perilously negative results. That's the difference between playmakers, uhm, athletes… with intuition and natural raw abilities aligned with mental acuity and wherewithal to survive viscerally. Athletes use adversity to empower them, throw their human instincts into another gear, and use danger like a stimulant rather than an impediment"</u>

Joshua and Heather were under attack, and Eric, Ray, and Tom... smelled Money!

Josh took slow, methodical breaths waiting to see if there were more soldiers approaching, just the one shown, then disappeared behind more brush. Heather was tense with her 22 Caliber Rifle resting on an outstretched limb. Heather was concentrating on the approaching soldier's silhouette and had lost the shot three now four times. Trees and boulders shielded the advancing soldier, and he was now invisible... Josh spun toward her, whispering, "ok, I'll take the silent shot with this dart gun you fire next. This is how we will do it put your foot, uh, heel, against my foot when you have a shot, press weight onto me. I will do the same if we press near the same time; I will fire, then you instantly fire to... you got it?" she nervously replied. "Yes."

Eric stealthily made it to the bend, which turned like an inverted Emoji face around the middle of the smile. He'd have a clean direct shot straight up at the Oak Tree. He dropped down into a crawl again; rocks and pebbles blasted down the hill from Tom's aggressive movements above. Creeping closer and closer blinked as a stone bounced off his helmet, crawling over a berm. Whoa, he could see both figures kneeling back-to-back with weapons of their own, damnit just a few more feet inching nearer to a perfect shot. He lowers down on the ground leveling the RFD at his targets, and places his index finger on the trigger, carefully spinning the scope's focus unh, almost!

Josh's heel is touched hard. He presses back they fire nearly synchronized precise shots. Josh's dart catches Ray in the neck. He staggers; the echoed 22 Caliber loudly takes down Tom with a shot to his left shoulder, followed up by a second shot to his stomach both hit their targets, and so did Eric.

Josh hears Heather scream out, turns, and watches a pattern of darts spread above him into the tree bark immediately rolls, pulling her down. She'd been hit several times. He couldn't see how many darts were impaled in her skin. He did the only thing he could, which was to play dead, yelling out a Beastly groan and growl falls for effect with his RFD pointing in the direction the shooter had fired... his head, with night vision still attached, didn't budge, only a slight breeze trickled past dripping sweat then... he heard it!

Eric had fired a second barrage at them, and by the time the whooshing echoes of the darts had silenced, he was sure both the criminals were unconscious. He checks his RFD; only 22 darts remain. He'd blasted 33 darts at the couple in less than five seconds. Eric peers through his night vision goggles, and there in his scope, he sees at least one body down in a prone position. Uh, no, they were both down-checked his weapon making sure it was still in automatic mode, picking up his Walkie-Talkie. "Tom, Ray come in...." nothing came back. Eric tried one more time again with the same result. Eric began to panic, wishing he'd not altered the three Walkie-Talkies, having changed out the crystals retrofitting them for private conversations only. Damnit, he couldn't contact anyone for help. It was a double-edged sword indeed. This slashed at his psyche, wondering if the shots fired by the perpetrators that echoed over the hills were reported. He hoped the communication center based at Redding Airport was scanning all the radio channels. This was ordered at the start of the occupation of Shasta County by Colonel Ruiz and Major Bryan; from day one, a separate crew was supposed to monitor all radio channels. Hopefully, his fellow soldiers were on the way to help him. Eric was terrified and hyped up at the same time, he bit his lower lip, thinking, heck, I deserve the total reward. I got them... shot them both. I didn't need Ray or the belligerent Tom, darn it, second-guessing, uh, damnit, I had to split the monies... a deal is a deal. 🐾

He pressed the speaker on the Walkie-talkie… "Breaker, we have an emergency above the Shasta Dam. Possibly two soldiers down, we captured the two fugitives, Josh Strong and Heather Otter. Need assistance at once… over." Now he shouts shrieks out loud, "Ray, Tom, are you alive? Speak to me?……" Nothing, Eric was now challenged inwardly melded into skeptical terror 'was his manhood valid?' Always known to be shy and a bit timid, his self-conscious awareness of what others his whole life had thought about him, verbally said about him labeling him weak, a faggot, a nerd without balls, sure he couldn't do 15 pullups or bench press 200 pounds wasn't a fast runner nor an athlete ugh could he do this? Fear and terror shrunk him flaccid was he man enough?' He shuddered, almost whimpered, dreadfully feeling the urge to weep to tear up. Eric froze like stuck in the mud, unable to move, petrified, and peed.

Josh had heard the stressed man's voice cry out from below about 15 to 20 yards off, glad that Heather had been raised a Tomboy hunted with her Uncles and father. She was a definite asset, shooting down one of their enemies. He had carefully pulled three darts buried deep in her body, one puncturing her left breast. The poor girl had wet herself. Ugh, I couldn't do anything about that. Now he wondered just how long it would be until reinforcements arrived, determined not to abandon her. He felt like a Captain going down with the ship. Then the gruff sound of an angry voice rang out from his left side. "Hey, Eric, I'm hit. I need to be medevac'd out with stomach and shoulder shots. Get me film help now, bro! I'm not going to last long bleeding out…." Eric didn't move even more, frightened, shaking nervously, still watching the two bodies. Though he'd seen some movement decided to be proactive and fired another spray… burst of darts at them, depressed the trigger off, and flew 11 more darts.

Josh heard the swooshing sounds at the same time. A flurry of darts tattooed the Oak Tree and buried themselves into the ground, another hitting Heather in the back, thinking was it wrong to use her as a shield, or was he doing so? No, uh, he was lucky that there was a small ridge of grass that grew up around the base of the magnificent Oak, relieved until he saw the trail of blood pump down her cheek, dripping from her chin OMLord not wanting to move, but he had to. Josh saw another two darts in her head and yanked them out, hearing a crunching noise from her Scalp. In all, Heather was hit seven times. Omg, would she live?

Eric picked up his Walkie-Talkie. "Tom, you know the radios are useless. I'll have to backtrack down to the Jeep and radio for help to airlift you out, buddie… what about Ray?… over." Silence for an instant, then Eric blurted out, "oh yeah, there's a chance they're monitoring all communications across all bands and frequencies and could zero in on us any minute, also that gunfire will be reported… over." "Wtf, Eric? What are you doing? Get moving; who gives an fk about Ray? I'm dying, bro…bleeding out. Hurry, Eric, hey, you can have my share of the reward. I don't care anymore…. over." gasping for breath, "fk I hurt dude okfk ash…. please Eric hurry up!… over."

Eric turns to the tree, scanning the downed bodies. There was no movement whatsoever in the same vein of thought…. where was Ray? Was he injured or dead? His analytical brain breaks it down. Tom and Ray are shot. Wait, he'd heard only two shots fired by a rifle, and Tom claimed to be hit in the shoulder and stomach… huh, so the fugitives must have stolen an RFD machine gun cause Ray hasn't replied. He had to be sedated like the couple is now. They will be sedated for at least seven hours can't carry them down the mountain… realizing what he must do! Again the radio bursts out, "fk, what are you doing? Have you left for help? Come on, dude… over." *Eric starts to whistle, humming into the Speaker one of his favorite old-time tunes by the Artist 'Queen' 'Another one bites the Dust.' Then* allows himself to laugh. "Hey, dude, Tommy boy, I betcha need another beer, huh loser!... over." "What the fk, Eric? Are you sick? Man, get me out of here. I don't...." Eric pushes down the mic blocking Tom's words, then releases to no sound. "Tommy boy, how's it feel you, badass Psychopath, you freak, meet Eric the Sociopath. No worries, don't stress, poor boy. Slow your heart rate down. You'll last longer and won't pump as much blood out."

"Uh, sorry, Charlie, I must attend to Ray now. Then I will put you out of your misery. Stay where you are. Don't go hiding on me, pal, uuh, poor baby Tommy!... over." "Eric, please stop fkn around this ain't uuh oh uuhhh meaning I'm in the worst pain... over." "ssshh little baby don't say a word daddy is going to fkn kill you! Yep, shut the Fk up!... over."

Josh shivers and thinks what a manifestation, a transformation worthy of a Steven King Novel, the docile sounding scaredy-cat mild mannered Jekyll & Hyde conversion don't know if this Eric guy is a Psychopath, but he definitely is a lunatic possibly breaking under pressure a dangerous guy, and he was on the move. He slowly lifts his head, periscoping about saw feet, then nothing in the Green glow listening. Yep, the guy was coming straight up the trail right at them, damn. He rolled the RFD up and laid his head down as if sequestered and Knocked-out seconds passed by before Josh realized that this Eric veered off the trail. Then some breakage of twigs and crushing leaves, he was going South.

Eric couldn't find Ray anywhere. "Ray, where are you? Hey Ray, it's me. I'm here to help you...." nothing. He sees a large boulder and climbs up to the top of it, searching, scanning a wide radius of the area, and finally spots him, inches himself back to the ground. "Hello, Ray, are you ok?" Eric reached down and rolled him over; Ray was shot with a dart right in his darn neck, 'damn idiot Ray buddy, I know you're not a bad guy, not really, but you're going to be a dead guy.' Eric reached to his side and snapped from his sheath a razor-sharp Buck knife and ran it across Ray's windpipe a few gurgles bam...

deceased. He wipes the blade, thinking he'd watched addictively all the CSI series... lessons learned. He'd wrap Josh's handprint around the Tang or handle of the knife. Of course, he grinned. He wore gloves. Eric took Ray's handcuffs. He would need two pairs to cuff up the couple. Off he went towards the last conscious person that could ruin his plan.... ironically, the Walkie-Talkie goes off, "Eric, help me... come on!" wheezing barely verbalizing like a split personality schizophrenic, he snaps back, remembering a serious misnomer contrarian foul-up blunder he started running back down the path and over to the North side of the hill towards where Tom should be.

Eric's mind tweaked paranoia-wise, thinking all of their conversations were or could be recorded by a tower or satellite via scanners on the UHF frequencies and could be monitored even now, or someone working in communications could have stumbled on the active channel they were speaking on huffing and puffing stops with this thought in his mind clicking on the mic. "Tom, sorry, I just lost it. I've never been in a skirmish or at war; as you know, I just played those simulated war games. I'm coming to help you speak to me... yell loudly so I can find you!... over." Eric started frantically searching for Tom, not worried about the couple who'd be out for hours depending on how many darts were injected into their system. "Hey, help me... Eric, I'm over here by the tall Pine tree... over." "I am going to try to stop your bleeding once I find you and then get to the Jeep for you to be air-lifted out... over," Tom moans and howls, screaming... fk Eric, "where are you?" "over here, over here, brother." Eric's intensity grasps him again, grinding his teeth "he needs to shut the asshole up!"

Josh had watched the guy flash by running past the opening on the trail. He didn't have a shot. He decided to clean Heather's face and felt her weak pulse. They'd heard that five to seven darts could be terminal depending on the person's tolerance to the drugs injected. Heather was hit with a total of seven darts. He was glad that they had kept some of what was in Captain Rory's First Aid Kit. It was in her backpack the antidote to the darts formula.

Josh worriedly and cautiously slid his rear end over, trying to grab the pack. Then he said to himself in anger, it's now the guy Eric against me, Josh taking a long stare at his girl. He rubbed her hair out of her face and kissed Heather's forehead, and whispered… "Yes, Heather, I do love you." Hoping she could hear him in her unconscious state, "I'll be back, babe. I can't waste any time. The guy will be coming here next. I'm going to surprise him." He jumps to his feet in one motion. Josh frowned into a grimace, grinding his teeth, and converted his pain and worry for Heather into a callus machine-like persona. He outwardly growled now… Josh was the epitome of concentrated determination… heart pumping vengeance for shooting his girl, tossed the RFD over his shoulder, and grabbed her rifle, scanning the horizon for the guy he'd nicknamed 'Eric the Psycho' off he went in the last direction he saw him run by.

Eric rounded a bend navigating the dirt and rocky soil through a Green glow, then turned up a berm. The thermal signatures flashing footprints were still in view paranoia struck him. Was he stepping into a setup like a Clint Eastwood Movie? He leans around a Pine Tree, <u>not wanting to shoot him with his RFD. Ray was shot with a different RFD ballistics would prove that.</u> Finally, he sees Tom, who isn't moving. Eric took out his 45 Caliber pistol, not wanting to fire it because it would lead directly to him… being registered in his name. What else could he do if Tom pulled his gun on him? Creeping up slowly, bending down, barrel pointed at the jerks head, blood-stained dirt piled up didn't want to pull a glove off to check for a pulse, kicked the Walkie-Talkie from Tom's grasp, then aggressively stamped on Tom's crotch one foot and jumped back…. nah ole Tommy was dead.

Sighed…. pressure left his aura, stress relieved now to get back and handcuff the fugitives a dream night indeed. A ghoulish scowl erupts from his face remembering Captain Rory looking down at the corpse. Will the animals come for dinner for Tommy and Ray? Ahh, what did the French say? Bon Appetit! *"Eric, don't turn around. Drop your weapons. One false move will be your last, don't tempt me!" Josh watched closely with the RFD held outstretched in front of his shoulder. Eric didn't move and had his back to him. It was the Green glow; they saw no moon, only low-lying clouds above.*

"Your slick dude played dead, huh? A bad miscalculation on my part, but I did get your bitch. I saw her fall. I already called both my headquarters and informed the Captain in charge that I had the infamous Joshua Strong, and Heather Otter pinned up on this mountain, even sending the GPS coordinates to them. It won't be long till this mountain is crawling with troops. Dude, you won't make it off this mountain," laughing, "drop your weapon now, this is your last warning while Josh moved closer to him. "Joshua, right? Uhm, you might have a chance at living if you give yourself up right now. I could talk Colonel Ruiz into giving you leniency. Ah, me and Ruiz are pretty tight." Josh doesn't reply, so Eric motors on, still not obeying Josh's command, "howya going to get Heather off this hill, huh you ever think about that?" Josh watches Eric through the glow of his night vision scope and barks back at the freak. "I sure have. You're going to help me carry her, Eric, down the hill." Josh closed in on him, now only five feet from the diminutive soldier. "Unless you want me to leave you tied to that Pine Tree naked like I did your Captain Rory either way, it doesn't matter much to me." the stare-off continued neither moved for an eternity, it seemed.

Eric replays an excerpt of the video from his drone that saved Captain Rory… the guy's body was hemorrhaging from every pore, and in his mind's eye, he saw the female Mountain Lion. Rory didn't resemble a human; his torn and fractured bloody figure was beyond recognition, his nude body chewed while being alive, toes literally bitten off. Ants, Ticks, Flies, and mosquitoes swarming covered his skin and groin area. Just imagine that pain... he drops his 45 Caliber pistol to the ground, then the RFD.

"Take the knife you used to cut your friend's throat and toss it down on the ground, what, Eric, are you so dam greedy that you didn't want to share the spoils, umh, the reward for Heather and me so you'd kill your pals? You're one sick bastard, Eric, a real freak. Put your hands up now...." "How'd you know I cut his throat?..." "I didn't; you just confirmed it. The sheath holding the knife is bloody. It was an easy assumption, right... genius." Josh slings his RFD over his shoulder, sliding Heather's rifle out of the way... confident he could physically handle this soldier stepped behind him and started to pat him down, kicking his feet and legs out wider. Eric felt Josh's two hands on him, which meant he couldn't be holding a weapon. Eric swiftly spins a rotating hammer fist and twists upward, propelling a backward elbow at Josh's jaw and swiveling around. Being proficient in Taekwondo, he went to put his body in his attack stance. Josh hit him as the elbow grazed his ribs, a left cross right on the button of Eric's chin, dropping him, then kicked him as if kicking a 51-yard field goal, a winner in the gut. Then booted him again, and dropped a flying knee into his sternum, hearing Eric gasp, losing his oxygen. Josh had lost his night vision goggles and could barely see him, he reached down and jumped on the figure that was doubled up on the ground, moaning and whimpering. Josh rolled the fool over.... "This isn't the movies, Eric, or one of your video games, your martial arts career needs practice. Oh, and by the way, if you had called your superiors, this mountain would be swarming with soldiers. Where's the helicopters and drones, man?"

Josh hits him again with a swift uppercut after he'd regained his footing and then a brutal punch into Eric's stomach. "That's for my girl!" Eric tripled up groaning, moaning almost now pitifully crying, his goggles displaced.... Eric balled up into a fetal position rolling in Tom's blood. Josh pulls him up by his hair, and a gloved hand takes Eric's Army coat off of him, finding another knife that was hidden and two sets of handcuffs. A few minutes later, Eric wore only his boxers and T-shirt with his Army boots tied tightly, taking his confiscated 5-inch switchblade knife and poking him, "get up, Eric, we're going."

"I'm freakin freezing, dude. Why does it got to be like this, man?" " I had to check you for weapons, and I'm glad that I did. Uh, then I guess I got a little carried away, and no, it's not even cold. It's perhaps 77 degrees. This is July, not January. You are lucky for that." Josh starts pushing him down the trail.

<u>Joshua leads Eric to his fallen girl.</u>

His girl lay; still, blood spilled over her forehead from the dart's penetrations. Seeing this, he kicks Eric in the butt, dropping him over a tree root taking the cuffs out, and rolled him onto his face and stomach. Josh Hog ties him up, Eric was whimpering, and tears flowed freely from his eyes, he thought he was a dead man. Josh shouts, "Either be quiet, or I'll put a pinecone in your mouth to shut you up! You stay still now. I need to take care of Heather." Josh decided to pack everything up and leave anything that wasn't needed. He searched what Heather had taken from Rory's First Aid Kit and had put into her backpack. Josh sighed with a big exhalation when he found the antidote needles... he grabbed them and relaxed a smidgeon.

Josh was fretting over the seven darts that the bastard had shot into her body gathered all necessities, cleaned Heather with antiseptic swabs, wiped her clean, gently kissed her forehead, then injected her with the antidote.... checking her pulse, only a shallow increase she didn't show any signs of awakening not wanting to inject her again for it might just kill her frustratingly lost in what to do… began the task learned as an Eagle Scout.

Tied Eric's uniform, pants, and jacket together, cutting slots in the tarp that Heather and he had laid down to rest on and made sort of a stretcher carefully took her body and laid it on the makeshift cocoon… and kicks Eric. "Here's how this is going to play out, soldier boy. We are going to carry her down the hill. You're taking the lead; the Moto Cross trail is around 15 yards away. If you drop her, I will knock a few of your teeth out… the next time. It will be a broken nose yuh get my drift there, Eric?" "What if I stumble or trip, fall on accident, dude? This ain't fair…." "Tell me about it. Life sucks, but what's the alternative? If you fall, your mouth will resemble a Meth addict, toothless or possibly a Halloween Pumpkin…."

Josh dwells like he always did, thinking back to his 'Glory Days' one of his favorite songs by 'Bruce Springsteen.' When Josh was a winning quarterback, and how each play had at least seven blocking schemes and contingency plans, what if the inside linebacker blitzed?

Now on the move wearing night vision goggles, they make it down to the Sacramento River without any problems, most importantly not being seen; he hopes and mumbles a silent prayer it's 10:45 pm. How does he get them to Bethel? Uhm, or the Sundial Bridge or even Turtle Bay? Come on, think fast, he mutters…. Quickly he started to move, taking out a section of nylon rope, pulling Eric to a tree limb, tying him up, and placing a gag in his mouth while he asked himself, 'what am I doing? Why…?'

Josh leaves both Heather and Eric in a grove of trees just on the West side of the River. The Shasta Dam was only 300 yards to the North, the monstrous Dam above them 600 plus feet in the air. The soldiers patrolling the structure only needed to peer down at the Sacramento River, which was being fed by the Dams release, and there they'd be. Josh hurries back up the mountain, hoping to locate Ray's body. If so, he'd take his uniform. After questioning Eric, the man was almost his size. There was no way Eric's uniform would come close to fitting…

lucky enough, in 15 minutes or so, he'd located Ray's body. His carotid artery had bled out gravity flowed the blood away. He quickly dressed; not a bad fit, he surmised a little snug it'll work… back down to where he'd left his girl and Eric.

Eric couldn't very well cross the small bridge to the East side of the river in his boxers… so he had to rearrange the stretcher doubling up the tarp, and off they stepped in the open this is where the vulnerability was at its maximum exposure. Josh kept his eyes on a swivel, looking for any humans down by the river. They covered the distance without any mishaps across the walking bridge. Josh remained vigilant, keeping one eye on Eric, who could shout out and blow up his plans, "where are you parked?" "Our Jeep is parked between some trees over there…" gasped Eric, huffing and breathing hard. "You know this is a strait bust if someone sees us carrying this girl in the parking lot…." "Move it to the Jeep!"

Wow, is there a chance that Heather and he could really escape this nightmare? Glimpses the Jeep Cherokee and loads Heather in the back bench seat "turn around, Eric," who mumbles, "no, don't shoot me here…" too late. Josh fired a dart between his eyes and another in his chest. He fell backward after struggling to clutch the car door. Josh kicked him, then rolled him into a thicket of Blackberry briars, being July-ripened berries hung from the vines…. Josh, now more relaxed, casually plucked some. ✳

-73-

Bethel Church Bound

Joshua had already achieved Yeoman's work… finally, he sighed with a flash of relief, lucky he had been firing on all eight cylinders without forward thinking he would have forgotten to take the keys from Tom's pocket at the scene of his death. Josh deliberately removed his goggles, placed Eric's soldier's cap on his head, and started the Jeep up. Tight against his hip was a 45 Caliber pistol. He drove away, leaving Eric hidden in a blackberry thicket. The ride was less than five miles, and thankfully, uneventfully, he blended in with the vehicles on the road… Army Jeeps and the occasional Humvee. Josh decided to go directly to the Turtle Bay Complexes… and saw the guards well before he was stopped at the gate. Which Josh fully expected; hence he had hidden the gun on the passenger side floorboard.

Little did Josh know if the troops that manned the gates were still Bethel spies that had infiltrated the occupation party of Government soldiers. If not, he'd be arrested, it was worth the gamble, for he didn't know how long Heather could make it without medical attention. Bethel had their disciples in place since the 7th of July. Before he was apprehended, he prayed that they still controlled the Turtle Bay Convention Center gates. Three soldiers walked to the Jeep, passing the painted White and Red crossing bars like a railroad crossing, two of the three had rifles posed directly at him. The leader came to his window. "Can I help you, soldier?" Josh only said an acronym FOE (forces of evil) that used to be the passcode he'd been told before he was arrested, leaving the meeting at U–Prep High School… like eons ago. Swiftly with precision, the cross bars were lifted. The leader hopped onto the running board. "Drive into the parking lot to the left… park underneath the Whippoorwill Tree."

The Bethel team was thankful the Jeep Cherokee was an older version stripped down with no tracking GPS chips or onboard computer systems, they parked it in the expansive Sundial Bridge parking lot, and the clock ticked past the bewitching hour, the 23rd of July 2025 was upon them.

In less than 35 minutes, Elder Jeremy had medical personnel on site and Heather and him tucked away in a hidden chamber so Josh could unwind. He went from energetically expounding on their survival experiences, sighing tiredly, and exhaling deeply, closing his eyes while speaking to Wanda. "Thank you all for being here for me...." "ssshh, Josh, I want you to relax. We have a Doctor waiting for Heather in one of our labs...." Just then, a couple of Nurses knocked at the open door, "come in, Sisters, please take care of Heather."

Finally, Josh could relax a little he was deliriously exhausted and was led to a room with a bed. Wanda said, "Joshua, you are a mighty man. God was with you, and the Heavenly Spirit saved you.... now I want you to take a nap and then a long, relaxing hot shower. Don't you worry your precious soul about Heather; she's in great hands. I have been informed that because she was shot with seven darts filled with caustic chemicals. It would be better for us to be careful when giving her the antidotes you brought with you. We also have to take into account that you already gave her one shot. Our labs have designed the latest remedies to counteract the chemicals in the darts but mixing adrenalin injections, ughhhh, many advocates have in these cases stated it could be dangerous to her heart, so we must be patient."

"What? I can't rest. Let me be with her...." Wanda stands, "no, she's in serious condition; five darts have proven fatal in over 50% of cases. The mixed tranquilizers have been lethal more times than we can count with just three darts. Heather was shot with double that amount. You listen, hear Josh; she's a strong young lady. Heather is going to be just fine, and we will all be praying for her!" "I'm not leaving her side...." as he sat in a chair next to Heather's gurney. Wanda's nose curled up, motioning towards a nurse, "please bring in a cot for Joshua." Strangely, another entity was lingering in the atmosphere supernaturally, mirroring the dimension that Wanda spoke with Josh within. Heather floated in this dimension, seeing her docile and unconscious body on a gurney. The words that were hoarsely whispered in her left ear still reverberated. _"Heather, you are not the one for my Joshua. You're a street tramp and whore, ugh, a drug addict. I'll make sure you never wake up. Your destiny has already been written in the sacred scrolls. You'll spend eternity in the underworld with Hades… your supreme leader!"_ Oddly, music played close to Heather's left ear… strange genre for Wanda to be listening to in her AirPods. 'Mask Off' was the song that Heather recognized the artist was 'Future.' What did this mean? Uhm, was Wanda wearing a mask? Heather was confused and felt locked in her soul. Unable to move… silent as a corpse.

Josh wakes up not knowing where he is… swinging his fist and kicking!

Josh didn't know what hit him. He woke with a wet cloth against his forehead, thought he was bleeding, and was back on Iron Mountain with Captain Rory standing over him. He pounced up enraged and bellowed out a grizzly howl.

A startled woman in a nurse's outfit bounced against a wall in the room, cowering away from him, raising her arms in a calming gesture at him. She pointed at a gurney showing him her compassionate liquid Blue eyes, which glowed back at him… those eyes, whose eyes? The eyes he'd known his entire life… she says, "Rest, son." He did while his Mother rubbed his head, a caressing kiss on his cheek. Exhaustion melted Josh… realized he was dreaming.

Latoya, Rocky, and Brock.

"I hope you boys are hungry. The biscuits will be out of the oven in less than 10 minutes," yells Latoya stirring her Mama's sausage gravy and eggs with Habanero cheddar cheese mix recipe, yum she *took another sample. I'm totally blessed to be standing in this rustic kitchen alive. The most challenging part of her consciousness was trying to assimilate and move into the present time. Future thoughts and hopes she couldn't respond to…. or absorb and digest, hell to even think about how her life was upside down imploded, uh exploded not only barely a couple of weeks ago!*

Here she stood making brunch for two White men shit, not that I'm racist, but shaking her beautiful brown face. I'm comfortable with my own people, no, not prudish or snobbish knowing she was an integral part of the upper-class society of educated professional Black men and women, not a ghetto queen like she'd been called by some fellow White students years back. Stopped stirring the gravy 'yep…. I never hung out with whites; much sure I had White friends that she worked out with.' Latoya thought about it for a second and realized she'd really never been to a white family dinner and didn't much relate with Caucasians. Guessing the most interactions with whites were at her family's Gymnastic Studios, where she was a trainer and instructor to many children. However, Latoya did keep some of the lighter variety of people in her social media accounts, especially from her College days. I had dated a few White guys, but there wasn't any chemistry to be had, kind of like Pepper and Salt.

Latoya did fall hard for a cutey pie Hispanic guy when she was 19 years old. It wasn't that her parents were against interracial dating, but they did make it clear there were plenty of credentialed Black prospects available, yep. One afternoon, Daddy had taken her to the side and subtly told me that he was sorry for how he'd treated a few of my dates. He told me he wasn't being fair when he purposely didn't make himself available to meet the off-black guys I brought home. Daddy disappeared after the introductions, snobby-like. I suppose I got the not-so-subtle hint and subsequently fell in love with a black man, Married….' "Hey, you need some help in their girl?…" "I got it 'hold your Horses' Brock!" she could hear their laughter in the Den.

Her 6-pack Abs clenched muscles tight, and she'd not hit the Uneven bars or her favorite, the Pommel Horse, in weeks. Latoya was called a natural at Gymnastics, an extraordinary athlete. She competed for herself and her family… race, and her country once she was so gloriously proud of her accomplishments, not any longer though it was like ancient news gone from her mind. Now it was all part of her superficial past life. Staring at the clock above the stove, almost 1 pm today, she'd be able to call home if the military occupiers did what they'd promised and were true to their words, the same law-enforcement types she'd witnessed killing her defenseless brother and husband. Terror filled her veins… squeamish and dour remembrances, anxiety, trepidation, and weariness filled her shrunken lungs, glued tongue dry. How could she ever begin to tell her mother, father, and her husband's parents about what happened?

Latoya lived for just that purpose. What the two white guys didn't realize was she only wanted to set the record straight, then she was done, never a quitter ugh hhh just need not live any longer, was all. <u>Latoya flinched and turned to see Rocky massaging her tight rotator cuffs "umh, thank you, Latoya, for cooking… wow, that is smelling enticingly delicious, girl," he shouted, "Brock come on, get your ass in here; it's a freaking feast…" Latoya had to admit she liked this man, ah, adored him… what was the ole saying? Ah, oh yeah, he was "White, but he was just Right!" she laughed to herself.</u>

Rocky did something internally to me not sure what it was, but it was like energizing me… his charming confidence combined with the man's straight-up arrogance, uhm, and those Copper Brown eyes seemed to magnetize me. "Stop it, Rocky; it's nothing special, just a recipe from my momma, is all." Brock rolls up next to them. "I'm starving all of a sudden, woman thanks!"

"Come on guys, just eat; it's not like…." Rock puts his forefinger vertically across her plump lips "sshh, now neither of us three has had nothing but cold sandwiches, soups, beef jerky, and essentially fast-made food. This is fine home cooking; you're an awesome Chick, come on, let's carry everything out to the kitchen table and pile up our plates and bowls. We can eat in the comfy living room…." Brock grabs the plates and bowls and adds, "There's supposed to be a bulletin due out by Colonel Ruiz coming up." "Chick," I chortled. "Isn't that so freakin White man, like from the 70s hippy days, or was it the 60s." They laugh while shoveling plates full of Brown Sugar and Honey butter biscuits, Orange juice, milk, and Rock cackles. "Yah, I thought you'd like the chick moniker. It had been decades since I'd used it," chuckling some more! "Chick, why chick" her grin contagious. "You promise not to take it the wrong way. I'll tell you, well, I was stepping into the kitchen behind you and saw your fine sway ass in that long apron that has Red Barns… White picket fences embroidered all over it with farm animals Roosters, Chickens in patterns thought you're one fine chick!…" Rocky spits, accidentally bursting dimples covering his face to hide all the non-chewed food "it was a moment all three of us fell about, leaning on one another, busting up hysterically. I giggled, slapping him playfully, wiping tears most fun I'd had since, I don't know… 'Loudly heard a name from the TV.'

<u>The bad news was forthcoming.</u> 🌐

Instantly the room's vibes and ambiance forever altered as if a furnace's heat hit their faces. Death Valley dried lids expressions of contempt, focusing on the screen staring at a montage of Rocky Blake's pictures in his many military uniforms and FBI Badge, but the narrator was careful not to show any medals nor any of his dozens of awards. This was a negative-styled broadcast like something from back in the day, a show called "America's Most Wanted." Next to hit the screen were pictures of Brock Dune, also with an FBI Badge attached to his suit. Scrolling on the bottom of the screen, 'Agents who turned on America, these two are the worse of, the worse bad cops that need to be held responsible for unfathomable carnage!"

Rewards for both of them had escalated to $225,000 per head. I held my spoon to my mouth, freezing up and noticing the guys were chewing away… joyously eager for their next mouthful, moaning in delight. I supposed their attitudes were fix the Colonel, and the rewards may be like the Western Days with what Jesse James did when he'd see wanted posters of him all over towns. He'd been known to take his pen out and put his 'John Henry' Jesse James autograph on some of them. Heck, if they weren't worried, why should I be?

Instantaneously my mood drastically changed in mid-spoon. There were three pictures of me, uh, her Latoya. I'm on the screen with a $75,000 reward named a complicit accomplice working with the two wanted mercenaries! Their appetites slowed as the roundup of Fugitives continued. One thing I noticed was that the names were always the same. Only a few additional criminals were added to their most wanted list. Which meant obviously they were not catching them, I mewed. "That wasn't a flattering exposé of me ughhhh, did you guys notice they didn't show anything from the last three Olympics, nothing positive about me?" Brock said what I thought aloud, "apparently, the powers to be haven't captured many fugitives funny, uh…." "Rocky throws in, "well, they're saving money not having to payout the rewards," cackles from the men. Their hunger resumes… like no big deal done.

Ooops, I heard a loud, long beep…. then a scrolling bar at the bottom of the screen in light Red 'Live update from the Sundial Bridge; BOLO (be on the lookout) the screen enlarged. "I'm Lieutenant Snags. We are looking for these two murderers; their

The cameras pan-out microphone sticks in front of a disheveled guy who had bandages wrapped around his head and looked severely beaten on a stretcher. He wobbled up onto the podium being held by Medics leans his bruised and battered face into the microphones. "Josh and Heather attacked us last night without humility like animals. I was able to get some shots off and shot Heather numerous times with my RFD. Josh must have circled around and got behind my friend Tom and shot him unmercifully two times, killing him. Then Josh shot my other friend Ray with Captain Rory's stolen RFD." Eric squints into the cameras and grimaces, speaking into a microphone.... "Then the vile predator Josh took a knife and nearly decapitated Ray cutting his throat, and then he put on Ray's uniform. Then he forced me to help him carry Heather down the hill and then stole our Jeep Cherokee...." Pan-out, switch cameras, the green Cherokee was parked with MPs standing beside it.

LT Sungs stood by somberly as the Medics helped Eric back on the stretcher and continued. "Somehow, the assailant, Mr. Joshua Strong, had switched out vehicles here under the tree line. Josh must have been aware of where our cameras were, for we don't have any other views, oddly ironic, we also couldn't pick up anything on satellite. We know that Heather was hit seven times with our darts; they were found emulsified in blood and mixed in a pile of leaves up on the mountain. Heather couldn't walk from here, so this criminal, Josh Strong, had help. At least one other accomplice, or possibly he's working with Rebels, this same couple is guilty of other murders up on Iron Mountain. We need the public's help to capture these outlaws!"

<u>Joshua and Heather were heroes in Rocky, Brock, and Latoya's book.</u>

Rocky slides another gravy-dripping biscuit into his mouth. Shaking his head Brock licks his spoon. "Well dammit, those two *have supplanted us on the most wanted list crap, at least our rewards are higher,"* lol. "Well, now we know the couple escaped the military's dragnet, that's way cool… I guess, as it turned out, we didn't have to help them out after all.   You have to give it to them; they're resourceful, good for them," yelps Brock. They both pop up. "I'm going for seconds this is scrumptious 'L'….." "Yeah, wildly delicious girl, you blacks no how to make these grits…." I had to smile and bark back… "You're a damn idiot, Brock those ain't grits," light giggles mixed with laughter. Grits these White men. Lol, did they know the fricken difference? Latoya followed to grab one more honey and buttered biscuit before they were all gone. She couldn't believe how hungry she was. They didn't seem bothered or nervous about what the Lieutenant reported on the television, not nervous a bit, so why should I be?... while in Rome, you know the saying. I saw the great big Grandfather clock and said, "only 25 minutes till communications should be up and running… I can't wait!"

We sat back down, working on seconds. The guys gobbled up third helpings. The frying pan was scraped clean I had to smile with a full tummy. It had been so darn long "you guys thrive on stressful situations. I noticed yesterday, with the Dogs barking and sniffing around the perimeter of this property, that neither of you was sweating. I had to admit I was biting my fingernails. Heck, there was a full platoon of soldiers less than

175 yards from us. I felt like I was nervously balanced on the edge of a cliff, but your perimeter system had the Dogs following a trail that led nowhere. Gotta admit it, that was clever!" Brock nodded "with your balance, you'd have no problem climbing on ledges, and I can't take credit for the doggie diversion. Latoya, the technology for that was an innovation from a laboratory in D.C. Actually, I buried specially manufactured silicon lines about three inches in the ground around the perimeter of my property. Talk about a five-week job! These silicon wires emit noises and humming tones that only Dogs can hear. As I've read, once the lines have been violated, they come alive, and the sound grows louder the further the dogs get from the original breach; therefore, the Canines are always chasing the sonic sounds. I ran the lines about one and a half miles right into Lake Shasta." Brock smiled "that's where the Feral Feedback Bloodhounds stopped hunting for us. ✿

"Thanks for the explanation," I said, then added, "you see, I watched you guys like you didn't even sweat when that happened, like you almost enjoyed it. I'd much rather be lying on a beach towel, laced out overlooking the Caribbean with a fruity drink in my hand. That's how I wanna relax!"

A high-pitched siren sounded off from the other room. Brock flew by with his bro behind his back. I followed, musing now what are we goin to be trippin' on… stepped down into the Den, and an image showed on three monitors; it was an Ultralight.

I was a spectator like a fish out of water listening to these Special Operations guys. Rocky said, "back the tape up…" Brock explained, showing him the wind speed from North to South was about 27 mph. "This is a rarity if the wind currents blow in this direction. The camouflage covering over this compound will wrinkle slightly, especially with wind gusts over 25 mph… look, the Pilot dropped a bottle onto the camouflage netting, which caused the alarm sensors to go off; we have major problems!" Scanning the radio waves, we hear these words "breaker, breaker this is UL747 come in Corporal Mendez please come in Oh I can't believe it ugh… shit it appears I've discovered their hide-out definitely an anomaly ingenious… over…."

Before the pilot had said another word Brock expeditiously moved lightning quick takes up his Walther WA 2000 Sniper Rifle, it was closer than his 50 Caliber McMillian walked abruptly out on the porch and aimed for what seemed a long time… he was a statue. The radio squawked, "Breaker, this is Corporal Mendez, come in… over." Brock squeezed the trigger bang ear blasting shot only one. I run back as I hear again, "Corporal Mendez here. What's up? UL747 come in. Do you have something to report?… over." The Ultralight flipped sideways, smoke buffeted out, then it fell from the screen out of sight. Another camera picked it up as Rocky switched the monitors to show the West side of Silverthorn Resort. I saw the aircraft crash down on Shasta Lake breaking into pieces.

Brock strutted back in, asking, "what else was said on the radio? Are we compromised, bro?" "No, but you know we should be leaving here by tomorrow at the latest, brother." Staring at the screen with me, he included. "It appears the Pilot wasn't wearing a parachute…." "Yes, the three of us need to have a Pow-Wow for sure. I'm going to clean my weapon." He disappeared from sight down a set of stairs.

I looked across the table at Rocky, now frantic even though he showed no worse for the wear "where are we going to? I mean, we were safe up here; you saw the TV. They have rewards. We're wanted dead or alive, they will shoot my Black ass without asking any questions. Uh, up here in Northern California, it's mostly White people. For you to understand how my situation is being Black, it would be like you walking through East Palo Alto in the Bay Area or Richmond, or Watts, a White man in Harlem at night!" He sauntered over and touched my arm "girl your right you stand out more than us it isn't that your Black as much as your gorgeous with an amazing mind and matching body!" Grinning at me teasingly, I shook my head, understanding his game. 'Change the subject with flattery!' Exasperated, I sighed and walked away, trying to hide a super wide grin, and biting my lip, playing my part. I turn to him "stop flirting with me. I'm being serious, Rock." "I was too; ahh meant nothing unreward wasn't like you are thinking… I wasn't flirting. Heck, you have been traumatized enough, Latoya. They killed your brother Tayshon and husband Devon. Remember I was there, Latoya." I nodded. "I am not hitting on you, girl. I merely wanted to disarm your tension, probably the wrong approach, but Latoya, truthfully, I think you're a Doll. We do have to leave tomorrow, and I won't let anything happen to you. I'm delivering you to your parents!"

"What could I say? What could I do? I reached up, snuggled a decent hug, and kissed his left grizzled cheek; whiskers poked me, and I had to follow up. "It was a little flirtatious, wasn't it?" he slowly released his grasp on me, peering down kisses my forehead… "Absolutely!" ✳

Radio blasts out, "shots fired, we have a Bird down fx omg Corporal Mendez… over," Mendez barks back right away. "I want all aircraft in the area re-directed to the last coordinates of the Ultralight now and deploy all drones possible to the area. I want our airplanes and drones to follow the flight pattern that he was on. There's no question the pilot saw something out of the ordinary, and I want to know what it was… get a crew over to the crash site now. He may still be alive; move it!… over.

I couldn't hide it. I was freakin nervous, my mind whirling at this latest transmission. Brock stepped up from the basement. "Don't worry, Latoya, this is to be expected. I've already lifted the rocker arms on the Camo netting to shift the bottle of water that the pilot dropped out of his Ultralight, most likely… accidentally." Also, he points to the wind currents. "It's now on the match, uh natural only 17 mph East to West it was just some wind gusts… we're cool!"

Rocky re-enters. I walked off, letting the guys converse, and decided to hop in the shower and get refreshed, ensuring my iPhone was on the charger. I'd hear my dad and mom's voices in a few minutes. I wanted vindication not only for myself but for my brother and husband that this wasn't going to go down as Law Enforcement wished. I would be proactive and ensure the culpable parties paid with their own blood.

Heavy rotors twirling sounds above the mountain fortress of cabins, the sky was under siege. Brock states, "Latoya doesn't seem too concerned; she's a good strong woman." "Yes, I told her not to worry, bro!" The monitors were filled with air traffic "your correct, of course, but once they download the satellite images video, they will be able to discern the trajectory of the shot that brought down the Ultralight, yuh think?" "Nope, I believe you are giving them too much credit look at the screens. They're way over on the West side. We've both flown your mountain many times, even knowing where the Camouflage nets were, and we couldn't tell where they started or ended…." "I guess you're right, Rocky, still, we have to get out of here. Heck, just this morning, they had Dogs at my perimeter; it's only a matter of time, brother!"

At 3:15 pm finally sounds from what seemed so long ago that people in Shasta County had taken for granted. Even at times, the sounds of phones chiming had been annoying but now welcome. Simultaneously their phones chimed… full signals, and satellite feeds up internet connections back online. "Wow, Rocky, they are actually following their schedule, that's one thing in their favor anyways. Yep, brother, good luck getting through on the phone. There's going to be a clusterfuck of a logjam to start with! Can you imagine the 10's of thousands of calls? Here look at the internet can't log on, just whirling busy prompts, but one thing remains a constant I can log onto the Dark Web via Tor."

The radio noise went back and forth, searching for the lone gunman who shot down the Ultralight pilot, searching troops on the ground and in the air. At a minimum, nine drones were working the area from Jones Valley Resort to Silverthorn Resort with swarms of troops with boats. Rock glanced at his lifelong pal... "The problem we have is they know only an expert marksman sniper could have made that shot. The target was almost half of a mile away. Evidently, the satellite images couldn't catch the muzzle fire from the Walther WA 2000 because Brock fired from underneath the Camo-net, a relatively easy shot for him. Left unspoken was their greatest fear, and that was one of the military Drones would fly in too low and try to drop below the tree line below the Camo-net. It would then get stuck, and they'd be sitting ducks.... Colonel Ruiz would call in the F/A 1BE/E Hornets or the F-22 Raptor heck, several times today, a squadron of F-16 Fighting Falcons had flown over them. They'd obliterate the entire mountaintop, and just debris would be left in their wake!

Three hours later.

It had been three hours plus, and still, the phones were useless, all locked up with full bars and signals without communications. The same could and would be said for computers, iPads, and Tablets. Nada, the wireless traffic came from both ways. The surge was sent from all over the World to Shasta. While Shasta citizens were trying to read text messages and log in on their Social Media accounts, no one knew how long it would take to be able to make a simple call. 7/23/2025 at 6:55 pm, Latoya joined them out on the deck. The Sun remained heating the earth from above them. She watched the boys working out; the temperature was nearly 101 degrees which in July could be deemed as only warm despite her shower earlier, it was like an addicted Jones. The guys were doing perfectly formed body weight exercises, pull-ups, chin-ups, push-ups, dips, and sit-ups. I couldn't just sit there and watch, nope. ✳

I spotted something that charged me up. I couldn't wait to have fun on the rope swings and mini zip lines. This was an outdoor paradise. Being a world-class athlete gymnast had always meant to her that exercising wasn't metaphorically working out, nah not work at all but fun at times needed healing of spirit and mind bodies moving fluently enjoyable. I found that if I didn't exercise on a regular basis, depression would seep into my mind, nervous pent-up tension–anxiety, ah energy stored and built up like a steaming kettle without any physical or sexual release. I just couldn't sleep as relaxingly, um, without working out. It cleared my mind and body, sweating out the body's waste from my skin pores. It was now a way of life after such a long time of doing so, a prerequisite to a dispositional mood regulator sweat equaled cleansing of body & soul. Besides that, I had to admit it kept me regular, uh, my bowel movements, lol.

It might sound funny, but our bodies are like an engine. At least that's what my first gymnastics coach had told me... and it has stuck with me ever since. <u>'If you run high octane through the motor and regularly blow out the built-up grime plus carbon and change the filters, the motor will last for a long time, same as our bodies if you pile up saturated fattening food ugh, garbage with processed foods, filled with preservatives. Fast food grime leads us to become sluggish and Sloth-like... without exercise, we soon become human Slugs!'</u>

—74—

<u>Ben, Cat, Cody, and Ali at Bethel.</u>

Ali and Cody sat in comfy recliners facing Ben and Cat, resting in a love seat... in the suite that Bethel had provided them. Ali said, "first of all, I couldn't imagine any of us taking suicide pills, man think about how insane that would be. Sorry just don't get it; why would they be trying to raise the dead? I mean, how long have the four of them been dead?" Cody jumps into the fray, "What the hell hadn't I told you about Bethel? There are a bunch of damn freaks. It's a damn cult, probably doing weekly sacrifices. Didn't you see the way Wanda described it to us, ahhhh with a gleam in her eyes, like a freakin ghoul, full-on enthusiasm boiling over that woman is a trip! They're going to do a ritual of raising the dead again! Tell me something, how did the four Bethelites die at the Bakery?" Cody didn't wait for any replies "let me tell yah all something else… that Venus girl she's rocking Hot what I'd give to be popping that Cherry!" Cat clamped her hands together, glaring at him…. "Shut up, Cody; you are such a sick, demented asshole sometimes. Whew, please keep your thoughts and fantasies to yourself…." "Now you two stop, please, Cody, Cat be respectful," yelped Ben.

"Okay, let us fill you guys in on how we got here, Cat; why don't you start?" Cat explained about the 'Sunshine's Sweet Goodness' confection shop, the search by the military for her and Ben, Father Rite, and Elder Jeremy and little Charlie being given to a family. That the four Bethelites took suicide pills, causing their hearts to stop beating… the foursome would rather die than be interrogated. Which by itself was weird, umh, kill yourself because of maybe getting arrested, something just didn't make any sense. What information or secrets were they trying to hide about Bethel Church? Cat then told Ali and Cody about their crazy escape to Turtle Bay and the African Exhibit and of them being restrained hooded in the tunnel under the ground on the way from Turtle Bay to the Church that they were at now!

Cat left little out Cody, and Ali sat still, wholly transfixed at times extreme expressions, mouths wide open in amazement like children being read a nightly Fairy Tale story. Other times they bit their lips in anticipation, clinging to Cat's next word.

Ben took over describing a thorough but quick overview of their meetings with Father Rite and Elder Jeremy, Wanda, and Venus oaths of trust, loyalty, and integrity signed contracts, that which Ali and Cody would also have to sign. Before either of them could complain, he went on about the meeting with Goliath and the spacious computer labs. Bethel's supposed objectives related to them because they were aligned with their own…. what they had offered them, and their group of activists proved they were on the same team.

Ben stressed out loud several times that Bethel had made it transparent, uhm, perfectly clear that we could leave anytime and that the organization had been in the foreground and background depending on your perspectives when it came to fighting against Martial Law and the quarantine of the citizens in Shasta. Bethel was a leading advocate and supporter of our freedom of speech. Bethel stood strong and staunchly defended The First Amendment of the United States Constitution… preventing the government from making laws up that regulate an establishment of religion or the right for the people peaceably to assemble and speak their minds. In Bethel's book, it was every person's God-given right to live an autonomous existence… being one of the largest institutions in Northern California didn't hurt their causes. Bethel had immense traction and political pull, not only in Redding but throughout Washington, D.C…

From the onset of the first Coronavirus Covid-19 way back in late 2019 and the beginning of 2020, the Church was proactive. Bethel's opposition to Governmental control was publicized, and their hierarchy stated it was subtly displaced manipulations that seemed surreptitiously or covertly designed for the powers to be to break and take the average citizen's resolve and freedoms away. Back in that era, Bethel Church was all over the newspaper's front pages, and even their movement was broadcasted nationally. They had concerts at the Sundial

Bridge right out in the open… masks were self-chosen. Most wore no masks right in front of Law Enforcement Agents.

Ben ended his monologue with, "we've united with Bethel, and we're on the same side with mutual objectives…" he nodded at Cat, who added. "This doesn't mean we have bought into their spiritual themes or beliefs. We are just in the infancy of learning what this church is about, don't equate our words or displayed strong emotions for what Bethel has accomplished to sway your belief that we are somehow brainwashed and blinded by what their ultimate goals might be. We're not wearing blinders, 'the Emperor wears clothes!' Ben and I do believe in the church's ideology and many of their philosophies… and feel Father Rite and his disciples have worthwhile principles to help guide us." Cody and Ali gawked at Ben and Cat, knowing they'd drank the Cool-aid. What the hell has happened to them? .

Cat once again took up the torch and let what was left to spill from the broken dam out… "As Ben has said, we're not into the way's uh, you know, believing all the Church's credos and manifestos." Smirking, "we are a long way from being freakin Baptized…" Ben laughed, Ali and Cody sat stoically, non-verbalizing. "You guys wouldn't be here and possibly alive without Bethel's interference saving you before the military had captured both of you. God knows where Karen and Maddii are, but you are safe with us now… for just their amazing gift of preventing you from being arrested, we are eternally grateful. This church has shown us loyalty and compassion… Bethel is friendly to our just causes. Bethel has too much to offer; you've heard what they're going to do for our activist group, uhm, at serious risk to the church's sovereignty… Father Rite has offered us safe meetings at the Turtle Bay Exploratorium. On top of that, he will protect our people and will help us scrutinize the attendees. Please check out where we are, huh? We're safe. Do you see the military prowling around the church? Bethel allows us to hope for a return to normalcy, and they have infiltrators inside the military. You are living proof. Look how they saved both of you with Dan and Jon dressed as spies, uh, soldiers driving a replicated military van; otherwise, where'd you be, Cody hmm, how about you, Ali?"

Ben pics back up "we don't have to do the Holy Roller stuff... Father Rite has asked nothing of us, actually uhm, ah." Ben looked at Cat "did I just say that? Heck, what does Bethel really want from us, babe? They're not helping us for nothing; what do they want in return?" They waited patiently, staring at Cat's bewildered look... no answers were provided. Yet they'd already come to the same conclusion. Cat' reaffirms... "I guess umh suppose ah speculate that possibly they'd want to recruit some of us along with our group members morph them into the Bethel ways, but they affirmed that we could remain steadfastly independent firmly freewheeling and so..." "Wait," shouts Cody, "have you guys gone off the deep end, there's no fricken water in the pool. In my short life, my dad has taught me to be skeptical. I have learned <u>that if it sounds too good to be true, then beware because</u> it isn't true! Also, another valued adage is um or saying is, 'no one does anything for you for nothing.' There's always a catch, uh ulterior motives!" Ali had been quiet, no more felt like jumping up hyped into the fray... nah then he thought better of it and leaned back down into his chair and calmly said, "you just made that one up, Cody shut up." Ali smirked, "I think we should observe them closely without our predisposed biases and possibly false assumptions about what we believe this church organization represents. Sooner than later, their true colors will shine through, and yes, I agree with Cody; they're not being forthright. There is something up their sleeves, no doubt they want to steal our members; that goes without saying!"

Ali wasn't done "he's got a point, though; what's in it for Bethel? Why did they reach out, risk their organization and themselves to rescue Cody and me, huh?..." Ben replied, "I haven't a clue Ali, but if it's for greed or self-interest, then they have four pieces of the puzzle and over $300,000 plus in rewards sitting within their grasp why not turn us in? Become a shining example to the military's occupational leaders." "Furthermore," Cat continues, "since you both are into quips, here's another from my Grandma, 'Don't ever look a Gift Horse in the Face!'"

"All right, the last time we saw you after the Mary Lake Conference, you two, with Maddi and Karen, were all heading to her family's ranch house. It's your turn to bring Cat and me up to speed on where Maddi and Karen are at…. what's happened since then?" asked Ben.

Cody stands up, perusing his friends… besides his parents and siblings, they were the closest of connections and reflections of whom he was. Hoping they'd be lifelong best friends. He began to pace in front of them. He went over important points and happenings, such as after waking the morning after the conference and reading Maddi's shocking note, she was sick with a fever. Maddi had assumed the worst-case scenario, ugh, that she had the virus was going to leave Karen's house before she infected any of them. Maddi wrote that she was going to find her parents…. that's all he and Ali knew. Originally they left Karen's house to look for Maddi and then their own families. We stopped at one of the designated drop spots for our activist letters and notes off Hwy 273 and picked up Wayne's correspondence about the next meeting where and when.

Ali joins in and then takes them from that point "we were still trying to figure out where to go Karen suggested her friend Kayla Green's Law Office. Suddenly, a Drone appeared, followed by soldiers and Dogs. Stupidly ugh, wrongly, we'd cornered ourselves; we didn't have many options with the drone watching us from above. We ran up some stairs in an office building. That's where the Dogs and luckily Bethels Dan and

Jon caught us instead of real soldiers they shot us with darts, believe me, we tried to kill them and shot our weapons strangely it wasn't like the video games we didn't even hit one of them!"

A long silence broke "next thing I remember is I woke up here with you....." "Yep," Cody agrees, "that's about the gist of it; things we have absolutely no clue of, like, how the hell Karen escaped or where she could be at?... It's all a blurred mystery, she had to of been shot by their RFDs they fired on automatic at us."

Solemnly with earnest, Ben spoke softly for more emphasis, "listen, we owe it to Tim, Kelly, and Trudy to at least be there at their Wake and funerals ah Church services. We'd just met the other victim Patti. Without their assistance um help Cat and I would have been arrested, and where the heck would we be now? So we are going to attend their services, it's not only that we're sort of obligated, but we're also wildly curious as to what Bethel is up to. You two don't have to." "Well, if you're going, so are we, and anyway, Dan and Jon saved us; we're indebted to Bethel also," obliges Ali, "but what's this Venus girl saying about raising the dead?" "I don't know, it's whatever it is," exclaimed Ben.

Cat had sat quietly thinking about telling them what Wanda had told them, then decided oh well, no secrets, "uhm, before we find someone to escort us to the Chapel for the services, I have to tell you what Wanda told us you're not going to like it one bit, there's no verification, but she said our families were dead the military occupation executed all of them and...." "No way, no, Cat not executed but dead babe again, all of its unsubstantiated, guys..." corrected Ben. Ali moaned. Cody placed his palms over his forehead and loudly spoke, "no, that's not plausible nor possible. Why would, uh, wouldn't make any sense? It's our own American soldiers; they're not here to murder us. Come on, please, it's totally illogical!"

Ben nods forward "your right, Cody; it is unbelievable and beyond that uncorroborated for sure, but we are in the blind heck. Think back to our last meeting at Mary Lake; we were supposed to get together every 48 hours or at least 72 hours, but that wasn't feasible. It's been over a week since, and we haven't gathered to cull positive or negative information about what's happening throughout Shasta County…. what we do know is there are hundreds of missing people, and our families are part of that group…. we must hold out hope for how insane would it be that in 2025 that there was a form of genocide occurring here… not possible, please think about…." "Yeah, honey, but where is everybody at? Are they in like prison camps?" asks Cat.

"Hey, aren't they turning back on the phones on July 23rd, all social media sites, and the internet? I heard Ruiz say in his last update that he's pulling out all Government soldiers unh. They're leaving Shasta County on the 27th for good, there only after us, our group, because we've revolted and rebelled against their silly rules like curfews and those Vaccination tattoos. It's unlawful what they are doing labeling people, and it's illegal ugh and unconstitutional…." "True, Cody, but they've vanquished all human rights, crap look at our freedom of free speech ahhhh squelched, shut down Social Media and our modes of communication. Damnit and this Martial law attacking our citizens, uh, shooting innocent people with those sleeping darts. Killing some of our residents accidentally… or maybe not" Ali slowly stopped speaking.

"Wait, Ali, stop. That's where we draw the line. We're not the older generation that has been conditioned and trained like docile puppets since March 2020. We will fight for our freedoms. Father Rite intimated that the military was selectively killing us. I know, crazy," declares Ben, his voice trailing off. "But what if?" Cat grasps his thigh "on a positive note, Bethel will allow us to have our next meeting at Turtle Bay and will help us with transportation and the deactivation of the GPS tracking chips that are hidden inside the Pyramid Tattoo's colors....." "Whoa, Nelly, what are you talking about? We never heard..." Ben dives in "yes, we just learned from Goliath that their techies discovered that the military is placing micro-dot-sized GPS chips under the skin inside of the supposed vaccination tattoos. Bethel has developed, uhm.... invented handheld devices that will temporarily disable and deactivate the chips so everyone can attend the Turtle Bay conference. Besides that, they will also provide us with security at Turtle Bay. What more can we ask from Bethel? We certainly owe them for that, right guys!"

Cody slams his open palm against the door "why again, why are they doing all of this to help us? For what reasons, guys, please, something smells fishy...." Cat and Ben could only shrug "let's play our moves out; we better get to the Chapel.... come on." Cat led them through the doorway and down a hallway; they stepped towards a closed door.

Unbeknownst to the group... Dan and Jon were watching the video monitors from the security cameras.... filming the four outsiders. Dan pops open the door, startling them "you make up your minds. Are you going to join us in the Chapel?" Three of the four nodded affirmatively, with Cody abstaining with a noticeable scowl-ish expression.

Up the elevator they went... from way down the hallway, you could hear the music exponentially getting louder, with each step sounding like a Rock Concert going on. The closer we got to the Chapel, the vibes from the Bethelites we passed were... like crazily pumped and outrageously excited. Positive momentum is displayed with an unrealistic uppity mindset.... instead of a funeral, uhm, or wake, you'd think it was a Wedding, like a wild celebration party. The atmosphere was on the hyped side. Cody's first thought was, damn; we're going to a Rave party. Why is everyone smiling and dancing around? Spring Break had nothing on this celebration, and heck, there wasn't any booze or drugs. The disciples were High On Life…

"Oh shit," muttered Ali turning around to his friends, "look, there's a bunch of 'em dancing in the hall weird like where's the reverence for the dearly departed, surprised they're not hooting and hollering…." Jon overhears him, "oh, that will come later. Don't worry, you are in for the experience of a lifetime…." The four of them close quarters now elbows almost touching, watching the Bethel adherent's joyful countenances exuberantly ecstatic, totally irrational.

Cody gets to the Chapel's double doors first and stops… he had enough of the weirdness and flips his head back to Dan "hey, correct me if I'm wrong, but aren't we going to a Wake… four of your congregation… are freakin dead!" "Not true, pal, not dead for long," he cackled loudly. Jon joined him with a snigger. Ali jokes, "where's the Molly undh LSD, beer bongs, and hookahs?" "We here at Bethel don't need mood enhancements or depressants to feel the Lord's Blessings. We are filled with positive endorphins. Our Drug is Omnipresent!" Cody, startled, stalled. "This is a ridiculous display of insanity; you should have this cultish stuff on video, man!" Dan chortles, "Oh, we are on video," and points to the cameras rotating now and gestures to Jon, who opens the doors to the Chapel to complete Chaos Cody's eyes blare out along with Ben, Cat, and Ali, not expecting the riotous scene.

People were jumping on pews. A freakin 5-piece band was on stage with balloons and banners with names on them. Cody stumbles and falls over a loose leg and is caught by a 3-some who returns him standing; he yells at Ben. "Where are the poles with Flin strippers?" Suddenly Cody was halted… both arms were snatched up, and his chest and body were wrenched up into the air by a shadow. His feet dangling like he was a damn infant, he was squirming. The others stopped, frightened, horrified, seeing their friend now in a tantrum, kicking and gesticulating. They hear a grumble over the piercing treble and the bashing bass blaring through enormous speakers. "Please, sir, there will be no profanity, cusswords, or expletives in the Lord's Chapel… in our place of worship. I am going to put you down now. Be respectful, for I don't want this to become an unpleasant experience for you or cause any problems, do you understand?" Goliath emphasizes his point with a breath expelled. Bear hug squeeze released. Cody is only able to shake his Red face forward in acceptance Ben reaches out shouts "put him down now Goliath!"

Cody is slowly released and dropped into their arms, Ben and Ali holding him up, his eyes bulging, straining outward, and popping out of their sockets, and he starts to speak, "Wtf…." Cat covers his mouth "Oh F…udge no whew," Dan yells. "Hold hands so we can get you to your designated pew. You are lucky you're in the 3rd row next to Tim's parents!" Banners were flying out from blowers. The music stopped the lead singer cried out, 'Welcome back, Tim, Kelly, Trudy, and Patti… God is Great!'

Cat can't quantify or believe the sight, and strangely, the faces she sees are mostly her age; an Organ hits some deep reverberating tones, keys…. the music starts a slow sequence of sound with lights above aligned with each note.

There couldn't be a doubt in anyone's mind that a supreme talent stood behind the Organ's mellifluous sweet notes, the woman's fingers and hands silky smooth fluttering across the keys. The Chapel was gigantic, larger than the entire gymnasium at U-Prep High School by three times. Cat thought it more resembled a huge theater… on stage, the band's music stops, then the person who was working the light board or the control panels flashed a flood light, uhm, spotlight, and out walks someone Cat had met earlier. Elder Jeremy, a microphone on a stand, stood forth. He grasps it, lowering his head into a bow.

It was extraordinary witnessing the immediate change of ambiance; all ruckus, commotion, and unrestrained exhilaration ceased to exist like someone had turned a faucet off. Yet vibes were lighting up the audience of Bethelites. A sense of flagrant passionate enthusiasm existed as they'd just watched the warm-up bands. Now comes the headliners....

Elder Jeremy takes the mic and cruises the length of the stage, then to each end, somberly nodding his head, then regains the center stepping up on a pedestal. "You all are aware why you're here this evening...." Cat could feel the air around her heavy breathings of anticipation.... for her, it was the unknown enormity of this immense gathering of pious believers that had her fully alert.

"We are joined in commitment, faith, and willpower with undaunting Spirituality we must find a oneness; through us, God shines. Do you believe this?" A quiet murmur starts in the back somewhere, and then a hushed chant gains momentum, the Cathedral moving forward slowly mystifyingly like a train nearing the station louder, louder 'I Believe, I believe... I Believe...

The spotlight flocks off total darkness, then a seated section on the stage lights up seven Red velvet high-back chairs where four men and three women stare out at the mass of humanity worshipers of their faith again unprovoked, a noise starts, clapping slowly. The Bethelites clapped louder all-around Ben and his friends. Exalting the seven who at once stand upright, palms over their hearts.... The crowd whips into a frenzy, jumping off their chairs to their feet. It's a standing ovation.... Cat didn't get it; what the heck just happened?

Cody fidgets about searching for the Giant freakin monster.... didn't have to look far... Goliath's Neanderthal Head was three times per a normal cranium. The dude's thick forefinger pointed at Cody, whirling in a circle. Then the crazed freak Goliath smiled at him. Cody was confounded at the size of his Crocodilian Pumpkin-faced grin. He shuttered stiffly, thinking I'm stuck here like fricken Superglue 3rd row from the front by a Caveman; there was no escape... Cody would never make it to the exit doors.

Elder Jeremy moves into the limelight next to a silent unwavering group of seven individuals who were standing still, bowing their heads in prayer, who seemed to demand the respect of the entire Bethel congregation. "Thank you for showing our Prophets your appreciation tonight; with their guidance and inspiration of divine intervention, we....." He spreads his arms wide above his head. "Do you feel it? ... feel the Holy Ghost is with us inhabiting each of our Spirits just as Christ arose from his crypt, so will Tim, Kelly, Trudy, and Patti. We will witness miracles this evening, but only if you all collectively believe in our supreme spiritual leader and Lord. Amen... Kumbaya, My Lord, yes, Amen!"

Instantly the lights in the cathedral were flipped off, then a spotlight found its way in front of the band, shining on a robust woman who stood smiling at the crowd, sublimely jolly and pretty. She puts her hand up, and music starts to be heard. Ali did not casually peer around. He was vigilant and wary. Everyone was singing Church Hymns; he supposed.... none of the four had ever heard the songs before. On the far left of the aisle was Cody, then himself, next Cat, and lastly was Ben. On all sides, ahhhh, around them were Tim's mother, father, and sisters; likewise, Ali saw the resemblances of other family members of the other poor souls who had died. They seemed to surround them, and he felt sad for them, especially being fed false hope and expectations of some miraculous resurrection. How wicked thought Ali for Father Rite to lie to the parents of Tim, Patti, Trudy, and Kelly's family and tell them that their children could possibly rise from the Dead. This was cruelty to the max as far as Ali was concerned.

Ben didn't know how the Elders could have got all the family members here during the lockdown siege, uh, Martial Law. Still, there was undoubtedly an older generation of people, most likely parents, and relatives of the deceased. Ben, periscoping around, had to guess the population inside the humongous Chapel had to be way past three times the people who attended their last meeting at Mary Lake. Ben paused and then made an estimation. He decided there had to be way over 5,000 Church goers inside this massive Chapel.

Ben wondered how many of his group of activists were already tattooed, seeing tattoos throughout the audience. Ben caught a glimpse of a man staring at him. Oh man, there was no doubt who sat nearby…. the resemblance to Tim was overwhelming. His father and mother were directly across from him, with mascara already streaking. How merciless could this Father Rite be? What a farce of indignant stupidity to give hope to suffering family members shook his cranium forward. This time I have to admit Cody was correct. They were surrounded by cultists, for all he knew they… he nearly chuckled then seriously finished his thought. The four of them might be on the Rotisserie spit uh sacrificed for this Lunatic Fringe in his mind as sweat commingled dropping down his cheek. They were trapped. It wasn't if they were going to raise the dead. No, it was if they would make it out of here alive! Paranoia mixed with irrationalities, he agreed with his inner-spirit Devil's Advocate, but his Spirit needn't worry. It was his skin that was going to be baked crispy.

Ben's imagination went wild, and sick-ass horror movies came to the forefront of his disturbed conscious state of being. He wouldn't be surprised to see a river of human blood flow down the aisles. Deranged warped minds surrounded Ben. Movies like The Living Dead, The Purge, and The Texas Chainsaw Massacre all morphed into one. Ben was a part actor in a Movie starring Ben, Cat, Ali, and Cody. We're all Victims…. we're probably on the dessert menu…. staring at all the wild eyes, unblinking. These people are Insane… like mass insanity! He cackled silently into a long-lasting grimace…. mulling over how'd they get to this point?

With a perpetually dry tongue, Cat observed mouths open in astonishment while the music changed; lights flashed and moved fluently as a Flutist played... OmLord, this was something out of the Las Vegas Strip, an Extravaganza put on by Cirque De Soleil, a gorgeous woman in shining shimmering glitter floated across the stage belly dancing provocatively, Tambourines and thimbles clacking in her paws. The Flute played as she gyrated beside a colorful straw-like round basket. No way... it wasn't a flute nope, it was a Pungi being played. Snake Charming instrument, what? 'Oh God no, R U Kidding me... it's really a King Cobra, and the charmer slings the top of the basket off... a slithering tongue flicks out, omg... oh fk no, each of them starts to elbow one another ugh, no one was laughing, stunned morgue-like, perched at the edges of their seats, petrified. This was some serious shit; she mused crazy that's when they noticed three other likewise round cylinder-like baskets, one on the steps up to the stage, not 15 ft. away. Cody bit his finger in the middle of whispering; his eyes were nonblinking, oh-damn.

Cody was fossilized; fear flaunted his direful reality... haphazardly and not so nonchalantly, Cody periscoped around, shaking and shivering in unadulterated terror, peering on each side of the aisle to see if any other baskets with the snakes were near him. Ali was streaming sweat. He had a severe phobia.... Ophidiophobia is an extreme fear of Snakes.... ready to hit the aisle, screaming deathly afraid, and yet he couldn't shut his eyes. Ali was trembling, and hearing his heart blasting from his chest, he started counting again. Ali was trying to keep his mind preoccupied, but it was in vain. Surely he would be in cardiac arrest any second. Omg, five of the straw cones had Cobras dancing to a tune. The serpents were erect up, bobbing, slithering, forked tongues flicking and whirling around, spying him.... displaying Evil pinpricked eyes staring right at him. He knew it; drool fell from his bleeding lower lip.

Sighs were heard throughout the Chapel, a tantalizing respite, then all the Cobras, in unison, slowly glided, swirling unnaturally, spinning their huge heads on a swivel. Then the Vipers dropped back out of view, like trained puppies… the snakes tucked down and disappeared into their cones once more. Then lights flicked off moments later, and the spotlight was on three men with microphones, one at the edge of the stage, one in the middle, and the other on the far-left side. The lead guy started to shout into the mic a different language wiggling, rocking like breakdancing OmLord gasps Cat to herself… 'Their Speaking in Tongues' 'Oh crap! There was a guy in the middle that emitted a deep growling yowl as if he was calling, Wolves to the Kill, uuh, a slaughter he was yelling and yelping.' Omg, another guy was bouncing around on the stage wearing a freakin Kilt in a one-legged… bent-over Scottish Dance; Bagpipes played loudly over the speaker throughout the auditorium. The wailing and shrieking colluded with the loudest drums on the planet, 'Lambeg drums.' The volume was slowly being sequestered then a Rapper started up from behind a curtain, rapping a mean-sounding tirade.

We sat, shoulders touching, shaking, panicked, then the lights came on dimly. "Oh crap, theirs more of them," shrieks Ben, the stage filled with crazed drooling trolls spitting with maniacal gesticulations, inhuman countenances, double-jointed freaks flipping like acrobats… on a trampoline in the middle of the stage, the demons bounced. Maimed, disfigured faces dripped with a fervor, clicking and clenching teeth, scowl-ish ghouls seemed to be beckoning them to the stage. Waving at them with deformed appendages, the entire fricken Bethel entourage started yammering and chanting they were possessed… flaming fire shot from the sides of the stage. Omg, the distorted savages suddenly populated the aisles. They were now trapped, then others joined the devils and were full-on Speaking in Tongues. The demons cowered impishly and shrank back silently into the abyss…

Instantly a troll popped up next to Cody... he almost jumped out of his skin trying to sit in Ali's lap. The ghouls clenched fists rotating dammit the Asylum; UGH, The Patients had taken control of the prison and were on the prowl. Ali shrunk as small as he could, screaming silently, his mouth wide open, matching his prisoner friends. Ali wasn't a fan of Horror films now cast in the middle... felt his pulse needing to pee badly, knowing farewell a heart attack was imminent. Zombies with makeup covering their extremities bounced all throughout the Chapel, cornering them in, and a few replicated Vampires slithered by. Ali was shaking spasmodically in agony, imagination running wild. He swiveled his head around at a female who was screeching non-words, chomping,... chomping her Feral Teeth. One row back in an enlarged aisle seat was the giant Ogre... Goliath, who was pumpkin grinning. Cody lost it. "Oh, Ft, help me get out of here!"

Ben stoically took it all in, amazed at the production. Ongoing, the Cobras were unreal. This had to take mega-hours upon hours to choreograph simply fricken amazing what a performance... never ever seen anything like it before a number-one hit in Vegas, no doubts, his appreciation for the costume designers, what the heck would they do for an encore... he spun his head to see fear in his friends... Ali seemed to be in a catatonic state. Unfortunately for Ben, this was merely, umh, symbolically only the third inning, ughhhh, the preliminary rounds. The Main Event wasn't going to start for another two hours. Ben, Cat, Ali, and Cody didn't know it, but they were going to be the scrumptious entrées, the lead actors on the stage that they looked upon. Yeppers....

Bethel; Resurrections, and Baptisms. 

Rantings from the Author

Not the Last Words… I hope! But yuh never know… do yuh?

I hope you enjoyed reading the first and second part of the Covid-57 debacle, the Covid saga continues not only in this fictional narrative but on earth. The third Covid book, takes us into a future that is filled with uncertainty, free people have to be nimble and creative to survive. Mandatory inoculations have the world's populace up in arms, many of the conditioned individuals, believers wearing 'rose colored glasses' kowtowed and joined the parade of clones. These worker bees are a necessary cog to keep the well-heeled and connected privileged 1 %... uhm, gold and silver spooned deserved people comfy and satiated.

This is the 7th book in the NIA series of 13 that have all been written. Unfortunately, I am the sole Author without a team of Editors. I don't have a Literary Agent; I will be Self-Publishing…. it's just poor ole me. Therefore, the many errors in my novels are all mine; I'm sort of old school. I use a notebook and different colored pens for plot changes; I'm aware my punctuation sometimes stinks, although rarely, it's purposeful.

When I started putting pen to paper, I didn't know what an undertaking I was getting into. Whoa, this is Work!... with a Capital W! I wish I could hire someone to do the hard part of bringing my writings to fruition because… I honestly enjoy putting pen to paper.

I'd much rather write than do almost anything else, but this work formulating a Book is mind-blowing, and yet I step into Libraries and Walls; there are books forever; I am in Awe of them all.

The Covid-57 series continues Book # 8 just needs editing. Tell me folks what do you think of this statement... _Really in this world, you never know, it has been declared too many times to number, 'Truth is stranger than fiction...but it's because Fiction is obliged to stick to possibilities: truth isn't!'_ ...I must declare, my Covid narrative is no doubt fictional but in many cases it wouldn't be hard to find some relative Non-Fictional scenarios. It was definitely challenging for me writing these books.... simultaneously adrenaline-charging and ominous to write. Speaking for the only person I can... me I enjoy and have fun getting lost in my imagination, where anything is possible. I find creative writing super-duper rewarding and oddly an exciting endeavor, filled with exhilaration and pride. I will publish books three and four in the Covid-57 series soon. ☺

I'm also hyped up.... about a partially written book titled 'The Clinic.' I will soon add a preview of this novel based in San Diego and Mexico. Within the words and pages of 'The Clinic,' there is much truth about covert prison camps throughout Mexico; these establishments are supported mainly by relatives that pay the guards to keep their relatives alive and unharmed; I've spent time interviewing family members with inside information about this ongoing travesty.

Non-Fiction accomplishments 'Charity,' 'Take a Chance,' 'Take a Chance 2,' 'Take a Chance 3'... 'S.C.J Sacramento County Jail,' 'Savant Style Trading,' an informative book about trading the Stock Market, nuances, and how to profit, using basic algorithms…

Since this is a Lone endeavor or enterprise, I haven't many individuals to thank. Still, I have a single person I want to praise… 'Gerald Ward,' employed by the Sacramento Public Library and the leading publisher at 'I-Street Press.' He just retired in December 2021. Gerry has been instrumental in this process of preparing my novels for print. Unfortunately, he's not an editor, but he is a fantastic photographer and knows his way around the Art of publishing… His extensive library of Photos has been used on the covers of the Feral Eyes books.

<u>Last but Never Least, I would be remiss if I didn't Dedicate all my writing to my Dear Mother! 'Barbara Jean Hayes Meyers.'</u>

As a small child, I watched her write page after page in notebooks; she wrote thousands of pages. Her Genre was Romance. She loved to write, always dreaming of one day publishing a book. Sadly never did. These books are for you, Mom… sorry, I am not talented in the Romance arena; perhaps one day, I will give it a College try.

Thank You for reading what I enjoyed writing, Glen 'Rocky' Meyers. Oh, BTW, I include in many of my novels this phrase 'From the Corner of his eye' or my eye. The reason for this…. is that it's my form of praise for one of my favorite books by 'Dean Koontz!'

I'm responsible for every error and mistake in my novels. I printed the first edition called an… 'ARC' book… or (Advanced Readers Copies) for some beta readers to let me know what they thought. Ugh, my first test books needed a lot of work… I had thousands of mistakes literally in my writing…The second edition will be cleansed, but it will not be perfect! Thanks for your time. Please visit my website, '<u>Gembooksrock.com</u>,' soon;

I hope to have a business venture also offer for you, not costing you a penny, only time… enough! >Glen Rocky Meyers @ Facebook, Instagram. Please visit my website Gembooksrock.com.

Thank you very much for your precious time…

Glen Rocky Meyers@GlenAuthor' Twitter. Soon to be on YouTube.